Praise for the Novels of Terri Lynn Wilhelm

"A delightful treat! Terri Lynn Wilhelm has crafted a wonderfully refreshing tale filled with fun, adventure, and soul-stirring emotion." —Lisa Kleypas

"A clever romp and an impassioned love story."
—Christina Dodd

"*Highland Jewel* delivers on every promise! This is truly one of the best Scottish romances . . . captivating characters and lyrical prose." —Teresa Medeiros

"Engaging . . . enchanting . . . compelling . . . witty, deeply emotional, and sexually romantic. Ms. Wilhelm uses clear, rich, intelligent prose to draw us into a magical world."
—Under the Covers

"Wilhelm again dazzles the readers with this compelling saga. . . . *The Moon Lord* shimmers with a captivating story-line and a star-studded lineup of enchanting characters."
—*Midwest Book Review*

"Enthralling. . . . Strong characters, lively dialogue, and of course, romance make this story a winner." —*Rendezvous*

"Wonderful, sensual, vivid . . . will leave you, the reader, breathless. . . . Pure romance magic." —*Gothic Journal*

"An impeccable storyteller . . . Ms. Wilhelm bedazzles with an enchanting tale that makes us smile in utter delight."
—*Romantic Times*

"A wonderful, unique romance that will charm your socks off." —*Affaire de Coeur*

"A great story with a wonderful cast of characters."
—*The Paperback Forum*

DECEPTION

Terri Lynn Wilhelm

A SIGNET ECLIPSE BOOK

SIGNET ECLIPSE
Published by New American Library, a division of
Penguin Group (USA) Inc., 375 Hudson Street,
New York, New York 10014, USA
Penguin Group (Canada), 90 Eglinton Avenue East, Suite 700, Toronto,
Ontario M4P 2Y3, Canada (a division of Pearson Penguin Canada Inc.)
Penguin Books Ltd., 80 Strand, London WC2R 0RL, England
Penguin Ireland, 25 St. Stephen's Green, Dublin 2,
Ireland (a division of Penguin Books Ltd.)
Penguin Group (Australia), 250 Camberwell Road, Camberwell, Victoria 3124,
Australia (a division of Pearson Australia Group Pty. Ltd.)
Penguin Books India Pvt. Ltd., 11 Community Centre, Panchsheel Park,
New Delhi - 110 017, India
Penguin Group (NZ), cnr Airborne and Rosedale Roads, Albany
Auckland 1310, New Zealand (a division of Pearson New Zealand Ltd.)
Penguin Books (South Africa) (Pty.) Ltd., 24 Sturdee Avenue,
Rosebank, Johannesburg 2196, South Africa

Penguin Books Ltd., Registered Offices:
80 Strand, London WC2R 0RL, England

First published by Signet Eclipse, an imprint of New American Library,
a division of Penguin Group (USA) Inc.

First Printing, December 2005
10 9 8 7 6 5 4 3 2 1

To Vinicio Hernandez, physician extraordinaire,
who has one of the most difficult jobs in the world.
Thanks for putting up with all my whining.

PROLOGUE

The merciless Indian sun bore down on the ranks of men standing at attention on the fort's parched parade ground. Perspiration trickled from beneath shakos and turbans alike. The smell of sweating males permeated the air. Through it threaded the scents of ghee and curry, and wood smoke from cook fires tended by wives and camp followers outside the north wall. In the distance, a dog barked.

Bitterness as hot as the sun above burned inside Captain Foxton Tremayne. Orders had been handed down from on high: An example must be made.

Without lifting his head to look, Fox Tremayne knew kites glided on the thermals far above this British mud-and-wood bastion. Keeping his expression unreadable in order to conceal his grief and fury, he gazed straight ahead, out over the seared grounds crowded with still, uniformed men.

Fox Tremayne, whose ancient Cornish forebears had battled at the right hand of kings, sweltered in his wool uniform and awaited an awful shame he had proved powerless to stop.

A rustling through the columns and footfalls on gravel signaled the approach of Colonel Michael Montgomery, commanding officer of this post.

The knot in Fox's chest tightened.

Striding behind the colonel came his captains, all of them stone-faced. None glanced directly at Fox.

Did they fear disgrace was contagious? Or were they eaten by guilt?

Colonel Montgomery halted in front of Fox, his escort arrayed by his side. A captain, whom Fox had befriended upon that man's arrival at this isolated post, now unrolled a sheet of parchment and began to read aloud, projecting his tenor voice so that it struck the limewashed walls and echoed back, demanding the attention of every man, woman, and child who was not stone-deaf.

One and all learned anew that Captain Foxton Verran Tremayne had disobeyed orders under fire.

There was no mention of Colonel Lord Everleigh's shocking conduct. The Marquess of Everleigh, who had given Fox his initial, ultimately fateful orders, was nowhere to be seen. That was, of course, because Everleigh was no longer stationed here. His powerful father, the Duke of Kymton, had arranged for him to be whisked away to Calcutta, where the marquess had doubtless been collected by an agent protecting the family's Indian interests.

That same powerful peer had also arranged that Fox should take the fall for Everleigh's misguided order.

Fox gritted his teeth against shouting out that it was only by his disobeying the order that even a third of the company had been saved from slaughter.

After the battle of Kurndatur, Fox had tried to make his case. Even Colonel Montgomery's letter on his behalf had met with no success. Fox would have given a year's pay to know what that last communication from the governor-general's office had contained. After its arrival, Fox had become persona non grata with his fellow officers.

And, when all was said and done, he, Fox Tremayne, *had* disobeyed an order.

A drum rolled. Beside the colonel, a junior officer produced a red silk cushion bearing a *khanjar,* its gleaming blade almost blinding in the harsh sunlight. Humiliation twisted in Fox's gut.

Without a word, Montgomery picked up the curved hand-knife. He sliced the epaulets from the shoulders of Fox's uniform coat. The uniform of which the Tremaynes had always been so proud.

Fox maintained his ramrod-straight posture. He swallowed hard, his throat rasping against his collar. With a will, he kept his fingers from clenching at his sides.

The blade flashed again in the colonel's white-gloved hand. One by one, the polished brass buttons of Fox's coat dropped to the ground. Each made a faint *ting* as it struck the sand—the death rattle of the military career Fox had cherished.

When Montgomery had removed every button from the front of Fox's coat, he restored the *khanjar* to its cushion. Then, in a commanding voice that had the ability to reach soldiers in the tumult of battle, he announced, "Foxton Tremayne, you have one-half of an hour to leave this post. Your mount will be held at the gate. If you do not leave within the specified time, you will be cast out."

Cast out.

For seventy miles, arid, barren, mountainous landscape surrounded the fort.

To his surprise, Montgomery did not immediately turn and march away. Instead, the colonel spoke, his voice low-pitched for Fox's ears only.

"Were I in your boots, Tremayne," he murmured, "I would leave India straightaway. This is no longer a good place for you. Try America," he added. "You'll not prosper in England."

ONE

Isabel Millington paused outside the library, her fist hovering over the surface of its paneled mahogany door. Her uncle Gilbert Millington had claimed the library as his office and sanctuary upon moving into Greenwood with his socially ambitious, hypochondriacal wife, Lydia, six months ago. He had pronounced the room forbidden to the household, save the occasional maid for the purposes of cleaning.

Only the urgency of her quest spurred Isabel to break an elder's decree. Her fist descended twice, thrice. Polite, not too loud, yet persistent.

"Come!" Gilbert's voice rang, edged with impatience.

Isabel took a deep breath, then let it out. She smoothed the skirts of her gown. Then she curled her fingers around the cool brass doorknob and entered her favorite room in what was now her brother's house.

Gilbert Millington, Isabel's uncle on her deceased father's side, was a tall, husky man of two-and-fifty years. At the sight of Isabel, his dark eyebrows rose.

She walked to the writing desk behind which he sat. Papers and a large, open ledger covered most of its surface. On a shelf behind him, Isabel spotted the precious book: Homer's *Odyssey*. Her father's last gift to her.

Gilbert studied her down his nose as he closed the ledger. "I own, this visit comes as a surprise, Isabel."

How like Papa he looked. Well, perhaps a more studious version of Papa, she corrected, for her father had disliked fussing with accounts.

"I know you have said that this room is out-of-bounds, Uncle," she said, "but I come to you on a matter of import."

"Ah." He smiled. "I should have known you would not disturb my work for a trifle. You are always a good girl, my dear." He waved her to the lyre-back chair beside the desk. When she was settled, he leaned forward, his gaze moving over her face. "Now tell me what troubles you, child. You know I'll do whatever I can to help."

She looked down at her hands clutched in her lap. How impertinent she felt! She didn't like questioning Uncle Gilbert. After all, had he not been Papa's indispensable right hand for years? Had he not moved into Greenwood to lift many of the burdens from Mama's frail shoulders as soon as that awful letter had arrived from the East India Company?

Isabel met the steady gaze of her uncle. "I fear you cannot help but take me for impudent, but I must know . . ." She swallowed.

"Yes?" Gilbert coaxed softly.

Isabel found courage in his kindly expression. "The demand for ransom was delivered over a fortnight ago, Uncle, yet you . . . you have not . . . responded." In her lap, her fingers gathered tiny folds in the fabric of her dress. "I fear for Rob. You know what barbarians those Spanish are. I've heard stories—horrid stories—of what they do to English officers."

Uncle Gilbert heaved a ponderous sigh. He eased back in the leather-upholstered chair. "I have not tried to hide from you the appalling financial state of Greenwood. Where am I to find all the gold demanded by your brother's captors? Indeed, where am I to find gold of any significant amount?"

"Sell the estate!" she cried, fear for Rob overpowering

her good sense. Yet even as she said the words, she knew she counseled the impossible.

"The estate is entailed." Gilbert did not point out that she had always known this.

With a great effort of will, she reined in her desperation. When she spoke again, she managed a calmer tone. "Can you not . . . can you not provide the funds? You know that Rob will reimburse you. You know he will."

Gilbert's eyes widened. "Rob's honor is not in question, child. Surely you could not think I would withhold, or even begrudge, the money if I had it? Why, I would send it in the wink of an eye! But alas, I have not above a quarter of what those filthy Spaniards want."

Gilbert sighed. "My own money is tied up in investments. Speculative ventures, you see, for they give the best return, and a man with an elegant wife must always keep his coin working for him."

"Speculative ventures?" Her uncle had never struck her as a gambler.

"Yes. Commodities. Risky, but their return can be quite lucrative, much better than the Funds."

"What sort of commodities?" Isabel asked. She'd heard of the Funds and knew an investor could extract his guineas if he chose, but of commodities she'd heard nothing.

"Oh," he replied, "timber, copper, wool—such things as our society uses in great quantity. There are always opportunities for a shrewd investor, particularly during times of war. However, this kind of investment must run its course before I see a penny of return. It ain't like the Funds, Isabel. There are no shares that I can sell and no market in which to sell them. These are private arrangements, put together by a broker, a man of business with experience in such matters."

"Could you not explain to this broker the circumstances? Surely even he would agree that the ransom for a brave British patriot must be paid."

"Doubtless he would agree—in sentiment. But he has already spent the money he received from me and from his other investors. That is the nature of investments, child. One must spend money in order to make money."

Desperation thickened in Isabel's throat, threatening to choke her. "We could borrow against the estate—" The expression of sadness that softened her uncle's face stemmed her words.

Gilbert reached across the desk and took her hand. He looked down at her fingers and sighed again. "Only Rob can borrow against the estate. When last he departed from Greenwood, your father was still here and in good health. I spoke to them about giving me legal power in the event of need, but they refused to listen. Superstitious men, the both of them." His fingers briefly pressed hers in sympathy. "You know how they were about business."

"Rob is still alive," she reminded him in a choked voice.

"And we shall pray that his captors are not so harsh as we fear. He is an officer, after all."

"When . . . when do you expect your investment to pay out?"

He hesitated, clearly reluctant to deliver more bad news. "The soonest I can hope to see any return is one year."

His answer struck Isabel like the blow of a hammer.

A year.

Could Rob survive for twelve more months?

"Are you certain there is nothing you can do?" Her words issued as little more than a whisper.

"I'm sorry, Niece," Uncle Gilbert murmured. "I truly am."

She nodded, unable to speak. Afraid that her composure would crack, Isabel fled the library.

A bent, elderly gentleman in an old-fashioned frizzed wig hobbled into the London offices of Battams & Tice, Accountancy. A chill breeze stirred the sable on the collar and cuffs of his greatcoat. One gloved hand pressed heavily upon the ivory head of his walking stick. The other clutched the handle of a leather portmanteau.

The sight of him caused a flurry amongst the three clerks working in the anteroom and sent one of them scurrying to the substantial walnut door of their employer, Mr. Elsegood Tice.

"Please go in, Mr. Syer," the clerk told the old gentleman seconds later in a tone reserved for only the most esteemed patrons. "He is expecting you."

As the old man entered the partner's office, Elsegood Tice, a portly fellow in his midthirties, rose from his green leather chair.

"Welcome, Mr. Syer," he said, just loud enough to be heard by anyone who might happen to be listening outside his office. "I trust you are well?"

Mr. Syer quietly closed the door behind him. He turned the key in the lock. Then he crossed the room and set the case on the desk with a heavy thud. From within came a muffled jingle.

For a moment, neither man spoke. Each stood still, listening. When a conversation started between the clerks in the anteroom, the tension in Elsegood's office eased.

The old man grinned. Oddly, the expression belied the myriad wrinkles on his face with a cast of far greater youth. He carefully removed his greatcoat, then his coat of fine, dove-gray wool and laid them neatly on a side table. For the first time, Elsegood noticed that the garments were sewn differently from a normal coat. Though that difference had been cunningly concealed by the tailor, these coats would hang perfectly only if the wearer stooped.

Mr. Syer straightened, drawing his previously bent frame up to a lean, impressive height.

Elsegood smiled back at him. "I can never comprehend how you manage to appear positively wizen. One doesn't even notice the breadth of your shoulders."

The other man placed his fists at the small of his back and stretched. "Being ancient plays hell with a man's body," he observed as he came upright.

"So I hear," Elsegood said. "Only I usually hear it from men who truly *are* ancient."

With a deep sigh of relief, Mr. Syer dropped into the cushioned chair beside Elsegood's desk and extended his long legs.

"How do you manage to appear so convincingly aged?" Elsegood asked.

"It's all in the tailoring," Mr. Syer replied lightly, his voice now its natural rich baritone. Without elaborating on his uncanny ability to shift guises, he leaned forward and opened the leather portmanteau.

It was filled with coins. Shillings. Spanish dollars. Crowns and sovereigns. All gleaming, glittering silver and gold.

Elsegood laughed out loud. "May I assume your venture was successful, sir?"

Mr. Syer's grin returned. In that instant he looked every bit as young as his nine-and-twenty years. "You may."

"Do you wish me to make the usual deposits?"

"Into the usual accounts, yes. I want everyone well paid. Especially the Ladies."

"It shall be done," Elsegood promised. "Shall I invest the overage for you?"

"Yes. In America this time. The United States. You know how I prefer to diversify."

"Very wise."

"That little country intrigues me. And I've noticed numerous opportunities there. If the United States survives, I think it could become something unique, possibly even something grand."

Elsegood allowed himself a look that silently expressed his skepticism.

Mr. Syer's wide mouth curled upward. "I know you'll do as I ask."

"I always do." For which he was generously compensated.

Mr. Syer clapped Elsegood on the shoulder. "Yes, you do." He rose and picked up his coat. "I noticed one of your clerks is missing. I believe his name is Thomas. Is he ill? Or . . . has he gone to another accountancy firm?"

Elsegood took his meaning. "Thomas was privy to nothing of yours. I attend those matters myself." He sighed and shook his head. "He has gone off to the Peninsula. Thinks to help Wellington win the war."

"Bloody fool."

"I tried to talk some sense into him, but he'd have none

of it. The glory, you see. Visions of it blind these young fellows."

"There is no glory in war," Mr. Syer said curtly. "There is only duty and pain, treachery and death."

He donned his coat and his luxurious, heavier greatcoat. As he did, before Elsegood's eyes, the tall, vital, younger man appeared to dwindle until, standing in his place, bent and leaning upon his ebony cane, was an old gentleman.

"Well, I must away," the old Mr. Syer said in his creaky voice.

After quietly unlocking the door, Elsegood opened it. Mr. Syer hobbled out of the office and into the larger anteroom.

Elsegood accompanied his patron to the outer door, which opened onto the offices' front steps. Beyond, pedestrians crowded the flagway. In the street, Mr. Syer's plain black carriage awaited amidst all the other carriages and blooded mounts.

At the outer doorway, Elsegood stopped. His smile faded. Meeting Mr. Syer's gaze, he felt impelled to express his concern. "Have a care, my friend," he said in a low voice. "'Tis a dangerous game you play."

Mr. Syer regarded him solemnly. "Who said I was playing?"

He turned, then, and made his way down the stairs, his crabbed progress painful to behold. His footman solicitously aided his passage through the river of pedestrians and his ascent into the unremarkable carriage. After shutting the door, the servant stepped up to his own place on the back of the vehicle.

Although it was scarcely past four of the clock, the retiring winter sun had already left the sky a grimy pewter color.

With a snap of the reins and a call from the coachman, the matched bays moved away from the posts. As Elsegood watched, the carriage vanished into the chaos of London traffic.

The moon had not yet reached its zenith that evening as Isabel Millington tiptoed up the narrow wooden steps. The flame from her slender rushlight filled the stairway with a capering glow that danced between the moonbeams falling through the window at the midlanding.

When Grandpapa had built the Greenwood mansion, he surely had not intended that his granddaughter be forced to use these servants' stairs, save, perhaps, to conduct some child's prank, such as sneaking out of the house to go riding when she ought to have been attending the instructions of her dance master. In that, her grandfather would have found her a disappointment.

She had never been daring enough to skip any of her lessons . . . or any other duty, for that matter. Consequently, miserable in her lack of grace, blushing and stiff with nerves, she had forced herself to learn by rote each movement of the dances. Hanging over her head like the proverbial sword hovered her knowledge that polite society would expect her to conduct herself with fawnlike fluidity through those same awful exercises when the time arrived for her first London Season.

If she could not be a fawn, Isabel had been determined that she would not be a clodpole. Jaw clamped tight, she had memorized each step and sway, every nod and gesture.

Much good it had done her.

There had been no London Season for Isabel Millington. Her parents had not given a lavish ball in their London house for her introduction into fashionable society. There had been no beautiful new gowns, no soirees, no picnics filled with laughter. Nor had there been any shy flirtation or steadfast beau.

Instead, the house in London had been sold, and the price it brought had been applied toward her parents' debts.

Cautiously, Isabel peered around the door frame, into the dark hall. Doors that marched along its walls opened onto a stately gallery, the library, a ballroom, the formal dining room, and several guest chambers. She looked first in one direction of the long, wide corridor, then the other.

Down the hall, a door creaked.

She froze in place. Wind thrashed across the slate roof tiles high above, whistled between chimney pots, and rattled windowpanes.

Minutes passed, and she heard nothing else. Finally, Isabel put the creak down to the door in the dining room, which was old and heavy, but so perfectly balanced on its hinges that the merest draft could move it. In a house as old as Greenwood, there were countless drafts.

She eased out a sigh of relief. Then, ashamed of that relief, she tried to cover the guilt she felt with a practical question—a question she had never before asked herself: *What is the worst that might happen if I am caught?*

An admonishment from her uncle or her aunt? Unpleasant, of course, perhaps even mortifying, but tonight she needn't worry about them. Tonight she was safe.

An acquaintance in a neighboring county had invited her aunt and uncle to a dinner party. Aunt Lydia and Uncle Gilbert were probably involved in a ripping hand of whist even as Isabel skulked on the landing. At this hour, the few servants of Greenwood would be abed. Which meant she had most of the vast Palladian house to herself.

Isabel stepped into the hall, the glow from her rushlight skimming across pastel-tinted plaster walls, marquetry side tables, and slim-legged mahogany chairs. Down the center of the polished oak floor, vividly colored carpets from Turkey formed a jewel-toned avenue.

Her worn slippers made no noise as she walked the plush path. These carpets had been one of her grandfather's many contributions to the family estate—the same estate her father's heedless spending had drained.

As she moved down the hall, she trod on the hem of her night shift. Stumbling, she hop-skipped a few steps, trying to regain her balance while retaining hold of the rushlight. Annoyed with herself, Isabel jerked her ruffled nightcap and dressing gown back into order with one hand as she continued toward the gallery.

There, moonlight poured through tall windows, gilding heavy frames and brushing images of people and treasured animals with a phantom's light. Isabel stopped in front of a life-sized portrait.

The glow of her burning rush revealed the image of her father. He stood beside a marble bust of Plato, which rested atop a fluted pedestal. A powdered bagwig covered his curly dark hair, and he wore a coat of azure velvet, black breeches, black stockings, and black shoes with silver buckles. Unlike most of his contemporaries, James Millington had chosen to smile, and how truly the artist had captured the appeal of it. Isabel found the corners of her own mouth lifting. She reached up and touched his hand, feeling the slick roughness of solidified oil paint beneath her fingers, but remembering the warm security of his clasp. Clear in her memory was the image of him holding a book. They had shared long hours of both companionable silence and diverting discussion in their favorite room, the library.

Isabel exhaled unevenly. She turned to the portrait of her mother, Annika Adkisson Millington. Mama had been born in Sweden and had insisted her children learn to both speak and write Swedish fluently. Her brother, Valfrid Adkisson, was a successful merchant who made his home in Göteborg, Sweden, though his work often took him abroad. Isabel had met her maternal uncle when she had been little more than a babe in arms, but they had exchanged a few letters over the years. Written, of course, in Swedish.

Mama had possessed an ethereal air that had been almost fairylike, and this quality had defied the painter's capabilities. Isabel supposed he had done as well as any mortal could. Mama, too, had chosen to smile, her lips caught forever in a winsome curve. Her sky-blue eyes reflected the joy she had shared with Papa and her children.

At last Isabel came to the painting of her brother, Robert William Millington. He stood tall and straight, his curly dark hair pulled back into the queue favored by so many of the military men. Rob had just turned twenty when this work had been executed. He wore his uniform, that of the Sixteenth Light Dragoons. The striking dark blue dolman bore a brave field of white cording on its chest and touches of scarlet at the collar and cuff. His snug white pantaloons were immaculate, his black Hessians polished, and his treasured saber hung by his side. In the crook of his arm, he held his fur busby.

That particular style of head covering engendered the

loathing of anyone required to wear it. The thing's towering form quickly fell off balance when a dragoon entered battle, it absorbed and held moisture, and it offered little protection against French swords. Until Rob had confided his dislike of the hat to Isabel, she had thought its appearance quite dashing. After she had learned how bothersome that busby was to him, she, too, had despised it.

"Who's there?" demanded a voice behind her. "What are you doing?"

Isabel whirled, her heart hammering in her throat. Then she recognized the voice as that of Mrs. Odling. At the same time, Mrs. Odling must have caught sight of Isabel's face.

"Miss Isabel, is that you?" the housekeeper inquired as she marched toward her, shielding her own rushlight with her hand. "You gave me quite a fright."

Mrs. Odling would have appeared severe were it not for the row of bobbin lace on the white linen nightcap tied beneath her chin and the tasseled crimson sash cinched firmly at the whip-handle waist of her plain dressing gown.

"I was just letting the cat out when I heard a stair creak," Mrs. Odling said. "Gracious, why are you roaming about at this hour?" Then the older woman glanced at the painting in front of which Isabel stood. "Well, I suppose that's a foolish question."

"Sometimes visiting them makes things a bit easier," Isabel said.

Mrs. Odling, who had been the housekeeper at Greenwood since Isabel had learned to walk, placed her arm around Isabel's shoulders and drew her into a comforting embrace. "You've had more troubles than any girl should have to bear, and that's the truth." She gazed up at the painting of Rob. "A fine-looking young gentleman, is your brother. He has always had a good heart, too. 'Tisn't right, your uncle refusing to pay the ransom to free him from those nasty Spaniards. 'Tisn't right at all."

Isabel's eyes burned with unshed tears. "It is not Uncle Gilbert's fault," she said. "His money is tied up for at least a year."

Mrs. Odling sniffed. "He had enough to buy himself that new hunter."

"That was at the last quarter day. Now his coin is invested."

"If only the master had paid more heed to his fortune."

Isabel knew Mrs. Odling spoke of Papa. The housekeeper had never referred to Uncle Gilbert as "the master."

After Papa's departure for India, it had grown to become general knowledge that he had frittered away his wealth despite Gilbert's pleas. "I *tried* to do my duty as steward," Uncle Gilbert was wont to say—far too frequently for Isabel's taste. It wasn't pleasant to be continually reminded that one's greatly reduced circumstances were due entirely to one's sire's insistence on purchasing more books, more horses, more gowns for his wife and daughter. Though, in truth, Isabel could not remember him spending so very much on those things. How spoiled she had been.

"What's done is done," she said, unwilling to rehash the tribulations of her family. "The challenge at hand is to find the money for Rob's ransom. I fear his captors won't wait a year to be paid."

Mrs. Odling, however, was not to be deflected to another subject before she had her spoken her piece. "'Tis a shame your dear father ever gave the accounts to another to keep. Begging your pardon, Miss Isabel, but it seems to me you did a superior job of balancing the accounts whilst you kept them. Humph. More than one lady has kept the accounts for her family and their properties."

"If only there were at least something for me to sell!" Isabel said, not for the first time. Nearly everything left was either entailed or mortgaged, and what remained of her personal possessions would not come near to fetching enough to free Rob.

She turned her gaze to her father's portrait. *Oh, Papa. How could you have spent your entire fortune and not even known where it went?*

"I fear for Rob," Isabel said, her cheek resting against Mrs. Odling's sturdy shoulder.

"Continue praying for him, sweeting. We all do, you know."

"Thank you," she said softly.

Mrs. Odling stroked Isabel's back in a comforting motion as she struggled unsuccessfully to stifle a yawn.

Reluctantly, Isabel pulled away. Mrs. Odling worked hard, and it was late. "It has been a busy day. Good night to you, Mrs. Odling. I'll see you in the morning."

Mrs. Odling glanced at the painting of Rob, then studied Isabel's face, hesitating.

Touched by the older woman's loyalty, Isabel replied, "I'll be only a bit longer. Sweet dreams to you."

"And to you, my dearie." Mrs. Odling turned and made her way down the long gallery, her rushlight bobbing into a pinpoint before it vanished around the corner.

"I go to fetch my book now, Rob," she told her brother's portrait. "Then I am for bed. It is up early in the morn for me. With so few servants, we all must do our part."

She had to retrieve her book. If she did not recover it tonight, she might not have another opportunity for months.

Uncle Gilbert had made clear his strong disapproval of women reading for pleasure. He claimed it "littered" their minds. She had never asked him for her book, afraid that it might become suddenly lost—or worse, sold.

Homer's *Odyssey* spoke to her of adventure, of family ties, of enduring love. More important, it had been Papa's last gift. To have it back, she would even break a rule.

Isabel left the gallery and went directly to the library. She had already met one person she had not expected to find up at this hour. Best if she proceeded with her mission and hurried back to her chamber before she encountered anyone else.

Nervously, she stuffed fugitive black curls back into her nightcap. From her pocket she pulled the extra key to the library door. She had forgotten to turn it over to her uncle when he had moved into Greenwood and promptly required all the keys to be placed in his possession. She had found it in her sewing box weeks later. A tiny demon had arisen in her as she regarded the key lying in her palm. Her uncle had

banished her from the room where she and her father had
spent so many wondrous hours poring over books. Gilbert
had already received a key to it from Mrs. Odling. What
could it matter that he did not also possess Isabel's? At that
moment, it had not occurred to her to ever *use* the key.

Now the door opened silently under her hand. Inside,
moonlight flooded through a bank of windows to pour silver
over tables, chairs, and shelves. She set the wicklike rush in
its tin holder on the desk.

Quickly she went to the nearly empty shelf where, months
ago, before the arrival of her aunt and uncle, she had placed
her *Odyssey*.

She pulled out the Morocco-leather-bound edition of
Homer's classic . . . and almost sent it flying. The thing
weighed not a quarter of what it should.

Isabel opened the book.

Or, rather, she tried. Handmade parchment pages refused
to part. When she carried the book to the light, she saw why.

They had been glued together.

Shock, then indignation soared within Isabel. Her dearest
possession had been vandalized!

On the verge of insolvency, Papa had bought it from a
used-book dealer and given the book to her just before his
departure for India. When most of the contents of Greenwood's library had been sold off, her mother had concealed
this precious book, saving it for her daughter.

And someone had destroyed it.

Its lack of weight suggested the core of the pages had
been hollowed out, making *Odyssey* into a cache, a mere
box! Who had done this? And why? Surely something so
important, so urgent as to cause a sort of madness must account for such desecration.

What might such an important hiding place contain?

Tentatively, she shook her book. A muted thump inside
answered.

Snatching up the rushlight, Isabel left the library with
Odyssey under her arm. She locked the door behind her in a

flurry of white lawn night shift and hand-knitted woolen shawl.

Once in her chamber, she placed the light on her dressing table and proceeded to examine the hollowed-out book.

As she searched for a way to open it, the thought occurred to Isabel that her mother might have forced herself to convert the book into a hiding place. Near her end, Mama would have known that neither Uncle Gilbert nor Aunt Lydia enjoyed reading. With relative safety, she might have concealed something. Something important. Something she meant only Isabel to find.

Isabel's fingers stilled. Perhaps there was something here that could help Rob.

Perhaps the book-box contained bank notes. Or a deed to property unknown to Isabel. Or a key and directions to a secreted strongbox.

Charged with hope, Isabel prodded and pressed various places on the tome, searching for a way inside. Each time, she failed. Then, when frustration nudged her like a knife, she pressed and slid the cover. She felt, rather than heard, the *click*.

With unsteady fingers, she opened the box. Inside lay a baize-lined compartment into which Isabel peered.

No jewels glittered in the rushlight. Instead, there reposed a small journal and bundle of letters written on ordinary writing paper, the kind one might find at any stationer's shop. Not the heavy parchment of a deed, a royal grant, or even a treasure map.

No! There had to be a false bottom. There *had* to be. Isabel turned the box upside down and shook hard.

No key fell out. No bank drafts. Not a single coin.

Standing there in her cold room, Isabel wanted to weep. Sniffling, she reminded herself harshly that her family possessed no wealth to leave in some ridiculous book-box.

That was why, upon his discovery of his near-insolvency, her father had sailed to India. He had hoped to earn a fortune to replace the one he had inherited. The one that had dwindled away before he had realized it. Failing that, he had hoped to at least earn a wage that might allow his family to live with a modicum of comfort.

But James Millington had managed neither. Instead, he had died of fever. His employer, the East India Company, had sent a letter telling of his death.

That had been six months ago. Six months. It was past the time for tears.

Gradually, the tension in her muscles drained away, leaving her feeling spiritless, hollow. Whatever these papers were, she would lay money they were *not* the miraculous salvation of Rob.

Numbly, Isabel lifted the journal from its hiding place. As she scanned the first few lines, her breath stopped in her throat.

The moon was nearing the top of its nightly arc as the coachman halted the carriage in front of a prosperous-looking house nestled amongst other prosperous-looking houses on London's Harley Street. Lamps lighted the walkway to the front door, casting their dancing glow into the cold darkness like a banner of welcome.

Fox Tremayne looked out the carriage window, impatient to get into the house and out of his uncomfortable disguise. The persona of Mr. Syer was extremely useful, but all that bending went hard on the knees and back.

Operation Pear Tree had been successful. The Assembly had pulled off their various parts with the precision of a clock's works. With each operation they improved their performance. They gulled the corrupt and the greedy while making a far better living than any of them had ever expected.

On an afternoon three years ago, after Fox had lost everything, he had sat nursing a watered-down cup of coffee in a chophouse, trying to stay warm and avoid the gimlet eye of the establishment's proprietress. She preferred patrons who took up a seat so long to order more than a single cup of coffee.

He passed the time eavesdropping. That day he overheard two dandies discussing various plans to get rich quick.

Each scheme was laced with holes and doomed to failure. If they could not see that for themselves, Fox could have told them. In fact, he did, in a tactful way, hoping to save them some pain. They jeered at him for his troubles, and their voices brought the proprietress, who finally ordered Fox out.

He took note of their faces. The next time he encountered them, he would recognize them, but they would not recognize him.

After returning to the hovel he shared with Mary, an overworked laundress, he sat on the pallet in the tiny space he rented from her, and devised an investment that would work for *him*. He based it on one of those the dandies had discussed, and his aim was that their pride would propel them into the financial folly. Folly, that was, for them. For him and Mary, if she agreed, it would end quite profitably. It involved the bait and switch of a prized horse. A horse he did not own. Nor, to their great distress, would they.

He applied a disguise to both Mary and himself, for Mary needed to look like a lady, and he needed to look like a respectable gentleman—something he had been once. He obtained their attire from the dustman and borrowed makeup from a prostitute who was a neighbor. He had once helped the daughter of delight to pass for a countess. They still laughed about it.

As he expected, the game would take time—a week in this case. Mary grew nervous several times, but managed to buck up. At last the dandies begged and borrowed the sum to purchase the horse. They handed over the ready one morning at the chophouse where a far different-looking Fox had tried to be helpful.

By nightfall, Mary and Fox had bid a glad fare-thee-well to Manchester and gone their separate ways.

It was then that Fox had realized he might have a future in confidence games.

For some time now, his operations had far surpassed that first one. They had evolved into far grander, riskier schemes that were often international in scope and always highly profitable.

Fox waited as John the footman, a scarred former soldier, opened the door. The liveried fellow handed him out of the carriage and onto the walkway. Remaining in character as long as the eyes of the outside world might observe him, Fox hobbled up a short flight of stone steps to the black lacquered front door.

Before he quite reached it, the door opened to reveal the somber countenance of Bartholomew Croom, fact finder extraordinaire. What the outside world saw at this moment, however, was a slim manservant in his midthirties, of midheight, with large brown eyes, cropped brown hair, and a wooden left leg.

As Croom closed the front door behind Fox, he gave him a nod and a wink, the signal that all was clear. With that knowledge, Fox went directly to his chamber, where he removed his old-fashioned wig and the expertly applied face paint and prosthetics. He changed into his own clothes, clothes that would allow him to stand upright.

"We did well, Croom," Fox said as he tied his cravat. "The best we've done yet."

"I knew we would, Cap'n. The Assembly works well together now, smooth as you please. Like a regiment."

Like a regiment *should* work. Although Croom hadn't said that, it hung silently in the air between them, a black memory for both.

Fox let the moment slide past. He reminded himself that he had moved on with his life. In these past few years, he'd played his cards cleverly enough that no authorities had ever become involved in his activities, and he had pinched the pocketbooks of men who deserved an even more thorough fleecing, but who would doubtless live long lives, then die rich.

Still, despite his progress, sometimes bitterness gnawed at him. The one man he wanted to hurt most remained now and forever beyond his reach. Fox was not averse to taking some risk, but he wasn't insane.

Croom held up an embroidered waistcoat. "So the Ladies will get their checks as usual?"

"Indeed." Fox slipped his arms into the garment, then

began buttoning it. "Wouldn't want them to feel forgotten, now, would we?"

"No, sir." Croom chuckled. "Wouldn't want that at all."

Fox slid into the dark blue kerseymere greatcoat Croom held for him. He shrugged it into place on his shoulders and admired the excellent tailoring in the tall mirror.

"A bit of a celebration might be in order, sir," Croom said.

A celebration. They certainly had cause. "Yes, Croom, it would. Have Nottage pull that excellent brandy Etienne brought with him last time he came to London. We'll all drink a toast or two. It's too late to ask Cook to make something special, but perhaps she could send round to Napsorts for some of their excellent apricot cakes."

Planning a celebration before he had actually finished an operation's business might bring bad luck, and Fox had no intention of risking *that*. Now that the last detail had been finalized, however, a certain degree of indulgence was safe.

"Too bad everyone can't be here to toast the success of Pear Tree," Croom said as he gathered up Mr. Syer's clothes to be cleaned and pressed for the next undertaking.

Having the Assembly come in from around the globe undoubtedly would make for an unique gathering, but it would also attract the attention of neighbors and passersby. Fox had spent the last three years making the avoidance of attention into an art.

"Someday. When we're ready to retire from the field of investments." He cocked an eyebrow at Croom. "Are you ready for that?"

Croom shrugged. "I am a rich man now, thanks to you. But I could tolerate growing richer."

"We all have our parts to play in these things, Croom, and because we have all been careful, we've all made a few bob. And we have done it without drawing the attention of the hangman." Fox's gaze moved to the window. Moonlight gilded the anthracite rooftops and chimney pots across the way with a blush of silver. The occasional *clip-clop* of hooves on paving stones accompanied by the rumble of wheels echoed against the tall houses that lined the street.

He was now a wealthy man pursuing an occupation at which he excelled. Why, then, did this gray mood persist? He could not change reality; he could only try to cope with it.

Fox turned back to Croom. "So," he said. "Just when were you proposing to begin these festivities?"

Croom grinned. "Your lovely aunt and that pretty sister of yours arrived a few hours ago. Cook has prepared your favorite dishes. Nottage and I helped Mrs. Browder lay everything out for a very handsome table."

Such unrepentant cheek prompted laughter from Fox. He should have grown accustomed to it by now. In the two years since Bartholomew Croom, formerly Sergeant Croom, had tracked him down, the only thing that had changed about Bart was his brighter outlook.

"No doubt everyone is gathering in the saloon even as we speak?"

It was Croom's turn to laugh. "Aye, Cap'n, they are, and they'll soon be growin' impatient. You know how Diana hates to be kept waiting." He shook his head and chuckled. "Who'd ever have thought plain ol' Bart Croom from Yorkshire would be addressing a baroness by her Christian name?"

Fox clapped him on the shoulder. "Who would have thought any of us would be doing what we're doing today, my friend?" As he led the way through the chamber door, he thought about his father, who had died before Fox's return to England. Martin Tremayne had been an upright man with a strict sense of honesty that would have made him deeply ashamed of his son, the confidence trickster. That knowledge seldom left Fox.

Croom waved an arm in the direction of the downstairs saloon, from which drifted voices in cheerful conversation. "They're waiting on us. Even though he could not be here now, Etienne sent another case of champagne from France."

"He certainly was confident Pear Tree would turn out well," Fox observed as they descended the wide oak staircase.

"And why should he not have been? 'Twas a good plan well executed."

They entered the formal saloon where the others had already gathered. Present were Fox's paternal aunt, Lady Diana Blencowe; his seventeen-year-old sister, Catherine; Ephraim Nottage, who had lost an eye in the Battle of Kurndatur and now kept busy in his capacities as a butler, spy, and first-rate forger; and Tsusga of Deer Clan, a full-blooded, Oxford-educated, Cherokee warrior who had found Fox's lucrative operations a way to aid his beleaguered tribe.

Aunt Diana swept across the elegant room to kiss her nephew on the cheek. She was as exquisite as ever in a gown of frosted blue satin touched with crystal beading. Diamonds glittered in her blond hair, at her throat, and on her wrist.

"You pulled it off! You are simply amazing." Her eyes sparkled with delight. "Catherine and I did not want to stay at Willow Hall and miss the celebration. Did we, Catherine, dear?"

Catherine blushed at having the attention of everyone in the room. "No, indeed," she said softly. With far less assurance than her aunt, Fox's sister came forward to greet him. Like her aunt, she was tall for a woman and her eyes were a warm brown. Like Fox, her hair was golden-brown.

"My two favorite ladies," he said as he gave them a courtly bow. "You are as ravishingly lovely as ever, Aunt Diana." And she was. Before she had accepted the proposal of her dear, late Hector, Diana had been the reigning beauty of London, as much celebrated for her wit as for her looks.

She gave her ivory and lace fan a small flutter. "Such a well-mannered boy," she confided to the occupants of the saloon with a confident smile and a roll of her eyes that brought laughter.

Fox regarded Catherine as he took her slim gloved hand. Attired in white muslin embroidered with white work and wearing a demure necklace of perfectly matched pearls, she was the picture of youthful womanhood. Seventeen years old. It didn't seem possible.

"And you, my favorite sister . . . well, you have turned into a fairy princess overnight. I can see I'll have to guard you carefully against the throngs of suitors who will want to take you away." Privately, he feared there might be a marked dearth of bids for the hand of an infamous traitor's sister.

As Catherine smiled politely, Aunt Diana lifted an eyebrow at Fox. She, too, knew that Catherine wasn't likely to meet any suitors, much less throngs of them, while buried in Willow Hall. "We'll speak of this presently," his aunt murmured to him.

Soon, too soon for Fox's comfort, his sister would deserve to have her introduction to Society. It was her right and his duty. Aunt Diana had offered to sponsor her, which would, it was to be hoped, fix Catherine in the minds of the respectable with an estimable baroness, as opposed to with a despised villain. Still, he worried for his sensitive sister.

Ephraim Nottage, a stocky man with a balding pate and a black eye patch, held up his glass of champagne. "A toast."

Everyone turned to him, smiling in anticipation.

"To success," he declared. "May we never know anything else!"

The group lifted glasses filled with pale gold liquid that glittered in the candlelight. Delicate chimes sounded as lead glassware touched amid exclamations of agreement.

Bart held his half-emptied glass aloft. "To the good life!"

"Oh, yes!"

"Right you are!"

"Hear, hear!"

Fox hung back a moment while the company sauntered out the door, heading toward the dining room, where the long mahogany table had been draped in white damask and laid with china, silver, and sparkling German glass.

When he was alone, he murmured his own toast to the future.

"To anonymity."

The moon hung low in the night sky. Isabel again sneaked up the back staircase, the shell of her *Odyssey* clutched in one arm. What she had read in that journal had filled her with grief and anger. Even now they burned in her chest like red-hot coals.

Uncle Gilbert was a liar and a cheat.

The letters in the box had come from a Mr. Syer in London and discussed the various investments her uncle had made in his own name. Investments made, Isabel now knew, with money embezzled from her father. The journal had been written in Uncle Gilbert's own careful handwriting, and the contents of it damned him as a thief who had been stealing from his older brother, *from Papa,* for years. He continued to steal from once-prosperous Greenwood even as he denied Rob's ransom.

How convenient it would prove for Gilbert should Rob die in prison. Being heir presumptive, her uncle stood to inherit Greenwood if Rob died without a son.

Papa's bewilderment over how he could have gone through his fortune so rapidly was little wonder. In truth, he had *not* squandered it. His inheritance had been stolen from him. By his trusted brother.

A chill skittered between Isabel's shoulders. If Uncle Gilbert did not scruple to steal from his sole sibling or to consign his nephew to die in a Spanish prison, of what other vile act might he be capable? What might he do to keep his deeds secret? Her feet slowed on the worn wooden steps.

Murder?

The thought sent her hurrying to the library, intent on returning the box to its place and scurrying back to her bedchamber, where she could lock the door.

Now in the *Odyssey*'s hidden compartment lay letters she had forged, her best duplicates of damning evidence. The originals she had secreted beneath the loose floorboard beneath her poster bed.

The forgeries were good, if she did say so herself. The stationery was similar to the original. She only hoped Gilbert did not look closely at the letters any time soon.

Isabel placed the book back in its original position on the shelf. Then she slipped back out of the library, once again locking the door behind her. She hurried toward her room, where the letter she had written to her uncle Valfrid awaited posting to Sweden. Unnerved by the night's discovery, Isabel had hidden even that. She prayed that her mother's brother could—or would—come to the rescue of his niece and nephew.

She had a little time left to her, since her aunt and uncle would only stay with their hosts to break their fasts before returning to Greenwood tomorrow.

As she all but ran down a dark hallway, Isabel felt she must do *something*. She just didn't know what that something ought to be.

She could not simply ride to the nearest justice of the peace and name her uncle an embezzler. She might have spent her entire life in the country, but she wasn't *that* naive. Gilbert would doubtless claim the journal and letters were her doing. In the end, it would boil down to her word against Gilbert's, a spinster's word against that of a respectable family man. The key word and element in his favor being "man."

What would Gilbert do if she made such a denouncement to authorities? Isabel didn't want to consider how he might retaliate.

She needed time to think.

A floorboard groaned in the direction of the stairs. Like a hunted mouse, Isabel went stock-still. When, after a heart-hammering eon she heard nothing more, she scurried on her way. Staying on the carpet to muffle her footsteps, she made for the back staircase. Only when she achieved the bare, utilitarian landing did she pause again. She cocked her head, listening.

A large hand clamped around her wrist.

· *Two*

It was well after midnight and the moon but a pallid smudge, low in London's starless sky, when Fox strode St. James's Street toward number sixty. Here and there lighted windows glowed like brands.

Back at the house, a few of the celebrants continued to revel. Those who had not already fallen into slumber believed he had retired to his bedchamber. Unknown to any of his cohorts, suggestions from his aunt and sister for Catherine's coming out had finally goaded him into this outing.

The wind blasted damp and caliginous through London's avenues and alleyways, ruffling the Brutus-cropped, ash-blond hair of his undetectable wig and the many capes of his greatcoat. He held his beaver top hat in place on his head with one gloved hand and gripped a rosewood walking stick with the other.

Tonight he was Simon Fullarde, eldest son of a well-heeled family. Salt of the earth, Simon, though a bit overworked. He moved from one estate to another, keeping a peregrine eye on their administration. This made his attendance at the usual Season festivities a sometimes thing. It also made the pursuit of a close acquaintanceship with him nearly impossible.

The persona of Fullarde had proved useful in many ways

to Fox in his rich career as a confidence trickster. This evening's foray, however, was out of the ordinary even for someone with such an unique occupation. He intended to test waters that had gone untried for three years.

Even as he turned into Brooks's Club, a blight of uneasiness shivered through him, like footsteps of crows dancing on a grave. The cavern-eyed phantom of rejection and loss rose to haunt Fox. With the skill of three years' practice, he thrust it back into the dark domain of memory.

With a nod, he rendered his hat, gloves, cane, and greatcoat to the porter, then strolled into the fashionable men's club where Simon Fullarde maintained a membership. Polished wood and fine upholstery appointed the den. Branched candlesticks, fireplaces, and chandeliers provided illumination. Tobacco smoke and the smell of expensive liquor hung in the air. Desultory masculine voices droned into a solid hum, interrupted only by the occasional short burst of laughter or an exclamation. At a table where four men played whist, Fox spied a fellow he had met before.

Each man there was attired as a gentleman, perhaps more conservatively than any other group in Brooks's Club. From the snatches of conversation he caught, Fox discerned that no serious gaming took place amongst those at this table.

"Ah, Fullarde," said a man in his third decade who bore a long scar across his left jaw. His empty left sleeve was neatly pinned to the front of his coat. "I didn't know you were in Town."

Sorting through his memory, Fox found a name to go with the square, pleasant face: Captain John Brunger, formerly of the Twenty-third Fusiliers, who had fought on the Peninsula and been released last year because of extensive wounds.

Fox smiled. "Even *I* weary of the country sometimes, Brunger."

At Captain Brunger's skeptical expression, Fox chuckled. He had played his part well if even a former soldier like Brunger believed him to prefer country living to the crush and thrill of the city.

"In truth, I've come to Town on business," Fox said, as if

conceding a fact. "But I found myself idle for a few hours and thought to pass the time here."

Introductions were made, and Fox came to learn the names of the three other men sitting at the table, one of whom decided to call it quits with the game so that he might pay a duty call on his father's sister.

"Sharp as a needle, my aunt," the gentleman said as he rose from his chair to go, "and quite dissatisfied with the world." He sighed as he laid down his cards. "Might as well get the business over with. Can't very well *not* call on her."

Fox was invited to become the new fourth, and the deck was dealt. As they played a few hands, they spoke of the weather and hunting, of horses and family. When a servant came by, and drinks were ordered, Simon Fullarde received some good-natured chaffing over his request for coffee.

He took a sip from his steaming china cup and smiled. "I'm nothing if not consistent."

Tall, slender, and currently unwed, Sir Mumfry Davidson— known as Mums to his friends—laughed outright. "Dash it all, Fullarde, you cannot possibly be as dull as you would have us believe. Just because one appreciates the charms of country living does not mean he's boring company. *I* enjoy a month in my house in Sussex. But"—his eyes twinkled—"when a fellow desires to rusticate endlessly, one must suspect that it takes entirely too little to excite his interest."

It was Fox's turn to laugh. "I believe I've just been insulted. Dull, am I? Why, I'll have you know that overseeing the dropping of seeds and the scything of grass can be most engrossing. Once one of the laborers stepped in a rabbit hole."

During their conversation, Fox had learned that Mr. Edgar Yarnold, upon receiving word of his father's death, had with reluctance resigned his commission in the Royal Navy. He had returned to England to manage the family estate. In doing so, he had taken the honorable path, for neither his young stepmother nor his infant half brother could oversee the properties with any competency, but it had meant leaving a way of life that he had known since boyhood.

He pulled a face over Fox's example of the thrills to be had in country living. It was a life, Fox knew, to which Mr. Yarnold still struggled to adjust.

"Go ahead, roll your eyes at me," Fox said, touching his voice with a knowing lilt. "You'll see soon enough that the country is the best place to be."

Yarnold snorted. "For me, the *navy* is the place to be. There I could hope to serve this kingdom with distinction."

Brunger took a swallow of his claret. "And not a little excitement or prize money, eh, my lad?"

Yarnold grinned. "Aye, when the sails are full, and you're bearing down on a French man-of-war that has seventy-four guns, and your frigate has only thirty, it *is* exciting, never you fear! The prize money can be good if luck is with you and you find an enemy to capture—and then manage to take her."

Fox set his cup down. It chimed faintly against the saucer. "I stand corrected. Perhaps sowing time is not quite as adventuresome as I had thought."

All the men chuckled.

Choosing his words carefully, Fox took the conversation in a new direction. "Was not Foxton Tremayne a member of this club?"

The smiles of the other three men vanished.

"Traitor Tremayne." Brunger spat the two words as if they fouled his tongue. "Do me the courtesy of not mentioning his name in my presence."

"Nor mine," Sir Mumfry Davidson snapped.

Yarnold laid down his cards. "I've no doubt he'll roast in hell when he finally has the grace to die."

A sick knot formed in the pit of Fox's stomach.

"Ask any man in this room," Yarnold continued, "and you'll find he feels the same. Tremayne has no friends among patriotic Englishmen. How did you come to hear that traitor's name these days?"

Fox regarded the fanned cards in his hand from beneath half-mast eyelids. When he spoke, his tone gave no evidence of his emotions. "I overheard him mentioned at Tattersalls as I was looking at a little mare for a neighbor's daughter," he said casually. "The fellow—I'm not acquainted with him—seemed to believe Tremayne will be coming to London."

"In truth," Sir Mumfry said, "I had thought him dead."

"Better it were so after his performance in India." Contempt seared Yarnold's words. "All those good men killed because he disobeyed an order."

Brunger regarded the contents of his glass. "Mayhap," he said without looking up, "we should desire that he comes to Town."

"Why?" Fox asked quietly.

Sir Mumfry took a swig of whiskey. "What would you do, Brunger?"

An unpleasant smile altered Brunger's mouth. "Me? Why . . . nothing. I would do nothing at all. Indeed, if history were to repeat itself, no one would do anything. No one would acknowledge him. No one would speak to him. He would be cut dead by all decent society. Shunned."

"As he was when he arrived from India," Sir Mumfry pointed out.

Brunger nodded. "Precisely so."

"Yes, I remember," Yarnold said. "If I hadn't lost a cousin in the battle of Kurndatur, even *I* would have felt pity for him. Heard he had been an outstanding officer, before." His thumb moved back and forth over the edge of his fine woolen coat sleeve. "Wonder what turns a good man like that."

By now the card game had fallen by the wayside.

Lord Fulcher, a wiry gentleman who had already seen the high side of sixty years, strolled over to their table. "I could not help but overhear. Do pardon me for interrupting. I knew Captain Tremayne's father," he asserted. "Good man, Martin Tremayne. The Tremayne name had gone unblemished—well, in any way that matters—until his son's appalling failure in duty managed to get so many British subjects slaughtered. And by heathen savages, no less. The disgrace is intolerable."

"Well," Sir Mumfry said, "Foxton Tremayne seems to have paid a high price for having tupped some maharaja's daughter. I wasn't in London when he arrived from India, but I was told that he had been engaged to be married, and his fiancée cried off. Called him a filthy coward."

Lord Fulcher examined his stemmed wineglass, holding it up to the gilded illumination of the nearest chandelier. "I heard the same thing."

"This is the first I've heard of it," John Brunger said.

In the street outside the club, the *clip-clop* of horses' hooves rang against the pavement, echoing against the buildings that lined St. James's. Carriage wheels rattled. A woman's laughter faded into the distance.

"She claimed he had humiliated her," Fox drawled, idly rearranging the cards in his hand.

Lord Fulcher passed his glass to an attendant for refilling. "Lost his family estate, too, did he not? Not even the Israelites would lend him money."

Yarnold's sandy eyebrows rose. "Even they have standards."

Lord Fulcher scowled. "Imagine being responsible for the slaughter of so many of your countrymen." He accepted the filled glass of claret. "Contemptible."

"He would be wise not to return to London," Sir Mumfry Davidson declared.

"Is he even in England?" Brunger asked. "I've heard nothing of him until today. Fullarde, are you certain you heard—"

"Perhaps I misheard the name mentioned. As an eavesdropper, I couldn't ask them to repeat what they said." Fox withdrew his watch from his waistcoat pocket. He directed a blind glance to the clock in his palm, then signaled the attendant. "Gentlemen, I must bid you good night. I'm used to country hours."

Yarnold smiled. "Up with the cock's crow, eh?"

Fox had donned his greatcoat, hat, and gloves. He took up his walking stick, then executed a civil bow. "Sweet dreams to you, gentlemen."

"Don't stay away so long next time," Brunger called to him as, with a calm and measured stride, Fox exited the stifling premises.

His pace did not alter as raindrops exploded against him like quicksilver musket balls.

Fox had plied his test.

He had received his answer.

A startled cry escaped Isabel's lips as she tried to break free of the iron grip on her wrist.

A tall, stocky figure stepped into the light from her rush-wick. "What mischief are you doing, roaming about at this time of night?" Gilbert Millington demanded.

Isabel's heart thundered like the hooves of galloping horses. "Uncle, wh-what brings you to Greenwood now?"

"Lydia forgot her sleeping powder. Now answer *my* question," he ordered harshly.

"You're hurting me—"

His grip tightened. He shook her. "*Tell me.* What are you about?"

"Nothing! I—I heard a noise."

"Oh, indeed? What sort of noise?" He shoved his face within an inch of hers. "Just what noise could you hear from your closed bedchamber?"

An alcoholic cloud enveloped her head. Her uncle had imbibed, and the spirits had drawn aside his curtain of courtesy and rigid self-discipline to reveal this violent, growling Gilbert she had never seen before. But then, she had never before defied him. She noticed that while he had imbibed, he had not drunk enough to impair his speech or coordination.

Isabel thought quickly. "Footsteps. I heard footsteps. The boards creaked through the ceiling above my bed."

Slitted eyes studied her face. "Footsteps, eh?"

She nodded. This man was not the person she thought she had known all these years . . . until tonight.

"How brave of you, Niece," he said mockingly. "And where did you go in search of this prowler?"

"The dining room." As she stared into his face, anger flickered in the pit of her stomach. Flickered and then grew into a flame that matched the chill of her fear. This man had destroyed her family. He *wanted* Rob to die.

Isabel lowered her gaze as her outrage fed her with a courage she had not expected. "Please. You'll leave a bruise."

He hesitated, then released her wrist, apparently believing her sufficiently cowed. "Is that the only place you went?"

"Yes."

His shadowed gaze drilled into hers. "You lie."

"I went to the dining room. I found no one."

"You went into the library—I saw you come out. *You entered my library!*"

At that her gaze shot up. "*Rob's* library! Greenwood belongs to *him*."

Gilbert backhanded her. His blow exploded against her cheek, snapping her head to one side.

"Not for long," he sneered. He grabbed her upper arm. "Give me the key."

The side of Isabel's face throbbed with pain. "Key?"

He shook her again. "The library key I saw you use. Give it to me."

Rage howled in Isabel's gut like a gale. Slowly she reached into her dressing gown pocket.

"From this night until the day I inherit Greenwood, you are not to leave the property. Do you understand?" he said. "You will not receive visitors, and you'll be locked into your chamber at night. Now give me that key, Isabel."

The fingers of her free hand curled around the large key in her pocket. The metal bit into her flesh. "What happens to me after you inherit?" she asked without meeting his stare.

"You'll be out in the road. And there's no need to try to bring charges against me. The whole county knows the estate is impoverished." He laughed, but it was an ugly sound. "And I'm doing nothing illegal."

So. He did not yet suspect that she had discovered his terrible secret.

His fingers tightened painfully around her arm. "*Now,* Niece."

She dragged the key up out of her pocket. Clearly, however, she did not move fast enough for him.

"By God," he swore, "I'll teach you who is master of

Greenwood. Little bitch, you'll wish you had never been born!" He raised his hand to strike her again.

Instinctively, Isabel used the large key as a weapon, driving it toward his eye.

The arm he had lifted to beat her now whipped up to protect his face. He loosed his hold on her to make a grab for the key.

She kicked him, and he stumbled backwards.

He swiped at her, attempting to latch onto her arm again, but she dodged his reach. Breathing hard, she lashed out again before he could recover his balance. She drove her heel against his knee, the impact jarring her teeth.

Abruptly, his arms flailed the air. Before Isabel's eyes, he fell backwards down the stairs, tumbling down the several steps to the midlanding. He came to rest in an pliant heap, his rump in the air and one coattail flung over his head.

Isabel stared at Gilbert. What had she done?

She hesitated to come within his reach. He made no move.

Was he dead?

The smell of smoke reminded her of the rushlight she had dropped at Gilbert's blow. Quickly she stamped out the nascent flames, then turned back to look down on her uncle.

Cautiously, Isabel descended the stairs to where he lay. Picking up one out-flung wrist, she felt for his pulse, as she had seen numerous doctors do countless times with Aunt Lydia.

She found it. His pulse beat against her fingertips, steady and strong.

She released a sigh of relief. At least she wasn't a murderer. As she leaned a bit closer, the moonlight revealed a swelling on his jaw. By late morning, he would sport a bruise. His vanity, however, would prevent him from admitting a mere female was responsible, of that Isabel felt certain.

Still Isabel fretted. Should she seek a physician?

Before she could reach a conclusion, a loud, guttural snore issued from his lax lips. Gradually, it assumed an even seesaw cadence.

Isabel backed away from Gilbert as the chilling knowledge of what the morrow would bring soaked into her stunned brain. Her hand went to the side of her face, and she winced.

She hated the fear that had clenched in her stomach when her uncle revealed the vicious nature he had concealed so well for so long. She had never thought of herself as a coward before, and the realization shamed her.

She tried to recall what Rob had said when they discussed the subject of fear just before he left to join his regiment. In her mind she heard him speak the words again: *Courage is not the absence of fear, Bel, but the mastery of it. The only way to master fear is to face it.*

At the moment, fear seemed to surround her like the gloom in the stairwell. The choice appeared to be that she either face her fear of Gilbert and endure captivity and possibly physical punishment to no useful purpose, or try to reach Uncle Valfrid in Sweden and enlist his help in saving Rob. Perhaps together, they could then seek justice.

Isabel glared down at Gilbert's somnolent form. "And I am not *little*," she informed him softly as she turned away.

Scant time remained before dawn. Only a few hours to escape.

"There. That's the one, miss," the urchin declared as he indicated a large brick house on Harley Street. He held out a filthy paw to Isabel.

Days ago, Isabel, the daughter and sister of gentlemen, had purchased the clothes of a Berkshire dairymaid. She counted on Gilbert expecting her to be dressed as a lady— one forced to live in genteel poverty for the past year.

"You're certain Mr. Syer lives there?" she asked, but even as she questioned the child, she knew the return address on the envelopes she carried in a hidden pocket showed this address on Harley Street. Without a guide, however, she would never have found the place in the little time she could afford for this foray.

The boy nodded. "That's Mr. Syer's place, right enough."

"What is Mr. Syer's appearance?"

"He's an owd gent, he is. Spectacles. Walks bent over, like. Has to use a cane."

Into the thin, outstretched hand, Isabel placed three pence from her too-small horde of coins. "Thank you, Jemmy."

The boy's fingers closed quickly over the coins. He grinned, his blue eyes twinkling in his grubby face. Quick as a blink, he darted up the street, back the way they had come.

Isabel regarded the house Jemmy had indicated. The three-story structure advertised prosperity with a restrained hand. She could see little to set it apart from the other handsome houses on this street.

Fatigue weighed on her. She ached with cold. Four days had passed since her flight from Greenwood.

Instead of bypassing England's capital city on her risky journey to Harwich, Isabel had decided she must at least to try to speak with Mr. Syer, the man of business who specialized in putting together moneymaking propositions for select investors.

At the ripe old age of nineteen, Isabel had witnessed enough of life to doubt her chances of success in this London venture. Still, she felt compelled to at least try to convince Mr. Syer to return the money. But not to the man from whom he had received it. Instead it must go to the rightful owners.

If the broker of investments refused, her only hope lay in reaching her uncle Valfrid in Sweden, to whom she had posted her letter three days ago.

Isabel glanced up at the smoke-layered November sky above slate roof tiles. She shivered in her gray felted wool cloak. Crammed inside her portmanteau with her other garments lay her mother's black velvet cloak, lined with fox fur. It was the only material thing that she had left of her mother.

On a black ribbon around her throat, she wore a miniature she had purchased for a couple of pence at a fair she had passed. The small portrait was of a stranger. A rather poorly painted stranger at that. Hence, no doubt, the low price.

A female traveling alone risked her virtue and her life.

With her parents dead and her brother a prisoner of war in Spain, Isabel could claim no champion, no protector.

So she lied. She transformed the unfortunate-looking man in the miniature into a brave fellow legendary in his skilled use of pistols and swords. A fellow who felt highly protective of Isabel, his fiancée. She gave this paragon her maternal uncle's name: Valfrid Adkisson. The good uncle. She hoped.

Uncle Valfrid would, if Fortune smiled, become her champion. Until she could reach him and discover how Fortune chose to favor her, Isabel must remain on the run, staying out of sight as much as possible, fearing for her safety and perhaps her life.

Isabel stood on the flagway for a moment, taking her bearings. Much lighter traffic visited this neighborhood than that which mobbed the streets bearing shops or places of entertainment. Pretending not to notice the disapproving stare of a liveried servant who walked a Russian wolfhound on a lead across the street, she gripped her portmanteau.

Fortunately, there were only two or three persons who might notice her, not counting, of course, anyone looking out a window. She drew back into the late afternoon shadows cast by houses.

"If only there was some place I might make myself presentable," she muttered. With so much on her mind, by the time she remembered her appearance, there had been nowhere to perform any semblance of a proper toilet. It didn't take a mirror to inform her of her less-than-dashing looks. Sleeping under hedgerows could not be recommended as a beauty aid.

As she considered her next step, a plain, glossy black carriage rattled to a stop in front of Mr. Syer's residence, two houses from where Isabel lurked. A groom leapt down to assist an old, bowed man from the vehicle.

Wearing spectacles, leaning on an ebony cane, the ancient hobbled to the house, the front door opening for him as he approached.

Mr. Syer was indeed at home.

What now? Isabel possessed neither invitation nor appointment, and her appearance certainly lent her no credit.

She considered what might ease her past the butler and into the presence of the wealthy man of business.

The letters concealed in her stays were addressed to Gilbert, not her. Besides, she had no wish to hand them over to anyone of whom she was even the least bit uncertain. Isabel eyed the closed door. She wanted to believe Mr. Syer stood innocent of Gilbert's conniving, but what if he did not?

Back to the first problem, which was to get past that door.

Inspiration struck. Calling cards!

In the chaos of packing, habit had guided her hand. Into her portmanteau she had automatically tossed her reticule, which contained several of her calling cards. What dairymaid could offer such an item?

In the finger-numbing chill of shadows, she dug into her mud-splashed portmanteau and extracted two items: her reticule and her mother's hooded cloak. Quickly she removed the felted wool cloak, squashed it into the case, then buckled that shut.

As she unfurled the luxurious garment over the shawl she had knitted, a faint fragrance of roses enveloped her. Moisture welled in her eyes as she recognized it.

Rose scent. Her mother's favorite perfume.

Oh, Mama, how I miss you!

Isabel blinked rapidly as she slipped on the kid gloves from her reticule. Then she brought up the cloak's cowl, carefully concealing her wind-mussed hair and drab, unfashionable bonnet. If only she had thought to pack a looking glass.

She felt around in her beaded and embroidered reticule until she came up with a calling card. There in the early twilight, Isabel considered the small, elegant card printed before the dark days. She had no idea what the box of calling cards had cost her father, but she knew that price was well beyond her now.

Isabel decided she would offer her calling card if it seemed the only way she might be admitted to see Mr. Syer.

With Gilbert on her trail, she disliked making free with her name. She no longer knew whom she could trust.

After stashing her leather bag behind a shrub at the base of Mr. Syer's front porch, Isabel adjusted her cowl and closed the cloak's opening to conceal any glimpse of her travel-stained country garb. Then she straightened her shoulders. Slowly she inhaled, then exhaled in an attempt to calm her pounding heart.

When she knocked, a slim man attired in a dark coat and pantaloons and an ivory-colored waistcoat opened the door.

Isabel smiled, trying to conceal her nervousness. "I would like a word with Mr. Syer."

The butler's gaze moved to the street, then back to her. His expression remained perfectly neutral. "Mr. Syer is not at home."

An eddy of panic rolled through her stomach. "I understand that Mr. Syer has only just arrived, and I would not consider disturbing him, were it not a matter of dire importance."

"Mr. Syer is not at home."

Her panic surged. Isabel drew herself up. "I am certain he would wish to speak with me."

"And you are . . . ?"

Despite his rudeness, Isabel hesitated. The fewer persons in possession of her name, the better. On the other hand, she needed to give Syer the same name shown on the calling card it looked as if she must now present. "Miss Isabel Millington."

He regarded her dispassionately, and Isabel wondered if there might be dirt on her face. Reluctantly, she handed him her calling card.

As the butler studied the card, Isabel noticed he was missing two fingers on one white-gloved hand.

When he looked up, he appeared to study her face as thoroughly as he had her card.

"Well, Miss Millington of Greenwood Park, Berkshire, I must repeat what I told you before: Mr. Syer is not at home to anyone now."

She reached for her card, suddenly wanting it back very badly.

He ignored her hand. "I'll give him your card. May I tell him where you are staying in Town?"

"When do you expect that he will be at home to callers?"

"I cannot say, miss. But I will convey your card to him and give him your present address, if I may know it."

Isabel gave him a fictitious address. Mr. Syer would not see her now, and she could not risk staying in London any longer. Uncle Gilbert might be on his way here at this very minute, if he had discovered her forgeries.

She made one more attempt. "I have no wish to discommode Mr. Syer or his household, but, truly, I do need to speak with him. The matter is most urgent, and I might be called out of London at any moment."

From the corner of her eye, she noticed a tall, shadowed figure standing behind the servant, just beyond the lighted entrance hall.

Doubts sprang up like dragon's teeth. This time when the servant repeated his line about Mr. Syer not being at home, she bade him good day.

Isabel turned away and heard the door close behind her. Despair gnawed at her.

What had ever possessed her to believe that a calling card might make up for the absence of a carriage or even an abigail? Without a previous introduction, her presence here was most irregular. If only she had more *time*. But time, she feared, was a commodity that was running out.

"Who was that female?" Fox asked. He had just removed his disguise and returned downstairs when he had heard voices—one of them belonging to a young woman—in conversation at the front door.

"Someone desiring to speak with you, sir. Someone I've never seen before." Butler and former Corporal Horace Leckenby, who possessed the ability to speak four foreign languages, handed him a calling card.

Fox stared at the card. "Millington," he murmured, trying to recall the name. "Sounds vaguely familiar, but I cannot place it at the moment." He walked into the small southern parlor. "And you say you've never seen her before?"

Horace shook his head. "A beauty like that, sir? I'd have remembered her for sure."

"What purpose did she give for her call?" Out of habit, Fox positioned himself so as not to be seen from outside the house. He regarded Miss Millington as she descended the front steps, her shoulders bowed as if in defeat.

As he watched, she caught her heel on one of the stone stair edges and stumbled. Her arms whirled in the air like windmills as she struggled to regain her balance.

A strong urge to catch her caused Fox's muscles to tense.

She recovered, but took the remaining stairs more cautiously. Then, to his surprise, the mystery woman thrust her arms behind a shrub.

Standing beside Fox, Horace also watched her. "All she said was that it was urgent she see you. 'A matter of dire importance,' she said. Have we skimmed the cream from anyone name of Millington?"

"Possibly," Fox replied without taking his gaze from her. "That's easily enough verified. And I wish to make certain she has not come as an agent for someone else."

Horace shot Fox a knowing look. "A worry, sir."

Fox absently tapped the card against the loose fist of his other hand. "I recall every female investor with whom we've worked. There have not been that many. The name of Millington was not among them, as either a real or assumed identity."

"She wore an expensive cloak, but there was a smudge o' mud on her nose, and her face was bruised. And she wore half-boots that have seen some wear."

"The cloak I saw. I was too far to observe any other interesting details."

Under Fox's gaze, the unaccounted-for caller had extracted a portmanteau from behind the porch shrubbery. Then, leaning to one side against its weight, she had trudged down the street.

No groom with a horse had attended her. No carriage, not even a rented one, had arrived to retrieve her. Surely an agent sent by the authorities would have sufficient financing to procure the trappings required by a lady owning an expensive cloak. On the other hand, Fox knew how close with a shilling the government could be. Any man who had served in the army or the navy could testify to that fact. Magistrates and sheriffs worked even more closely to the cuticle.

And there was that portmanteau.

His gaze returned to the elegant calling card. "Have her watched."

"Aye, Cap'n."

Without looking up, Fox said, "We will adhere to the old Arab proverb."

"Which old Arab proverb would that be, sir?"

"Keep your friends close, and your enemies closer. Until we learn whether Miss Millington is, or represents, a friend or a foe, she will be our bosom companion . . . even though she doesn't know it."

The alewife looked Isabel up and down, making no attempt to conceal her annoyance. "You come for the job?" she demanded, nearly echoing Isabel's earlier, more politely spoken words as she had entered the kitchen-office at the rear of the village alehouse.

Long pine worktables and cooking implements surrounded them. A small cluttered desk huddled in a corner.

By now, Isabel had already ascertained that it might have been a mistake to wear her own clothes today. Apparently nothing available in Felgate could equal the quality of her violet velvet bonnet, slightly squashed from its sojourn in her portmanteau, her velvet-trimmed violet merino pelisse and her lilac sarcenet gown. Even the black half-boots that she had worn for the sake of practicality came from better days when she could demand the best.

She cleared her throat. "Yes."

The fact that the alewife couldn't see that the bonnet had been trimmed and retrimmed and both pelisse and gown had been reworked more than once to update their style and conceal worn places might have been taken as a testimony to Isabel's skill, but it did nothing to procure employment.

"Have any idea what it takes to brew ale and work in an alehouse?" the alewife demanded.

Tension knotted in Isabel's stomach. She had already endured two mortifying interviews today, and thus far the conversation did not augur well for this one.

"No," she admitted. Ale for Greenwood had been purchased in the village along with other food staples. "But I could learn. I'm an excellent student."

Instantly, the alewife's expression warned Isabel she had chosen the wrong word. The knot in her stomach clenched tighter.

This was her last chance. Both she and Mrs. Densham had scoured Felgate for possible work, but had come up with only three persons even willing to speak with Isabel. The first two had already rejected her.

"Student." The alewife snorted. "I need no student. A strong girl unafraid of work is what I need."

"I am strong," Isabel said quickly. "I very much want to work. If you'll just show me what you want done, I will do it."

"Take off your gloves."

With a sense of impending doom, Isabel complied.

Abruptly the alewife seized her wrists, causing Isabel to wince as callused fingers pressed against the bruise left by Gilbert's mishandling. The older woman turned them to expose smooth pink and alabaster palms and fingers. Despite the decline in fortune, persistent applications of homemade salve and the use of gloves had kept Isabel's hands those of a gentleman's daughter.

"Look at 'em," the alewife scoffed. "Not a callus anywhere. These are the hands of a girl who don't know how to work."

Isabel nearly laughed. She had effectively been mistress of a large country house for years. A large country house, of late, too short of staff.

As abruptly as she had grabbed them, the alewife

dropped Isabel's hands. "You're a fine lady. I don't need a fine lady. Good afternoon to you."

The woman opened the back door of her kitchen-office, indicating the interview was over.

Desperation kept Isabel where she was. "I assure you, I am not afraid of calluses. Were you to engage me, I promise you wouldn't be sorry." Seeing no response in the broad features of the alewife's face, Isabel swallowed the last bit of her pride. "Please. I need this job."

The alewife continued to hold the door open.

Struggling against crushing defeat, Isabel drew herself up. She accorded the alewife a crisp nod. "Thank you for your time," she said, then hurried toward the door, her thoughts in turmoil. Blindly, she bumped the corner of a worktable piled with empty drinking tankards. As she stepped outside, into the rank alley behind the building, she heard a clattering crash in the kitchen, followed by a shriek of feminine fury.

It had happened again. Grace had deserted Isabel. Indeed, it was as if some evil imp placed things directly in her path.

She caught her bottom lip between her teeth. Should she go back to help the rude alewife or just swiftly vacate the area? Bearing no love for the woman—and certain the sentiment was mutual—Isabel chose the latter.

The small village of Felgate sat on the edge of the vast marsh known as Oakum Fen. She had never intended to visit Felgate. Until yesterday, she'd had no notion either Felgate or Oakum Fen existed. That was when the driver of the public coach in which she traveled had set her and her portmanteau on the side of the road. He had pointed in this direction, unmoved by her outrage at having her ride—a ride for which she had paid from her few remaining coins—prematurely ended. Neither he nor Isabel's fellow passenger had reacted to her wrath or her repressive, politely worded request to know why she was being put off the coach. When she thought how she had *agonized* over spending the money to hasten her trip to Harwich, where packets regularly left for Sweden . . . well, it was enough to make a well-bred female throw a tantrum.

Eventually, Isabel had stumbled upon Felgate, a few miles down a remote country track that would, in the spring, be virtually hidden by thick-trunked, sheltering trees. In November, however, those trees lined the lane like a towering army of skeletal hands. And that eerie country lane had turned out to be nothing less than a portal to a different world.

In the village closest to Greenwood, where she had spent most of her life, Isabel had never encountered such *caution,* for want of a better word. While the inhabitants of Felgate were not precisely brusque, they were not overly civil, either. Only Mrs. Densham and her family seemed to believe Isabel did not promise trouble. Perhaps it came of living on the edge of a misty fen.

Now Isabel marched briskly toward her lodgings, telling herself that a walk in this bracing air was just the thing to restore her spirits.

The only thing the cold, damp air restored was her circulation. Her spirits, as well as her hair and clothing, sagged beneath the chill moisture. By the time she climbed the steps to the largest structure in Felgate, the Blue Dragon Inn, despair also weighed on her like a wet wool cloak. The effort required to lift her hand to the door latch drained what little energy she retained after three humiliating interviews and a walk through the village. The latter required that she be courteous to persons who clearly viewed her with suspicion.

She had wanted to shout that she was not here to steal from them. All she wanted was honest work.

Work. If she were not so dejected, the word might have made her laugh. But in Felgate, options for impoverished gentlewomen on the run appeared limited.

To the everyday concerns of an alewife, a baker, or a seamstress, of what use was the knowledge of French, Italian, and Swedish, the ability to play the pianoforte, or the skill to run a large household with few servants? Isabel had also studied tracts written on a wide variety of subjects, but this also had failed to produce an offer of employment. Only Mrs. Densham had listened to her list of abilities with a sympathetic ear.

If only Isabel had never gone to her "in case of" stash of bills to ease the most painful of Greenwood's household budgetary strains! Then she would have had sufficient cash to make the journey to Sweden. Of course, if that treacherous coach driver had not put her off the coach, she would now be in Harwich, where her skills might have found a better market. There she stood a better chance of earning enough to pay for passage to Göteborg and her uncle Valfrid.

Now she had only sufficient coins for another two nights in her modest room at the Blue Dragon, along with two small meals. After that, she would be destitute.

Destitute and alone.

Isabel paused, blinking rapidly against threatening tears. Her fingers touched the place on her pelisse collar under which she wore the miniature of the stranger on a ribbon around her throat. It had become a talisman after it had discouraged the unwanted attentions of a few men along the way, most particularly that thug employed by Lord Kymton, who had taken time from his task of burning the dwellings of those poor souls his master had ordered evicted. Along the road, she had met too many families driven from their homes through the offices of the horrid Duke of Kymton.

If ever she had needed a talisman, it was now.

Determinedly, she inhaled a long breath. Melancholy thoughts must be purged. Self-pity accomplished nothing. There must be another way to earn money open to her; she simply had to find it.

Before she did anything else, though, Mrs. Densham deserved a report on the outcome of the three interviews she had arranged.

Rolling back her shoulders, Isabel entered the receiving hall of the village's only inn, an oddly large and prosperous inn for the small size of Felgate. Straight ahead, the main staircase led to the two upper floors of guest chambers. Behind the closed door to her right lay the quaintly appointed private dining room. Resisting the impulse to scurry straight to her room, Isabel turned left, into the common room, where tasty meals were served along with a choice of tea, coffee, or ale—brewed by members of the large Densham brood. Isabel deemed it an amazingly well-provisioned inn, considering its remote location and no visible signs of carriage trade. This morning, as usual, the Blue Dragon common room bustled with patrons of both genders.

Thin sunshine poured through high windows. Thick, rough-hewn beams contrasted with limewashed plaster that covered the rest of the ceiling and the walls, save for the oak wainscot. Fire crackled in a brick fireplace large enough to roast an ox, inviting patrons to shed their coats and cloaks. The cozy settles with tables lining the walls and the stout tables and chairs in the central area of the chamber accommodated both guests of the inn and local folk alike.

Isabel found the short, wiry Mrs. Densham helping a stout fellow out of his redingote so that he might be seated. Already waiting to advise him of the available dishes and then take his order was the eldest of Mr. and Mrs. Densham's numerous, rosy-cheeked offspring, all of whom worked at the Blue Dragon. A more fully staffed inn one could not hope to find. So fully staffed, alas, the innkeeper could not hire Isabel.

When Mrs. Densham saw Isabel, she lifted her feathery eyebrows in query. Isabel shook her head. To her surprise, Mrs. Densham didn't look at all disappointed. In fact, she beamed as she clasped Isabel's arm, ushering her into the unoccupied private dining room across the hall.

After the innkeeper's wife closed the door, she turned to Isabel. "I've good news, my dear, which I'm bound to believe you could use now."

Never had Isabel needed good news more.

The twin pink circles high in Mrs. Densham's cheeks were even ruddier than usual, bright against the white of her lacy cap. "Captain Foxton Tremayne will be here shortly. He's seeking a tutor-companion for his sister. A fair-natured young lady she is, too, though painful shy."

Isabel blurted, "*The* Foxton Tremayne? That notorious person responsible for all those poor soldiers dying in that battle in India?"

Mrs. Densham scowled. "You'll do well to speak no ill of him in *my* inn, Miss Smythe."

Isabel Smythe was the name Isabel had given upon arrival. She wasn't proud of it, but the fewer people who knew her true identity the better. Gilbert would be hunting her, and *he* had the resources to travel swiftly.

Astonished at Mrs. Densham's change of temper, Isabel said, "The man is a traitor! He disobeyed an order—"

"Don't you believe everything you hear of him, my girl."

From what Rob had reported from Town at the time of the traitor's return to England, Tremayne's actions at Kurndatur had been indefensible. "My brother wrote me that all of London spurned him when he arrived from India."

The usually kindly face of Isabel's only ally grew shuttered. "We'll say no more on the matter," Mrs. Densham said crisply. "Are you interested in the position or are you not?"

No! Isabel wanted nothing to do with anyone as dishonorable as Foxton Tremayne. That he was free and doing well enough to hire a tutor for his sister—while Rob, a brave patriot, rotted in an enemy's prison—offered insult to all that was right and just.

But the fact remained: If Isabel did not immediately find employment, she would be stranded, facing starvation out in the road. For all she knew, her letter to Uncle Valfrid might never have reached him, leaving Rob no closer to freedom. And then there was Gilbert. . . .

"Yes, Mrs. Densham," she said, feeling as if she had swallowed a large stone. "I am interested."

The older woman gave a curt nod. "Very well. Mr. Tremayne resides not far from Felgate. He desires a companion for his sister, Miss Catherine Tremayne. This companion must speak Swedish, which you told me yesterday you speak fluently. He wishes his sister to learn Swedish." She peered over the top of her spectacles in question.

Isabel had no intention of remaining in this swamp-burg long enough to teach someone to speak a language, but she needed to keep her few options open. "I can teach her."

The innkeeper's wife folded her hands at her waist and nodded. "I took the liberty of sending a note, you see, when

I heard he was seeking someone with your qualifications. Just in case your first three appointments bore no fruit."

"Did you tell him that I was a gentlewoman in diminished circumstances?"

Mrs. Densham's cheeks pinkened again. "Yes, well. I didn't like to tell him your business, but it seemed the best way to assure him you are Quality."

Isabel suffered her own twinge of guilt. She wasn't feeling very Quality at the moment. Mrs. Densham had merely repeated to Traitor Tremayne what Isabel had told her about being an orphaned gentlewoman in reduced circumstances. It was true. Well, most of it.

One hour later, Mrs. Densham's flustered eldest daughter knocked on Isabel's door with the news that Captain Tremayne had arrived and awaited her in the private dining room.

Isabel walked down the stairs, smoothing the skirts of her Clarence blue, high-waisted gown. She had done what she could with it, but there were still more wrinkles than she would have wished. Abandoning her attempt to remove them as hopeless, she instead patted her hair, which regularly defeated her with its profligate curls. An angel must have guided her hands this time, for it appeared more orderly than usual.

Outside the closed door of the private dining room, she paused, trying to quiet the gamboling butterflies in her stomach.

Her knock was answered by a baritone "Enter."

She reminded herself to smile, then opened the door.

Foxton "Traitor" Tremayne stood across the chamber, next to the fireplace in which danced bright flames. He held in his hands a teacup and saucer.

Isabel didn't know precisely what she had expected to find, but it certainly was not this. Why had no one ever mentioned it?

As she dropped an abbreviated curtsy, she managed not to gawk.

Tall, broad of shoulder, narrow of hip, Foxton Tremayne presented a vision of striking masculine beauty. Classical perfection created from a golden palette. Surely he must resemble every self-respecting woman's secret dream prince. Isabel had always held the opinion that the perfect man must be dark. This man, however, made her reconsider.

Although cropped in an acceptable style, his thick chestnut hair lacked the pomade favored by so many gentlemen. Firelight and candles' glow gleamed upon clean hair.

The arrangement of his immaculate cravat appeared deceptively understated, as did the excellent cut of his ginger-colored coat. Beneath the latter he wore a sienna waistcoat embroidered with pear trees. His long, well-muscled legs were clothed in snug, tan pantaloons and polished brown Hessians.

It seemed to Isabel that if "beauty is as beauty does" were a physical law, Mr. Tremayne ought to be a warty troll, not a towering Apollo.

She sensed something about him. Something . . . submerged. It was as if Foxton Tremayne had thrown a cloak of invisibility around his person, leaving only a remote fraction of his true self within the world's sight.

His sculpted lips curved in a polite smile. "I am, as I'm certain Mrs. Densham has told you, Foxton Tremayne. You are Isabel Smythe?"

"I am she."

"Please, Miss Smythe, pour yourself some tea."

And what a loud crash the cup would make when it leapt from her nervous fingers, she thought. "Thank you, no."

One bronze-colored eyebrow lifted. Humor danced in his amber eyes.

"I assure you, Miss Smythe, I have not drugged the tea."

She could use a few swallows of tea to cure her dry mouth. "The thought did not occur to me, sir."

"Then you would be one of few."

She could not argue with that statement, though in her corner of Berkshire, he had ceased to be a topic of conversation years ago. The prince's—now Prince Regent's—excesses, the war in the Peninsula, and the rising cost of everything had usurped it.

Isabel went to the tea tray, where she managed to pour as

gracefully as her mother had taught her. Mr. Tremayne waited until she had taken a sip before he spoke.

"I desire that my sister, Catherine, learn Swedish. It is possible that she will soon make her home in Sweden, when she marries."

"I comprehend."

Mr. Tremayne cocked his head. He studied her intently for what seemed like a very long minute.

Really! Isabel thought indignantly. At least when *she* had scrutinized *him,* she had not been obvious about it. She hoped.

He seemed to arrive at a decision. With a quiet movement, he set his cup on its saucer.

"I had been given to believe you were not a mouse, Miss Smythe. Have I been misled?"

She stared at him in astonishment. "A . . . mouse?"

"A mouse."

Events of the past seven days rushed through Isabel's mind. She'd had to muster all her courage to approach Gilbert in his—no, in *Rob's*—library. Since then she had been accosted by a despicable cheat, fled the only home she had ever known in the dark hours of the morn, slept under hedgerows and in barns, and dragged her portmanteau countless miles.

Gilbert hunted her. She had spied him changing horses in the courtyard of a coaching inn. It had been that sighting that had driven her to spend precious coins on a stagecoach to Harwich.

For all the good it had done her.

A mouse.

Laughter burst from her throat. A mouse! To her horror, the laughter possessed a hysterical edge. She could not stop it.

Foxton Tremayne's expression sharpened to one of concern. He placed his cup and saucer on the mantelpiece and crossed the distance between them in three strides. Quickly he took her cup from her and then guided her to a chair.

"Sit," he said.

She sat.

"Lower your head and bend over."

Her eyes widened as she felt caught between panic over her inability to stop those ragged sobs of laughter and dismay at such an unseemly order.

His palm stroked her shoulders in a soothing caress. "Lower your head and bend over. Go on, now. I promise not to look at anything but your face. It's turning crimson, you know."

She bent over.

Her ears rang. Her face pounded.

Her laughter grew more jagged and she gasped, struggling against a sense of suffocation.

Tremayne continued to rub her shoulders, his touch light, his hand warm through the sarcenet of her gown. She should not have been so glad for that bit of human contact, particularly with the likes of him.

"You needn't fight for air," he murmured to her. "It will come in a second or two."

And he was right. Inhalation grew gradually easier, the dreadful laughter dying to an occasional hiccup.

Sweet oxygen rushed back into her lungs at last. When she had breathed her fill several times and no longer feared asphyxiation, Isabel recalled that she sat with her legs agape, her head between her knees. Abruptly she lifted her head.

And nearly brained Foxton Tremayne in the process. Fortunately, the man possessed lightning reflexes. He dodged the collision.

They stared at each other, their noses scarcely an inch apart.

THREE

He broke the silence.

"How did you come by that nasty bruise on your cheek, Miss Smythe?"

She gave him the answer she had given everyone else. "I dislike admitting to my clumsiness, but I fell."

"I see."

Relieved to be past that subject, she sat up, which brought her side by side with him. An unfamiliar tension gripped her. She rose to her feet and made much of smoothing her gown.

"And is that bruise around your wrist also a result of your fall?"

She restrained herself from tugging at the edge of her glove to thoroughly conceal the mark.

Tremayne stood. Isabel remained silent as he poured her a fresh cup of tea, then handed it to her. She took a swallow to ease her raw throat.

"We must make certain you have no more such unpleasant accidents," he said.

She shot him a glance over the edge the cup, but only met with his mild expression.

"We were speaking of a mouse," he continued as he retrieved his cup from the mantel and then went to the tea tray.

"More specifically, sir, you inquired if I was a mouse."

"Well? Are you?"

She sighed. Oh, but how comfortable her life as a mouse had been. Until the discovery of her father's insolvency and his departure. Alas, once a mouse lost the security of her hidey-hole, the world transformed into a frightening place. Everything—every task, every claim, every fear—grew so much larger than oneself.

She had not realized it at the time, but she had taken the first step out of her mouse skin the moment she had slid her key into the lock of the library door. No, that wasn't quite correct. Her mousehood had begun to slip away when Uncle Gilbert had told her he would not be sending the ransom to free Rob. Rob, her companion since childhood, her hero.

Wouldn't he be surprised to observe her now? At the rate she was transforming, if she survived another sennight on her own, she might qualify as a feral cat. Or, more likely, a ferret.

Carefully placing her cup on its saucer, she said, "No, Mr. Tremayne, I can safely say I am not a mouse."

"Good."

"May I ask the significance of your question? I take it you refer to my character, not my physical attributes."

He grinned, and the expression transformed his beautiful face into something . . . glorious.

"No one could ever mistake you for a rodent, Miss Smythe."

"Not even a ferret?"

He shook his head. "Especially not a ferret."

Isabel put his statement down to his brief acquaintance with her, but it pleased her anyway. She had not treasured her comparison to that cousin of the weasel. Still, the beasts could be fierce and cunning when necessary. In her present circumstances, that stood as an improvement over "mouse."

"My sister is of a retiring nature. Too retiring, I believe. It would be beneficial for her to spend time in the company of a lady near her own age who is more like my aunt Diana, known as Lady Blencowe to the world in general."

Even in Greenwood, Isabel had heard of Lady Blencowe.

Elegant, intelligent, lovely, and spirited, the widowed baroness, at the advanced age of fifty, still reigned as one of the premier hostesses in both London and Bath.

"Lady Blencowe is your aunt?" she asked, then immediately wished she could take back her incredulous tone.

"As astonishing as it sounds, we are related."

Isabel felt her cheeks warm. "I did not mean—"

His eyebrows arched. He wasn't fooled for a second.

"That is to say," Isabel amended quickly, "it seems to me Lady Blencowe would prove the perfect example from which Miss Tremayne might learn confidence."

"One would believe so, but it seems not to have taken. Catherine lived with Aunt Diana for three years after my father died."

As if he could hear the question in her mind, he added, "I was still serving in India at the time."

India. Where his disobedience had wrought disaster.

"Perhaps having a companion closer to her own age will make a difference. I fear she leads a life somewhat isolated from other seventeen-year-olds. And Diana does not know Swedish."

Isabel nodded absently as she mulled over what he had told her about his sister. Catherine Tremayne had been even younger than Isabel when she had lost her father. Isabel's heart went out to her over that loss.

Since he had not mentioned Catherine's mother taking over the care of her daughter, it might be presumed the woman was either dead or in disgrace. Or worse, did not care. The poor child!

Seventeen and apparently about to be affianced. Why promise her at such an early age? Of course, engagements in which the female had attained only sixteen or seventeen years were certainly not unheard of. Here Mr. Tremayne stood, expressing concern over his sister's lack of confidence. Did he believe a husband could endow that quality?

It didn't fit. Tremayne might be a rogue, but he did not appear to be stupid.

"How does your sister feel about your engaging me as a companion for her?" she asked.

"Once word arrived from Mrs. Densham that she knew of an amiable young lady who spoke fluent Swedish and might be interested in the position, I confess, Catherine immediately commenced making arrangements for your bedchamber. A trifle premature, I grant, but her enthusiasm bodes well."

Aside from the fact that her employer would be one of the most widely despised men in Britain, it appeared a safe hiding place had presented itself.

She had miscalculated.

As Isabel gazed at the spiked brown carpets of rushes and water plantain that surrounded them, she realized that she ought to have started her trek to her new employer's manor earlier. Sparing the purple and russet sky no more than a glance, she looked back the way they had come. At least, she *thought* it was the way they had come. The fen in that direction appeared the same as in every other direction around the flat, blunt-bowed punt: dark water from which rose rushes, like streams of shifting spears, interrupted by an occasional small island. These mounds scarcely qualified for the description of "island," as they measured little larger than a barouche. Still, they were the only places trees seemed to survive. Be it a single white willow or a copse, their silvery leaves shivered in the breeze gusting from the east, adding their rustle to the restless whisper of the rushes and the hoarse, echoing cries from migrating birds.

Yes, she had certainly miscalculated.

And then there was Catherine. Isabel stared into the opaque water that swirled silently behind the boat, but in her mind's eye she tried to imagine what the young woman looked like based on her brother's fond description.

From things Foxton Tremayne had mentioned, the unknown Catherine had reached out to pluck responsive chords within Isabel's breast.

Catherine needed something. Or someone. She was, according to Mr. Tremayne, lovely, mild-natured, and shy. Far too shy. Isabel's heart went out to the girl. How she must have suffered for her brother's crime.

Courage slept within each person—that Isabel believed. It lay dormant or perhaps even muffled by fear. It might be great, as in heroes, or a minuscule bit, as was what she had found within herself. She had been fighting fear for eight stomach-knotted days now. While she knew she could not be called brave, at least she did not think she could be called a coward.

The taciturn boatman guided the small craft along a path only he knew, stirring the dark, brackish water of the fen with his pole. His coat and breeches of homespun marked him as a local man, but where any folk lived in this mysterious wilderness of marsh, Isabel could not guess. Certainly she had seen no evidence of human habitation since she had stepped into this flat-bottom boat at the Blue Dragon's dock.

She huddled more closely within her fox-lined cloak, chilled more by the aspect of this desolate vista than by the wind off the endless water.

"How much farther?" she asked the boatman. Minutes passed with no answer. Perhaps he had not heard her. She cleared her throat and raised her voice. "I say—"

In an abrupt whir of wings, ducks rose to her right, startling her as much as she had clearly startled them. Pressing her gloved hand to her breast, as if such a gesture could calm her pounding heart, she watched them in their flight.

"We're here," the boatman said.

Isabel eased out a breath of relief, which formed a small white cloud. Yet she noticed no change in the landscape. Was he toying with her? The thought increased her uneasiness.

He guided the boat around one small island, and then another. Finally, as if by magic, a house surrounded by bare white willows came into view.

As the boat moved toward the structure, she amended her first impression. Perhaps "house" was not an adequate description. It did not begin to encompass the extraordinary edifice before them.

Broad stone stairs rose from a quay to three separate landings until they reached a simple, dark Jacobean entrance to a sprawling pile that had been built by different men of vastly differing tastes—or one insane man. Jacobean, Palladian, imitation Gothic, and something that looked like a picture she had seen in a book about India. Just about every building material imaginable had been used in one part or another of this architectural hodgepodge. Isabel had seen many a house that had been built over the course of centuries. They were not unusual in England. Naturally, styles varied somewhat, but usually builders strove to blend the old and the new into something harmonious.

Not so the builders of Foxton Tremayne's residence. Her gaze moved over the strange conglomeration. Clashing, independent ideals had been stamped onto an alien landscape that she suspected had seldom, if ever, supported anything other than stilted, bound-rush structures.

"This is Willow Hall?" she asked.

"Aye, miss. It is." The boatman eased the craft up to the stone quay.

In the gloom of late twilight, she searched the towering manor house for even the glimmer of candlelight, but found none. Mr. Tremayne had said today, she was certain of it. He had said he expected her.

She noticed that the boatman was waiting on her. Isabel fumbled with the catch of her reticule.

"Nay, miss," he said gruffly. "Mr. Tremayne does attend to that."

She felt relief to hear it, for she had little to give him.

Returning her gaze to Willow Hall, a part of her wanted to offer the boatman the few coins she had left to take her immediately back to the Blue Dragon. The Blue Dragon, at which one arrived by carriage, not by a poled boat. The Blue Dragon, where nice Mrs. Densham clucked over her as if she were a starving chick.

But Isabel could ill afford to pay for a room at the inn. There was no turning back now.

Placing her gloved fingers into the boatman's gnarled hand, she stepped out of the boat and onto the quay. Above them, the house towered, silent and dark.

She turned back to her guide. "I would like to make certain Miss Tremayne and her brother are at home. Will you wait for me?" she asked, wishing her voice didn't hold that note of anxiety.

He shook his head. "Nay, miss. I cannot." Even as he spoke, he swung her leather portmanteau onto the stone slab, beside her feet. He placed his pole back into the water and pushed away from the stone landing.

Isabel's heart clenched as she watched him depart, gliding swiftly away, then out of sight. Finally, reluctantly, she turned toward the house and ascended the avenue of stairs.

Although most of the house looked to be as old as Methuselah, this part, at least, appeared fairly new. The limestone steps were evenly cut, with generous room for her feet. For that she felt grateful, since the light rapidly dwindled.

As she made her way to the simple entrance, a short, stocky man with a black eye patch appeared at a window above her, bearing a branched candlestick of lighted tapers. He set it on the sill and then vanished from sight.

The candles' gold illumination acted as a balm upon Isabel's spirit. She had not been forgotten after all.

Encouraged, she climbed the remaining stairs more rapidly. At the ribbed Jacobean door, she used the gargoyle-headed knocker to announce her arrival.

She waited.

Standing in the growing dark, feeling more and more alone, Isabel recalled the sinister-looking black eye patch the man with the candles had worn. Behind her, a marsh bird loosed its plaintive cry. The sound echoed eerily over the black water.

Why would anyone choose to live in this desolate place? she wondered. Casting an uneasy glance over her shoulder, she knocked on the door again, more forcefully this time.

It flew open. Facing her stood the one-eyed man. He now held a candlestick with a single taper. At this proximity, he looked somewhat less ominous. The reason for this might have been his round, pink cheeks. More likely it was the fact that he stood two inches shorter than Isabel.

"I heard ye knock the first time," he grumbled. "Would ye have me leap from yon landing above to get to this door?"

Isabel made no attempt to respond to such impertinence.

He cocked a bushy eyebrow at her. "I suppose ye be Miss Isabel Smythe, then?"

"I am."

"Well, come in, come in. No use ye standin' out there. Where is yer trunk?"

She indicated the portmanteau sitting at her feet. "No trunks."

He eyed the case as he accepted her bonnet and cloak from her. "Mr. and Miss Tremayne are waitin' on ye."

He left her in a cozy sitting room. A swift glance revealed a beamed ceiling and walls paneled with carved oak. Chairs upholstered in crewelwork and a settee covered in green brocade were clustered around a brick fireplace. Accompanying the seats were a game table, a sewing table, and two side tables. One of the latter bore a clock in a satinwood case, the other a collection of elephants carved from onyx, ivory, amethyst, and lapis lazuli.

The door opened, and in walked a lovely young woman who, judging from Mr. Tremayne's description, must be Catherine. She wore a smile so sunny, no one could have doubted her pleasure over Isabel's arrival.

"Hello," she said in a soft voice. "I am Catherine Tremayne."

They accorded each other an abbreviated curtsy.

Isabel returned her smile. "Pleased to meet you, Miss Tremayne. As you probably already know, I am Isabel Smythe." The lie suddenly sat heavy on Isabel's conscience.

"When you did not arrive before dark, we became worried."

Without thinking, Isabel took her charge's slim hand and gave it an encouraging squeeze. "I pray you forgive my tardiness. My ignorance of this area is responsible for my poor timing."

Slim fingers clasped Isabel's. "As long as you are well, that's all that matters."

"Catherine." The word spoken from the doorway behind Isabel moved through the air of the parlor like the deep tone from a golden gong.

"Fox, Miss Smythe has arrived safe and sound."

Before she had even turned to face Fox Tremayne, his presence seemed to reach out and stroke Isabel's nape. It unsettled her.

He accorded her a bow. "I'm happy to see you have arrived safely." The master of Willow Hall smiled, and Isabel felt a little bereft of breath.

"I do apologize for being so late. I hope I've not discommoded you in any way," Isabel said, feeling a bit off-balance. What with sleeping in barns and under hedgerows in cold weather, she supposed she might be coming down with a fever.

"I requested the innkeeper to make arrangements for your transportation. I'm certain he engaged a boatman as early as could be." Mr. Tremayne looked at his sister. "Catherine, would you be so good as to have Cook prepare a platter to be taken to Miss Smythe's chamber directly?"

As Isabel was wondering why he didn't just tug that embroidered bellpull behind him to summon a servant to take the message, Catherine murmured her agreement. She left the chamber with a parting smile to Isabel.

Mr. Tremayne gestured toward a chair behind Isabel. As soon as she settled against the cool brocade, she realized she was deeply fatigued.

"My sister is pleased you are come," he said.

"I am honored."

He took a chair across from her, resting one booted ankle on the other knee. "When last we met, you gave as your previous employer the Earl of Merlawe."

Abruptly, she forgot her weariness. "I did."

A lie. He had assumed her change in circumstances, as Mrs. Densham mentioned in her note to him, meant Isabel had been forced to earn her way in the world in the usual occupation of a displaced lady: governess or companion. Unwilling to give him any information that might allow him to trace her to Greenwood, she had given as a reference the father of her childhood friend and neighbor, Frannie Twickham. After all, she had taken the surname of Frannie's last tutor, Isolda Smythe. The earl had constantly confused Isolda's and Isabel's names.

"Since your letter of reference has been so unfortunately lost in your travels," he continued, "I've taken the liberty of writing the earl to ask for another for you."

Isabel clutched her reticule. From everything she had heard about Fox Tremayne before yesterday, the man was nothing short of a recluse, rejected by polite society. She had believed he would not have the audacity to intrude upon the attention of a nobleman, particularly with such a minor concern.

How easily her ruse might be exposed. With just one word amiss, one rare, right word . . . if the Earl of Merlawe troubled to respond to Mr. Tremayne's inquiry at all.

Suddenly this island in a swamp seemed like a trap.

"I believed you would not want to be without such a useful letter."

"Of course." Her voice sounded faint, even to her ears. She infused it with more vigor. "I appreciate your concern." This late in November, would Lord Merlawe still be in his Berkshire marquessate, or would he have traveled to warmer climes by now? Frannie's father detested the cold. "I am certain you'll find Lord Merlawe's response quite satisfactory."

If there was one.

Privately, Isabel hoped there was not.

Fox studied Miss Isabel Smythe, wondering why she was using that name now.

She stood taller than most women. Like his aunt and sister, who were also tall, she was slender and well formed. From the conformation of her upper arms, revealed by the unsuitable capped sleeves of her gown, he surmised physical activity came as no stranger to her. Miss Smythe's carriage spoke rather of a gently born lady than the smudge-faced young woman in a sorry disguise who had knocked on Mr. Syer's front door and handed over her calling card.

The calling card, as it turned out, bore the same last name as one Gilbert Millington, a particularly greedy fellow who had swindled tradesmen in counties surrounding the one in which he dwelled. Millington had been invited into an investment Mr. Syer represented by an even more corrupt fellow, who had been one of the real targets of the operation. To Fox's surprise, Millington had returned to invest with Mr. Syer a few more times, preening himself at rubbing elbows with men of superior rank. Some persons took longer to learn their lessons than others.

These things recommended Miss Millington to the invented position as his sister's companion.

Fox was not completely easy with allowing her near Catherine before he had ascertained her purpose in seeking out Mr. Syer. She remained an unknown element until Croom unearthed more information about her. But Catherine had been entreating Fox to allow her to play a part in the operations. He disliked the idea of her involvement, but to deny her request might demolish an opportunity to diminish the distance between them. She wanted to be a bona fide part of his life, something he wanted every bit as much. He only wished his enterprise were safer for her, like that of a merchant or a . . . a baker. Just in case, Fox had assigned Nottage to keep a sharp lookout for her safety. In addition, he knew his young sister would be watched by everyone else in the household as she went about the mansion. "Miss Catherine" was held in affection by those who knew her. Particularly her brother.

Now his thoughts returned to the female before him. Those large, gray-green eyes, that retroussé nose, and those full, rose petal lips added to the picture of feminine innocence, as did the cloud of curly black hair. Indeed, she presented a vision of sweet promise. A vision that surpassed even the one Everleigh had fallen prey to in India, the young fool.

In this case, a vision bearing bruises. At the thought, Fox again experienced the wrath he had felt upon discovering the marks on her fair skin. She might have received them in a fall, as she had said, but if she had, it had been a fall come by with assistance. That bruise around her wrist resulted from someone's brutal grip, of that he felt certain.

Miss Smythe met Fox's gaze, then looked down in that

way women often used to secret their thoughts behind the guise of modesty. She sat with her lashes demurely lowered and her hands folded in her lap, clasping her reticule, a velvet, beaded thing.

Odd that something so unrelated to his purpose as some small, female accessory should capture his attention. Perhaps it was because the gewgaw had cost a pretty penny. As had her lilac gown and her incongruously sensible half-boots. Of course, it was common for a servant or a companion to be garbed in the castoffs of her employer, and an earl's daughter would command a handsome wardrobe.

Yes, Miss Smythe presented an intriguing puzzle. One that would soon be solved. Between Croom's gift for uncovering information and his own letter to the Earl of Merlawe, written in his guise as Simon Fullarde, he would doubtless be well on the way to discovering what Miss Smythe wanted with Mr. Syer.

FOUR

The door to the sitting room opened, and Catherine entered. "Miss Smythe's portmanteau has been taken to her chamber, and so has her dinner," she said. "Cook is fretting that it will grow cold."

Fox smiled at his sister. "We cannot have Miss Smythe eating a cold supper." He looked at the newcomer. "I'll have Nottage show you to your chamber." The room he had chosen for her was situated as far from the accoutrements of his work as possible, so it would take her a while to get there. That placed her an inconvenient distance from Catherine's quarters, but he felt it was a necessary precaution.

Catherine hesitated. "I'll be happy to be Miss Smythe's guide," she offered softly.

"Oh, good," Miss Smythe chimed. "We will have a chance to become acquainted." She appeared completely sincere.

Fox rapidly weighed the risks. Then, deciding Catherine would be safe until Nottage caught up with them, he inclined his head in agreement. "*Bon appétit,* Miss Smythe. We'll speak again in the morning."

After Catherine led her new companion away, Fox tugged the bellpull in the afore-planned code that would send Nottage in search of Catherine. Then he turned to the fireplace.

Isolated as she was in the fen, ignorant of the house's floor plan, surrounded by possible hostiles, Miss Isabel Smythe would be a fool to try anything untoward. He did not believe her to be a fool.

Into his memory swam the image of her large gray-green eyes. Her gaze had remained steady on him, despite the reaction that had caused her fingers to tighten on her reticule when he had mentioned the letter to Lord Merlawe.

It didn't take a gypsy's crystal ball to see she was determined to keep something from him. The question was, what?

Fox took the poker from its rack and idly jabbed at the burning log in the fireplace. He watched as it shed a glowing red nugget.

Although he doubted she had known just how far out into the fen she would be ferried at the time she had stepped into the boat at the Blue Dragon, at first glance it struck him that she must be desperate to have come here to Willow Hall. True, it had been his man who had put her off the coach and directed her toward Felgate. And according to his informant, Mrs. Densham, Miss Smythe had come alone and allegedly penniless. Oh, yes, Mrs. Densham had been most efficient in maneuvering Miss Smythe into Fox's employ. But then, the energetic innkeeper's wife liked Miss Smythe and trusted Fox.

Some of the sharpest tricksters he knew would *appear* to be alone, when, in fact, they were surrounded by their associates. To make certain this was not the case, Fox's people had checked the village and combed the fen, but had found no sign of anyone who might be in collusion with Isabel Millington-Smythe.

Perhaps she was waiting. For what? Whom? Did she run a confidence game of her own? Or, worse, did she work with the authorities? He doubted any of his fleeced "clients" would be willing to make their greed or gullibility known, even to underpaid public servants, but there was always the slim chance. Fox had no wish to explain his enterprises to someone with the power to have him or any other member of the Assembly transported or hanged.

Fox thrust his poker into the flames as he considered. The turned log burned brighter for an instant, sending sparks up the chimney.

Then he reached into his pocket and withdrew her calling card.

Branched candlestick in hand, Catherine led the way down the hall, away from the parlor. "Was the trip from the Blue Dragon too unpleasant for you?" she asked, casting Isabel a concerned look.

From the moment they had met, Isabel had sensed Catherine's general incertitude, and her heart had gone out to the girl. Now she made her first move to reassure her.

Isabel smiled. "Not at all. 'Tis only that I am unused to, uh, marsh."

Swamp. With forests of whispering reeds and the eerie cry of wildlife.

They entered a part of the house that had been built in the Palladian scheme. There they climbed a wide, marble staircase. It bore fine oak handrails atop wrought-iron balusters that likely would have done justice to any of the Prince Regent's residences.

"I, too, had no experience with a fen when my aunt brought me here to live with my brother," Catherine said. "I found it . . . frightening. In time, however, I came to appreciate its special character."

Special character, in Isabel's private opinion, was a description open to a wide range in interpretation.

As Catherine described Oakum Fen in spring, they entered a gallery. The patter of her slippers and the muted thud of Isabel's half-boots that had echoed on the stairs were now subdued by hand-knotted Moorfields carpets on the polished wood floor and by the pale green damask that covered the high walls. Light from the tapers Catherine carried danced capriciously across massive gilded frames and the portraits they enclosed. Lashless eyes set in solemn faces seemed to watch the two intruders as they passed.

As the fragrance of melting beeswax trailed in the air, Isabel gazed up at the paintings, curious about the lives that had been captured in only a span of hours by an artist.

"Family?" she asked. The high, barrel-vaulted ceiling endowed the word with a hollow quality.

"Yes," Catherine replied. "Fox brought them here after—" Abruptly, she broke off.

Isabel halted Catherine's progress with a touch on her arm. "With me, you needn't talk about anything that makes you uncomfortable." She grinned. "Except Swedish, of course."

Chewing on her lower lip, Catherine's gaze scanned the portraits, almost as if she feared they could hear her. Then, appearing to arrive at some decision, she released a long sigh. "You'll learn about it sooner or later, I suspect. He brought these here . . ." She lifted an arm toward the paintings. She stopped, then tried again. "He moved here after he lost Tregarn."

"Tregarn?"

"Our home in Cornwall. Our family had lived there since the reign of Queen Elizabeth. I was twelve when Mama fell ill. Fox was already in India. Papa consulted physician after physician, desperate for her to regain her health." In the candlelight, the expression on Catherine's delicate face had shifted to a haunted barrenness. "Father . . . he turned away from everything but Mama." As her softly spoken words faded, deep silence enfolded them for a moment. "Tregarn, the tenants, the animals, all suffered for it." She said nothing of the child who must have felt shut out. "There was . . . debt."

Her last words were almost whispered. Then, as if she had caught herself in a social faux pas, she drew a sharp breath.

"Debt is the companion of hard times," Isabel said.

Catherine smiled, though that tentative curve of youthful lips conveyed a sadness that pierced Isabel's heart.

"Mama died, of course," Catherine continued. "So did Papa, less than a year later. Aunt Diana came for me, and I lived with her until three years ago."

So Catherine, too, was an orphan. Only someone who had endured the loss could ever know the ache of losing both parents so close in time. Their deaths split the fabric of one's life. Into the tomb with them went so much of one's own life's history. One felt left behind. Diminished. Alone.

At least Catherine still had her brother. Unlike Rob, Mr. Tremayne was very much a free man. Indeed, he dwelt in splendor compared with Rob's prison cell.

The loss of Tregarn went a long way toward explaining this remote location and Catherine's lack of confidence. That and Mr. Tremayne's public status as a disgraced officer.

Isabel held out her hand to Catherine. After a slight hesitation, the younger woman grasped it. The tension in her fingers conveyed a longing. If it had been possible, Isabel would have made their link a conduit and poured into it all the encouragement she could muster. Lacking the magic to bring that about, she settled for giving Catherine's hand a reassuring squeeze.

Catherine's brown eyes glistened. She blinked rapidly, but in vain. "Oh, I'm so silly," she murmured, then released a hoarse, self-deprecating laugh.

Without thinking, Isabel pulled her one and only handkerchief from her reticule, then gently dabbed at Catherine's cheeks. "I'm glad I am come." Her throat tightened. During the past several days, she had spent too much time on the verge of weeping to remain unaffected by someone else's tears. "Where else can I learn what sort of ducks make such a din? A veritable chorus. I couldn't see them, but they certainly saw us, for they promptly ceased their noise and concealed themselves when the boatman poled me to your steps."

As Catherine accepted the handkerchief from Isabel, a watery giggle escaped her. "Those are *frogs,* silly."

Isabel was glad her mistake had helped to cheer Catherine. "Frogs? You're certain? Is it not too cold for them to still be out?"

Catherine shook her head. A muffled chortle escaped from behind the wad of lace-edged linen. "Soon."

"You see?" Isabel said. "I've not been here above an

hour, and already I've learned something. Perhaps tomorrow you might point out such a creature to me. I desire to see the frog that quacks."

Brown eyes widened. "You would not be repelled or — or afraid?"

Isabel's laughter rang through the gallery. "Afraid? Of a *frog*? I should say not." There were too many other, more frightening things. She linked arms with Catherine and continued in the direction they had been walking. "Why, if my brother ever heard that I had shied from a frog, I should never hear an end to it."

Catherine's face lighted. "You have a brother?"

"I do."

"Older or younger?"

"Older by six years." Isabel flashed Catherine a mischievous smile. "I learned to adore frogs out of self-preservation."

"You *adore* frogs?"

"Well, perhaps 'adore' is too strong a word. Tolerate might be more accurate."

"Where is your brother now?" Catherine asked.

Isabel tapped a fingertip on one of her reticule's beadwork roses. Perhaps she should have painted herself a single child. Too late now. Besides, she disliked lying to Catherine.

"He is a prisoner of the Spanish," she said, thinking it best to keep as close to the truth as possible.

"Oh! How frightful for you!"

"Rather more frightful for him, I should think."

Hurried footsteps sounded ahead of them. A point of light bobbed, finally revealing itself as the flame of a single candle. "There you are," a man's voice declared querulously. As he marched closer, Isabel saw the voice belonged to Mr. Eye Patch.

"Yer brother is wonderin' what happened to ye when ye didna return to the sittin' room, Miss Catherine," he said. His breath came quickly. He had been hurrying. "Thought ye would be in yer room by now, Miss Smythe. Food must be gettin' cold."

"We—," she began, but he had already turned back to Catherine.

"I'll see Miss Smythe to her room," he offered, though it sounded more like a command. "Yer brother is waitin' on ye," he added pointedly.

"Oh. Well. Thank you, Nottage," Catherine said, with all the enthusiasm of a condemned prisoner hearing her sentence. She gave Isabel an uncertain smile. "I'll see you at breakfast tomorrow?"

"Yes. Of course." *My. Aren't we the proper tyrant,* Isabel thought, casting Nottage a gimlet glance. She leaned forward and placed a bolstering peck on Catherine's cheek, as if her kiss were a protective charm or shield to ward off the power to make Catherine feel small or foolish. "What time shall I join you in breaking our fast?"

Catherine beamed. "There is a clock in your chamber. When it reads eight, breakfast will be served in the morning room."

They bade each other good night, and Catherine hurried back the way they had come. Nottage marched in the opposite direction. Isabel hastened to catch up, then fell into step beside him as they passed out of the gallery.

They entered a great saloon empty of furniture. Their boots clacked against the parquet floor. Suspended on long gilded chains were three chandeliers, composed, Isabel observed, of what must be thousands of droplets of cut glass, dingy from years of neglect. From each chandelier hung tattered gray tapestries of cobweb that fluttered as they strode beneath.

The light from Nottage's single taper exposed walls covered in acres of azure brocade, stained and rotted in places. Across the room stood an empty fireplace with an overmantel of alabaster, flanked by sienna-veined marble columns.

Clearly, Traitor Tremayne did little formal entertaining.

Isabel had to keep up with the taciturn Nottage, who left the saloon and vanished around the corner.

Just as she wondered for the third time where this alleged chamber of hers was located, they finally arrived. Relief flooded through Isabel when she saw that, unlike so much of what she had seen, the room was not long-abandoned at all. Her portmanteau sat upon the bed.

Nottage lit the candle on the bedside table with the one he carried. Then he headed for the door.

"Good night, Nottage," Isabel called sweetly.

"G'night to ye, Miss Smythe." The door thumped closed behind him.

His "good night" had sounded so grudging as to have been almost insulting.

With a sigh, she dropped wearily into a wooden armchair. It had been her experience that servants took their cue from their masters. If even a butler could bully Catherine, then Isabel's self-appointed task was going to be more difficult than she had imagined.

Isabel's thoughts continued to plummet toward gloom. The only person outside this household who knew her whereabouts was Mrs. Densham. The letter to her uncle containing what directions she could give to her present location must wait to be posted until opportunity took her to Harwich. She could not feel easy posting it in Felgate, not when so many in the village seemed suspicious of her. She intended that only her uncle Valfrid read what she had written.

Isabel took her first good look around her new quarters. The walls were newly painted a creamy yellow. A patterned cotton of a slightly deeper shade had been used for the curtains drawn over the two windows and those draping the tester bed. A place setting had been laid on an old-fashioned table of walnut, along with the cup of milk and napkin-covered plate. A fire burned on the hearth.

It was a cozy chamber, and, judging from the trek she had just made, Isabel certainly would not lack privacy.

She ate her dinner, then set about unpacking and arranging her clothes on the shelves in the carved rosewood wardrobe. As she worked, uncertainty assailed her again, this time from a different direction.

Willow Hall struck her as far too isolated—with too many abandoned rooms—for any sensible man. It was one thing to inherit a place like this. In that case, the heir might be tied to the house by family tradition or, quite possibly, penury. Mr. Tremayne did not appear to suffer from a lack of funds. And Willow Hall was not Mr. Tremayne's ancestral home. It was his hiding place.

An image of Fox Tremayne coalesced in her mind. Handsome. So very handsome. Tall. Lean. Broad of shoulder, narrow of hip, with long, well-muscled limbs. He dressed conservatively. His garments possessed quality and an elegance so understated as to almost become nondescript.

Isabel did not know why, but it seemed to her as if, beneath that image of a country gentleman, something rippled, leaving her with a prickling sense of the unseen. It was as if she had heard the growl of a tiger, felt its deep vibration, yet caught no clear sight of the dangerous beast. Even stronger than the impression of danger had come that of sharp, patient intelligence.

If it were not for the excellent reputation of Lady Blencowe, whom Isabel had been told stayed at Willow Hall often . . . if Catherine were not so clearly in need of the help the right companion might give her . . . well, Isabel would have been even more worried.

Gentlemen left the company of their peers behind for many reasons, she told herself as she eyed the creases in her only other gown. Often they retreated from society over matters of pride. Of honor.

Or of its loss.

Isabel covered a yawn with one palm. This day had seemed to last a twelvemonth. She went to the door, where she found the key protruding from the lock. Mr. Tremayne, it seemed, trusted her more than she trusted him. But then, what reason could he have to mistrust *her*?

She turned the key in the lock, then went about making herself ready for bed. As she slipped beneath the covers, she decided she was probably better hidden from Gilbert here than anywhere else in England.

If Uncle Valfrid had received the letter she had posted the day after her flight from Greenwood, then he knew of Rob's dreadful position and of Gilbert's treachery. As soon as she encountered the opportunity, Isabel would send him another letter—in case the first letter had not reached him—reiterating Rob's plight and informing him of her present situation and location.

The pillow accepted her cheek in its cool, soft embrace.

While she earned enough to pay for her passage to Sweden, Isabel decided to be the epitome of all that was perfect in a language tutor and to apply herself to boosting Catherine's self-confidence. Meanwhile, she was as safe as she could be until Gilbert met with justice. With a sigh, she drifted toward sleep.

Then her eyes popped open. She sat upright in one bolt.

She had left her monogrammed handkerchief with Catherine.

FIVE

The following morning, Isabel woke to a moment of confusion, until she remembered she was now the companion and Swedish-language tutor to Traitor Tremayne's sister. This was her room in his odd, rambling mansion.

A mansion with—based upon last night's experience, at least—relatively few servants. Since Lady Blencowe's reputation was one of refinement, taste, and fashion, this apparent lack surprised Isabel, who knew that maintaining a standard of elegance required a cadre of skilled assistants. Mama, too, had been a woman of discernment.

Her gaze moved around the chamber. Of course, she would have preferred that Willow Hall not be isolated in the middle of a swamp, but beggars could not be choosers. This cheerful, cozy room certainly ranked above the hedgerow under which she undoubtedly would be now huddled had she not accepted Mr. Tremayne's offer of employment. This location also brought the added benefit of being difficult for Gilbert to find. Alas, it did, however, pose a challenge to safely posting a letter to Uncle Valfrid. She had no desire to make known to her new employer or his servants that she was alone, a runaway from her thief of an uncle, and that she planned to hie off to Sweden as soon as she had the money for passage to Göteborg. Some persons read all the corre-

spondence of those in their hire. The Countess of Merlawe—
Frannie's mother—was just such an example.

Isabel pushed aside the covers. A watery sunbeam shone
in her face, as if seeking to drive her from bed. Glancing at
the clock on the mantel, she saw she had time to dress and
get to the morning room . . . wherever that might be located
in this vast pile.

The fire had died out in the night. Wriggling off the high
tester bed with a speed encouraged by the cold, Isabel scurried to the washstand. For want of a better place to put it, she
emptied the water she had used for last night's ablutions into
the chamber pot beneath the bed, then filled the basin with
the remainder of the icy water from the pitcher. After bathing,
Isabel donned her blue wool gown. She stepped into her
slippers, then checked the clock again. There remained
enough time to dress her hair.

Swiftly she brushed it out, leaving the short hair around
her face to curl naturally, while gathering the longer mass
into a knot high at the back of her head. Rather, she *tried* to
gather it into a knot. When she checked the looking glass,
the sleek knot she had attempted to create appeared a bit less
than sleek. She sighed. It usually did.

The mantel clock told Isabel it was time to seek out the
morning room. Having been tardy once, she refused to keep
the Tremaynes waiting again. As she breezed out of her
chamber, she noticed the clock read seven thirty-eight. *This*
time, she would not be tardy.

Pleased with her punctuality, if not her hair, Isabel hastened down the hall, certain of her path. Some of her certainty dispelled when she reached a hall perpendicular to the
one in which she stopped. She chose the direction she believed correct.

She turned into another hall . . . then another . . . and another. Doubt gnawed at her. Nothing looked familiar.

Silence filled every room and passageway she walked
past, disturbed only by the increasingly faster patter of her
slippers.

She attempted to retrace her steps back to her bedchamber so that she might try again to find the correct way.

Instead, she became ever more misplaced. Isabel hurried through corridors that were large and stately, and others that were old and narrow, but she failed to come across the gallery through which she had walked with Catherine or even the saloon through which Nottage had led her.

Finally, consumed with frustration, Isabel came to a halt. She was lost. Worse, she was doomed to be late again.

Abandoning all semblance of decorum, she broke into a run to reach the end of the hall in which she now found herself. Pale cobweb draperies fluttered from staghorn wall sconces as she rushed by. She was certain she had not seen this place before. Quite certain. Wasn't she?

Her steps slowed. Isabel worried her bottom lip with her teeth as she considered her alternatives. This was not the first time she had become lost in a great house. Indeed, she had been in too many of them to avoid the experience. Of course, *then* there had been no pressing need *not* to be lost, and servants had turned out to retrieve her.

Since she had departed her bedchamber, Isabel had not seen one room in which people might have gathered or dined within the last several years. She had caught not so much as a glimpse or heard even a footfall from another soul. Nowhere to be found was a functioning bellpull to summon help.

She passed a statue in the hall and wrinkled her nose at a spiderweb suspended from the bronze elbow of Apollo. Or maybe it was Ares. It was difficult to tell with such thick dust.

Clearly, if she was ever to find the morning room, she must resort to drastic measures.

"Help!" she shouted. "I'm lost!"

A faint, brief echo murmured through the hall and chambers beyond like an eddy after a splash, fading finally into quiet. Isabel's temper began to simmer. If Mr. Tremayne treated all his employees in this negligent manner, she didn't wonder why there were so few of them.

"Hul-l-l-*o-o*," she bellowed. "Will *someone* please *help* me?"

Again, her only answer was silence. She pounded on the

floor with her heel, but slippers were not designed for use as hammers, and shortly she was forced to abandon that tactic or incur a bruise.

She waited, hoping for a sign of impending rescue. As minutes passed, she seethed. Clearly she was on her own.

She looked around until she found a window. Carefully she nudged aside the holland cloth that covered it, fearful its burden of dust might avalanche down on her.

To her amazement, the view that met her eyes was nothing like what she had seen last evening as she had approached the front of the mansion. Below was a garden, though winter-barren, and beyond that a frost-seared lawn and a faux temple.

She took note of the direction from which the sun shone and surmised it was likely still in the eastern sky at this hour. Last night the breeze had come from the east. As she had faced the entrance to Willow Hall, the wind had blown against the front of her. Therefore, if she walked in the opposite direction of the sun—westerly—then she should end up at the front of the house. Perhaps there she would find a staircase down and, eventually, someone to direct her to the morning room.

Feeling better now that she had a plan, Isabel peered out each window she came to, until she more exactly gauged the sun's position. Then she struck off toward what she hoped was the west, pausing periodically to shout for help.

As she turned down a hall, a tall figure abruptly stepped through a doorway in front of her.

Isabel let out a startled yelp.

The master of Willow Hall lifted one eyebrow. "Late again, Miss Smythe?"

Her heart hammering in her breast, Isabel glared at him. He stood tall and handsome and possessed an air of masculine vitality—and she wanted to throttle him.

She demanded waspishly, "Is it your custom to lurk about and startle people out of their wits, Mr. Tremayne?"

"My apologies, Miss Smythe, if I gave you a fright, but you seem quite in possession of your wits."

"I've been trying to gain someone's attention for some

time now, sir. Did you hear me call out?" Call out, indeed. She had bellowed.

"I heard nothing. I simply noticed it was late and you were missing."

Ah. Deductive reasoning.

"I cannot think why it did not occur to me to throw down bread crumbs last night," she said, "when I had a *guide* to this other side of the moon."

He cocked his head. "I perceive you find your chamber a bit far from the rest of the household. I thought you might value your privacy."

"Your consideration is appreciated, Mr. Tremayne, but do you not feel there is a difference between privacy and isolation? It cannot be convenient for Miss Tremayne to have her companion quartered miles away from her."

"Of course. But alas, presently that is the only available room that is suitable."

With a house this size? Isabel found that difficult to swallow. Nonetheless, he was her employer. Out here in the middle of the swamp, Isabel was at his mercy.

She tried to keep the disbelief from her voice. "The decision is yours, of course. You are, after all, master of Willow Hall," she said stiffly.

"Kind of you to remember." Amusement warmed his words. "If you will but endure the inconvenience for a while," he added, "I shall see what can be done to accommodate your wish. You understand, I am certain, that procuring good help out here often proves difficult."

"Doubtless it is," she murmured. Like as not he would still be trying to recruit that good help as she waved good-bye from her Sweden-bound ship. Well, there seemed to be no help for it. She would simply have to learn her way about the place. String? Bread crumbs? She would give the method some thought. "You are the soul of patience," Isabel told him.

She, however, was not. And the letter informing her uncle Valfrid of her whereabouts still needed to be posted. With the possibility that the Earl of Merlawe might actually respond to Tremayne's inquiry, time had become even more critical.

Before she could say anything further, her employer turned to indicate the direction from which he had come with a short sweep of his forearm.

"Allow me to escort you to the morning room, Miss Smythe," he said. "We are expected."

"Certainly." She suppressed a sigh. Once again, she had kept people waiting. At this rate, everyone was going to think her the most incompetent creature to come down the turnpike.

As he accompanied her toward the stairs, Isabel tried to make note of the turns and their directions along the way, but she became confused before they could even begin their descent.

"Thank you for rescuing me," she said as they progressed down the handsome staircase.

"When Nottage returned from your chamber without you, and you had not yet made an appearance in the morning room, I thought it wise to seek you out."

She had only seen the man three times, and on two of those occasions she had been late. Considering that, she had to admit he displayed patience. Her father had always despised tardiness. Thus, she, her mother, and brother had learned to be prompt. In their household, there had been no such thing as "fashionably late."

"I believed I could remember my way to where I came in last night. I do apologize. It was not my intention to discommode you or Miss Tremayne," she said.

Hands folded behind his back in a contemplative manner, he seemed to consider this. When he spoke again, his question caught her off guard. "Did you experience such problems in the Earl of Merlawe's residences?"

The question made her uncomfortable. She stuck with the truth as much as possible. "'Tis not that I am unacquainted with large houses, Mr. Tremayne. It's only that I am used to them having a certain . . . *logic* to their pattern. If Willow Hall possesses such a plan or order, I fear it escapes me."

"It escapes us all, Miss Smythe," he said, humor twinkling in his golden eyes.

They walked in silence for a few minutes. Isabel fretted over being late again. She wondered at the odd flutter, that breathless hurly-burly inside her that his direct gaze had brought.

She wished he might reveal something of what occupied his mind, but his expression remained neutral.

At last he broke the silence. "I don't like surprises." So comfortably modulated was his voice that he might have been politely reporting the weather.

"I understand," she murmured, perceiving a warning. Now more than before she felt determined to keep secret her letter to Uncle Valfrid.

"Miss Smythe, I confess to you I have a shortcoming."

"Indeed, sir, haven't we all?"

"Yes, but this particular shortcoming can be remedied with your cooperation."

Isabel regarded him uneasily, but made no reply.

"I have a quarrel with time."

She blinked.

"There never seems to be enough of it," he said. "Please attempt to be on time in the future."

"I did try!"

He held out his hand to her, palm down. "As I believe I have already mentioned, I sent Nottage to show you the way, but you had already left your chamber."

"Oh." Isabel placed her palm upon the back of his hand and allowed him to guide her down the stairs. She did not recall Frannie's father ever showing Isolda Smythe—the *real* Miss Smythe—such a courtesy. "Had I realized someone would be sent to me," she explained, "I would not have left. And I would still have been late." She trailed her free palm over the cool, polished oak handrail. She lifted it to find a dark smug of dust. Quickly she curled her fingers into a fist, which she concealed amongst the folds of her gown's skirts. "Your sister told me that the morning meal at Willow Hall was laid at eight of the clock. I took her to mean that I should attend then, so I left my room before the hour."

"Eight? There must be a mistake."

A mistake. Doubt gnawed at her. "Did I misunderstand? Do you prefer I dine with your staff?"

For Isabel, this was unexplored territory. She knew that in some homes, companions and tutors were treated as family, in others as servants.

"You are welcome to take your meals with my family, Miss Smythe. Indeed, I will have it no other way." Instead of giving her the reassurance she would have appreciated, the commanding tone in which he delivered the statement informed her she had no choice in the matter.

"The mistake," he said, "was the time. Breakfast is always laid at seven. It is not yet eight of the clock."

Seven? She had been weary at the time, but Isabel felt certain that Catherine had mentioned eight o'clock, not seven.

As they progressed down a hall paved with white marble tiles intersected with small diamonds of black marble, she agreed that there had been some confusion.

Restless, her fingers sought the miniature she wore on a ribbon around her neck. The portrait nestled on her lace tucker.

"What is that you finger so assiduously, Miss Smythe?" Tremayne inquired.

Now that he had called attention to the miniature, she was glad he had noticed it.

Isabel beamed, hoping she looked like a woman in love. "This is a miniature of the man I will marry."

"Indeed? May I see?"

She nodded and released the small painting into his palm.

Although he drew no closer than was proper, Isabel noticed he smelled of wood smoke, leather, and sandalwood soap.

"What is the name of this fortunate man?" he inquired politely.

"Mr. Valfrid Adkisson." She had chosen her uncle's name because it would be easy to remember.

He repeated the name, but she could extract nothing from his tone. "And where is Mr. Adkisson?"

She had decided that having him fighting in the Peninsula would place him too far away to protect her, although she thought that would have displayed his courage. He couldn't be in London, because too many people went there regularly, which might lead to awkward questions.

"Sussex," she said. "He's in Sussex." That placed him not too far to come to her aid, but far enough to explain why he didn't visit her.

"I take it he plans to come for you?" he asked.

"Yes," she said quickly. Perhaps too quickly. She had never been much good at lying, but with all the practice she had been getting lately, she reckoned she should soon improve.

Tremayne placed the painting back into her hand without touching her.

"You are affianced?"

"Betrothed." She saw that as a more unbreakable bond.

"This miniature, it is his love token to you?"

"No." At least *that* wasn't a lie. "A gift from his family."

"So your marriage has been arranged by your parents?"

"Yes, but it is a love match. Mr. Adkisson adores me. And—and I love him. Very much. But he is too proud to wed me until he can become established," she added dramatically. Sweet angels in heaven, she was babbling.

"Which, I presume, he has not yet accomplished."

"Not yet."

"I would dislike losing my Swedish tutor before Catherine has become fluent in the language. Is there a chance your beloved will soon appear at my doorstep to sweep you away to Sussex?"

"It is improbable. But he might choose to visit—"

"Unexpected visitors are not welcome at Willow Hall, Miss Smythe," he said sharply.

A fist clenched around Isabel's stomach.

In a more moderate tone he added, "I find they can complicate household operations."

It was possible, she tried to reason. A small staff, the necessity of provisioning so isolated a house . . .

"Simply request Mr. Adkisson notify us of his intention

to visit beforehand, so that provisions might be obtained and accommodations made."

A not irrational requisite, she supposed. "So, he will be welcome here as long as he has made arrangements with you beforehand. When, of course, he can take the time to journey here."

"From Sussex."

"Yes. To see me. His betrothed." She was babbling again. "I see."

Oh, she hoped he did not!

"Mr. Adkisson's eyes appear to go in separate directions," Tremayne observed as he glanced at the miniature. "Would this not prove inconvenient?"

That little matter had bothered Isabel since she had purchased the miniature, but her only other choices at the tinker's stall at the fair had been women, children, and elderly men. "That," she said primly, "is the artist's failing."

Tremayne straightened, his expression bland. "A comfort to you, I'm sure."

Before she could reply, he walked on, and she hastened to catch up with him.

Tremayne brought her into a large room. November sunshine slanted through the tall windows that marched along the outside wall. Near the fireplace at one end of the chamber, a settee upholstered in yellow damask and two armchairs covered in pale green silk had been arranged for conversation. Side tables were populated by small, brilliantly colored, demonlike creatures, the likes of which she had never seen before. On the shelf of the carved alabaster chimneypiece stood a large garnet elephant, its trunk upraised.

The far side of the room held a handsome sideboard set with various morning delectables. The fragrance of hot chocolate wafted to Isabel, and she breathed it in, savoring it like a rare perfume. She had drunk no hot chocolate since . . . well, many months.

At a medium-sized dining table sat Catherine and a woman who Isabel assumed was Lady Blencowe. According to word of mouth, the baroness had been widowed five years ago by her husband's weak heart. The hand of the graceful baroness was much sought-after. Stories of her wit had reached even into the schoolroom where Isabel had listened to them recounted by a tutor who had thrived on gossip about the *haut ton*.

Introductions were made, and Isabel made a small curtsy to Lady Blencowe.

Nottage burst into the room. He drew up sharply when he saw Isabel and sent Tremayne what Isabel thought to be an odd look. Then he straightened smartly, fixing her with a disapproving eye. From the dusty, disheveled look of him, the poor fellow must have been conducting a desperate search for her. Clearly she had disturbed his morning and caused him no little concern. She cast him an apologetic look over her shoulder as Tremayne steered her to the table.

The scent of warm ham and curried eggs teased Isabel's nostrils. Her mouth watered as she remembered the faint salty flavor of sweet, butterlike ham and the spicy tang of creamy-solid eggs on her tongue. Once she had taken such meals for granted.

"I quite apologize," Catherine said, her pretty features shadowed with consternation. "I should have told you someone would come for you. I haven't forgotten how confusing Willow Hall can be until one learns one's way about the place."

Isabel smiled. "We were both fatigued last evening. I suppose I should have stayed in my chamber until someone came for me, but I honestly believed I could find my way. And you had said the clock in my chamber—" Abruptly she broke off, her eyes widening.

The clock in your room . . .

The error regarding the actual hour became clear to her. "The clock in my room doesn't give the correct time, does it?" She sensed rather than saw Tremayne move to stand behind her. The temperature in the room seemed to leap a few degrees, which was, of course, quite ridiculous. She put the heat down to being unsettled over becoming lost and arriving late again.

"No," Catherine replied, "that clock has not kept proper time for years. It insists on being precisely one hour late. But it is reliably late, so in its own way, it does keep time."

Fox moved to the table, where he paused to examine the cuff of his wool coat. "Just not the *correct* time."

Catherine pressed her lips together and regarded her brother with large, brown eyes. "I apologize, Fox. I could not bear to throw it out."

"Have it repaired."

"I've already taken it to an excellent clockmaker in London," Lady Blencowe said. "The silly thing refuses to be altered."

Tremayne pulled out a chair for Isabel and waited while she sat.

"It is amiss by only one hour," Catherine pointed out.

Nottage assisted Isabel with her chair as his master took his own place at the head of the table.

"You know how I feel about things that don't work properly," Mr. Tremayne said. His voice was neither sharp nor harsh, but an edge of steel carried to the ears of anyone listening. "Why would you wish to retain a timepiece incapable of keeping accurate time, Catherine?"

Catherine dropped her gaze to her plate. When she spoke, her words were so softly uttered as to be almost inaudible. "It belonged to Mama."

Tremayne went still in the midst of arranging his napkin. Several seconds passed in the silent room before he spoke. "Catherine, I would not have you part with anything precious to you. Simply . . ." His eyes turned toward her, and his expression softened. "Don't save something that does not work only for the sake of economy. And warn me if you know something is not operating properly. That's all that I am saying."

She lifted her eyes to him. "Yes, Fox."

Again, his face was a study in neutrality, but Isabel saw a muscle jump in his jaw. He pulled in a long, quiet breath. When he released it, it sounded to Isabel more like a sigh than a controlled exhalation.

Was he simply feeling frustration over a long-standing

dislike of accumulating useless odds and ends? Or was it his sister's submissiveness that bothered him?

It occurred to Isabel that beneath the practical woolen coat and modest waistcoat of the self-possessed Mr. Tremayne, there might beat the heart of a flesh-and-blood man. A man with a great deal to answer for, to be sure, but still a man. One who might even care for his sister and want her to be happy.

"How good to meet you, Miss Smythe," Lady Blencowe said. "I'm delighted you decided to accept Fox's offer." She cast a fond glance toward Catherine. "My niece will enjoy the company of one closer to her own age."

Isabel felt as low as a mole's toe. She hoped the others at this table would consider her lies justified, should they ever come to know of them. Not that she intended for that to happen.

Polite conversation during the remainder of the meal revealed that Lady Blencowe would leave at noon for Bath, that a gentleman known as Etienne would be arriving at Willow Hall for a visit, and that Catherine, Isabel, and Tremayne would leave early on the morrow to go into Harwich. There a bookseller had received some books written in Swedish, and Catherine was to visit her mantua-maker for the first fittings of the wardrobe that would set her launch into Society.

Isabel experienced relief at not having to broach the subject of going to Harwich herself. Now all she had to do was find a way to post the letter once they reached the port town.

Tremayne and Lady Blencowe finished breaking their fast and left to attend to their affairs. Today, it seemed, Catherine and Isabel were on their own.

Isabel smiled at Catherine. "If you will teach me about the fens, I will teach you about Sweden."

For the first time since Isabel had arrived in the room, Catherine's face lit. "Oh, yes! We'll have an *adventure*!"

After they pulled on their pelisses, bonnets, and gloves, they hurried down the stately oak-paneled corridor, abruptly suppressing their pace to a decorous stroll when they encountered the perpetually scowling Nottage. As soon as they were out of sight from him, they looked at each other and burst into giggles. They raced through the entrance hall and out the front door, their half-boots ringing on the flagstones. They descended the stairs more slowly until they came to the water's edge, where they plunked down on the steps.

A pale mist hung in the morning air, drifting over the dark water like a restive wraith. Moisture gathered on their skin.

"Where are they?" Isabel asked, peering into the forest of reeds that edged the side of the stairs. "I don't see a thing."

Catherine immediately understood. "We've frightened them, silly. If we stay still for a while, the frogs may grow brave again and return."

"Oh. Would they mind if we spoke softly?"

"Perhaps not."

"Well, then, shall we talk about Sweden and Swedish while they rally their courage?"

Catherine nodded shyly, her eyes twinkling.

"May I ask if you speak French?"

"Yes, of course."

"Does that mean you speak French or that I may ask if you speak French?"

Catherine's smile widened. "I speak French."

"Italian?"

Catherine shook her head, and the damp fox trim on her bonnet cast droplets onto the shoulders of her moss-colored wool pelisse.

Isabel smiled. "I gather felicitations are in order."

Catherine's face went pink.

Surprised at Catherine's reaction, Isabel patted the girl's hand. "Please, if you consider the subject too personal, we needn't spend another second on it."

The younger woman took a deep breath and let it out. "No." Her cheeks deepened in color. "The subject discomfits me a bit." She looked away.

Isabel studied her student's sweet young face for a moment. Then it came to her why Catherine might be so dismayed over speaking about her impending engagement. Sympathy for her welled up inside Isabel.

Perhaps Fox Tremayne was an even worse bounder than the rest of England knew.

SIX

Isabel didn't like to believe that Fox Tremayne would force Catherine to wed against her inclination.

Arranged marriages were not as common as they had once been, but they were by no means rare. On the other hand, while sons and daughters were still expected to do their duty by their families, these days one heard more and more often about love matches. Of course, Isabel thought as she looked around at the fog-shrouded, alien waterscape and the peculiar, isolated mansion, a love match might prove rather difficult to bring about when there were no eligible gentlemen—nor even roads by which to import them—for miles.

She could see that Catherine needed her help even more urgently than Isabel had realized. What with her plan to leave for Sweden as soon as possible, time was of the essence. She came directly to the point.

"Do you love this gentleman who would take you to live in Sweden?" Details regarding Catherine's intended remained vague.

Catherine colored. "I . . . I . . ."

She gave Isabel a helpless look. Perhaps she was still trying to decide.

Isabel sighed. "Do you at least esteem him?"

Catherine plucked at the edge of her pelisse with gloved fingers, refusing to meet Isabel's eyes. "I suppose so."

"Your enthusiasm is overwhelming."

"He is . . . respectable."

How dry that sounded. It lay as far from a declaration of love as England lay from India.

Isabel stilled Catherine's nervous fingers by taking her hand between her own kid-gloved palms. "I am pleased to learn he is respectable, but my question remains unanswered."

Catherine's gaze slid sideways to meet Isabel's eyes. "He is . . . um . . . handsome." Her lips jerked fractionally upward.

Isabel met that tentative smile with one fully realized. "That is as it should be, sweeting. *You* are a beauty."

Catherine's color deepened.

"Do you not wish to answer my question?" Isabel asked.

Catherine pressed her lips inward.

Isabel looked down at the hand she held. The well-made gloves revealed long fingers and a slender palm smaller than her own. "Do you dislike him?"

"I am . . . unacquainted with him."

"If you did not wish to wed him, would you be allowed out of the arrangement?"

"Allowed? By whom do you mean?"

"Everyone involved."

An expression of dawning realization moved across Catherine's features. "You mean my brother," Catherine said flatly.

"I mean everyone involved. But your brother's support of your decision could mean the difference between being forced to wed against your feelings and being released from an alliance that is unacceptable to you."

Catherine's brown eyes searched Isabel's face. "Fox would never press me into marriage. My happiness is important to him."

Tension that Isabel hadn't been aware was tightening in her stomach eased at Catherine's words. She nodded, feeling unexpectedly relieved. It seemed Fox Tremayne was a sufficiently good brother to bring his sister to his defense.

"Look," Catherine said abruptly in a low voice. "There. Watching us."

Isabel froze. "Who?" she asked in a hoarse whisper.

Catherine's fingers twitched in the direction of the reeds directly beside them, and Isabel's breath stilled in her throat. Her heart thudded in her ribs.

"There," Catherine whispered. "To the right. See?"

Without moving her head, Isabel cautiously turned her eyes in that direction. The only thing to be seen besides vegetation and water was a small green and brown frog.

"It has been so cold lately," Catherine continued in a low voice, "I am surprised they haven't tucked away for the winter."

Isabel released her pent-up breath on one quiet exhalation that sent a long, thin cloud of white into the air. She felt torn between embarrassment over her initial dread and amusement at the silliness of it. Well, perhaps not so silly, considering she had spent the past sennight on the run. And until she reached Sweden, there was still the chance Gilbert could catch her, could silence her. Forever.

"Clearly, Miss Tremayne, you breed a hardier sort of frog in these parts," she told Catherine as her heart gradually slowed to its normal pace.

Catherine grinned. "Please, call me Catherine. I feel as if we've been friends forever. May I call you Isabel?"

"Certainly."

Together they studied the small amphibian, trying to get a better glimpse without sending the creature leaping away.

"He is smaller than I anticipated. An unassuming fellow to possess such an intimidating croak—or quack, rather. I had expected something more duck-sized. Something, at least, with fierce red eyes instead of those pretty gold ones."

"Fox says 'tis the quiet ones who are usually the most dangerous," Catherine said as she watched the frog watch them.

How odd to place the words "dangerous" and "frog" together. But then, Catherine had not said "frog."

"Indeed?" Isabel murmured.

"Oh, yes," Catherine replied solemnly.

"May I assume your brother was not speaking of frogs at the moment he uttered this minim of wisdom?"

Catherine's eyes crinkled into merry crescents. "The conversation began with frogs, but it might have shifted elsewhere." She lifted her shoulders in a delicate shrug without taking her gaze off the croaker. "Frogs or people, do you not believe it is a truth that applies to both?"

Isabel released Catherine's hand and sighed. Her breath unfurled as white mist. "I believe that altogether too many persons are not as admirable as frogs." Frogs didn't steal from their brothers.

"Did you know that frogs are cannibals?"

Apparently, however, frogs did eat their brothers. At least Gilbert hadn't done *that*.

Probably only because the need had never arisen, Isabel thought darkly, not inclined to give Gilbert even a particle of credit.

"Cannibals. Hmm. Interesting," she said.

Catherine shot her a querying glance. "You weren't speaking of Fox just now when you said frogs were more admirable than some persons, were you?"

"No, of course not." But a minute more and she might have worked around to the comparison.

Isabel turned the subject briskly. "We were discussing whether or not you wish to wed a certain gentleman."

Catherine offered no response.

"Do you at least know if you would like to become better acquainted?"

Catherine hesitated. Suddenly she gave Isabel a brilliant smile. "Pray do not worry about me. I'm certain everything will turn out well."

Isabel knew when a subject was being avoided. She would try again later. In her own experience, ignoring a disagreeable fact only gave the thing time to grow even more disagreeable.

Isabel concealed her concern with a smile of her own.

"Well, I know another way to appear optimistic about the possibility of your engagement."

"What would that be?"

"Learn to speak Swedish and gain some knowledge of that country."

"Er . . . yes. How surprised he will be when I speak to him in Swedish."

"Tell me first what you know, so I don't bore you with repetition."

For a moment, Catherine considered. "I know that Sweden is across the North Sea from us."

"Yes," Isabel coaxed.

"And that it has a king."

"A king, yes."

Catherine shrugged apologetically. "I fear that's all I know, except that Vikings came from there."

"Some of them," Isabel agreed. "Oh, good. That leaves us a great many things to talk about."

Catherine gave her such a skeptical look that Isabel laughed. The startled frog leapt away with a splash.

"I promise I will endeavor not to become a droning windbag."

That drew a surprised squeak of laughter from Catherine. "Oh! I never meant to imply—"

Isabel waved away any apology Catherine seemed about to offer. "I've had all too many droning windbags as tutors. The prospect of becoming one appalls me."

Catherine giggled again. Her giggles grew into infectious laughter that caught Isabel like a shower of silver butterflies and carried her along, the sound of her mirth unexpectedly lifting from her throat to mingle with that of her student. She had laughed little in the past sennight. It felt good.

The spate of merriment left both of them gasping for breath.

"I cannot imagine you ever becoming a droning w-windbag," Catherine managed.

"Well, you must pinch me if I do."

Catherine cocked a slender eyebrow. "I shall remember you said that."

"Now, where were we? Oh, yes." Isabel cleared her throat. "Suppose we start with learning how to say the name of Sweden in Swedish."

"A distinct advantage, knowing how to say the name of the country." Catherine smothered her laughter.

Isabel's lips quivered. "'Tis a kingdom as you know, and its true name is Kingdom of Sweden. In Swedish, that is *Konungariket Sverige*. Let's say that together."

They said it together several times—or at least tried. Catherine had difficulty getting her tongue around the foreign words, particularly the first one. When she at last neared the correct pronunciation of the first, she failed with the second.

Isabel sensed Catherine's mounting frustration might cripple any hope for success. Time for a new direction. "Perhaps it would be easier if you could see the written words. Shall we go inside and find paper and pens? And perhaps even some shorter words?"

"A fine idea," Catherine quickly agreed.

As they rose to climb the broad steps, a boat rounded the willowed bend, slipping silently through the mist, bearing a single occupant.

The door to Willow Hall's library flew open, and Fox turned from the window where he had stood watching his sister and Miss Millington-Smythe, drawn there by the effervescence of their laughter.

In strode Etienne de Fortier, fourth in that once-arrogant line known as the Comtes de Sivigny. Mist-moistened dust layered his usually impeccable multicaped box coat. Mud spattered relentlessly glossy boots. In his haste, he had failed to remove his flat-topped, broad-brimmed hat. The face over which ladies were known to swoon bore at least three days' growth of red-gold beard and lines of fatigue etched in a mask of journey grime.

In short, Etienne appeared very unlike his typically elegant self.

Fox moved across the room to greet him. "You've been traveling hard," he observed. "To what purpose?" He smiled. "Are you pursued by some determined miss? Or by her father, perhaps?"

Etienne grinned at Fox, his teeth startlingly white against the grayish-brown dust and the beard. "I carry news," he said.

Grumbling over the dirt, Nottage divested Etienne of his box coat, hat, and riding gloves. He left the room, returning in the blink of an eye, looking for all the world like a curmudgeonly pirate with a black eye patch, bearing a tray with a bottle of claret and four filled, stemmed glasses. He offered the first to the tall Frenchman.

Etienne accepted the glass. "Thank you, my friend," he said to Nottage. He sniffed at the wine appreciatively, then took a long swallow. "Very nice, Fox. Always you manage to obtain the excellent wine."

Fox waved him to a leather-upholstered chair as he took a glass from the proffered tray and thanked Nottage.

"Sit, 'Tienne," he said. "You look ready to collapse."

Croom entered the room, his peg leg thumping softly against the paved floor. Nottage closed the library door behind him. Fox locked it. Then he sat in the remaining armchair and took a sip from his own glass.

"I knew you would desire to hear this *immédiatement*," Etienne said.

The sound and images of his sister and Miss Smythe laughing together lingered in Fox's mind, but Etienne's statement snagged his complete attention. "Yes?"

"I was on my way to my humble cottage, returning from my last bit of business in Pear Tree." White teeth flashed again as he used the name of their latest undertaking. "We did well in our little project, eh?"

Croom chuckled. Slim and dapper, he held his glass up to the light coming through the window. "We certainly did."

Etienne took another swallow of wine. "As I was saying, I was returning to my *petit* cottage when I was intercepted by a courier bearing an urgent message from the Watcher in Dorset asking me to attend him." He rolled his eyes. "*Mon Dieu,* but you have provided poor Ralph Jesty the dullest of little farms!"

Excitement simmered in Fox, but he forced himself to lean back in his chair. Etienne loved the drama of suspense. It wouldn't do to rush him.

"Watchers are supposed to blend into their surroundings, 'Tienne. You know that. For a Watcher, dull is good."

Etienne shrugged. "As you say. It has worked well for this Watcher."

"Regarding . . . ?"

The Frenchman's eyes met Fox's. "The Duke of Kymton."

Fox straightened in his chair.

Wineglass forgotten in the pinch of his fingers, Etienne leaned forward, his blue eyes gleaming with excitement. "The duke, he has perhaps made the fatal error."

All extraneous thoughts and perceptions dropped away from Fox. Every fiber of his being tensed, alert to Etienne's words. "Tipped his hand?"

Etienne slowly nodded.

Three years ago, the Duke of Kymton's lie had destroyed Fox's life.

Every day of those three years, Fox had burned to return the favor. He was not, however, fool enough to believe this might ever come about. He had learned the hard way how far Kymton's power extended, and the lesson had cost him everything but his life, his sister, and the staunch support and affection of Aunt Diana.

Fox had come to terms with the impossibility of unleashing his rage on Kymton. Only a fool failed to learn from experience.

Even so, he kept a close eye on the duke. The duke and his son, George Foss, Marquess of Everleigh. The former Major Lord Everleigh. Fox's onetime superior officer.

Since his return to England, after escaping his just deserts over his responsibility for the slaughter at Kurndatur, Everleigh had seldom been seen in public.

"What have you and Ralph Jesty learned?" Fox asked quietly.

"Are you acquainted with the name Didier Perreault?"

"He's a French scavenger."

"Ah, *oui*. Scavenger. A good name for such a creature. He

trades with either side, republican or royalist, and both allow him to exist only because, like rats during a siege of Paris, he is useful."

"Word is," Fox said, "he fobbed off a shipload of ruined gunpowder on the royalists. But what has he to do with Kymton?"

"Monsieur Perreault has been calling on Piltunne with some frequency."

Piltunne was Kymton's Dorset estate. "Indeed?"

Etienne took a swallow of claret. "Monsieur Perreault applies stealth to his visits."

"He calls after dark, I presume?" Fox considered this news, turning it over in his mind. Kymton was in residence at Piltunne now. At the end of December, he would depart for his magnificent London house, where he would likely dwell until the end of the parliamentary session.

"Long after dark. So furtive, is our Monsieur Perreault." Etienne grinned. "One would suspect he did not wish to be discovered."

Reluctant to build his hopes until he obtained more intelligence from his operatives, Fox ventured a suggestion. "Assignations with a lady?"

Etienne lifted a grimy golden-blond eyebrow. "Perreault?"

"Not even Lady Kymton?" Nottage ventured.

Etienne snorted. "What man would risk his life to lie between the thighs of a woman whose spirit has been so thoroughly broken?"

Fox privately agreed. The only thing one could feel for such a creature was pity. Her husband treated her no worse than he treated anyone else. Her curse lay in her inability to escape, even briefly, his realm of influence.

"Very well, what purpose, if any, has my Watcher discovered behind Perreault's visits?"

Etienne stood. From within the top of one riding boot, he withdrew a folded sheet of stationery that had been sealed with green wax. This he handed to Fox.

"Monsieur Jesty contacted me only because he knew that I would reach you sooner than he, and because he knew you would not wish him to leave his post at this interesting moment. You are the master." He bowed from the waist with a graceful sweep of his free arm. "We are but your loyal servants. We endeavor to anticipate your wishes in all things." His feigned humility brought a grin from Fox, who accepted the paper.

"Ah, yes," he said, his gaze moving over Etienne, Croom, and Nottage as his fingers broke the seal. "My meek servants."

Croom and Nottage grinned.

Etienne laughed. "Perhaps not so meek, but most certainly loyal. And through your genius, growing rich."

While most of the Assembly were now wealthier than they had ever expected they would be in their lifetimes, none were as rich as the de Sivignys had once been. The revolution in France had seen Etienne's family and friends slaughtered. Etienne had escaped with the clothes on his back.

"I work with only the best," Fox said as he opened the letter.

Etienne assumed a dramatic pose of majestic dignity. "I *have* always been incomparable."

Nottage and Croom hooted.

One corner of Fox's mouth curled upward as he scanned the note. "And modest."

"Kymton *is* in debt up to his hocks," Croom reminded them.

"Likes to gamble," Nottage said, unnecessarily.

They all knew the cause of the duke's debt. They also knew most were reluctant to try to collect from him.

"And the villain does enjoy a bit of risk, of danger about his nefarious doings," Croom said.

"Aye," Nottage agreed. "The bastard."

"What does it say, this note from Ralph Jesty?" Etienne asked.

"Perreault has visited the Duke of Kymton for eight straight nights. Always in secret."

Fox wondered if these stealthy visits could be related to the sizable withdrawal made from Kymton's account at the

Bank of England by his man of business a fortnight ago. Was Kymton investing in cargo for Perreault's ships?

If Perreault already dealt with both French republicans and royalists, why should he hesitate to do business with an English duke? Unless Perreault had changed his mode of business, such cargo would almost certainly end in the hands of the French republicans . . . and turn a shameless profit. If Kymton invested in such cargo, he would be aiding the enemy of Great Britain during a time of war.

Fox already knew Kymton was corrupt. Of course, it would not be the first time a peer and member of Parliament deserved that label. But to go from "corrupt" to "traitor" remained unthinkable.

And now for the powerful Duke of Kymton, that leap might not be a far one.

SEVEN

The trip to Harwich would be made in a modest black carriage pulled by four bays. These were waiting for Catherine, Tremayne, and Isabel outside the front door of the Blue Dragon. Isabel made note of the door through which they had entered the inn, a back door that faced the dock.

As they made their way through a maze of windowless hallways lighted by lanterns on the walls, passing one closed door after another, she realized there was a whole other aspect of the respectable inn that she had never suspected. Since there was no reason that she could see for such caution—after all, Mrs. Densham had already made her sympathy for Tremayne quite clear—Isabel could only conclude that the former officer had encountered an even more difficult time since he had returned to England than she had realized.

She wondered what would greet them when they stepped out of the carriage in Harwich. An outraged mob, such as the one that had met him when he had arrived in London three years ago? That thought winked out of Isabel's mind almost as soon as it entered. She didn't believe Tremayne would risk the safety of his sister. Since no armed outriders accompanied the plain-looking vehicle in which she rode, Isabel could only suppose it was either better to remain unnoticed or that the residents of Harwich offered no threat.

She hoped it was the latter. She decided to take her cue from Catherine and her brother, who seemed perfectly at ease. Apparently they expected this to be nothing other than the ordinary shopping trip it would have been for anyone else.

A shopping trip that might advance Isabel's plan to reach Uncle Valfrid in Sweden.

The port town of Harwich came as a surprise to her. She hadn't expected such a bustling place, though upon consideration, she didn't know why. The town sat on the Haven estuary of the Orwell and Stour rivers, which provided the only safe harbor between the Humber and the Thames on the eastern coast of England. For centuries, this fact had been appreciated by the masters of both military and trade ships. Three years ago, in 1808, the redoubt fort, with its breastwork, parapet, and heavy guns, had been built to protect the town from an invasion by Napoleon's forces. The men who wore gold braid in Whitehall knew, as did any local farmer or fisherman's wife, that if an enemy could win its way past Harwich, its army would find a clear path inland to London.

The pandemonium of pedestrian voices, punctuated by the occasional piercing whistle from an ostler and the bellows of street mongers hawking their wares, merged with the rumble of wagon and carriage wheels and the clatter of hooves. Every so often, the imperiously mournful clang of a bell from the harbor somehow managed to drift through.

The carriage stopped in front of Pegrum's Book Emporium on a street crowded with shops. A groom unfamiliar to Isabel opened the coach door and let down the steps. As he handed the ladies out of the conveyance and onto a walkway, Isabel noticed a savage scar across his chin. Tremayne's servants certainly were a battered-looking lot.

Behind Isabel came Tremayne, attired in a blunt beaver top hat, a multicaped box coat and top boots. With two long strides he outdistanced Catherine and Isabel to open the door of the shop. A small bell tinkled inside.

With a fractional bow, he held the door for them. "Ladies," he murmured.

As they entered the shop, a stout woman of middle years was on her way out. Tremayne held open the door for her.

The woman glanced at him, and in the middle of offering him a civil nod of thanks, her glance grew sharp. Abruptly she pulled up short. With calculated disdain, she scoured Tremayne with her narrowed gaze. Then, dramatically sweeping her skirts aside so as not to touch him, she stormed out of the shop, nose in the air.

Isabel had never seen the cut direct given with such self-righteousness, nor delivered in such a crowded place.

Sympathy for Tremayne welled up in her. How hurtful! How mortifying. Surreptitiously she slid a glance at him from the corner of her eye.

His beautiful face was void of emotion, his amber eyes shuttered and unfathomable.

Without a word, he escorted Catherine and Isabel through the ogling crowd of customers, who parted hastily before him, as though he were a known carrier of plague.

Standing next to Catherine at the counter, Isabel noticed that her student's unnaturally pale face sported two berry-pink splotches high in her cheeks.

The sight sparked anger in Isabel. Catherine had harmed no one! The shy young woman lived in near-isolation, and when she did come into the society of others, the first thing she encountered was humiliation. Isabel turned to glare after the Guardian of Morals and caught her watching the results of her snub through the shop's display window. Encountering Isabel's disdainful look, she flounced away. Off, no doubt, to inform her neighbors and friends that she had put Traitor Tremayne in his place. The horrid biddy.

Isabel slipped her gloved hand beneath Catherine's slender elbow and linked arms with her, giving her a little hug in the process. She met Catherine's surprised look with a smile.

"Swedish will be so much easier to learn with a book or two," she said, patting Catherine on her gloved hand as she steered her to the counter. "Easier to teach, too. A book concerning the geography of Sweden would also prove helpful." Determined not to have Catherine's outing ruined, she turned to the tall man with shuttered expression standing next to her. "Don't you believe that advisable, Mr. Tremayne?"

In response, she received one quiet, baritone word. "Indeed."

A short, wiry-looking man in his third decade hastened through a door from the back of the shop, apparently summoned by one of the clerks. Isabel had noticed him disappear through the same door upon Tremayne's entry into the establishment.

The wiry man's attitude, as well as his respectable green coat, somber waistcoat, and dark pantaloons, marked him as one in charge. He beamed as he greeted Tremayne. The wide smile struck Isabel as being genuine.

"How good to see you, sir," he said. "Have you come to claim the books we discussed?"

As he came closer, Isabel noticed the three-inch scar separating the hair on his left temple.

Tremayne's expression relaxed into a smile. "It is good to see you, too, Caspar."

He looked around, and a few of the other customers averted their eyes. Two scowled. Some actually smiled at Tremayne, and to these persons he nodded acknowledgment.

"It looks as if business is good," Tremayne commented as he watched two clerks transacting sales at the counter.

"Aye, Captain. I've been blessed, and no mistake." He turned to Catherine. "You are in fine looks this morning, Miss Tremayne. Feeling well, I trust?"

"Yes, Mr. Pegrum, thank you. I don't believe you have met my tutor, Miss Isabel Smythe. Miss Smythe, may I present to you Mr. Caspar Pegrum, *the* Pegrum of Pegrum's Book Emporium."

"An honor," he murmured as he bowed.

"So pleased," Isabel returned as she gave the abbreviated curtsy. "I was delighted to hear you had books in Swedish."

"We're not far from Sweden, as you know. There is a good bit of trade between our two kingdoms, and not a few Englishmen have taken Swedish wives."

"Which has proved fortunate for Catherine and Miss

Smythe," Tremayne said. "I can see you're busy, Caspar, so I won't detain you long."

"Yes, sir." Pegrum went behind the semicircular counter and brought forth a small stack of books from a shelf below.

"Miss Smythe," Tremayne said, "would you please look through them and determine what you need?"

Isabel did as he bade her. She found an intelligent assortment that would prove useful. "A book on the geography of Sweden would help Catherine learn more about the country in which she might be living."

For a second, Pegrum looked startled. He glanced at Tremayne, and his face abruptly shifted into a polite smile. "Of course, Miss Smythe. I have a very nice one that arrived just last week, complete with several colored plates."

"Add it to the pile," Tremayne told him.

After the books were wrapped and the purchase concluded, Tremayne escorted Catherine and Isabel back out onto the bustling street.

Isabel studied the buildings, conscious of the letter in her reticule that had yet to be posted. Signs of various shapes and colors vied for the eye's attention, but on none of them did she read anything to suggest where she might post her letter. She chewed her lip. Maybe she should take a chance and simply ask Tremayne where she might post something.

She thought about how she had lied to him, to his aunt, to Catherine about her identity, and how she lived in his house under false pretenses.

Then she thought about Rob.

And about Gilbert.

Isabel maintained her silence on the subject. She needed to post the letter to Uncle Valfrid, but she must do it without anyone living in Willow Hall learning.

Tremayne ushered Catherine and Isabel a short way up the street and into a public house. There they were shown through a draped doorway into a private dining room, complete with a lighted fireplace and a small window that afforded a view of pedestrians hurrying by on the street outside. Without so much as a word uttered to the host, three neatly attired servants filed into the cozy chamber bearing a tea tray and steaming platters. Clearly, her employer had been expected.

Isabel's mouth watered as she inhaled the aroma of freshly baked bread, roast chicken, buttered vegetables, and a brandy-laced poppy-seed cake.

As she watched the food being set out on the table, she wondered when she had grown so hungry. The realization that it was already time for luncheon, and she had yet to find a way to post her letter, nearly banished her appetite.

The first thing to do was discover *where* a letter must be taken in order to have it shipped across the North Sea to Sweden.

"Where is the privy?" she whispered to Catherine, her gaze upon Tremayne as he stood at the hearth, his back partially to them. His masculine presence dominated the room.

Catherine smiled. "I'll show you."

"No, no," Isabel said. "Stay in here where it is warm. Just direct me."

Catherine whispered the simple directions through the public house to the privy located in an alley in the back.

Isabel had not made her way past the curtained doorway before Tremayne turned his head and fixed her with his tawny eyes. "Where are you bound, Miss Smythe?"

"The, uh, privy," she replied, feeling a blush move up her cheeks despite her lie.

"Take care you don't become lost."

What did he mean by that? Was he suspicious? He didn't trust her!

Why that should make her indignant when she was lying to him, Isabel couldn't fathom, but she found it annoying all the same.

Repressing a tart reply, she slipped through the heavy curtains and, following Catherine's directions, made her way down a shadowed hall through which a steady stream of servers raced, carrying food or empty plates. She exited the back of the establishment, stepping into a narrow alleyway. Through it flowed the murmurous traffic of laborers, servants, and clerks. The *clop-clop* of a horse's hooves echoed against the high brick walls on either side of the passage as the beast towed a cart filled with cackling, caged hens. To Isabel's right stood the wooden structure of the privy.

It was, however, the wet brick alleyway that interested Isabel.

Fox gazed at the curtains through which Miss Smythe had just passed. The female grew increasingly confounding. He had not missed the way she'd promptly aligned herself with the Tremaynes when that old harridan had cut him at the bookshop. In that moment, his first thought had been for Catherine.

So had Isabel's. She had offered his sister reassurance and comfort in a subtle, yet seemingly genuine manner. He would also have been willing to bet the glare she had focused on the woman had been authentic.

The previous evening, he had consulted the meticulous records he kept for each operation. Gilbert Millington had indeed invested with Mr. Syer. More than once. Millington had given an address not far from the one printed on the calling card Isabel had presented to Leckenby at the house on Harley Street. What was the man to Isabel? And was the relationship even pertinent to Isabel's visit to Harley Street?

What if Miss Isabel Millington-Smythe was nothing more than what she presented? A companion and language tutor?

It would be easy to believe. For one thing, he wanted to believe it. He found himself attracted to the elfin, dark-haired woman. Clearly Catherine liked her. She deported herself as a lady. So easy . . .

Except for this *feeling* he had about Isabel. Why had she given Smythe as her last name? And those bruises.

She might be a runaway, in which case she could pose a problem. It wouldn't do to have an angry father or husband or betrothed follow her to Felgate, even though Fox knew it was unlikely they would manage to get any closer than that. Long ago, Fox had learned to trust his instincts, and they had rarely failed him. Certainly they had been correct at Kurndatur.

No, something about his sister's tutor felt just a bit off-kilter, and until he found out precisely what that something was, he didn't plan to relax his vigilance.

Catherine went to the tray with the covered pot and the cups. "Tea, Fox?"

"Please," he said.

Fox watched as his sister gracefully poured from the pewter teapot. From the pretty, charming child he had left behind when he had sailed to India, she had grown into a quiet, beautiful woman. Was she happy?

Happy. What adult could, with any truth, claim to be happy? Happiness was a domain exclusive to children. To anyone with the least bit of sense, it was strictly the rubbish of poets. Satisfaction, contentment—those were the best for which one might hope.

As he gazed at his sister, Fox felt his chest tighten. Was she at least content?

How content could she be, whispered the soft, dark voice of his conscience, when she was isolated from all the things girls her age favored?

Yet she had never complained. And that gnawed at him.

Catherine walked to where he stood at the fireplace and offered him his tea. She smiled up at him.

"I was glad to have Isabel with us at Pegrum's," she said. "I do believe she was actually *angry* at that horrid woman."

Fox's fingers tightened on the fragile handle of his teacup. "I'm sorry you were forced to endure that female's bad manners, Catherine. I would give anything to keep you safe from such embarrassment—"

"Pooh. The shame goes to *her*," Catherine said lightly. Too lightly. "Someday the world will learn that you are innocent of the charges laid upon you at Kurndatur. Then that woman will feel like a fool, along with all the rest of them."

"I would not hold my breath for either event," he told her wryly.

Her flowered teacup nestled in its saucer in one hand. With the other Catherine tugged playfully on one of his coat lapels. "I know you are innocent. Our friends, the people we care about, know you are innocent." She regarded the lapel of his rust-colored coat for a moment. Then she gave a quick shrug that struck Fox more as a painful contraction of muscles than an indication of indifference. "Perhaps that will have to be enough."

"I want you to have a normal life," he said, his voice low. "You deserve parties and dances, a flock of worshipful beaux, and, in the fullness of time, an adoring husband and several beautiful children. What I have thus far given you is so much . . . less."

She laughed, and the natural sound of it surprised him. "We have parties. Sometimes when you complete an operation, we celebrate success with a very fine party. And occasionally we even dance."

"I meant with persons your own age, Catherine—"

"I know what you meant. Dinners and balls in London."

"Yes! And dinners and balls in London you shall have. Soon. Aunt Diana will see to it. But I cannot promise they will be easy for you. There is always the self-appointed patriot ready to snub or insult because of what I am purported to have done. I can only promise that Diana will do her usual excellent best to insure that your introduction to London Society is a pleasant experience."

Catherine smiled up at him. "The beaux, the adoring husband, and the beautiful children . . . well, I am hardly on the shelf, you know. Perhaps it is not too late."

Now Fox laughed. Some of the tension in his shoulders loosened. "You have time yet. Would you like your new tutor to accompany you?"

Her eyes widened. "I would like that very much. Have you changed your mind about her?"

"To tell the truth, I don't know what to make of her. For all the world to see, she appears to be what she claims. Still, I have this feeling . . ."

"But you don't believe she is dangerous?"

"Not to you. If I did, I wouldn't have allowed her near you."

"Shall I continue to keep an eye on her for you?"

Fox almost laughed again. She had badgered him to be included in the Assembly, wanting to take an active part in the operations, but he had kept her out of it. If the authorities were to discover the activities of the Assembly and manage to apprehend someone, it would not be Catherine. On that head he remained determined. But he had seen in Miss Smythe an opportunity to allow his sister to feel included in the family business without actually knowing exactly what that business was. While she supposedly watched Miss Smythe, others who were less tenderhearted and more experienced also watched her.

"Proceed as you have been doing. Let us see how much Swedish you learn." Fox grinned. "Perhaps she will surprise us all."

Catherine's gaze dropped to the cup she cradled in one palm. "I hope so. I find I like her. 'Twould be a happy discovery that revealed she is no agent."

"It would indeed. Speaking of Miss Smythe, she's been gone a long time for a simple call of nature."

Catherine's slender eyebrows drew together. "Oh, dear. I'd best go inquire at once. Mayhap she's become unwell."

"Or lost," Fox muttered. He set his cup on the table. "Go ahead and eat before the food gets any colder, Cath."

"But 'tis my job—"

His lips curved in a firm smile. "I'll see what detains our Miss Smythe."

The awareness of passing time pressed upon Isabel as she made her way through the crowd in the alley. The passageway between the two tall rows of buildings turned out to be much longer than she had supposed.

She stopped a woman carrying what looked to be bundles of laundry on each hip. "Could you please tell me where to post a letter addressed to Göteborg, Sweden?"

The woman shook her head and continued on her way.

Isabel quickly looked around, then stopped a man leading a large dog burdened with panniers full of cheap fans.

"Don't know, miss," the man responded when she questioned him.

After unsuccessfully taking her inquiry to a boy leaning against the wall, hands in pockets, Isabel knew she had run out of time. She hurried back toward the public house. A sharp creak of hinges alerted her to the fact that someone was coming out the inn's rear door.

Worried that someone might be Catherine or Tremayne, Isabel surged forward to fling herself into the dim, malodorous privy. As quietly as she could, she slipped into place the worn wooden bar that served as a lock. She tried to calm her breathing without inhaling too deeply.

Standing close to the door, Isabel focused all her consciousness into listening. Bold footfalls rang against the paving, moving closer and closer. A sharp rap against the boards behind which Isabel hid made her jump.

"Miss Smythe?" came Mr. Tremayne's voice.

"Yes?" she managed, her heart racing.

How close she had come to being discovered absent!

"Are you well?" he asked in a low voice through the door.

What sounded like a note of genuine concern surprised Isabel as she stood in the gloom, breathing shallowly. Did he worry for her health?

Or her possible defection?

Could she be imagining bogeys where there were none? The muscles across the back of her shoulders ached with tension. Since her discovery of Gilbert's betrayal, it seemed as if she had come to suspect the motives of everyone.

"Miss Smythe . . . ?"

"Uh . . . yes. I'm—I'm well. I'll be only another minute."

Her face heated as she realized he must think she had spent an inordinate amount of time in the privy. She remained still, waiting to hear him return to the inn. *Please let him return to the inn.*

"I'll be just outside when you're ready," he said.

Isabel sighed. She would have to face Tremayne sooner or later.

Opening the door, Isabel stepped outside. She inhaled deeply of the fresher air, then slowly exhaled. Her breath frosted the air like a disheartened wraith.

Tremayne studied her face. "You're pale. Come. You'll feel better with some food in your stomach."

With one hand he gestured toward the inn. The other hand he placed lightly at the small of her back. Through her cloak and the wool of her gown, the firm pressure against her flesh felt large, warm, and incontestable.

He guided her toward the inn.

EIGHT

He did not withdraw his touch until they entered the small private parlor where Catherine awaited them.

After a luncheon marked by conversation that centered on such neutral subjects as the weather, the war, and the Prince Regent's activities, the three of them departed the inn on foot for the mantua-maker.

To Isabel's surprise, Tremayne accompanied them into the feminine bastion. Neither her father nor brother had entered the establishment of her mother's—and eventually Isabel's—mantua-maker. Of course, Catherine required a proper chaperone, but Isabel certainly fulfilled that requirement.

Gloved hands clasped loosely behind his back, Fox wandered idly about the displays, inspecting the exquisite garments more closely than seemed, well, *proper* for a gentleman. Yet, as Catherine's guardian and the head of the Tremayne family, he was entitled to approve or refuse garments intended for his sister's wardrobe.

His wide, sculpted mouth drew her gaze. Unlike the Earl of Merlawe's statue of the Greek athlete, to which Tremayne so favorably compared, the mouth she studied possessed the color of warm male flesh, the mobility of . . .

One corner of those lips lifted in a rakish smile as he looked at a delicate muslin evening gown.

Abruptly Isabel turned away to feign scrutiny of a walking dress. No adult male ought ever to be so appealing. No cashiered officer ought even to be noticed.

She reminded herself that Rob rotted in a Spanish hellhole, while this man, who had refused to obey an order from his superior officer during battle, lived comfortably in a large, if odd, house, owned a carriage with a matched team, and could afford the services of a mantua-maker for *his* sister.

Not that she begrudged Catherine elegant clothing. Isabel did not. She did, however, want her brother back. That retrieval, and the plans to accomplish it, must remain foremost in her mind.

Easing her clenched fingers, she took stock of her surroundings. This front portion of the shop, partitioned as it was from what she guessed were the changing rooms and work area, was quite spacious. There was room enough for several persons to browse among the forms attired with examples of Madame Billaud's exquisite work or samples of fabric and lace. Judging from the quality of furnishings, the mantua-maker did an excellent business.

As Tremayne passed near Isabel, the room seemed to shrink, the temperature to rise. Disturbed, Isabel bent her attention to the walking dress in front of her. In this handsome garment of cloud-soft, pearl-gray merino, she discovered not only style, but flawless workmanship and a sophisticated attention to detail. She drew her fingertip along the edge of a *point de France* lace ruff.

Tremayne stopped beside her. "While we are here, Miss Smythe, you are to select some things for yourself."

Isabel stiffened. She felt like a pauper who had been caught with her nose pressed to the window of a fragrant bakery.

To her knowledge, Frannie's father had never given the real Miss Smythe—or any other governess or tutor of his children—so much as a handkerchief. He'd expected her to provide for herself out of her pay and the castoffs of his wife and daughter. Her own father had been considerably more generous, but probably most were not. So what was Tremayne's game? Not for a moment did she believe him to be anything like her father. That left her with the question: Did he have seduction on his mind or did he expect her to pay for any garment she ordered? Either was out of the question.

"That won't be necessary, Mr. Tremayne," she informed him coolly. "I have sufficient, thank you."

"I believe you are wearing the majority of your wardrobe," he said, his voice mercifully low. "You have worn this same gown and cloak almost every time I've seen you. I take leave to doubt that bag of yours could hold much in the way of additional clothing. Am I mistaken?"

Isabel frowned at the walking dress, refusing to meet his gaze and wanting more than anything to be able to tell him he was quite, quite wrong.

"I have one other gown," she finally admitted. "And a shawl I knitted." And her night shift, of course, but she certainly had no intention of mentioning *that*. She had disposed of her countrywoman's attire just outside of London in favor of gaining a meal and lightening the weight of her portmanteau.

"I prefer to provide my own clothing," she said.

He lifted his gaze to the window. "Ah, wouldn't that be ideal for both of us? Alas, we are faced with reality, Miss Smythe, and reality is that you have precisely two dresses, a pair of half-boots, and a pair of worn slippers in which to accompany my sister."

Stung by his brutal, but accurate, assessment of her belongings, she snapped, "Accompany your sister about a remote house in the fens, sir. How many dresses must one have for that?"

One bronze eyebrow lifted. "Do you suggest that those who dwell in Willow Hall have no appreciation of fine things?"

Struggling to swallow a heated retort, Isabel limited herself to one safe word. "No."

"I'm pleased to hear it." He turned his head to look at her.

"I would not like to think you hold us—any of us—in low esteem."

"I am a practical woman, Mr. Tremayne. As long as I'm presentable, there is no need for me to expand my wardrobe."

"There is need if I say there is." His tone brooked no argument.

Her reply dropped off her lips like two chips of ice. "Very well."

She didn't look at him, certain he could read the resentment in her eyes. Isabel knew she needed clothes. She didn't *like* wearing garments that had been reworked and mended so often their next stop would be the rag bin. Two reasons set her back up against accepting them from Tremayne: the manner in which the offer—no, *order*—was made, and the fact that they came from Tremayne when her brother lay in peril because he *had* followed orders.

"By God, woman, most females in your situation would welcome new finery."

Her gaze shot to his face. "And just what *is* my situation, Mr. Tremayne? No one has inquired of me directly, but I took that for a delicacy of sensibilities after Mrs. Densham informed you of my circumstances in her note."

"Make no mistake, Miss Smythe. You'd not be allowed close to my sister if I believed you were a threat to her."

Isabel cut off a laugh of astonishment. "So much for my theory regarding your delicacy of sensibilities."

Tremayne sighed. "Let's cut to the chase, madam. I sometimes entertain business associates and friends at Willow Hall—ah, yes, I see I have astounded you." His mouth crooked in a half smile. "Surprised to learn that there exist persons other than family who willingly associate with me?"

Isabel tried to cover her embarrassment with an air of hauteur. She told herself she had nothing over which to feel embarrassed, but she sensed she had hurt him, which pricked her heart.

"My sister," he said, "will soon be introduced to Society in London. She will, of course, be guided by Lady

Blencowe, but it's my belief that she will also benefit from the company of someone closer to her own age.

"Catherine is burdened with an unpopular brother. Too many individuals will delight in finding fault with the sister of Traitor Tremayne. I don't intend that her companion's meager wardrobe should provide additional fuel for their critiques." His gaze bored into Isabel. "She's young, and she's shy, Miss Smythe, but she is no coward. If I had my way, she would never set foot in London, but both she and my aunt insist that she must do this if she is ever to have anything resembling a normal life."

Who could help but sympathize, at least a little, with any man so clearly fond of his sister? Isabel imagined some of the hurt Catherine might be in for and privately cringed. Like Tremayne, she wished that the girl would forgo the debut experience.

"I cannot reimburse you for new clothing," Isabel told him bluntly. "My earnings are required for something else."

He made a small, impatient sound. "Did I suggest I expected you to pay for any new clothing? No. Consider the clothing as a sort of uniform necessary to the fulfillment of your position."

Isabel hesitated. "How soon is Catherine to come out?"

"In January, when Parliament convenes."

One month away. "Well, there will be decidedly fewer people in Town then than if she came out in spring."

"Exactly. Fewer gossips."

"Fewer parties and dances." Her intended might object to her dancing and laughing with numerous other men.

Tremayne studied the *point de France* lace ruff on the walking dress. "So . . . no more argument?"

She would have preferred being able to board a packet ship for Sweden, but that remained beyond her reach. Her best chance of reaching her Swedish uncle now was in posting the letter in her reticule.

"I have no wish to cause problems for Catherine," she replied.

"Ah, Monsieur Tremayne!" exclaimed a heavily accented female voice from behind them. "Mademoiselle Tremayne!

I am so 'appy to see you. A thousand pardons, I beg of you, for not coming to greet you sooner. A small difficulty regarding a gentleman's vest required my attention."

Isabel turned to see a handsome brunette of medium height sweeping through the draperies that covered the shop's interior doorway. She wore a high-waisted gown of sapphire muslin that exactly matched the blue of her eyes. Isabel estimated her age to be around thirty-eight or forty.

"I was unaware that you made men's clothing, Madame Billaud."

She laughed as she came forward. It was a gay, trilling sound. "Ah, but I do not, monsieur. This was a special item. One cannot refuse nobility, yes?"

Tremayne inclined his head. "Yes, of course, one cannot."

The mantua-maker beamed at Catherine, who looked up from a book of watercolor dress sketches. "You 'ave come for your fitting, *n'est-ce pas?*"

"Yes, I have," Catherine said, rising from the brocade-upholstered chair.

"Madame Billaud, I wish to make known Miss Smythe," Tremayne offered smoothly. "She has undertaken the task of teaching my sister to speak Swedish."

The mantua-maker and Isabel each bobbed an abbreviated curtsy.

"She will be accompanying my sister to London," Tremayne continued smoothly, "and has need of Town clothes."

Isabel suppressed the urge to tread heavily upon Tremayne's well-shod toe.

"But of course," Madame Billaud said brightly. "I 'ave illustrations and dolls showing the very latest in London styles. If I might know exactly what Miss Smythe requires?"

"One gown—" Isabel began

"Everything," Tremayne said firmly. "Now," he continued before Isabel could voice her protest, "if you are ready, madame, perhaps Miss Smythe's measurements can be taken while my sister tries on the items you have made her."

Isabel had learned enough about the future's uncertainty

to know she might very well end up in London for a while in order to earn her passage fare to Sweden. She offered no further protest.

"*Certainement,*" Madame Billaud replied. "Please follow me, Mademoiselle Tremayne, Mademoiselle Smythe. I believe you will find my dressing rooms most comfortable." She tugged a velvet bellpull. "Violette," she said to the small, mouselike young woman who appeared promptly in answer, "please see Monsieur Tremayne to the parlor. Bring to him a decanter of the *best* brandy."

Apparently different patrons rated different qualities of brandy.

Catherine and Isabel followed their guide to separate dressing rooms. When the door of her own chamber closed behind her, Isabel turned to survey this latest development.

"Opulent" was the first word to enter her mind. Pink satin swags dropped from the center of the ceiling, giving the impression one stood inside a luxurious tent. More of the gleaming cloth covered the walls. A sofa covered in plum brocade promised comfort at one side of the room.

In less than a minute after Violette's exit, a strapping, silver-haired woman bustled in, armed with a smile and a measuring string of knots. In short order, she disrobed Isabel and took her dimensions, all the while keeping up a cheery barrage of chatter.

When she was finished, she helped Isabel dress. "Now, if you please, miss, I'll show you to the parlor where you can join Mr. Tremayne. The sample books are there."

Isabel knew this would be her only chance for even momentary escape. "Uh . . ." She needed to stall. "First I must make a necessary visit. Where . . . ?"

The woman directed Isabel to a small room near the back door, which was furnished with a carved and polished wooden seat over an empty china chamber pot. It seemed Madame Billaud had provided that none of her clients must brave inclement weather to answer nature's call.

Isabel waited until she heard the woman leave, then cracked open the door to peer in both directions. Upon finding the area empty, she slipped out, quietly shutting the door behind her. Then she darted out the back door.

Sharp cold caused her to tense. Her cloak remained inside, where she dare not ask for it.

She knew time was short. Isabel hastened down the dim, narrow passageway. Unlike the busy alley behind the bookshop, only one soul was to be seen behind the mantuamaker's establishment. A girl close to her own age, bundled in a bonnet and a felted wool cloak, hurried toward the street onto which the alley emptied.

Isabel fetched the coin she had concealed in her shoe. Then she abandoned decorum and called to the girl, who stopped.

When Isabel caught up to her, she launched directly into an apology. "I am sorry to intrude upon you, but I'm new to this town and must find where to post a letter to Sweden."

"Where in Sweden do you want it to go, ma'am? There's a packet leaving shortly for Göteborg." Noticing Isabel's surprise, she added, "My brother is a pilot on the *Albatross Wing,* which plies the North Sea out of Harwich. I've learned something about the schedules."

It would be only minutes before someone came looking for Isabel. At luncheon, Tremayne had said he meant for them to return to Felgate after they left Madame Billaud. She must post the letter to Uncle Valfrid *now*.

Isabel knew she must take a risk.

"What is your name?" she asked.

The girl drew back at such bluntness, but answered just the same. "Tilly Lagden, miss."

"Miss Lagden," Isabel said in a rush, "I must have this letter"—she withdrew the folded, addressed, and sealed document from her sleeve, where she had slipped it when she had dressed—"delivered to my uncle in Göteborg as soon as possible. Would you please see it into the right hands to have it properly delivered? This is of dire importance." The precious coin burned an icy circle into her hand. Surely it would cover the price of posting the letter and a nice tip for Tilly. "I'll pay you for your time and trouble."

Tilly regarded her. Doubtless she thought Isabel a bit odd.

"Doing this for you won't bring trouble to me, will it?" Miss Lagden asked.

Isabel shook her head, trying to keep her teeth from chattering.

"It must be important to you, miss."

"He should know his sister has died."

After studying Isabel a little longer, Miss Lagden seemed to come to a decision, for she gave a nod. "Here now, you're turning blue. I'll see your letter posted. Worry no more about it. Tilly Lagden keeps her word."

Isabel pressed the coin into the young woman's mittened palm. "Thank you, Miss Lagden," she said, every word heartfelt. Then she turned and hurried into back to the mantua-maker's establishment.

She only hoped Miss Lagden made good on her word.

Shortly after her return to the dressing chamber, one of Madame Billaud's assistants arrived to take her to the parlor. Tremayne sat in an upholstered armchair, the booted ankle of one long leg crossed atop the knee of the other. As the assistant vanished back through the draperies that covered the doorway, he indicated Isabel should take the armchair facing him across a small table. Albums of fabric, lace, and ribbon samples lay stacked on the marquetry surface.

Like a golden-eyed demon spreading temptation before a faltering soul, Tremayne reached out a negligent finger to flip open the cover of the top one, exposing swatches of velvet, satin, and silk.

Despite her resolve, Isabel drank in the sight of them for a second. It had been so long since she had known the sweet caress of luxury against her skin. At times, it seemed that those days had belonged to someone else, that she, Isabel Amelia Millington, had never known anything but genteel poverty, anxiety, and anger.

She tore her gaze from the glimmering cloth, only to have it collide with that of Tremayne. He had been watching her.

Her temper sparked, but when she went to turn her eyes elsewhere, Isabel found she could not. Unwilling fascination and flagrant curiosity sprouted within her, their roots denying logic, refusing to be crushed.

She had been told over and over that this man possessed no honor, which meant only a fool would trust him.

But what if this man was not the monster the world believed him to be?

"Can you be bought for the price of a few gowns, Miss Smythe?" he asked, his voice deep and gentle.

Strangely, Isabel felt no outrage. He had beckoned. What caused him to now retreat?

She glided a fingertip over the swatch of velvet. "Why? Do you wish to purchase me, Mr. Tremayne?"

He scowled. "No. Of course not."

"How fortunate for both of us."

For a moment Tremayne regarded her. "Why is that?"

"Because I am not for sale."

Tremayne eased back in his chair. He took a leisurely swallow of brandy, then examined the dark gold liquid remaining in his glass. "I am glad to hear it."

For a moment, Isabel sat there on the edge of her chair, back sword-straight, hands folded loosely in her lap, uncertain whether she ought to examine fabric for clothing that might no longer be offered. Fox Tremayne had managed to leave her feeling unsettled and perplexed.

"If you do not select what you want, I shall choose for you," he said.

"I said one dress," she replied more sharply than she'd intended.

"You may say what you like. *I* shall do as I please, and it pleases me that Catherine not be accompanied by a companion attired as a bankrupt's daughter."

Isabel flinched as the cruel words struck too close to the painful truth. She didn't want to go to London. It was too logical a place for Gilbert to look for her.

Perhaps he had already searched Town and moved on. That thought cheered her. Perhaps the hunt had ended when they'd failed to find her and no king's men had shown up at Greenwood Park to arrest him for embezzlement.

Absently, her fingers went to the miniature she wore at her throat. *Please, Lord, let my letter reach Uncle Valfrid soon.*

She picked up a set of pastel drawings illustrating a variety of gowns. Even as she winnowed out those gowns she considered overly ornate or too daring, doubt assailed her. What did she know of the latest fashions for Town apparel?

Feminine voices softly filtered in from other rooms. As difficult or humiliating as genteel poverty might be at times, Isabel reminded herself that it rated far higher than the raw squalor of a Spanish prison or even the impoverishment that she'd glimpsed in parts of London.

"I know little of London fashions, Mr. Tremayne," she admitted, absently fingering the miniature at her throat.

"You have called my bluff, Miss Smythe. In faith, I am too ignorant of women's styles to choose for you. We shall consult Madame Billaud. Her taste is excellent, and she is most knowledgeable about the latest fashions in Paris and London."

Isabel nodded, relieved that he would not select her clothing. It would be too familiar. Too . . . intimate. Despite herself, her gaze moved to his nearest hand, which cradled the full, round body of the brandy glass. Quickly she looked away, back at the drawings on her lap.

For a long, excruciating moment, the chamber filled with turbulent silence.

"Have you found something you like?" he asked, his voice deep and disturbingly masculine.

"No."

"Since you have looked at that one drawing for so long, I thought the gown might have caught your fancy."

She shook her head and turned the page, having scarcely noticed the illustration mentioned.

"Where do your loyalties lie, Miss Smythe?" he asked softly.

Isabel rubbed her thumb along the corner of the drawing,

her heart beating faster. "A strange question, Mr. Tremayne."

"We have strange circumstances, do we not? A lovely young woman, clearly of gentle birth, arrives in an isolated village on the edge of a marsh rumored to be a hotbed of smuggling. She has no companion, no servant, no wardrobe to speak of." He regarded her. "From whom are you running?"

Her heart missed a beat. "R-running?"

He held up the brandy, examining it against the flames of the crystal chandelier suspended from the center of the small room's ceiling. "At first I suspected you might be an agent of some sort, hoping to discover me in some nefarious activity. Such as smuggling. Tell me, do you believe I'm a smuggler?"

"I . . ." Her voice died in her throat.

Tremayne lowered the glass to observe her over its rim. "Yes?" The single syllable resonated softly within the silk-lined walls of the small parlor.

Back and forth, back and forth went her thumb against the heavy paper. "I thought it might be possible." Best to stick to the truth whenever possible.

"And yet you accepted my offer of employment."

He was cutting too close. She straightened and looked him directly in the eye. "In truth, sir, that concerned me less than your notorious reputation as a disgraced officer."

He made no reply. He did not blink. His gaze remained steady, focused, searing.

Isabel forged ahead. "I accepted your offer of employment because of Catherine."

One bronze-colored eyebrow lifted.

"It has struck me that she needs . . . more than Swedish lessons."

"Indeed," he drawled. "What conclusion have you come to?"

His relaxed posture revealed only casual interest in her answer, but something about him, some *intensity,* warned her that judgment rested on her next words.

Isabel breathed in, sharply cognizant of her need for this job. "I believe she wants for confidence."

"I see."

"Perhaps a companion near her own age, one who sincerely esteems her, will help." How pretentious it sounded now that she spoke the words aloud.

Madame Billaud entered the parlor, and Tremayne took his leave of the room. With businesslike efficiency, a modest wardrobe was selected, one just sufficient enough not to disgrace Catherine during her debut.

Tremayne and Catherine stood in the outer reception room buttoning their coats when Isabel emerged from the parlor. She donned her bonnet, and then a girl helped her on with her cloak. Earlier, Madame Billaud had pointed out that a pelisse and an India shawl were both more fashionable than Isabel's fox fur–lined cloak. More fashionable, Isabel thought as she now snuggled into her mother's old garment, but not nearly as warm.

She observed Tremayne from the corner of her eye, not knowing what to expect. She had just ordered clothing for which she could not pay.

His expression gave her no clue to what might be brewing in that brain of his. With his usual good manners, he held open the door for Catherine and Isabel.

An icy breeze struck them as they stepped onto the walkway outside the shop, causing Catherine to gasp and shudder.

"Here now," Isabel declared, surging forward, other thoughts forgotten. "Let's get you into the carriage. You're much too susceptible to the cold to be out in this flimsy little pelisse. Fur is what you need." She hurried her toward the carriage.

"But my pelisse is fur-lined," Catherine protested half-heartedly, allowing Isabel to guide her into the black lacquered vehicle.

Leaning into the cab, Isabel snatched up a lap rug to tuck around the younger woman. "Then you need something more," she said firmly. "I'll put my mind to it."

Satisfied when she saw Catherine snuggle into the

squabs, Isabel caught up her skirts, ready to mount the carriage steps. She promptly discovered Tremayne's gloved hand held out to her, offering aid into the compartment. He smiled.

Butterflies flickered in her stomach. Before she could take the proffered hand, laughter drifted to them from across the street.

The hair stood up on the back of Isabel's neck.

NINE

She tensed. With anxious eyes she scoured the street.

Across the crowded thoroughfare stood her uncle Gilbert Millington.

Preoccupied by his conversation with a well-dressed man in front of a haberdasher's shop, he appeared not to have noticed her.

Quickly she stepped sideways, so that the carriage blocked her from his sight. She peered through the two sets of windows in Tremayne's carriage to see her uncle end the conversation. He bid good-bye to his acquaintance, then walked a short distance down the way, where he stopped another pedestrian. He appeared to make inquiries.

He was searching for something.

Or someone.

Isabel lunged into the carriage. Pressing herself into the squabs, she remained out of view from the window, her heart pounding.

"Isabel, what's the matter?" Catherine asked. Concern etched her delicate features. "Your face has gone quite pale."

"Just a chill." Isabel tried for a reassuring smile.

Then she remembered to pick up one of the lap rugs to spread over her. Catherine assisted.

Tremayne entered, taking the seat across from them. The vehicle lurched into motion, entering the clattering river of carriages, wagons, and hackneys.

He regarded Isabel for a long minute. "You must have a care for your health, Miss Smythe," he said. Pale gray light from the window cut beneath the brim of his beaver top hat, glinting on thick bronze lashes. Amber eyes watched her. One side of his mouth lifted. "It would be a pity to have your new clothes go to waste."

Gilbert is here! Gilbert is here! Gilbert is here! The thought, like a panicked moth, beat against her brain.

Tremayne must not find out. She did not trust him—or anyone—enough to place herself in his palm. She had believed she could trust Gilbert. . . .

"Indeed," she replied with numb lips. "Most thoughtless of me."

At this rate, her behavior would cause the worst of dullards to be suspicious, much less two intelligent persons. Isabel struggled to focus her mind on something constructive, something that would divert attention from herself.

"I believe I have just the ticket for keeping you warm," she told Catherine in a breathless rush.

"Splendid! I am all ears."

"Do you know how to knit?"

Catherine's slender eyebrows rose in surprise. "Why, no."

"It is not a skill gently bred women ordinarily learn, but I assure you, 'tis perfectly respectable. In the north, reputable countrymen and -women knit so that they might stay warm."

With the metallic clink of tack and the rhythmic thud of hooves, the team of horses turned onto the road out of Harwich.

"Miss Smythe, are you suggesting my sister must dress as a countrywoman in order not to freeze?" Tremayne asked.

"I'm suggesting Catherine take advantage of good common sense. We wear knitted garments every day, do we not? They're pliable and they're warm."

"I could commission an artisan to make whatever it is that you propose, Miss Smythe," he said. "Then Catherine would be assured of quality. I doubt my sister wishes to look like a bumpkin."

"Nor would I wish her to, sir. The garments I'm suggesting are worn under one's gown."

Catherine blushed.

Life in the country had taught Isabel to respect the hard-working, resourceful women who dwelled on farms. She had no idea what they wore under their dresses; knitted small clothes were her idea.

She smiled at her student. "Would you like to learn how to knit? 'Tis an intriguing, useful skill, unlike embroidering serviettes. The world has sufficient ornate serviettes, don't you think?"

Catherine darted a glance at her brother, who offered no comment. "Yes," she answered.

"Sweden is colder than Felgate, England," Isabel continued. "So this clothing ought to prove even more useful. I've found that knitting also helps to calm the mind."

"Gadzooks, this skill should be learned by everyone," Tremayne drawled.

Isabel could see by the gleam in his eyes that he teased.

She pressed on. "I'll be happy to teach both of you to knit. I had an excellent teacher."

Mrs. Odling's many years of experience had stood Isabel in good stead.

"I believe I'll decline your generous offer," Tremayne said. He looked at Catherine, who nodded almost imperceptibly.

Isabel arched an eyebrow. "Afraid you won't manage, Mr. Tremayne?"

He smiled. "Ah. I'll not be pulled in by that old ruse. You shall have one eager student. That will have to suffice. Now, tell me what materials the two of you will need."

By whatever magic Tremayne worked, as the winter sun set over the fens, Joe the boatman delivered skeins of pink silk yarn and a collection of knitting needles in various sizes to Willow Hall.

Lady Blencowe declined Isabel's offer to teach her to

knit, but she seemed to find nothing objectionable in her niece's learning.

After supper, the four of them sat in the parlor. The three women chatted and laughed while they wound yarn into balls. Tremayne read a newspaper from India. Nottage kept the fire bright and crackling on the hearth and brought them tea.

Anxiety over Gilbert gnawed at Isabel. She kept telling herself that he would probably not search for her in the middle of a fen. It was doubtful Gilbert could even *find* Felgate, much less question anyone there regarding her whereabouts.

She told herself that again and again. But what if he were to make inquiries at the public house where she and the Tremaynes had dined? Or at the mantua-maker's shop?

Later, as she tossed about in the curtained bed, far from the rest of the silent household, sleep escaped her.

Now she made her way through the maze of deserted rooms to join the others for luncheon, knitting in hand. Hours of Swedish lessons had occupied the morning. She could almost feel the dark circles under her eyes growing heavier.

Lady Blencowe had told her they would be joined by two guests: a Frenchman and a Cherokee Indian from the former colonies. Birth had created Etienne de Fortier, the fourth Comte de Sivigny; the French revolution had taken that title along with his wealth and his family. William Talloak, who hailed from the mountains of North Carolina, had also lost much. Many of his people had died in the war between the American colonists and the British. Allies of the latter, they had been forced to cede much of their lands to the victorious Americans.

Had Tilly Lagden posted the letter as she had promised?

Had Gilbert spoken with someone who had seen her with the Tremaynes?

As she sailed along occupied with these thoughts, the toe of Isabel's slipper caught the edge of a dusty carpet. She stumbled. Her needles, knitting, and ball of yarn tumbled to the floor. The yarn bounced, then rolled, leaving a trail of fine pink silk in its wake.

"Ugh!" she muttered as she chased it, fretting over all the dust it must be collecting.

As the ball rolled merrily toward the opulent fireplace, the prospect of ancient soot loomed. Putting on a spurt of speed, Isabel managed to snatch up the yarn before it reached the blackened maw. In doing so, she overshot her balance. To save herself from slamming into a sienna-veined marble column, she threw out her arm, her fingers splayed against the intricate carving of the alabaster overmantel.

The saloon seemed to spin. Isabel blinked.

Then she realized the chamber wasn't moving.

She was.

Without a sound, the hearth and the fireplace, complete with high overmantel, revolved on some sort of central pivot.

A squeak of alarm escaped Isabel. She gripped the edge of the mantel with one white-knuckled hand and clutched the pink ball in the other. The saloon passed out of sight as a room with windowless stone walls surrounded her.

A room in which Fox Tremayne worked a printing press.

Absorbed in what he was doing, he labored in his shirt-sleeves, his clothes protected by a printer's apron, turning out rectangles of bordered paper too far for her to view clearly. Three Argand lamps illuminated this Spartan chamber. The smell of burning rapeseed oil and ink saturated the air as the press's carriage rumbled a stilted rhythm.

Isabel stood unmoving, stunned.

As Tremayne lifted a specimen of his handiwork, he caught sight of her. His eyes widened. "What the devil—!"

"Uh—"

"How—?"

"I—I dropped my yarn." She held up the ball as if to verify the truth of her claim. "It rolled to the fireplace. I . . ." She cleared her throat, not liking to admit to her miserable lack of grace. "I stumbled against the overmantel, and found myself in here."

He laid down the rectangle of paper. Quickly he removed his apron and snatched up his waistcoat from a peg on the wall. Not waiting to button the garment, he grabbed his coat from another peg and then slid his arms into it.

"What is this place?" she asked, wandering into the room.

A secret chamber. She had heard stories of smugglers using such things. Did smugglers operate printing presses?

Fox Tremayne caught her elbow in a gentle yet firm grasp and ushered her back to the fireplace. "Oh, just a place to which I can escape when I want to be alone. Will you look at the time? We'd best be moving along before we're late for luncheon. Don't want to keep our guests waiting, do we?"

"How fortunate I happened along to remind you," she observed dryly. Isabel recognized when she was being hurried out a door.

"Fortunate. Yes." He looked down into her face.

Silence expanded into the boundaries of stone walls. Tension hummed all around them.

Isabel was the first to look away. "You enjoy coming here?" She glanced around the austere, windowless room.

He shrugged. "Not especially. It's just a place where I can be alone to think."

She thought of all the well-furnished, neglected rooms—with windows—in Willow Hall. "Alone."

He pressed something on the overmantel, and they began to move. "Yes."

"Just you and your favorite . . . printing press."

They arrived in the abandoned saloon, and the fireplace fit quietly back into its place.

"Er, yes," he replied.

She looked at him, expectant of a more complete answer than that. When he didn't offer one, she asked, "What do you print on your printing press?"

Isabel picked up her knitting and needles, dusting off the yarn.

Tremayne began walking. Gazing straight ahead, he said, "I print things."

Isabel hurried to keep up with him. "Indeed? How cunning of you to use it for that purpose." She indicated his gaping waistcoat.

He glanced down. His fingers went to work fastening

buttons. "I don't suppose you'd accept that I find it amusing."

She shrugged. "I will if you tell me you do."

He gave her a keen look, then sighed. "I don't. But I'm working on the first newspaper for Felgate."

What hamlet needed a newspaper? Based on her experience with the tiny burg closest to Greenwood, so few souls could not supply sufficient news to fill even a couple printed pages.

Her expression must have been one of scepticism, for he continued with no prompting.

"A local squire's wife and Mrs. Densham of the Blue Dragon are attempting to cultivate an, uh, improved social life for Felgate. A small assembly building is planned. Certain local persons have promised to write elevating articles on the arts."

"Uh-huh." The enterprise was doomed. As she had witnessed of neighbors to Greenwood, amateur authors of "elevating articles" either bludgeoned their subject into tedium, or were called upon to write one article after another until their enthusiasm petered out. With this area being so sparsely populated, how many willing authors could there be?

"I perceive you are doubtful," he said.

"You are kind to undertake such an endeavor. The residents of Felgate are fortunate. I believe, however, that you, sir, will find yourself having to write most of Felgate's gazette."

He smiled as they started down the stairway. "We shall see."

"I should be most interested in reading a copy of your noble undertaking."

They entered the hall that led to the dining room. "Ah. Yes. Well, there's still much work to be done yet."

"Oh, but I thought that's what you were printing."

He opened the door for her. "Purely a rough draft. Nothing worthy of your notice."

"But so many—?"

"The press has just undergone repairs. I was testing it.

"Will! How good to see you again," he continued in an

enthusiastic tone directed toward the tall, broad-shouldered man sitting next to Catherine at the table.

The man Will possessed elegant facial bones, light coppery-tinted skin, and black hair worn in a conservative cut. The tailoring of his midnight-blue coat and embroidered gray waistcoat could not be faulted.

After Isabel placed her knitting in a lyre-back side chair against a wall, Tremayne performed introductions.

Only slightly shorter than William Talloak, Etienne de Fortier presented a sharp contrast in coloring. His modishly styled hair was blond. Large blue eyes seemed to take in every detail without being obvious. If his plum coat and black-and-green-striped marcella waistcoat did not proclaim him more interested in fashion than Talloak, then the elaborate knot of snowy linen at his throat did.

After she and Tremayne had gone to the buffet to fill their plates with ham, oatcakes, boiled eggs, and herring, Isabel was pleased to find her place beside William Talloak. She had already met plenty of once-wealthy Frenchmen. It seemed no gathering in Britain was complete without at least one.

"What brings you to England, Mr. Talloak?" she asked. Certainly not that unpleasant episode in America. That had been settled years ago.

He smiled. "Business. And friends."

"I've always been told the two don't mix," she teased lightly.

"Often they do not. But some friends can be relied upon in any situation."

Did he mean Fox Tremayne?

She changed the subject. "I hope I don't sound presumptuous, but the name William Talloak sounds so . . . well . . . English."

"It *is* English."

"But I thought you were a Cherokee Indian." Rob had told her that most of the Cherokee nation had sided with the British against the colonists in the American rebellion.

"I am. Among my people I am known as Tsusga, but most English have trouble pronouncing it. My clan decided to send me to Oxford to learn the ways of whites, and it seemed foolish to use a name that made me more foreign to them."

Isabel swallowed a sip of hot chocolate. That he had attended Oxford surprised her. Oh, very well, the fact that he wore a normal suit of clothing instead of skins and beads surprised her. Clearly her ignorance of his people was profound. "Were there many of you sent to English schools?"

"Bird Clan sent one of their sons to Cambridge, but he succumbed to smallpox not long after arriving in your land." He took a bite of ham.

He possessed admirable table manners. That she took note of them at all reminded her of her ignorance. "Are you from a different clan?"

"I am of Deer Clan."

"Were you . . . young when you made the journey to England?" Isabel asked, thinking of a small boy separated from his family, living among strangers in an alien country.

He finished the food on his plate. "I was sixteen years old. I had received schooling with the children of a local farmer and a minister. When I arrived at Oxford, I found I had been academically well prepared."

Sixteen. When Rob had turned that age, his family had gathered around him, inviting friends to join them in a celebration that included a feast, music, and dancing. "You must have been very homesick." She knew she certainly would have been.

"Tsusga, are you being examined?" Tremayne asked, amusement coloring his tone.

Tsusga shrugged. "She is inquisitive."

"Yes," Tremayne agreed. "She is."

Isabel's cheeks grew warm. "I did not mean to presume—"

"I took no offense, Miss Smythe," the American assured her. "You merely made conversation . . . and perhaps learned something of my people."

She aimed a narrowed look at Tremayne. "So I thought."

Tremayne grinned.

"I notice Mr. Tremayne has no difficulty pronouncing your true name, Mr. Talloak."

"He has had many years in which to practice. He, also, attended Oxford." His smile returned. "If you can pronounce my name, Miss Smythe, you may use it."

Her knack for languages served her now. "Tsusga."

"Excellent."

"One might expect," Etienne de Fortier said, his words marked by his native language, "that a woman proficient in Italian, *Français,* English, and Swedish would have little trouble with one little Cherokee word."

"A little word," Tsusga drawled, "that you continue to mutilate, *mon ami.*"

From the corner of her eye, Isabel saw Tremayne studying her.

"I am flattered to be the subject of consideration, sir," Isabel told de Fortier, not flattered at all. It made her uneasy to have strangers know even unimportant details about her. She hoped Mr. de Fortier did not know Gilbert or his wife, Lydia.

The Frenchman inclined his head solemnly, but humor danced in his blue eyes. "I did not go to school with them, mademoiselle, and so I am downcast. To make up for my shortcoming, I have troubled myself to learn what I could about my friend's guest."

The polite smile on Isabel's lips froze.

"Etienne met Fox on board a ship on his way to India," Catherine said, not seeming to notice anything wrong. She took a dainty bite of her oatcake.

"You've been to India?" Isabel croaked. She took a swallow of chocolate to ease the abnormal dryness of her mouth.

"Ah, *non.* I was on my way to Spain to visit my uncle, who, I regret, had already fled to the West Indies, to keep his sons out of the war." He stared into the dark ruby depths of his wine, his blue eyes seeming to see beyond the liquid, into the past.

Isabel remembered that she had been told de Fortier had lost his parents and siblings to the guillotine. The war had taken his uncle and cousins from him as well. A small motion caught her attention. She glanced at Catherine to find the younger woman trying to direct her attention by a slight narrowing of eyes and small jerks of her elegant head toward de Fortier. Apparently without Lady Blencowe there to act as hostess, Catherine wanted a bit of aid to distract de Fortier from his memories.

"Mr. de Fortier," Isabel said before she could clearly think out *what* she might use to distract him. "Have . . . uh, you ever been to . . . to . . . Sweden?"

Turning to her, de Fortier looked baffled. "Sweden? Why would I wish to go to Sweden? Why would any self-respecting Frenchman travel to such a country?"

Isabel lifted an eyebrow. Her mother had spoken fondly, longingly of Sweden. "Have you forgotten that Sweden may be destined to become Miss Tremayne's home?"

A bland expression came over the Frenchman's features, and he turned to Catherine. "A thousand apologies for my so boorish comment, mademoiselle. I had . . . forgotten."

"'Tienne, how could you forget that Catherine's intended is an assistant to our ambassador there?" Tremayne chided.

"I, uh, could not bring myself to believe that he would remain there." De Fortier turned to Catherine. "Of course, your love for your, uh, husband will cast an enchantment over that backward land."

"Yes. Of course," Catherine murmured.

"Have you been to Sweden, Miss Smythe?" Tremayne asked.

"No."

"How came you to learn the language so fluently? Smythe is not a Swedish name. Was your mother Swedish?"

Isabel rubbed her thumb back and forth against the silver handle of her knife. "Yes."

"Ah, *non*!" de Fortier exclaimed. "I have managed to offend both our ladies!"

Tremayne's mouth twitched, but he managed a somber expression when he asked Isabel, "And your father is British?"

"Yes." She darted a glance toward Catherine's plate and saw it was finally empty. "I dislike playing the hard taskmistress, Mr. Tremayne, but it is past time for Miss Tremayne's lesson," she said.

Tremayne stroked the body of his etched wineglass with the tip of one long finger. "Which lesson?"

Isabel looked at him in confusion. Her instincts warned her to cut short his stream of questions.

"A knitting lesson or a Swedish lesson?" he elaborated.

"Swedish," she shot back. "Gentlemen," she murmured, including Tremayne and his guests in her glance and nod.

Catherine excused herself. As the two young women swept from the dining room, Isabel felt Tremayne's gaze following her.

Fox watched Isabel leave, noticing the way her dark curls bobbed against the nape of her slender neck. She had not liked being asked about herself. Did that mean she was hiding something?

Not necessarily. But a hushed, niggling voice that whispered at the back of his mind insisted Miss Isabel Smythe was indeed concealing something.

He no longer believed she might be an agent for the authorities—not unless they were employing amateurs these days—but she might be working on behalf of a disgruntled investor. Not a few of them would be foolish or thoughtless enough to exploit a green girl.

But even a green girl might stumble hard enough to upset Fox's applecart.

"Your Miss Smythe is a lovely creature," Etienne said.

Tsusga poured himself a cup of coffee from the silver pot at the buffet. "And quite a conversationalist, until the subject turns to herself." He wandered back to the table.

Fox sat back in his chair. "She's not *my* Miss Smythe, but you're correct. She seems unwilling to talk about herself."

"Unlike Etienne," Tsusga said, then took a drink of his coffee. Above the rim of the china cup his brown eyes twinkled.

"I am interesting," Etienne replied with a smirk.

"Will you keep an eye on her?" Tsusga asked. "These op-

erations have proved profitable to my people. I should dislike seeing them come to an end."

"As would I," Etienne agreed.

"That's why she is at Willow Hall," Fox told them.
"'Keep your friends close and your enemies closer.' I'm not
certain she's an enemy, but I can keep a watch on her here.
Unfortunately, she has discovered the printing room."

Tsusga and Etienne looked at each other; then both
turned to Fox.

"How?" the Frenchman asked.

Fox sighed. "She fell against the overmantel."

Tsusga frowned. "What was she doing in the old ballroom?"

"She passes through it to go from her room to the rest of
the living quarters. Her chamber is as far away from most of
the hidden rooms as possible."

"*Mon Dieu.* Such luck! She is an accident waiting to
happen."

"Please remember, my friend," Tsusga said to Fox, "you
are not the only one at risk."

"Do you think I could ever forget that?" Fox asked
quietly.

For a moment, silence surrounded the table.

"No," Tsusga said softly.

Etienne shook his head. "We do not doubt you, Fox. But
this girl. She *fell* against the mantel? How could this happen? What was she even doing there?"

"Her yarn dropped and rolled away. I imagine she was
rushing to keep it from getting filthy in the fireplace." He
smiled, remembering. "She has moments when grace
deserts her."

Tsusga's keen eyes studied Fox. "You find it appealing,
this lack of grace?"

"In her, it has a certain charm." The smile abruptly vanished from Fox's lips as he realized those rare moments
were not the only appealing thing he found in Isabel
Smythe. His fingers tightened on the stem of his wineglass.

"She, Catherine, and I went into Harwich yesterday to
purchase some books and for a fitting at Catherine's

mantua-maker. While we were in town, she twice made long trips to the privy."

"Either she had the grippe or she was up to something," Etienne said knowingly.

"As it turned out, she was endeavoring to mail a letter."

Tsusga stopped stirring his latest cup of coffee. Etienne's wineglass halted on its way to his mouth.

"It was addressed to her intended. Apparently he has left Sussex and gone to Sweden."

"She is engaged?"

"To a weasel-faced fellow whose damned miniature she insists on wearing 'round her neck," Fox said, annoyance scraping like sand against his nerves. "She entrusted the letter to Tilly Lagden, daughter of a local ship's captain. My man tried to persuade Miss Lagden to let him deliver it in her stead, but she's like her father: She honors her promises. She refused to hand it over. The fellow did at least discover that the letter was addressed to Valfrid Adkisson in Sweden. Miss Smythe had already told me her intended's name and that he's trying to make his fortune."

"And what of the girl's family?" Etienne asked.

"She told Alice Densham at the Blue Dragon that her parents had perished when the ship they were on went down in a storm. She isn't aware of any other relations. Her mother and father were cut off when they wed."

Tsusga leaned back in his chair. "Has she no brothers or sisters?"

"One brother, if what she told Catherine is the truth."

Tsusga lifted a jet eyebrow. "You doubt the truth of her words?"

"Let us just say that I'm a suspicious man."

Fox fingered the folded square of lace-edged linen in his coat pocket. The exquisite embroidered initial at one corner was not an *S* or an *I*. It was, in fact, an *M*. As in "Millington."

The name on the calling card.

TEN

The following morning, Isabel's breath emerged as a faint, translucent cloud as she stood in the unused room.

If she was ever to learn her way around this mad mansion, she must deviate from the single path she knew. Thus, having departed her chamber earlier than usual, she now tested a different route to break her fast.

Unlike the jewel-tinted carpets she had so far observed in Willow Hall, the one in the hall outside, beneath its covering of holland, was woven of cream-hued wool bearing a pattern of flowers and vines in green, rust, and gray-blue.

She had chosen this room at random, with the thought of eventually visiting every chamber on this floor. As on so much of this story of the house, the pale covers on the furnishings gave an impression of waiting ghosts. Waiting for what, she had no idea. She put the impression down to her imagination.

A pastoral mural of exquisitely clad shepherdesses tending pristine sheep covered the walls. Isabel gave a snort of disdain. She knew from her country life that raising sheep—or livestock of any kind—was not for the faint of heart.

Carefully avoiding the thick layer of dust, she folded

back a corner of the holland on a large piece of furniture. A black lacquered cabinet of approximately three feet in height sat on a stand. Five ornate brass hinges attached each of the two doors, both of which had been intricately painted with dishes of flowers in gold, red, green, and yellow. The table supporting the chest was gilt wood and carved with female heads emerging from flowers as well as with countless curling acanthus leaves, scrolls, and sprays of flowers. Many would call it lavish. "Overdone" was the word that popped into Isabel's head.

A key stood in the engraved brass lock. What exotic articles might lie within such a chest? she wondered. A casket of uncut rubies? Love letters, written on vellum and scented with myrrh?

The large limestone mantel over the fireplace was a profusion of carved acanthus leaves, acorns, and pomegranates. Isabel smiled. She had heard about houses with secret stairways and rooms. The tales usually spoke of gaining access to these concealed places by lifting an old portrait or pressing or turning a bit of sculpture.

She pressed an acorn. Nothing happened. Then she attempted to twist a pomegranate. Again, no hidden door was revealed. Well, it was all just silliness anyway. She had not really expected to find anything.

Then Isabel recalled discovering the correspondence and ledger revealing her uncle's treachery. Grimly, she eased the cloth back over the chest and its stand. She needed no new surprises, thank you. She still endeavored to deal with the first one.

Another lifted covering revealed a large wall mirror framed with woodland abundance carved out of limewood. Isabel regarded herself in the old looking glass, thinking the extravagance of the frame must always outshine the reflection. No one could ever grow puffed-up with vanity while looking in this.

A male chuckle reached her ears, and she went to the window to see who enjoyed himself this cold morn.

The view from the window looked down on the dock in front of the house. There, in the water some yards from the

stone steps, sat Fox in a peculiar boat. She had seen drawings of it in books. A canoe, it was called, and he handled it
with the ease that came from experience. Beside the slim
craft floated a duck. It followed Fox, staying close to the
boat, quacking at him. In and out, he executed smooth loops
in the water. In and out, the duck followed him.

Finally, he docked the canoe and lightly leapt onto the
quay. The fowl scurried up from the water onto a duck-
sized paved path that led to the dock. It beat its wings as
it hurried, but no flight occurred. When the duck caught
up to Fox, it assumed a sedate waddle, following at his
heel.

At the first step in the staircase to the door, Fox lifted
the duck in his arms, talking to it, stroking its sleek feathered head. The creature nuzzled his ear, and he chuckled
again.

Fox climbed the many stone stairs that would have been
nearly impossible for the duck to mount on its own. Together, man and duck entered the house.

Isabel's interest in the room abruptly waned. She hurried
out, closing the door behind her. The prospect of breakfast
had just grown more interesting.

In the morning room, Isabel found Fox, Catherine, and
their aunt already making their selections from the sideboard.

"On my way to join you, I vow I heard a duck," Isabel
said casually as she tried to appear interested in the platter
of Wigs. She chose one of the spiced rolls at which Cook
excelled.

No one replied immediately.

Going to her chair, Catherine cleared her throat. "Indeed?
A duck?"

Isabel took a dollop of marmalade. "Yes. I believed all
such fowl would have migrated farther south by now, so you
can imagine my surprise."

"Perhaps it was a frog," Catherine suggested.

"I am certain it was not."

Lady Blencowe cast her nephew an amused smile.

"Then it occurred to me," Isabel went on, "that Willow Hall might keep domestic poultry and fowl."

Finally, Fox sighed. "You heard a duck."

She munched a bite of her toast. After swallowing, she echoed Catherine's words. "Indeed? A duck?"

She met Fox's gaze with an innocent look. To her surprise, he pinkened.

"The creature's mother was killed, and all her eggs but one were destroyed by the hounds of an intruding hunter."

"And you managed to hatch the surviving egg?"

"I did."

"The duck's name is Oscar," Catherine volunteered. "He follows Fox wherever he can. He is now in his little house just outside the kitchen."

Crimson crawled up Fox's neck to color his high, sculpted cheekbones. "Shed," he muttered, buttering his toast. "It is called a waterfowl shed."

Catherine grinned. "A shed, then."

Isabel tried to think of a single adult male of her acquaintance who would have bothered. No one came to mind.

She studied Fox for a long moment. Images of a butler missing two fingers, a badly scarred groom, a peg-legged valet, and an ill-tempered manservant with a black eye patch filed through her mind. "Now you wish to keep secret your kindness?"

The edges of his ears flushed even darker.

Amusement at his discomfort dissolved as Isabel discovered she had no wish to embarrass him. She turned to a subject unrelated to Oscar.

"A goodly bit of yarn is left from our knitting project." She caught Catherine's eye with a smile.

The sleeved camisole and the warmers they had made did not come close to making use of all of it, but Catherine had insisted Isabel not knit another stitch on her student's behalf. Finally, Catherine had admitted to having no patience for knitting. Isabel's idea was nothing less than brilliant, but in the future, someone *else* could labor for her warmth.

Catherine plucked back the edge of one sleeve to reveal the pink knitted silk.

"Miss Smythe, it is yours to use as you please," Fox said, his eyes directed toward the slice of ham he was cutting on his plate.

"So generous," Isabel murmured. And it was. She could only imagine the cost of the yarn.

"Well, you are on your own," Catherine teased. "I have knit my last stitch. At least with embroidery, one works with only one needle at a time."

Isabel *tsk*ed. "Are you warm?"

"I am, you clever puss. It is such a relief!"

Catherine had the luxury of employing others to make her clothes. Isabel did not begrudge her friend this good fortune. No doubt Madame Billaud would find a source for Catherine's future knitted undergarments, perhaps one who would even embellish with lace.

"Perhaps we should undertake a lesson now that you are feeling more comfortable," Isabel suggested.

"Oh, *ja*," Catherine agreed.

As Isabel and Catherine excused themselves from the table, Isabel glimpsed Fox regarding her with an unreadable expression.

After breaking his fast, Fox went to his office to attend to some business before he joined Etienne, Tsusga, and a handful of operatives at the Blue Dragon.

A brief knock sounded on the closed door. "Come," Fox barked. As Nottage entered, a plush carpet muted his footfalls.

Onto the lapis lazuli and silver salver at one corner of the desk, he deposited a neat bundle of newly arrived correspondence. Beside it he laid the newspapers and journals from various points around the world.

"Thank you, Nottage," Fox said, glancing up from the letter he was writing to Elsegood Tice, his man of business in London.

Nottage gave a curt nod. He left the chamber, closing the door behind him.

Fox completed his epistle to Mr. Tice, then replaced his pen in its brass-elephant stand.

Another of the Ladies' sons had reached an age where a decision must be made regarding his future. From all reports, the lad was the studious sort, clever with words and excellent with numbers. His marks had been good enough to warrant continuing his academic education, rather than apprenticing him with a suitable master tradesman.

This would not be possible unless Fox increased the quarterly allotment to the boy's mother. This could be done if Elsegood fabricated some distant relative from whom the widow might "inherit." The terms of the will, of course, would require that the bequest be paid directly to either of the usual two schools in the form of tuition.

Another tap on the door. This time it was Croom who entered.

"Are you away?" Fox asked. The sooner Croom departed, the sooner he would uncover the details regarding Isabel Millington-Smythe's true identity.

"I am, sir. Shall I deliver your letter to Mr. Tice?"

"Jove, man, how did you discover my correspondence was intended for Tice?" The intelligence-gathering talents of the former sergeant never ceased to impress Fox.

"I read the outside of the letter, Cap'n."

"Oh."

With a smile, Croom pointed to the address. Since it was almost completely concealed by another sheet of paper, Fox didn't feel so foolish.

"Yes, do post the letter, if you would be so good. Here are some others that need to go out, too."

Croom carefully tucked the wax-sealed envelopes into the leather pouch slung over his shoulder. As ever, when on such a mission, he traveled light.

"Instructions as to your Ladies, sir?"

Croom's sister had been one of the Ladies. A destitute mother of two, and widow of a corporal who had fallen at Kurndatur, it had been her receipt of her first "government check" that had sent Croom off on his quest to locate the actual source of that benefaction. He was the only person who had ever been able to track Fox.

Now Croom could afford to support not only his sister and her children, but his mother and aged but spry-as-a-wren grandmother.

"All the Ladies are lucky to have you," he said stoutly. "Not many men could serve them as you do."

"Off with you, Croom, before you put me to the blush. Godspeed."

At that moment, they heard a metallic sound outside the door. A sound, Fox thought, like a knitting needle dropped on the floor. Both of them strode to the door to find it slightly ajar.

"Sorry, Cap'n," Croom said with an apologetic look. "I thought I had closed the door all the way."

"Don't worry about it this time. If anything, you may have created for me the reputation of a potent ladies' man."

Croom grinned as he took his leave, possibly because Fox was anything but a ladies' man. Since the nightmare of returning to London, physical contact with the so-called weaker gender had been rare. And since Isabel's arrival, Fox would say too rare.

After cleaning ink from his fingers, he picked up the stack of mail and began sorting through it. One piece caught his attention. It bore the wax seal and title of the Earl of Merlawe.

Fox smiled wryly as he opened the envelope. Had he used his real name when he'd written Lord Merlawe to inquire after a reference for Isabel Smythe, doubtless the peer would not have responded.

As he opened the letter, something tightened in Fox's belly. The message on the expensive stationery in his hand would expose Isabel's ruse. It would reveal her as a liar.

He remembered all too clearly how her lovely face had blanched when he had announced his intention to write the Earl of Merlawe, whom she had claimed was her previous employer. She had not believed he would dare contact a peer—or anyone else of quality. What she had not counted on was that he would do so under a false name.

Fox read the earl's reply. Then he read it again.

"Jove," he swore.

Lord Merlawe vouched for Miss Isabel Smythe. He wrote that she had been an excellent tutor and companion to his daughter, Frances. Miss Smythe had been engaged to an officer—whose name the earl could not recall—fighting on the Peninsula. The fellow had been sorely wounded and sent back to England. The estimable Miss Smythe had given up her enviable post in the earl's household to fly to her intended and nurse him to back to health.

Alas, her intended had died. Or so Merlawe had heard.

Fox wondered if it was Adkisson the Weasel who had died, or if he was a new intended.

If Fox discovered this to be true, Merlawe's letter continued, the earl asked that his own condolences be conveyed to Miss Smythe. And if she was not satisfied with her position as tutor and companion to Miss Fullarde (Fox's fictitious niece), would he, Mr. Fullarde, then please assure Miss Smythe she would be welcomed back with open arms to her old post with Merlawe's family.

Fox scowled. The audacity of the man! Trying to inveigle away Catherine's Swedish tutor, as bold as brass. Wasn't that just the way of a peer?

He refolded the earl's reply, then placed it in the proper drawer. His annoyance with Lord Merlawe withered to a wisp of smoke as he considered the facts.

He, Fox, had engaged Isabel as a Swedish tutor Catherine did not need, to coach her in the language of a country in which she would never live, wed to an ambassador's assistant who did not exist.

Audacity, thy name is Fox.

Even so, Fox had not failed to notice the change in Catherine since Isabel's arrival. He did not know if Isabel had wrought some personal magic, or if anyone Catherine's age could have nudged his formerly reticent sister into becoming the swanlike creature of smiles and engaging wit who now graced Willow Hall. Ha! No wonder Merlawe was eager for Isabel to return.

A dark thought opened in Fox's mind like the unfurling

frond of a venomous fern. Perhaps it was not for the sake of his daughter that the earl desired the return of Isabel.

Glossy black curls. Large gray-green eyes. Luscious bowed lips. What man would not want her? Desire her?

Fox shoved back his leather wingback chair and stalked to the fireplace. Grabbing the poker, he delivered three stabs to the coals, sending flames leaping higher. Devil take Merlawe and the rest of his nobly-born kind. Croom would discover the truth regarding Merlawe's past relationship with Isabel.

But for now, Isabel Millington-Smythe wasn't going anywhere.

Isabel scurried away from Fox's office as she heard Croom's footsteps approaching from the inside.

The Ladies? Not many men could *serve* them as did Mr. Tremayne? She wouldn't have thought it, but . . . was he a skirt-chaser? Even the consideration sent disappointment plummeting into the pit of her stomach.

Odd, but now that the subject had entered her mind, Isabel discovered that she truly would not have thought it of him. He had struck her as being more honorable than that. Honorable in the bone-deep sense of the word. Some men, womanizers amongst them, wore their honor on their sleeves, touchy and vocal about it with their peers.

Fox wore no feeling or philosophy on his sleeve. Indeed, with Fox, it seemed to Isabel all remained hidden. Until unexpected persons caught her by surprise and forced her to observe more closely: A respectable innkeeper's wife. The scarred owner of a bookstore. A one-legged valet. A curmudgeon of a butler. A devoted duck.

There were more. Just about anyone who served or worked with Foxton Tremayne seemed genuinely loyal to him. They had given him their trust.

As the door to the office opened, Isabel ducked through the first portal that presented itself. That of the kitchen.

The spacious room possessed limewashed walls and a high, vaulted ceiling only partially blackened with smoke from the fireplace and the modern roasting range. Clerestory windows allowed sunlight to flood in, glinting off immaculately polished copper pots, pans, and molds. Large rectangular tiles of mottled gray-and-wheat-colored stone paved the floor.

The sudden silence reminded her she was not expected in this area of the house.

Cook was a muscular widow, whose customary gray gown was wrapped by a long white apron, and her carrot-hued hair contained in a generous gray cap with lappets. She dusted flour from her hands and strode across the kitchen from a long wood worktable.

"Are you lost, Miss Smythe?" she asked briskly. Clearly, Cook did not cherish the distraction of unexpected visitors.

"No. No, I am not, Mrs.—"

"Just 'Cook' will do, miss."

Isabel looked around at the handful of kitchen and scullery maids. A couple nodded to her. One briefly smiled. The rest seemed to find their work too absorbing to flick a glance at her. They had no cause to do more, she reminded herself. She was an outsider. And when all was said and done, she, too, was paid for services rendered. Like an iron file against flesh, her fall in circumstances grated against her pride. She rolled back her shoulders.

"Very well—Cook," she said. "I have come to . . ."

To hide like the common eavesdropper she was? That wouldn't do at all. Then inspiration struck.

"I've come to make the acquaintance of Oscar," she announced pleasantly.

Cook's furry eyebrows rose. "You? Come to meet Oscar?"

"I am."

"Oscar is a duck, you know."

"Part of his charm," Isabel assured her.

"Uh-huh." Finally Cook waved an arm toward a door at the opposite end of the kitchen. "You'll find him just outside."

"Thank you." Isabel started toward the door, then stopped. Viewing Oscar had grown into more than a scheme to avoid being detected as an eavesdropper. Now she wanted to meet the creature whose affection prompted Fox Tremayne to tolerate embarrassment.

"Do you have anything I might feed him?" she asked.

Cook did not immediately answer. Almost grudgingly, she replied, "He does like his greens."

"Do you have some to spare?"

Cook sighed. "Go on. I'll have some brought to you."

Isabel smiled. "Thank you."

Oscar the duck dwelt in a well-kept waterfowl shed surrounded by a small, clean, gravel yard, enclosed by a fence. From the finishing details of the structures, Isabel discerned they had been built by an expert carpenter. She guessed the fence served more to keep predators out than to keep Oscar in.

As soon as Isabel arrived, Oscar waddled out of his private shed, which shielded him from the cutting breeze, quacking softly, as if muttering to himself. When he arrived at the fence in front of Isabel, he fell silent as he inspected the intruder.

"You are quite a handsome fellow," she told him.

He cocked his head and eyed her.

She looked around. "Have you no duck friends for company?"

"He don't want nothin' to do with other ducks," said a voice behind Isabel.

She turned to find a little scullery maid bearing several wilted bits of salad greenery. "Hello." She accepted the greens from the young child. "Thank you." The need to know more about her surroundings and the people who shared them with her prompted her to continue. "I am Miss Isabel Smythe. May I know your name?"

The girl stared at her in surprise. "Lizzie, ma'am," she said, bobbing a curtsy. "Lizzie Kesh."

"A pleasure to make your acquaintance, Miss Kesh. You say he shuns the company of his fellow fowl?"

"Aye, he does," the grimy youngster replied. "Ain't seen nothin' like it."

Isabel sadly regarded the lone figure of Oscar. "Perhaps he is confused."

"What's he got to be confused about?" Lizzie wanted to know. "Has a nice house. Plenty of food. Don't need to worry about the axe."

"Perhaps he believes he is something he is not."

Lizzie peered up through the ash-brown hair that escaped from her cap. "What would that be, I'd like to know?"

"A person."

The child squatted in front of Oscar, who came to see if she had brought him something tasty. "He *is* a person. To us as knows him."

Thoughtful, Isabel handed Lizzie a piece of green. The girl offered it to Oscar, who nibbled vigorously on the choicest portion of it.

"You're quite right, Lizzie. I've known certain dogs and cats, and even a horse who were persons. Perhaps 'person' is not the correct term, then, for what I mean," Isabel mused. " 'Human' might be a better choice."

Lizzie made no reply, but Isabel sensed the little scullery maid considered what she had said.

"He is lost, but he does not know it," Isabel said as she came down to sit on her heels, conscious that her slippers would have done better without this exposure to damp gravel.

Lizzie cast Isabel a worried look. "I wish Oscar would find a lady duck. A lady duck would keep him from being lonely."

Isabel held out the remaining green to Oscar. Promptly, he waddled to her and went to work on her offering. "Before he will want the company of a lady duck, Lizzie, I fear he must accept that he, too, is a duck."

Lizzie pressed her lips together. She nodded.

The door from the kitchen burst open. A flushed Catherine came flying out.

"There you are," she cried upon seeing Isabel. "I've been searching everywhere for you!"

Lizzie quickly rose and excused herself to Isabel as she hurried back into the kitchen.

With a parting glance for Oscar, Isabel stood. She smiled at Catherine as she brushed the back of her skirts.

"I wished to meet Oscar," she said. "A fine, feathered fellow he is, too." Isabel slipped her arm through a flustered Catherine's. "I certainly did not mean to discommode you, my dear. Come. Let us return to the shelter of the house, and on our way to the warmth of the sitting room fire, you must tell me what service I can do you."

Catherine fell into step with her. "No service. I simply fretted over your absence."

"I am honored."

"The fens are full of danger," Catherine insisted.

"Such as?"

"Oh. Drowning—I cannot swim—and the mire. It is far too easy to become lost—"

"I can swim, though this water is far too cold—and dark—to suit my taste. As far as the mire and becoming lost, it seems those pose danger only if I propose to wander off Frog Island. Which, as you can see, I did not."

As they passed through the kitchen, Isabel smiled and nodded at Cook. Lizzie was not to be seen. Likely she had returned to the scullery.

"Frog Island," Catherine echoed as they left the kitchen behind. "What is Frog Island?"

"*This* is Frog Island. Or rather, that is my name for it. What is its correct title?"

"I am not certain it has one. I've heard it called only The Island or Willow Hall Island." Catherine smiled. "I prefer Frog Island."

"Home to quacking frogs."

Catherine laughed.

"If you will gather your needlework—embroidering more serviettes, I believe?" Isabel said with a wicked smile, "I will take up my knitting, and we can review those new verbs."

"I already know more Swedish than I will probably ever use."

"Having second thoughts about the diplomat's assistant?"

"Er, no. 'Tis only . . . 'tis only that the persons with

whom I converse will probably also speak French. I already speak French, you see."

"Most of your household staff will speak only Swedish."

Catherine sighed. "I will fetch my needlework and meet you in the east sitting room."

ELEVEN

The heavy, nail-head-studded door of Willow Hall shut with a thump against the cold, drizzling dusk. In the greeting hall, flames tipped the tapers of two branched candlesticks on either end of a narrow table. In the shadowed room, light flickered over the oak panels.

Croom took Fox's wet top hat and caped box coat from him.

Fox smiled. "Welcome back, Croom. When did you arrive?"

"Shortly after you left for your business meeting in Harwich, sir. I hear that your carriage is soon to be filled with ladies' apparel."

Naturally, Fox had ignored Isabel's initial refusal of his offer to provide her with a wardrobe elegant enough for London in January. Her rejection disagreed with his plans, but strangely enough, her pride and caution pleased him.

"You hear correctly. My offer of a handsome bonus to Madame Billaud for completing Miss Smythe's wardrobe in time to accompany Catherine to London appears to have wrought nothing less than a minor miracle. I imagine, however, that Miss Smythe—or should I say, Miss Millington— might be displeased with me."

Croom looked surprised. "I was of the understanding that ladies *liked* elegant clothing, Cap'n."

"As was I, Croom, as was I. Miss Millington, however, wants nothing but her pay from me."

"The lady has pride." Croom adjusted the coat and hat in his arms. "And no small bit of influence on Miss Catherine, either, if I may say so."

Fox had not failed to observe that Isabel did, in fact, hold some influence over his sister. He had also noticed it was an influence gently wielded and bright with encouragement. Isabel seemed to possess a sincere affection for Catherine, whose shyness usually made friendships slow to bloom. Although Catherine's instant bond with Isabel had surprised him, Fox felt loath to disturb the relationship.

"So you decided to send Miss Smythe to London with Miss Catherine after all," Croom said.

"I have. Unless you have discovered something that sheds a different light on her?"

"No, sir."

Bartholomew Croom had the knack of being able to track down the most elusive fact, object, or individual. Three years ago, he had managed to locate Fox, who had believed his trail well concealed. Now Croom was a valued member of the Assembly, using his unique talents as an intelligence officer extraordinaire.

Croom rubbed his nose. "Did find out something about Miss Smythe, though."

That captured Fox's attention. "Pray, what did you learn?"

"Not much. Her parents are dead, but not in a shipwreck as she told Mrs. Densham. Her father perished of fever in India. Her mum pined after him and finally gave up the ghost. There's a brother—Robert Millington—who is an officer with the Sixteenth Light Dragoons. He was taken prisoner and is now held for ransom by Spaniards."

"Not part of a prisoner exchange?"

Typically, officers taken prisoner by the French in this war were exchanged with prisoners taken by the British.

"An isolated warlord, perhaps." Croom shrugged. "Her

paternal uncle, along with his wife, live in Robert Millington's estate."

"What are their names?"

"Gilbert and Lydia Millington."

Gilbert Millington. "Gilbert Millington has invested with
us. In fact, the fool has done so more than once. Both times
he reaped a small profit in addition to the return of the capital. Small fry."

Realization struck Fox like a thunderbolt. Jove! He had
swindled Isabel's uncle!

Croom cocked his head and gave Fox a wry smile.

Fox pinched the bridge of his nose between thumb and
finger. "Please continue. What's the name of this estate?"

"Greenwood, in Berkshire. That's where Miss Isabel
Millington lived, too. Until she went missing about fifteen
days ago. An 'I. Smythe' worked for a neighbor, the Earl of
Merlawe, but she left a few months ago. The *I* stands for
Isolda, though, not Isabel."

The devious elf, Fox thought. Devious, but not consistent. It was the lack of consistency that tripped up amateurs.

The question remained: Why?

Why did she leave her home—an estate, no less—to call
on Mr. Syer in London? What was her "urgent" reason for
wanting to speak with him? Fox could still see her in his
mind's eye, standing at the front door, trying to talk her way
past Horace Leckenby to an audience with Mr. Syer. Had
she come to beg for the return of her uncle's money? That
did not make sense. Her uncle had thought himself well off
to get back his capital and a small return.

Fox went on to the next puzzle. "Why was she on her
way to Harwich when I arranged to have her put off the
coach?"

Croom shook his head.

"With a name like Valfrid Adkisson, her intended is
probably Swedish. Perhaps he has returned to Sweden,"
Fox murmured, more to himself than to Croom. "Perhaps
she was trying to join him there." That weasel-faced Mes-
mer. Fox's gaze cut back to Croom. "Find anything about a
betrothal?"

"No, but I did find out an interesting fact or two otherwise."

"Meet me in my office in a quarter hour."

"Don't usually say this, sir—"

"What don't you usually say, Croom?"

"Something about her makes me believe she means us no harm. Can't say what it is, exactly." He shrugged. "Just a feeling I have."

Fox heard a tiny splash in the silence of the greeting hall. His dripping coat and hat had created a small puddle on the floor.

"Go on, man," he said. "You're becoming soaked."

"Aye, sir."

Croom took three steps, then stopped. "Meant to tell you: I heard something about Kymton while I was out and about."

"Oh?"

"You know he owns a good bit of land in Berkshire."

"I do."

"Well, there's talk he's planning to turn out all his tenants there and build a manufactory. Locals are speculating it will produce cannons or something else to profit from the war."

One of the Ladies lived in a cottage on the land of which Croom spoke. She and the two children had lived there all their lives. Even after the battle of Kurndatur, she had been loath to move, and so Fox had seen to it that poverty had not forced them from their home.

"Thank you, Croom," Fox said softly.

The valet/intelligence agent bore the wet clothing off toward the kitchens, his wooden peg thudding an uneven rhythm against the flags.

Damn Kymton.

The dark hour before dawn saw the departure of Etienne and Tsusga. The two would assume new personae and keep their noses to the wind for the latest scandals and windfalls amongst the wealthy corrupt.

They would also visit many of the glassworks, cloth manufactories, and other businesses owned by the Assembly, under a multitude of different company names. These establishments were operated so that workers could be assured of decent working environments and fair wages. Most such enterprises were the largest employers in their areas and therefore wielded political might. To the best of their abilities, the Assembly used that might to ensure favorable conditions for the men, women, and children whose voices had been ignored by the privileged.

At breakfast, Diana announced that she had secured the private dining room of the Blue Dragon for luncheon that afternoon.

"I believe we all require an outing," she said.

Fox paused in the midst of buttering a wedge of toast. He noticed she had also commanded the attention of Catherine and Isabel.

"Do you indeed, Aunt?" Fox responded. "And what brought you to this conclusion?"

"Our activities have fallen into a rut. Without an occasional change, we risk becoming dull."

Fox laid down his knife. "Dear heavens, say it is not so."

Diana smiled. "I fear it to be true. On this island, we cannot go out for a ride. There are no neighbors to visit. The weather is gray. You continue to do"—she languidly waved a manicured hand—"whatever it is that you do, Nephew. Catherine studies the Swedish Isabel teaches her, and when they are not involved with their language lessons, they occupy themselves with needlework." She spoke the last word as if it released a faint, unpleasant flavor on her tongue. "If this continues, we will all run mad."

"I think you may exaggerate somewhat," Fox replied, aware of the two younger women's hopeful gazes. "We have all played cards a time or two in the evenings. Or read."

He saw his sister cast a questioning glance at Isabel, who smiled at her. Although he could not hear their whisper, he saw the tutor's lips form the words "go on."

Catherine cleared her throat. "I would much enjoy a visit to Felgate, Fox."

A little surprised, but pleased, at her speaking her mind, he smiled. "I see I have been remiss in my duties as brother.

You must be bored indeed if a visit to temperate little Felgate would grant you joy."

"'Tis only that a change now and then would be welcome." She turned to Isabel. "Would you not find luncheon at the Blue Dragon agreeable?"

Lusciously ripe lips moved. "I would."

Despite the distance of the dining table's width between them, Isabel's presence brushed against Fox like the steam from a hot spring. He noticed that this morning her glossy hair had been gathered into a smooth knot high at the back of her head. Tendrils spiraled in front of each ear, and a few dark wisps kissed her alabaster nape.

Fox's gaze wandered down her slender neck. Then it encountered that irritating miniature lying atop the delicate pulse point at the base of her throat.

Annoyed, he brought his attention back to the discussion at hand.

Diana was right. A break in their daily affairs was needed. Between the dreary weather and being confined to this small island with the distracting company of Isabel, *he* was certainly in want of one. An afternoon in Felgate offered the least disruptive prospect.

"You are entirely correct, Diana," he said, reaching for his cup of coffee. "An afternoon in Felgate and luncheon at the Blue Dragon will do us all good."

As the conversation turned to the proposed outing, Fox surveyed Isabel.

Like Croom, Fox sensed she might be trusted with his secrets, but only if push came to shove. He would not lightly put at risk the lives of so many in the Assembly.

Mr. Densham, the owner of the Blue Dragon, stood on the dock to greet them and aid them in stepping out of the punt. Standing beside him, Mrs. Densham beamed and made much over Catherine, Lady Blencowe, and Isabel.

"And how are you getting on at Willow Hall?" she asked Isabel as they all strode into the welcoming warmth of the inn and on into the private dining room.

"Very well, thank you. They are all that is kindness. I feel most fortunate in having secured the position." Isabel smiled. "I have you to thank."

Mrs. Densham pinkened. "Fiddlesticks."

Fox raised his baritone voice only enough to gain their attention. "My aunt wishes to speak."

Everyone fell silent and turned to look at Lady Blencowe.

"I thought we would each find a cup of tea and a spice cake fortifying against the chill of our boat ride," she said, "before we visit the shops in the village."

As if by magic, a freckled Densham boy bore a tea tray into the private dining chamber, and a slightly older Densham daughter carried in a plate piled with glistening spice cakes.

"I have asked that luncheon be served in this room at one of the clock," Lady Blencowe continued. "That will give us approximately two hours to do our shopping. Is that agreeable to everyone?"

It was.

As Isabel moved into the dining room with the others of her party, she tried to recall what she could of Felgate's mercantile offerings, but all she could remember were the hardened expressions of those who had rejected her when she had so badly needed work, and the desperation and despair she had felt.

Lady Blencowe sauntered up to Isabel as she sipped from her cup. A faint fragrance of orange wafted up in the curl of steam.

"You are in need of a new pair of slippers," she said, setting her cup in its saucer. "I have taken the liberty of placing coin in your reticule."

Faced with the sedately worded order, Isabel discovered it more difficult to argue with Diana Blencowe than her nephew.

"I cannot repay you," Isabel finally said.

"It isn't a loan. What I presume is your only pair of slippers is no longer serviceable. Your half-boots are inappropriate for the house." Lady Blencowe's eyes twinkled. "I would not have my niece fret over the possibility that her friend's toes are cold."

Not tutor or companion. Friend. The revelation warmed Isabel.

"Thank you," she said.

After everyone had finished their tea, they drifted out of the chamber.

When Isabel joined Catherine, she was informed there were a handful of shops in Felgate, and a few of them even offered an admirable selection of wares.

When Isabel finally peeked inside her reticule, she saw a small package wrapped in silk and tied with a fine satin ribbon. With a thumb and forefinger, she tugged slightly on the neat bow, and the square of silk fell open to reveal six gold guineas.

A fortune.

Once she would not have thought so. But then, once she would not have left Greenwood save to marry a wealthy young landowner.

Would six guineas be enough to pay her passage to Sweden? She didn't know. But the point seemed moot when Lady Blencowe expected her to purchase a pair of slippers— slippers Isabel did, in fact, need if she were not to appear shabby.

"What is it, Isabel?" Catherine asked softly. "You look as if you've discovered the eighth wonder of the world."

Isabel held out her open reticule.

Catherine peered inside, then looked at Isabel in question.

"The generosity of Lady Blencowe," Isabel said.

A smile stole across Catherine's face. "More than enough to purchase stockings, gloves, slippers, and, perhaps, a length of muslin."

Isabel knew she was sorely lacking in these items. Indeed, she had mended her stockings until there were more of her stitches than original stocking. There had been only so much time to pack, only so much room in her portmanteau.

If only she were now in Harwich.

Alas, she was not. She *had* sent her uncle two letters. Why had he not responded? What if he were . . . dead?

That grim possibility had occurred to her before, and it left a cold lump in the pit of her stomach. Uncle Valfrid was all she had left in this world whom she could trust.

Isabel's gaze slid up to encompass Catherine, and then, beyond her, Fox Tremayne, who stood on the walkway engaged in friendly conversation with the eldest son of Mr. and Mrs. Densham. Her fingers felt the weight of Lady Blencowe's gift. Would these folk be allies in her quest to free Rob, or would they, like most law-abiding citizens, return her to Greenwood and Gilbert?

No, she knew Fox would never turn her over to the law if she were to explain her circumstances. But even still, she sensed that there was much more to Fox than he let on. She couldn't put her finger on the precise reason why she felt this way, yet Fox left her with a strong impression that he was a man with secrets. There was so much she still did not know about him, and she dare not risk putting all her trust in a man she could not fully understand. He might very well use her desperation against her, to put her at his disposal in any way he chose.

She was Rob's only hope. Her brother's life was at stake, and if telling Fox might keep her from reaching him . . .

It was a chance she couldn't take. Better to wait for Uncle Valfrid to get her letter and send the money necessary to free Rob.

For the time being, she decided to continue to await a reply from Uncle Valfrid.

"Where might I find good stockings at a thrifty price?"

Catherine showed her. Together they scrutinized the wares in different establishments as they teased each other and laughed.

As they moved down the unpaved high street, visiting the shops, Isabel grew aware that Fox was moving with them at an inconspicuous distance.

"Why is your brother following us?"

Without looking away from the braid-trimmed glove she examined, Catherine said, "He is cautious."

"Cautious? About what?" Did the tiny burg of Felgate harbor a terrible secret?

"He protects the reputations of two young ladies."

"Oh." Isabel smiled. "I thought you meant there might be a murderous lunatic who occasionally escapes his chains in his family's cellar."

Catherine laughed. "No, of course not. Wherever did you come up with that idea?"

"One hears things," Isabel replied airily, feeling a little foolish. Country living brought with it the perennial rumor or two: a monstrous offspring chained in a dungeon. A mad wife locked in an attic. The identical noble twin secreted in an isolated country estate. The more remote the neighborhood, the more fanciful the rumor. And Felgate was as remote as a place could be. Well, excepting, of course, Willow Hall. Even it possessed a secret chamber and a publicly disgraced traitor.

Not that Isabel was convinced he was a traitor. Not intentionally. Fox was . . . kind. Respected. Perhaps his disgrace stemmed not from treachery, but from a moment of cowardice.

"Oh, yes. One does hear things about the inhabitants of isolated villages," Catherine agreed. "The murderous lunatic story is new to me, though. This is more of a mad-wife-locked-in-the-attic sort of place. Of course, being situated on the fens, Felgate is subject to unfriendly smugglers. But that is rare," Catherine added as she laid down the gloves. "The last attack came three years ago."

"I hadn't thought about smugglers being a threat to Felgate," Isabel admitted. "I suppose the fens are a good place for them to hide."

Catherine picked up a blue kid slipper. "This would go well with your gown, Isabel."

Ah. A not-very-subtle change of subject. Perhaps the tales of smugglers attacking the residents of Felgate made her anxious. "Yes. But a nice gray would be more practical."

Isabel tried on slippers while Catherine issued opinions, something, Isabel realized, she would not have done when Isabel had first arrived at Willow Hall. Gray-green slippers with green trim appealed to Isabel, but she reluctantly set them aside, as they went with nothing she currently possessed. She finally decided upon a pair of black kid slippers embellished with bows of gray grosgrain. Catherine tut-tutted, still preferring the blue leather, but Isabel maintained black was more versatile.

As they left the shop, they encountered Fox, who had been observing them through the front window.

"Do you not think Isabel ought to have chosen the blue slippers?" Catherine asked him as he held the door open for them to join him outside on the narrow wooden walkway that shielded pedestrians from the muddy street.

Fox turned his eyes toward Isabel, who immediately felt the personal touch of his gaze.

"I preferred the gray-green pair," he said.

The fact that he had actually noticed the shoes she had tried on surprised Isabel. It was not a detail Rob or her father would have detected. Indeed, Rob's eyes would probably have glazed over shortly after her decision to try on any slippers. Women's fashions had never interested him. Papa had possessed excellent taste, but the particulars of clothing amongst the females in his household had been entrusted to Mama.

Isabel found unexpected pleasure in Fox's attention. She smiled up at him, only to discover his warm, golden gaze spellbinding.

"Why the gray-green pair?" she heard herself ask softly.

"They match your eyes."

Fox knew the color of her eyes.

Warm, tingling astonishment left her speechless.

"It is time for luncheon," Catherine pointed out. Only the smallest of trills in her voice told Isabel she had noticed the momentary tension between her brother and her friend.

Fox pulled his watch from his waistcoat pocket. "Right you are, Catherine." He smiled at the women as if he had never revealed his knowledge of Isabel's eye color. "After you, ladies."

They walked in a single file along the narrow plank walkway, as it was not sufficiently wide to accommodate two persons striding side by side. Fortunately, there appeared to be few persons out and about the high street of Felgate at the moment.

As they made their way in the direction of the inn, Isabel began to feel foolish. Fox had acknowledged he knew the color of her eyes. All that meant was that he wasn't completely blind. Hardly a proclamation of devotion.

Not that she *wanted* a sign of affection from him, she told herself hastily. The very thought was silly.

The man was merely observant, not smitten. If she asked him, he likely could tell her the hue of Croom's eyes, or those of Nottage. Or Oscar's.

Just ahead of them, a large man attired in good-quality homespun wool stepped out of the baker's shop onto the plank walkway. He headed in their direction. When he caught sight of them, his ruddy face broke into a pleased smile.

He doffed his short, broad top hat. "Good afternoon to you, Cap'n. Ladies." He stepped off the plank walkway, into the muddy street, to allow them to pass. The mire darkened his stout boots.

"A fine day to you, Mr. Swaine," Fox replied, touching the brim of his own hat. "Most kind."

It certainly wasn't a civility Isabel had expected to be rendered Fox. Not after Rob's report of the goings-on in London upon Fox's arrival from India, nor after hearing the tales related by Greenwood's neighbors.

Catherine and Isabel greeted Mr. Swaine as well, adding their thanks for his courtesy.

The big man inclined his head. "'Twere my pleasure."

Once inside the Blue Dragon, the trio went directly to the private dining room. They were the first ones there. As they removed their coats, hats, and gloves, Mrs. Densham herself entered, bearing a well-equipped beverage tray. Behind her came two of her offspring carrying steaming platters of meat pies, slices of roast chicken, as well as vegetables glistening with melted butter and smelling of tarragon.

"Where is Aunt Diana?" Catherine asked. "I've never known her to be late."

Fox accepted a mug of ale from Mrs. Densham. "My thanks," he said with a smile. He took a swallow, then answered Catherine. "She sent word she might be a few minutes late. A delay with a merchant."

As Isabel sipped her tea, Catherine's mention of unfriendly smugglers came to mind. Smuggling was common in coastal and river areas. Rum, wine, lace, tea, and silk were all popular commodities, particularly when the customs fees could be avoided. Isabel would not have been surprised if many of the goods in the shops she had just visited, and the spirits available for sale at the Blue Dragon, had been purchased from smugglers. Isabel had sensed Catherine's reluctance to discuss the topic, and so she had not pursued the subject.

She had heard only a few tales of smugglers clashing with townsfolk, but they had been sufficiently grisly to leave an impression. Felgate was small and isolated. Some of the larger smuggling gangs—members armed to the teeth— might present a serious threat.

She caught Mrs. Densham's eye. "A word, if you please," Isabel murmured. "In private."

Mrs. Densham darted a glance around the room. No one was looking at them. She nodded.

Lady Blencowe swept into the room, smiling despite the cold air accompanying her. Seconds later, Mrs. Densham and Isabel slipped out into the hall.

"I'm a stranger to these parts, as you well know, Mrs. Densham."

"Not a stranger, dear. A newcomer." The older woman smiled encouragingly.

"You're very kind. I don't wish to offend, but you surely know that Mr. Tremayne's reputation is widely held amongst the citizenry of Britain to be . . . well, low. Yet here in Felgate he appears to be held in high esteem."

"That's true, dear."

"May I know why?" Isabel asked.

"Shortly after Mr. Tremayne moved into Willow Hall, despite our, er, aloofness, he saved us from smugglers who had repeatedly used Felgate ill. They hanged poor Mr. Burke by the neck, in a well. They whipped, then buried alive, Harry Timmer. And they attacked young women." Mrs. Densham's gaze shifted into the distance. It grew hard. "One was my daughter."

Mrs. Densham had three daughters.

Isabel's shock must have been reflected in her face, because Mrs. Densham nodded.

"Terrible men, they were," she continued. "Their crimes against us were many. They would come here when they wished, but no one knew when that would be."

She lifted her chin in proud triumph. "Then Mr. Tremayne moved into Willow Hall. When the smugglers descended upon us again, he led his and the men of Felgate against them. The smugglers far outnumbered us, but *he* devised a cunning plan. He was as heroic as Alexander the Great. Put his own life in peril for us."

Isabel thanked Mrs. Densham for her candor, then returned to the dining parlor.

As she sat at the table, enjoying the tasty meal and listening to the conversation and laughter, she knew that her latest theory regarding the cause of Fox Tremayne's catastrophic downfall was flawed. Mrs. Densham's revelation of Fox's defense of Felgate confirmed what Isabel, in her heart of hearts, wanted to believe.

Fox was not a coward.

He was an effective officer.

So, what—or who—was really behind the disaster at Kurndatur?

TWELVE

Isabel drew her knitted shawl more snugly around her as she gazed down at the barren garden from one of the many unused rooms on her floor. Dust motes drifted on the chill slant of light that poured past the drapery she held to one side.

Not for the first time, the small structure on the crest of the hill beyond the garden drew her attention. A small Greek temple. The towering hedge that wended around the island, shooting out from the house, cradled the temple as well. From this distance, she could make out little of the temple's detail, but from what she could see, it appeared a noble example of classical architecture.

Perhaps it might be a good place to walk to during a Swedish lesson. Catherine would benefit from more fresh air than she seemed inclined to take.

Isabel dropped the curtain. She had not entered this room before. The furniture was covered with holland cloth. Curious, Isabel lifted a hem, turning her face from the swirl of dust. The white marble top of the gilt wood table had been painted with roundels of fawns and decorated with garlands of bellflowers.

A fortune in finely crafted furniture decayed in Willow Hall. A comparison darted into her thoughts to stab her mind. Abruptly, Isabel let go the cloth. She strode from the shadowed chamber, into the hall.

All of Greenwood's beautiful furnishings had gone up for auction, that the creditors might be paid. Isabel and her mother had stood side by side, rigid with hard-won dignity, as they watched their possessions bled away: the green leather chair where Papa had sat while reading stories aloud to Isabel and Rob when they were little more than toddlers. The carved walnut four-poster bed that, against all custom, Mama and Papa had shared devotedly. The gleaming rose-wood dining table, where their family had gathered to celebrate birthdays, holidays, and the company of guests. Breakfront bookcases from the library, where Isabel and her father had spent so many pleasant hours. Bit by bit, their past was sold off.

Later, Isabel had discovered Uncle Gilbert had purchased much of the inventory, and at a fraction of its worth. He had told Isabel and Mama that he had done it for *them*. At the memory of how tearfully grateful she had been, Isabel's stomach clenched. Mama, however, had already slid bless-edly into her final decline. She could maintain the belief that her trusted brother-in-law had kept Greenwood from being stripped bare. Or perhaps Annika Millington had already discovered the truth about Gilbert. Isabel would never know. Her mother spoke not a word after that auction. She took to her bed, and three weeks later, she joined her husband in death.

She never saw that Gilbert had rearranged the furnishings in Greenwood to his own taste.

Isabel decided on exploring one more room before going on to her own bedchamber. The more she learned about the layout of this floor, the smaller the chance of her becoming lost again.

Bypassing the next several rooms, she played a small game to determine which one she would investigate. Before she could make her decision, her feet slowed and came to a stop outside a closed door.

There, in the gloom of the covered windows and the win-ter's twilight, a pale fan of light crept out from beneath the door. Where the holland cloth had slipped back to reveal a fraction of carpet, crimson, green, and lapis blue glowed.

Isabel stared at the light brushing the toes of her black slippers. Aside from her own, never before had she encountered any trace of occupancy in this or any other room on this floor. Well, any room save the hidden one where Fox labored to produce a gazette for Felgate.

She placed her hand upon the tarnished brass doorknob. Listening carefully, she detected no sound. Lightly, she rapped on the cream-colored panel in front of her face. And she received a response.

"Go away!"

The querulous voice was one she would recognize anywhere. She also knew Nottage's quarters were not on this level.

"I'm coming in, Nottage." Her fingers turned the knob, and she stepped into the room.

There, huddled in an antique armchair in front of a weedy little hearth fire, sat Nottage. Except for his chair and one side table at his elbow, the furnishings were covered.

"What are you doing *here*?" she asked, stopping in front of him so that he was forced to either stand or crane his neck to look up at her.

He did neither. "Be on yer way."

Now Isabel noticed the quavering quality to his voice came not so much from his usual foul temper, but from the fact that he shuddered. A glance at the fingers gripping the arms of his chair revealed the bluish tinge under his nails.

It was somewhat chill in here, but not nearly *that* cold. She strode to the fireplace and began feeding the flames with coal from the copper bucket beside his chair.

"Go away!" Nottage snapped. He winced, as if the movement involved with speech or breathing pained him. "Don't need yer help."

"No, of course you don't," she replied, wielding the business end of a poker in the fire until the flames grew. "It's much merrier to suffer." When she had a nice blaze going, she replaced the poker in its half-veiled stand of fire irons, then straightened. "Foolish man," she muttered.

"Foolish, am I?" he exploded. Instantly he grimaced and hugged his ribs.

Isabel set her fists on her hips. "I've never understood whether you are rude because you dislike me or because you are simply a curmudgeon."

Still holding his torso, he rasped, "Curmudgeon! I'll have ye to know I do my work right and proper. Ain't no one's complained. No one but ye."

Suspicion nibbled at Isabel. She looked around, then pulled the cover off a footstool, which she then pulled over to Nottage's chair. She sat down upon it, sending his eyebrows flying up, scandalized.

"What are ye doin'? It is not fittin' for a lady to sit on that footy little stool, whilst I—" He struggled to stand. His pain became more obvious.

She pressed him back into his chair. "Oh, do sit down, Nottage. I've not noticed a surfeit of formality at Willow Hall. I rather like that, don't you?"

He glared at her. "And what do ye mean by *that*?"

Isabel smiled. "Only that I am glad there won't be a fuss over my sitting comfortably on this footstool."

Nottage grumbled to himself.

"What's that you say?" she inquired sweetly.

"Naught for yer ears," he said, though a fraction less grudgingly. He seemed not to be holding himself so tightly now.

Isabel cast a glance at the fire, which gave off a lovely warmth now that it had been tended. The blue had gone from Nottage's fingers.

"Would you like some tea?" she asked, gesturing toward the earthenware teapot and empty cup on the side table. Without asking, she whisked the cup and pot to the hearth, where they would stay hot.

"Never ye mind about that," he said gruffly. "Go on, now."

"I have no intention of leaving just yet," she informed him cheerfully, "so you might as well take advantage of my offer."

His one eye studied her. "I've only the one cup."

"That's all you need, I should think."

"But—"

"I've had tea enough to hold me for hours yet," she assured him.

Without another word, she filled his cup and set it beside him on the marquetry table. Then she sat on the footstool near his knee.

With clear reluctance, he lifted the cup to his lips. His gaze caught hers, and his hand stopped.

"Go on, now," she urged pleasantly. "It will warm you."

She made a show of occupying herself with arranging her skirts. From the corner of her eye, she saw him finally drink.

They sat in silence for several moments. He cradled the steaming cup between his hands, drinking occasionally. The smell of coal-fueled fire filled the chamber.

"Fair shawl," he said.

She traced the edge of the cream-colored wool with a forefinger. "Thank you."

"Did ye knit that, too?"

Isabel nodded. "A friend taught me to knit." A friend, who, pray God, had not suffered at Gilbert's hand for having aided Isabel these many years. "Mrs. Odling is a practical woman. Knitting is—or can be—a practical skill. A knit shawl is much warmer than a sewn one, and fur was out of the question."

"Aye," he agreed. "Fur does raid the purse. This friend of yers, she was a neighbor?"

Isabel's mouth curved up. "You could say that. A close neighbor."

Neither said anything for a long minute. Nottage finished his tea and set down the cup.

"Do ye miss her?" he asked quietly.

"I do. She was a kind teacher and a staunch ally."

"Sounds a true friend."

"The rare sort."

"Aye. True friends are rare. But ye know when ye have one."

"You have such a friend, by the sounds of it."

Nottage's weathered face creased in the first smile she

had seen on him. "There's no doubtin' him," he said, "if ye have the honor to know him."

"A quiet man?"

"Nay, not so much quiet as . . . well . . . unknowable. 'Tis something like seeing a house. Ye observe the strong walls, the high roof, and the fair design, but ye cannot see what lies inside until ye are allowed through the door."

How closely he described Fox Tremayne. She had yet to be allowed through that locked door.

"Saved my life, he did," Nottage continued. "Aye, and the lives of many another man as well."

Most of England had heard only of the lives that had been lost. Perhaps Nottage did not speak of Fox at all.

She went to the hearth, where she tended the fire a minute or two. "Good friends are blessings."

"Aye."

After pouring Nottage another cup of tea, she returned the pot to the hearth. He seemed less uncomfortable now.

"'Tis not my intention to be impertinent, but when I entered this room, it seemed to me you had pain."

He straightened carefully in his chair. "No such thing."

She lifted an eyebrow.

Nottage sighed. "An old wound pains me when the weather grows cold."

"In your ribs?"

"Aye. In my ribs."

Isabel thought a minute. Then she dug her knotted string out of her pocket. "Stand up, please."

Eyeing her suspiciously, Nottage nonetheless complied.

Swiftly, Isabel took measurements, then thanked him. He settled back into his chair.

"I've a lesson to prepare," she told him, "so I must go now. Would you like your last cup poured before I leave?"

After a slight hesitation, he assented. She poured one last steaming cup of tea.

At the door, she smiled and nodded. He nodded in return.

Not long after she left the chamber, she returned bearing a blanket in her arms. This she arranged around Nottage's shoulders despite his halfhearted fussing.

Back in her chamber, Isabel made a few calculations based on the measurements she had taken with her knotted cord. Then, as she planned Catherine's future Swedish lesson, she took out her knitting needles and a ball of pink silk yarn and began to cast on stitches.

After the evening meal, Fox, Lady Blencowe, Catherine, and Isabel withdrew to the sitting room. Catherine and her aunt sat on the green brocade settee, where they discussed Catherine's introduction to Society in London this January. Their soft voices gradually receded into a murmurous flow. Pierced by the occasional crackle of flames in the fireplace, the quiet sound offered a sort of comfort to Isabel, who knit, ensconced in an armchair closer to the hearth.

She might have found serenity had not Fox Tremayne occupied the chair beside hers, separated by one paltry side table.

He appeared absorbed in a gazette from a town in the United States of America of which she had never heard. Indeed, she might have been a speck of dust, for all the mind he paid her.

That was precisely the way she liked it, Isabel assured herself as she wrapped the pink silk between her needles to produce another knit stitch in the neat row. Her goals remained clearer and life much less complicated when Mr. Tremayne did not converse with her—as he had in the parlor at Madame Billaud's establishment when Catherine had gone to have her fitting and outside the shop in Felgate when he had told her she ought to have purchased the gray-green slippers because they matched her eyes.

If only she still believed him to be the villain of Kurndatur. Or a villain of any kind. How could a man who had liberated a town from smugglers be a coward? Did men such as Nottage and Croom lightly accord their trust—nay, devotion? What of Lady Blencowe, who had experienced a wider world than either Catherine or Isabel? Would a woman of such high repute openly keep company with a traitor, even if he were a blood relation? Even a duck bore Fox affection.

"Have I grown warts, Miss Smythe?"

Startled by Tremayne's low voice, Isabel dropped her knitting.

Feeling conspicuously clumsy, she quickly bent to pick it up. In her haste, her shoulder slammed into his as he leaned forward to gallantly retrieve her project.

Isabel barely managed not to fall out of her chair. Mortified, she sat bolt upright. It was impossible to hope that Mr. Tremayne had not noticed her lack of grace; she only hoped that her awkwardness had gone unnoticed by Catherine and Lady Blencowe. She clenched her hands in her lap.

He handed her the needles and yarn. "Are you unharmed?" he asked softly.

She flushed warmly. "I am, thank you. My thoughts wandered, and I did not pay attention to where my gaze fixed."

Not completely a lie.

"So it was not my warts that distracted you?"

She could not help but smile. "You appear to be quite free of warts, sir."

One corner of his mouth lifted slightly. "I am greatly relieved to hear it."

No, he was as beautiful as ever. He also exuded a magnetic masculinity impossible to ignore.

Or was that magnetism actually her mounting conviction of his unsung bravery? Of his kindness?

Of perhaps even his innocence?

Refusing to speculate further, Isabel resumed work on the garment draped in her lap. Yet, despite her determination to focus on her knitting, his presence remained a distraction, like a warm breath against her skin.

Fox made no move to resume his reading. Instead, he seemed to study her.

She dropped a stitch.

"Have I grown warts, Mr. Tremayne?" she asked, exasperated.

A smile tinged his words. "You appear to be quite free of warts, Miss Smythe."

The false name was beginning to gnaw at Isabel.

Fox lifted his glass from the side table. Against the glow

of the fire, he idly examined the brown-ruby color of the port through the bowl of the small glass.

"How did you meet Vapid?"

It took her a second to realize what he meant. "His name is *Valfrid.*"

"Certainly. Just as I said. How did you meet him?" The question conveyed no more than idle interest.

Isabel set about recovering the dropped stitch. "He was an acquaintance of my mother. She . . . uh . . . introduced us."

"Indeed? How reassuring to have one's parent make an introduction."

"Yes. Yes, of course."

"Yet the impecunious fellow permitted your mother to introduce you to him. Curious."

"Valfrid is a gentleman's son."

"You said he had gone off to make his fortune."

"The gentleman had invested unwisely and lost his fortune."

"Hence the necessity of Valfrog making one."

"Valfrid," she corrected automatically. "Many men do. Make their own fortunes, I mean."

"No, Miss Smythe. Most men never do."

Her father had not managed. But then, he'd had little time in India before contracting the fever.

"Valfrid has," she told him curtly. "And he will come for me. Soon."

"So you say." Tremayne shrugged. "It is not impossible that he has succeeded in accumulating a fortune."

"I should say not."

"So your father and his father bore something in common, then?"

Isabel thought furiously. What had she said to make him think so?

"Both lost their fortunes?" he prompted gently.

"Wh-what would make you think that?" she asked, wishing she were a more convincing liar.

"Because you are here, in Oakum Fen, working as a

Swedish tutor and companion, equipped with a minute wardrobe."

"My parents died penniless." That last word nearly choked her. They had been robbed, betrayed by someone they trusted.

"Yes. Mrs. Densham told me. Or rather, she told me you are a gentleman's daughter who has been orphaned. I came to my own conclusion regarding your financial status." His long, lean fingers dallied with his wineglass. "Am I mistaken?"

Isabel hesitated, feeling exposed. "No."

With a grace she admired, he unfolded from his chair. "Your tea must be cold. Allow me to fetch you another cup."

Typically, he did not ask her permission, but rather merely informed her of his intent. Before she could respond, he had scooped up her cup and saucer and sauntered to the tea table. He exchanged a few words with his aunt and sister. After filling Isabel's cup and adding a bit of sparkling sugar, he returned to his chair.

"Thank you," she murmured as she accepted the cup and saucer from him. She took a sip. Sweet warmth coursed through her.

He picked up his glass of port. "Well, clearly you have named Valmoose your champion, but aside from him, you seem all alone in the world."

That was the last thing a female on her own wanted anyone to believe. "I have a brother," she said. "An elder brother."

Fox smiled. "Do you now?"

"I do."

"Where is he?"

She tilted her head and regarded him from beneath half-lidded eyes. "I confess your sudden interest in my family surprises me."

"It shouldn't," he said, his beautiful face smooth and unrevealing. "These are inquiries I ought to have made sooner, but as you were traveling alone when Mrs. Densham met you, and you appeared to have no one, I didn't like to cause you concern with my questions until you came to see how harmless I am. But I am not insensitive to the concern my . . . reputation . . . might cause you."

Harmless, indeed. Isabel could not shake off the feeling that there was more to him than met the eye. Still, she wanted to believe in her instincts, which told her Fox was a good and compassionate man. That he didn't have the blood of so many soldiers on his hands. But . . . how could *she* be right when most of England branded him a traitor?

A light tap at the door announced Nottage. "Might there be anything I can fetch ye, sir? Ladies?" he inquired, glancing at Lady Blencowe, then Catherine.

"I believe we are finished here. Thank you, Nottage," Lady Blencowe told him.

Picking up the tea tray, Nottage withdrew from the chamber.

Isabel's gaze followed him until he closed the door behind him.

Nottage believed in Fox Tremayne. In fact, the curmudgeon seemed to admire him. As did Croom. Catherine. Lady Blencowe. Mrs. Densham and her family. Mr. Swaine. None of them appeared to give a dancing fig for what the rest of their countrymen thought of Fox.

She dragged her attention back to her knitting, weary of this indecision. As she plucked out one consistent pink stitch after another, Isabel found comfort in the gentle rhythm of her needles, in the texture of the silk.

"Your brother," said Fox, "he is doing well?"

"Well enough."

A pause stretched between them, filled only with the low, feminine murmur behind them, occasionally spiced by a trill of more animated conversation, and the crackle of the hearth fire.

"Have you no aunts?" he asked, shifting fractionally in his chair, a move that brought him closer to Isabel. "No uncles who might wish you to reside with them? It seems so unsafe for a young woman to be traveling so far from home, all alone. One might even see it as an act of desperation."

Isabel's head swung up, her attention to her knitting sundered. Her startled look crashed against his steady gaze, sending a panicked shockwave through her body.

He knows! Her heart beat like that of a cornered mouse. *He knows!*

How could he? As Isabel tried to rein in her alarm, her thoughts churned. He couldn't know, she told herself. It was her fear, her anxiety that spurred her reaction to a commonplace remark. A remark that she had heard, in variously couched forms, several times on her trek between Greenwood and Felgate.

As she gazed into his eyes, Isabel felt herself swept into intense color.

Topaz and gold, bronze and citrine scintillated in the candlelight. They seemed to swirl around her, creating a gentle current transporting her inward, to a place where instinct and emotion prevailed. Gradually, her anxiety eased. The clatter of her heartbeat slowed, assuming a different, powerful rhythm.

"Have I grown warts?" he whispered, his breath warm on her face.

A hesitant smile curved her lips. "We all have warts, Mr. Tremayne."

"Fox. I would have you call me Fox. And I shall call you Isabel."

She knew such a familiarity was inappropriate to their stations, even in a household as peculiar as this one, but Isabel discovered she didn't care. Instead, she felt an odd, warm glow.

"As you wish," she murmured.

His gaze lingered on her face for the timeless span of heartbeats. Then he edged back into the embrace of the wingback.

"It seems too cruel that you possess no relations who might offer you succor against this hard world," he said.

Isabel weighed her next words, finally determining them vague enough to be safe. What could he know of her treacherous uncle Gilbert?

"Sometimes," she said, "the hardness of the world is

preferable to the hospitality of relations. Uncles are no guarantee against cruelty."

*   *   *

The morning sun shone bright in the sky over Harwich as
Fox gazed idly out his coach window, taking in the usual
early traffic crowding the streets. His gaze drifted to a walkway, noting a bakery doing a brisk trade. A steady stream of
wives and servants entered with reed or wicker shopping
baskets hanging on their arms, intent upon supplying their
households with the excellent quality bread and cakes Fox
knew this particular baker provided.

Down the street and around the corner, a fishmonger
braved the chill temperature to loudly drone his list of wares
to any who would listen, beginning and ending with
"Fresh!" His cries competed with those of the paperboy, the
clatter of a multitude of shod hooves, and the rumble of
wagon and carriage wheels.

Earlier Fox had deposited two separate, but identical,
letters—from Tsusga to his chief in North Carolina—into
the trust of two separate ships' captains. Dual sets offered a
better chance that at least one would arrive. Winter voyages
were always risky.

Suddenly, he brought his attention fully to the walkway.
Striding into a popular chophouse was the man who had disturbed Isabel when she had caught sight of him across the
street from Madame Billaud's establishment. She had remained subdued most of the trip back to Willow Hall.

Abruptly, Fox knocked on the ceiling of the passenger
compartment. Negotiating the steady stream of other horses
and vehicles, the coachman directed the team over to the
side of the street, slowing to a stop. Swiftly, Fox exited the
carriage.

Knowing that his coachman never felt dressed without
his pocket watch, he instructed him to have the carriage at
Pegrum's in two hours time.

Then Fox strolled into the chophouse and took a corner
table that allowed him a view of the entire room, while
keeping a wall snugly at his back. A well-tended fire in a
large brick fireplace cast its warmth and illumination over

much of the room, but threw the occupants of corner tables into shadows.

Smoke curled up from the pipes and cheroots of patrons to mass in a haze that seemed to absorb the sun's pale rays pouring through the large front window. On every indrawn breath swam a collage of aromas: the yeasty smell of newly poured ale, the mellow-acrid scent of lighted tobacco, the warm perfume of baking bread, and the mouthwatering fragrances of roasting ham and pan-seared onions in butter. A shout of laughter or a female's giggle occasionally breached the low thunder of predominately male voices.

Busy serving girls laden with mugs and plates threaded their way between tables where patrons shared the latest gossip and debated everything from art to zealotry. A man didn't come here for a tranquil meal.

Fox glanced around the crowded room until he spotted his quarry. Upon this closer look, he recognized him immediately. Stylishly attired, tallish, husky, with thinning dark hair, the fellow looked to be around fifty years. Oh, yes. This was Gilbert Millington, erstwhile greedy investor. And, it seemed now, probable relation to Isabel. Were they working together to corner one Foxton Tremayne? Or Mr. Syer?

Millington sat alone at a small table, a pile of handbills at his elbow and a spoon in his fist. As Fox watched, the man ate black pudding with gusto. He had been distributing handbills to passersby when Isabel had spied him, and, unless Fox missed his guess, had engaged a few urchins to do the same on other streets about Harwich. Apparently hunting down someone was more difficult than one would think, because it certainly appeared to produce a healthy appetite.

A serving girl arrived at Fox's table, a tray of empty mugs and bowls propped on one hip. As soon as he told her what he wanted, she disappeared back into the mob.

Only minutes later, a different girl showed up at Gilbert Millington's table with a mug of ale. Ale and wine were the only drinks offered at the Two Georges chophouse, and anyone who had been here before knew to take the ale.

Along with the mug, she set a platter of pork chops in front of him, expertly dodging the casual hook of his arm.

He accepted her rejection without a word. As she danced away to other duties, he polished off the last bit of ale in his first mug and then tucked into his meal.

Minutes later, Fox's own food and drink arrived. As he observed Isabel's varlet of an uncle, the man became "Gilbert," not "Millington." Millington was *her* name.

So. Uncle Gilbert. *Not* Valfrid the Bloody Magnificent. Well, that made sense. Had Isabel glimpsed across the street the weasel represented on that miniature she insisted upon wearing so faithfully, she probably would have run to him with outstretched arms and cries of gladness.

There had been quite definitely no gladness in Isabel's expression when she had caught sight of the fellow now mowing through his luncheon.

Fox wanted a close look at one of those handbills.

Rising from his chair, he headed toward the tap area at the far end of the packed common room. This brought him directly by his subject. Choosing his moment, Fox stumbled against the table. The nearly full mug toppled, spilling its aromatic contents down the front of Gilbert. The pile of handbills scattered over the tabletop and rained onto the well-trod floor like dry leaves.

With a bitten-off oath, Gilbert launched himself to his feet. Ale dripped from his green kerseymere coat, cream-and-brown-figured waistcoat, and once-pristine white cambric shirt.

"Devil take it," Fox swore. "'Tis this crush. There's nowhere to place one's feet!" He whipped out his linen handkerchief, which he handed to his prey, who hastily mopped at his soaked garments.

"I do apologize most heartily," Fox continued with his best earnest sincerity, grimly pleased with Gilbert's discomfort. "A fine thing when a gentleman cannot eat his luncheon without being accosted by clumsy fellows."

"Only one," Gilbert said through clenched teeth.

"Pardon?" inquired Fox innocently. The wet, yeasty ale had to feel cold.

"Only one clumsy fellow."

"Aye, so far. I truly am most sorry, old man." He hailed a

serving maid and ordered a replacement round of ale. "And bring a nice wedge of Mrs. Clarke's excellent rum cake, too, please," he added.

"I know ale and cake can't possibly make up for my blundering," Fox went on to Gilbert after the little maid had headed for the kitchen. "But Mrs. Clarke does make an exceptionally fine rum cake."

By now, Gilbert had soaked up all he could with his own and Fox's handkerchiefs. The drenched cloths sat in a small, sodden heap on the table. Fox's betrayed no clue to his identity. He owned nothing monogrammed. Nothing, at any rate, that was monogrammed with his real initials.

Gilbert's handkerchief bore a blue embroidered *M*.

Resuming his seat, Gilbert sighed. He motioned for Fox to take the chair across the table from him. "I accept your apology, sir. Anyone who ignores the offer of good rum cake must be a boor indeed."

Fox grinned as he sat. "Or without a sweet tooth."

Gilbert laughed. He introduced himself as he offered Fox one stubby-fingered hand sprinkled with black hair on the back.

Fox shook Gilbert's hand and introduced himself as Talbot Adamson.

They exchanged a few remarks regarding the crowd and the quality of ale and food in the establishment before Fox steered the conversation to the handbills.

"At least none of these were ruined," he said, scooping the ones on the table back into a pile and picking up the pages closest to him on the floor.

"More's the pity," Gilbert said. "I've given out a hundred of them this morning, or so it seems. Been handing them out for days."

Fox picked up a handbill from the top of the stack. "May I?"

Gilbert shrugged. "Be my guest."

The headline caught Fox's attention immediately.

RUNAWAY.

With bruises, Fox thought grimly. Gilbert wasn't looking for Mr. Syer or Foxton Tremayne. He was after Isabel.

Below the headline followed the description of "Isabel Amelia Millington, a tall, slim girl with curling black hair, fair, unflawed skin, and gray eyes."

Gray eyes, indeed. Isabel's eyes were gray-*green*.

A reward of one hundred pounds was offered for information leading to her recovery.

"Sounds a pretty girl," he said casually. "Your daughter?"

Gilbert's mouth flattened into a tight line. "My niece, damn her eyes. A troublesome creature."

"And her name is Isabel Millington."

"Have you encountered her?"

"No. I feel certain I should remember a woman of this description."

Gilbert nodded grimly. "She's a beauty. And smart. Too smart for her own good."

"Smart and beautiful," Fox said. "A dangerous combination in a woman or a horse."

Gilbert laughed. "Right you are! And Isabel must be as fleet as a horse, because I've tracked her from Berkshire and haven't caught her yet."

Uncles are no guarantee against cruelty.

Anger simmered in the pit of Fox's stomach as he went to fetch his own meal and drink to Gilbert's table.

He hooked his booted foot around the leg of the empty chair and pulled it out. "Might she be taking passage on a coach?"

"She has no blunt."

"Then why do you want her back?" Fox asked, careful to maintain his facade of innocent curiosity. "Is she an heiress?"

Gilbert cut Fox a sharp look.

The new mug of ale and the fragrant wedge of rum cake arrived.

"I've already got a ball and chain," Fox lied after the serving woman had gone. "Brought some useful relations, too."

"Isabel is poor as a church mouse." Gilbert quaffed his ale. "But she is an orphan, and I feel a certain responsibility.

My sole brother died in India earlier this year. She is his only child."

"Ah, the responsibilities of family," Fox murmured. *Bastard.*

"Her mama died a few months later. Of heartbreak, like as not. She was never strong-spirited."

"Not like her daughter, eh?"

"No." Gilbert scowled down at the pile of handbills.

"Had any luck with your campaign here?"

"Campaign?"

"Has anyone come forward with clues to your niece's whereabouts?" Fox clarified.

"No one. Harwich has been a waste of time. I thought for certain—" Gilbert stopped. A shadow crossed over his ruddy face, as if he had caught himself before saying too much. "I plan to move on to Tollesbury as soon as I pass out the rest of these bloody handbills."

Fox gave him a sympathetic look. "You're worried about her." *She must be holding something that could work against you.*

"Uh . . . worried. Yes."

After Fox pretended to consider the situation for a moment, he volunteered to pass out the remaining handbills and inquire after Isabel, so that Gilbert could get under way on his search of Tollesbury.

Gilbert's expression lighted for an instant, then dimmed. "No, I'd best do it."

Leaning forward, Fox said, "Why? I'm as capable as anyone need be when it comes to passing out these things on the streets of Harwich. And I believe I can frame an intelligent enough question to coax out information, if there's any to be had. If you will give me an address where I can contact you, I'll notify you of the results. Come, allow me to make reparations for spilling your drink."

In the end, Gilbert agreed. Fox accompanied him to the inn where Gilbert had been staying. His packed belongings were brought down and the bill settled. Outside, Fox watched Gilbert swing up onto the saddle of his hack—and a fine piece of horseflesh it was—before he waved him off into the dim afternoon sun.

On his way to Pegrum's, Fox dumped the stack of hand-bills in an alley privy.

THIRTEEN

Fox slowly dipped his pen into the inkpot, his thoughts far from the business letter he composed.

Isabel Smythe was, in fact, Isabel Millington. She was a woman on the run, and her uncle sought her. By aiding her, Fox broke the law. Ha! *Another* law. What concerned him more was the fact that Gilbert might track Isabel to Willow Hall. Secrecy was the Assembly's most treasured commodity.

He remembered the ugly purple, green, and yellow marks on Isabel's face and arms at their first meeting, and her tone of voice when she had spoken the words "Uncles are no guarantee against cruelty."

He also remembered Gilbert. The man's dislike of Isabel had corroded the air around him, despite his paltry attempt to appear the evenhanded uncle. Fox would be willing to bet a good hunter that Isabel's visit to Uriah Syer's residence had something to do with Gilbert, something he wanted to keep quiet. Perhaps even where he had obtained the monies he had invested. Her brother was probably heir to the estate—Greenwood, was it?—in which Gilbert dwelt. But her brother was held by the Spanish. How convenient for Gilbert.

Fox watched as the ink dried on his pen.

Isabel Millington. He knew her real name. Why did he not confront her with it? Or tell her that he had sent her uncle on his way?

It had occurred to him that she was hiding from her uncle. Perhaps it was the only thing keeping her at Willow Hall. If she knew Gilbert had left the area, might she leave, also, making her way to . . . Valfrid Adkisson?

The office door opened, and Aunt Diana entered. He knew by her expression she bore unfavorable news. He placed his pen in its holder and focused upon her his full attention.

"Your grandmother believes she is dying," Diana announced without preamble.

Fox sighed heavily. "Again?"

His paternal grandparents—his only surviving grandparents—had distanced themselves from him upon his inglorious return from India, but they had maintained a connection with Catherine, despite her loyalty to him. Fox had taken care never to reveal his hurt to his sister. She already felt torn between those she loved, and he had no wish to wound her more.

Diana seated herself in the leather wingback armchair across the desk from him. "I've lost count of Mama's deathbed scenes. Sometimes, I think, she even believes it to be so. Be that as it may, she has sent a messenger to Riverside," Diana continued, naming her primary estate near Woodbridge, "to ask for Catherine." She shrugged. "Who is to say but that the old basilisk might not be correct this time?"

Fox sighed. "Then I suppose Catherine cannot refuse her. You must, of course, take Miss Smythe with you, but that should not present a problem. She has excellent address."

"Oh, but she cannot accompany us, Fox. You know how your grandparents feel regarding strangers. I cannot even take my maid with me or your silly grandmother will expire for certain. And your grandfather will sulk. I learned long ago not to tolerate such behavior, but there is no doubt it would make the visit even more difficult for Catherine."

Fox frowned. "Someone has to watch Miss Smythe. *I'm* trying to put together the next operation."

"You have plenty of time to play spy, and well you know it. My only concern is that there should be another female here to protect her reputation."

Fox scowled. "She is an employee, Diana. Her reputation should be safe enough."

"She is a lovely, young, *unwed* lady reduced to acting as companion and teacher to earn her bread. Do not think I've missed the way you look at her when you are unaware anyone is watching."

His eyebrows shot up with indignation—sparked by a phantom of guilt. "Indeed? And just how *do* I look at her?"

As soon as the words were spoken, he wished he had not asked. His aunt was not one to hold back when challenged.

Leaning forward, Diana looked him straight in the eye. "Do not play the innocent with me, my boy. I know yearning when I see it."

"Yearning? Ridiculous!" Restless, he stood. He stalked to a bookcase, from which he plucked a leather-bound volume of maps.

Did he yearn for Isabel?

He found pleasure in her piquant company. She was intelligent, educated, and beautiful—what man would *not* take pleasure in her presence? Yet there was more to her than looks and intellect. Isabel possessed a bewitching combination of reticence and candor, of character and wit.

She made excellent company on this isolated island. Only a fool would fail to appreciate the circumstances.

Diana was no fool.

"Her reputation will be safe," Fox said firmly. "Above a handful of people, all of whom know how to keep a secret, no one will ever learn that for the space of a seven-day or so, she was not shielded from my *yearning* by you or my little sister."

Diana followed him to the bookcase. "I fear less for Isabel's reputation than for her heart," she told him softly. "And yours."

His lips curved faintly in a humorless smile. "Her heart is

in no more danger from me than her reputation, I assure you. She has already given it to Valfrid Adkisson." The name grated on his tongue. He stared at the gold letters shining on the binding of the book he held. "As for me, I am content with the life that I have."

"You should have a wife, Fox, and children—"

"Who would forever be hostages to my . . . career." What respectable woman would accept as her husband a disgraced officer and a successful cheat?

Diana searched his face for a long moment. Then she flicked open her ebony and silk fan and strolled toward the office door. "You might be right."

Her swift reversal stirred suspicion in Fox. Narrowly, he watched Diana. "Take Catherine," he said. "I am sure Mrs. Ivey"—he no longer called her grandmother—"will wish to hear every detail you have planned for her granddaughter's introduction into Society. Let her exclaim over all the clothes and fripperies obtained for the occasion." He smiled. "You'll need an additional carriage."

His grandparents had turned him from their door when he had lost everything and the wolves were closing in for the kill. Now it gave him a certain additional satisfaction to be able to outfit his sister in a style worthy of nobility.

"You can pick up Catherine's things from Madame Billaud's establishment on your journey to the Iveys' estate," he said. "I'll pick up Isabel's finished garments within the next few days and bring them back to Willow Hall. They'll be waiting here for you when you assemble the Great Cavalcade to depart for London."

Diana arched an eyebrow at the use of Isabel's Christian name.

Fox held up an open palm, as if solemnly swearing an oath. "Have no fear. She is completely safe from me."

The day following found Catherine and Lady Blencowe still at Willow Hall, though clearly occupied with packing.

"Is your grandmother not on the brink of death?" Isabel finally asked.

Catherine had taken a reprieve in her packing to work at

her embroidery in the morning room, where the winter sunshine poured in the tall, mullioned windows.

"It is difficult to say, so often has she professed to be at
Death's door," Catherine replied. "Always, in my experience, she has made an astonishing recovery."

"Good fortune?"

Catherine coughed delicately. "Rather, one might say, she
is prone to be premature in her declarations of imminent
extinction."

"A hypochondriac?"

"Sometimes."

"And sometimes manipulative?"

"I fear so." Catherine sighed. "I wish you were coming
with me. You would know how to make Grandmama behave
properly. I find myself caving in to her autocratic tempera-
ment."

Isabel laughed. "You reckon me too capable! Your
brother would be up to the task," she suggested, not for
the first time wondering why his presence had not been
required.

Catherine sighed. "Grandmama and Grandpapa all but
disowned Fox when he arrived from India under a cloud of
disgrace. Later they apologized, and he accepted with, I believe, extraordinary generosity. But he has rejected any further overtures they have made."

Fox had been stripped of his career, his intended, and his
home. At a time when he had needed their confidence, his
grandparents had turned their backs on him. Their disloyalty
must have cut him to the heart! Indignation swept through
Isabel. She sat silent for a minute or two, considering.

"Well, my dear," Isabel said, rising from her chair, "I
wish you well. Your grandmother sounds a trial." She
grinned wickedly. "Show off your new knowledge of all
things Swedish."

"Knowledge, I am certain, for which she has eagerly
awaited," Catherine returned wryly.

Isabel laughed as she left the morning room, but she
sympathized with Catherine, who must face the machinations of her grandmother alone.

After a trip to her bedchamber, Isabel went in search of Nottage.

She finally located him in the kitchen, seated at a table by one of the fireplaces, polishing silver with a shammy leather. He was listening to Cook, who also sat at the table. With one muscular arm she beat the contents of a large bowl held tilted in her lap. At the sound of Isabel's footsteps on the stone floor, they both turned to look at her.

She nodded a greeting to Cook, who nodded back. "Nottage, when you have a moment, I would like a word with you."

"Aye, miss," he said in his gravelly voice.

He rose from the table to join her, and she led the way out into the hall.

Isabel turned to him. "I'm sorry to interrupt your work," she said, "but I wanted to give you this." She presented him with the paper-wrapped bundle.

He stared at it blankly. "A present?"

She smiled, feeling awkward. "Yes."

"For me?" He glanced up from the package, meeting her eyes as if he didn't trust her words, or perhaps his interpretation of them.

"Yes, Nottage, for you. Here. Take it."

His eyes narrowed. "What do ye want of me?"

This was becoming even more embarrassing than she had feared. "Nothing. Nothing at all. I wanted to give this to you, that's all. And now I've done so."

Without another word, she turned and hurried away, the patter of her slippers echoing in the dim hall.

Tsusga arrived at Willow Hall shortly after luncheon. Promptly, he and Fox withdrew to the haven of Fox's office.

The myriad details of arranging Catherine's first time out in London had closeted Isabel's student with Lady Blencowe, leaving Isabel with the luxury of a bit of free time.

Isabel tied the ribbon of her bonnet under her chin, then straightened her mother's cloak across her shoulders.

Several times since her arrival at Willow Hall three weeks ago, Isabel had sought to persuade her student of the healthful aspects of spending time daily in the fresh air. Isabel wasn't used to being cooped up inside all day, save in the worst of weather. At Greenwood, before her father's ruin, she had gone riding daily. After the family's horses had been sold, Isabel had walked about the estate, to the village, and to visit neighbors.

Catherine had proved most unreceptive to Isabel's suggestions of their walking about the island or pushing out a skiff to spend time exploring the fen. Apparently sensing Isabel's frustration and puzzlement, she had explained her dislike of the chill air and the heavy, dampening mists.

Poor dear! Isabel thought now as she passed through a deserted kitchen and out the back door. She headed for the gardens she had seen from upstairs windows. Catherine must be even more miserable than anyone suspected in this place of frequent mists. Of course, much of England experienced fog, but not so much as Frog Island.

With Catherine's possible husband-to-be a member of England's diplomatic staff in Sweden, she might eventually take up residence in Stockholm, a far cry from Frog Island or Felgate. Then her isolation would finally be at an end.

Eager to explore the island, Isabel set a brisk pace, her half-boots crunching against the gravel walkway. From either side of Willow Hall ran twin pairs of thick evergreen hedges that formed a sort of tunnel. This island was covered with them. Since it would have taken many years for the plants to grow so high and dense, Isabel could only assume some previous owner had loved follies but had missed the concept of concentrating the hedges in one area.

Isabel breathed in the thick, pale air. With it came a rich, peaty amalgamation of scents from dark, slow-moving water and frost-stricken flora. Eddies of silvery mist caressed her cheeks like moist fingers.

Nothing bloomed in the garden now. Bare rose branches reached toward the winter sky like brown, skeletal hands. Beside long umber beds sat a lichen-encrusted stone bench. Next to the bench stood a large stone pot filled with—she frowned, trying to recognize the lumpen contents—something quite dead. Spring would need a whirl of replanting and repotting, if this place were to compare in beauty to Greenwood's garden.

Her pleasure in being released from the closed doors of Willow Hall dimmed. Aunt Lydia took no interest in gardens. Gilbert's wife had never troubled herself to cultivate skills with which to nurture growing things. All the hours Isabel and her mother had spent tending, and the deep pleasure they had taken in observing nature's gradually unfolding beauty, would not help Greenwood's garden now. Perhaps Lydia's need to impress the world or the desire to avoid censure from her neighbors would prompt her to cozen Gilbert into hiring a gardener.

Isabel could hear her conniving aunt in her mind's ear. With a woeful sigh, that woman would tell Frannie and Frannie's mother, Lady Merlawe, and anyone else who would listen, that Lydia had *tried* to step in for Isabel's poor, departed mama, but that Isabel had refused to accept her well-intentioned help. The familiar nasal voice declared again that Isabel *liked* being mistress of Greenwood and would brook no interference.

Which was true to an extent. Isabel did like being mistress of her own domain. She had, however, always believed that someday she would marry and become chatelaine of her husband's house. Greenwood belonged to Rob. When he took a wife, *she* would reign there.

Before any of that took place now, Rob must be freed from his Spanish captivity. At this rate, Aunt Lydia would remain mistress of Greenwood for life.

Isabel thrust the depressing thoughts from her mind. At the moment, nothing could be done to resolve the problems that caused them. Determined to enjoy her outing, she looked around to notice she had passed through the winter-barren garden and out the doorway in the far boxwood wall. She stopped to spy out the lay of the land before her.

Through the drifting fog, she saw a vast, scrubby brown lawn, edged by a towering evergreen hedge. Here and there stood stone statues of gods and goddesses, and more benches and urns. All of them went forgotten when she lifted her gaze. There, on the crest of what must certainly

qualify as the closest thing to a knoll in Oakum Fen, surrounded on three sides by bare white willows and tall
hedges, stood a classical Grecian temple.

Heavens above, a swamp sanctuary.

In the winter air, it glowed like the moon. The structure
possessed slender columns and elegant symmetry, which
soothed the eye. Isabel set off toward the temple.

She considered what it had taken to create such an edifice
here. Marble, mortar, trained masons, and artisans—all must
have been transported by boat. What must the workers have
thought as they traveled through Oakum Fen?

Even Greenwood did not possess a temple. Papa had
thought it too ostentatious. Instead, he had commissioned a
simple limewashed stone pavilion to be constructed, a place
of shade and shelter where the family could assemble to
dine and play when weather and schedules permitted. Isabel
smiled. More than one butterfly had eluded her and her
brother's childish nets

As she climbed the small, winter-browned hill in solitude, her thoughts wandered. Like pins to a magnet, they
flew to the reverberating presence that haunted her these
days: Fox Tremayne. Tall, handsome . . . and believed to be
a villain by most of the British population.

Once she had thought him a villain. Then, later, a coward. Now she could not believe even that of him. But perhaps he had changed? Had his experience in India, and the
resultant shunning in England, transformed his character?
She shrugged off the questions, uneasy with the answers she
kept coming up with.

She imagined lashes half-concealing amber eyes lighting
with amusement, one corner of his mouth, his perfect
mouth, quirking up in a half smile. And that melting, masculine baritone voice . . .

Isabel stumbled. With an annoyed tug, she freed the hem
of her skirt from the toe of her half-boot. That's what came
of daydreaming like some lackwit mooncalf.

What was she *thinking*? The man seldom smiled, she told
herself, irritated with her own silliness. Too often, one could
not even decipher what was going on in his mind. 'Twas as

if he sought to hold the world away from him. Away from his heart.

Lifting her skirts as she stalked the incline to the temple, Isabel gave a little snort. *His heart.*

The man had been drummed out of his regiment, hissed at, spat upon, jilted, rejected, and generally shunned. He had lost his reputation, his intended, his ancestral home, and, for all she knew, his sanity. After all, he had chosen to dwell in a swamp. He ignored most of his once-splendidly furnished mansion, living in a relatively small portion of it, along with his sister, sometimes his aunt, and entirely too few servants, while leaving the rest of Willow Hall to spiders and dust.

In short, he did not appear to be hunting a wife.

Frog Island—Isabel's name for this swamp lair—hardly qualified as a marriage mart. No flirtation flared between Fox and Isabel. None at all. Certainly she was in no position to become . . . involved. Rob lay in chains. Uncle Gilbert had stolen every penny of Isabel's dowry, and she was willing to wager her only other gown that even now he tracked her as a huntsman tracks a deer.

Oh, yes. Prime matrimonial material.

Not that she was looking for a husband. No indeed.

She mounted the crest of the rise, disturbing mists that swirled away to reveal a classical Carrara marble portico dominated by a majestic alabaster sculpture of Pallas Athena. Athena, Greek goddess of wisdom and war.

Isabel smiled as a thought, a bright fancy, curled through her mind. Within a Greek temple veiled by English fog, who knew what mysteries might be found?

Fox wiped his hands with a rag as he regarded the top copy on a stack of freshly printed certificates with satisfaction. A master printer could do no better. They looked real.

"Nice work," Tsusga said.

Both men stood admiring the certificates that Tsusga would being taking back to America with him to begin Operation Coffee Bean. Etienne would accompany Tsusga for Coffee Bean. The French were still popular in the United States.

"Yes," Fox agreed. He grinned at his friend. "Quite official-looking, don't you think?"

Tsusga smiled. "They always are. You are an artist among thieves. I salute you." He offered a flamboyant bow.

Fox gave him one in return. "You put me to the blush, sir. But you do speak only the truth."

"Ever the modest fellow."

"Yes, yes. So true." Fox removed the heavy printer's apron and hung it on a wall hook. "Now I must return to my persona of swamp squire." He removed his coat from its hook and slipped it on.

"You are attracted to the lovely Miss Smythe." Tsusga did not ask a question.

Like a well-aimed arrow, the statement pierced the layers of obfuscation around the subject of Isabel. Around what Fox felt for Isabel. Or thought he felt.

As if he could read the resistance and confusion that brawled inside his comrade, Tsusga placed his hand on Fox's shoulder. "It is time, my friend. For too long you have kept at arm's length all who have come to you after Kurndatur."

"Isabel has not come *to* me, Tsusga. She'll be passing *by* me. By all of us, if we're lucky." Fox stared unseeing at a small ink smudge on his palm as he thought of Isabel exiting his existence, taking her fierce loyalty, her pride, her unconscious ability to enchant, and leaving behind . . . emptiness.

"She will pass *you* by if you say nothing to her," Tsusga persisted. "It is seldom a woman's way to speak her heart until a man reveals his." A quiet note of self-deprecating humor crept into his voice. "In some ways, they are wiser than we."

Fox curled his fingers into a fist, erasing the smudge from sight. The risk . . .

"You have two wives, do you not, Tsusga?"

"I do."

Two. Fox could not acquire *one*.

"I would recommend marriage," Tsusga told him in a quiet voice. "With the right woman."

Fox trod on the cunningly concealed floor lever that opened the staircase leading out of the hidden chamber to which he had relocated the printing press.

"It is good to have someone to whom you matter," Tsusga persisted as he followed Fox down the steps into another secret room one level below, on the same floor with the family's living quarters.

"I have many someones to whom I matter," Fox muttered. "Perhaps too many."

"True enough. But the love a woman holds for a man is different from the ties you have with the rest of the Assembly, or the responsibilities you assumed for the Ladies. The Ladies are but dependents. Those of the Assembly are your associates, some even your friends." Tsusga smiled. "But the right woman—ah, the right woman—*she* will become not only your friend, but a part of you. A part you will wish never to lose."

Tsusga pressed the mechanism disguised as a plaster acanthus leaf and the staircase closed, leaving behind them only oak paneling in a limewashed wall. "When a woman gives her heart to you, you matter to her for your own sake. Your pain is her pain. Your delight, her delight. Your defeats sear her as they do you, and your triumphs uplift her as though they were her own."

Fox turned a bland look on his friend. "I'm not completely without experience, you know. I did plan to wed a woman once."

When word of Fox's disgrace had reached England, Miss Ariadne Gilbard had cried off the engagement with the righteous blessings of Society. Unfortunately, her letter had gone on to India while Fox sailed back to England. He had received no word of the jilt until he had called on Ariadne and been turned away at the door.

Tsusga grunted. "I never understood your wish to bind yourself to Ariadne Gilbard. *I* would have sold her to the Iroquois. She was not worthy of you, that one."

Fox led them down another corridor.

"A great many British would disagree with you, Tsusga,"

he said. After Kurndatur, she had been considered by the population at large to be much too good for Fox.

"The British. They left my people—their allies—to twist in the wind when they made peace with the American colonists. I have no wish to be like them."

"That was over twenty years ago."

"And my people pay for it yet."

Fox did not bother to inquire why it was to Britain that Deer Clan had sent Tsusga. The two men had discussed the matter years ago. The future lay with the former colonists, but the British schools, and the contacts and experiences that came with them, were deemed superior and more sophisticated than those available at the time in the new United States.

The two men walked without speaking for a while, the only sounds the soft thud of their footfalls echoing in the hall.

"Did you love her, Fox?" Tsusga asked.

For the past three years, Fox had refused to think of her. While she, herself, had faded in his recollection, the memory of her rejection still carried sting.

Now he considered Tsusga's unexpected question. Fox had been prepared to bind himself to Ariadne for the rest of his life. But had he ever loved her?

He suspected what he had felt for Ariadne had come from living among men, from being a stranger in a strange, exotic land far from England. But then, Ariadne been the prettiest girl at the Cavalier's Ball. He had stood up with her two times that sultry evening in Calcutta, where she visited an aunt. Ariadne had been someone from home. And she had been filled with, he later realized, preposterous romantic notions. When he had fallen short of the image she cherished, she had repudiated him.

He had not loved Ariadne. He had scarcely known her.

Feeling awkward, he admitted as much to Tsusga.

"That is well," the Cherokee said solemnly. "If you did not love her, then you lost nothing valuable."

"It was a humiliating experience, nonetheless."

"Yes, but it is you who laughs the last."

"In what way, I'd like to know," Fox said, faintly annoyed that a painful episode in his social and financial ruin was not accorded more sympathy by his friend.

"She married a man who has lived up to her most strenuous romantic expectations."

"How nice for her." *And how completely expected.*

"But she cannot live up to his," Tsusga said, surprising Fox. "She is unable to please the fool, despite her efforts to be a perfect wife. I heard him upbraid her at a dinner party in London."

Oddly, Fox felt little like laughing. Ariadne had taken pride in her womanly skills and promised to make some man—clearly not Fox—an excellent wife.

"She humiliated you before all of London once. Now she is forced to endure humiliations every day." Tsusga's tone remained unrevealing.

Fox made no reply.

"The gods prefer balance," Tsusga said gently. "It is only that we do not always take notice when they impose it on others."

Unwilling to discuss the subject further, Fox said, "I hope Catherine isn't forced to stay with the Iveys long."

"What of Kymton?" Tsusga persisted.

Temper spiked in Fox. "I don't know yet."

"You manage intricate operations with the Assembly, commanding the loyalty of men and women who do not easily give it. Why can you not manage to extract revenge on the duke?"

"What about the gods?" Fox sneered. "Will I not get in their way as they trundle about putting everything back into balance? When are *they* going to fix Kymton?"

Tsusga refused to rise to the bait. "Sometimes the gods require that we do our parts."

Fox stopped abruptly. "I know where this is leading, Tsusga. We've discussed this before, and I have not changed my mind. I am not interested in putting things back into balance, or taking revenge—whatever you wish to call it."

Tsusga regarded Fox calmly, which frustrated Fox even more.

"The Duke of Kymton is a powerful man," he ground out. "His tentacles spread everywhere. His actions in India robbed me of nearly everything. Do you comprehend? *Everything.* It has taken me nearly three years to recover from that brush with His Nobility. I do *not* desire another." Fox marched on his way without looking back to see if his friend accompanied him.

They quit the corridor, stepping out of concealment through a door in the butler's pantry. They passed through the main kitchen, with its high ceiling and bank of windows, its long pine worktables, massive fireplace and roasting spits, and its great dressers laden with the *batterie de cuisine*. Cook and her helpers acknowledged them briefly with smiles and nods, then returned their attention to their individual tasks.

Inside the stillroom that Fox and Tsusga strode by, another veteran of Kurndatur concocted dyes for use in forging old-looking documents and letters.

When they entered the east sitting room, they found Diana and Catherine conferring over guest lists, swatches of gauzy, glittery fabrics, and advertisements from London shops of various kinds.

"Where is Isabel?" Fox asked, concealing his disappointment in finding her absent.

Catherine's face, animated with excitement generated from her discussion with her aunt, went suddenly blank. "Is she not in the green saloon? I—I thought she was knitting there."

"Why is she not here with you?"

"She wanted us to go for a walk, but I persuaded her it was too unpleasant outside." Pink rose in her cheeks. "Then Aunt Diana wished to discuss the ball with me. . . . Isabel grows bored with such discussions."

Fox turned on his heel. He headed toward the green saloon. Catherine, Diana, and Tsusga stayed tight on his trail. When Fox thrust open the tall double doors, he discovered the green saloon to be empty.

"She is not here," he said, opening the chamber's doors wider so that they might see for themselves.

Catherine's expression became one of alarm. "I never

thought she would walk without me! I thought we had agreed not to go!"

Fox restrained himself from pointing out that, at her own insistence, Catherine had been given the task of keeping an eye on Isabel. Not that Fox any longer believed her to be a king's agent. But it went without saying: The less she knew about what went on at Willow Hall, the better for everyone.

"Do you have any idea where she wanted to walk?" he asked curtly.

S'truth, he didn't need this now!

Her face pale, Catherine squeezed her eyes shut as if trying to focus her thoughts. They popped open. "The temple. She wanted to explore. That's why I persuaded her to stay inside."

"*Tried* to persuade her, it would seem."

Diana's eyebrows rose. "What harm could come of her exploring? Everything worth concern is concealed."

"But the temple—," Catherine began.

"Appears to be just that—a temple," Diana said. "A well-kept building, nothing more."

"To you or I it would appear such," Fox said, "and probably at first to Isabel. But she has a way of stumbling onto secret latches to hidden entrances. I had best retrieve her."

"Do you wish us to help?" his aunt called after him.

"No."

Fox headed back to the butler's pantry at a brisk clip. He thought of the fireplace in the upstairs saloon, then broke into a run.

He pounded down one hall after another, his boots ringing on the flags. As he tore through the kitchen, the workers lifted their heads to stare in surprise. Fox nipped into the butler's pantry and through the secret revolving wall. It let him out onto the path between the high hedges that connected the house with various points around the island, one of which was the temple.

The greater portion of the island had been engineered by the first owner—most likely a smuggler who had grown rich in his chosen profession. Because of the high water table, he could not dig tunnels to allow for escape. Instead he had planted these evergreen hedges. They concealed pathways that radiated out from the house to various points on the island, most them involving methods of escape.

Cursing under his breath, Fox hurried through the green, foggy corridor. He wanted no witness to his chicanery, especially Isabel.

As he approached the entry to the temple, he slowed. Quietly, he slipped through the concealed door in the wall of the temple. Pressing his ear to the cold, damp marble, he listened. And he heard something unexpected.

A melody sung in a sweet, slightly off-key, alto voice.

It was an old country song about a woman whose beloved had gone off to war and never come back. Grieving, she had cut her long tresses, rent her clothes, and wandered the roads "of England-O." Different men had sought to console her, each offering something desirable—gold, a castle, children— but she would have none of it if she could not have it with the man she had loved.

Like the song of a tone-deaf Lorelei, it drew him. He moved along the wall, following that throaty, mostly mellifluous sound until the end of the passageway prevented him from going farther. Judging her to be on the other side of the imposing statue of Pallas Athena, he silently slid back a marble-faced pocket panel and stepped out into the misty inner temple.

Here, the architect had practiced restrained elegance. More slender Ionic columns supported a towering ceiling skirted by relief work, which related several of the goddess's better-known beneficent intercessions on behalf of mankind. Long-legged bronze braziers stood, cold and unlighted, at intervals along the walls and on either side of the statue.

Isabel had not noticed him as she wandered about the temple, studying the frieze. He watched her as she trailed her fingertips over the moist, polished surface of a column, leaving a faint, silvery track that would vanish as the fog closed in again.

Fox glided to a place where he could better see her upturned face, surrounded as it was by her bonnet. Large fringed eyes took in the beauty of the relief work. The haunting sadness of her still expression caught at him, piercing him like the barbs of a thousand tiny hooks.

As he gazed at her, an indefinable tension gripped him. A look of aching loss touched those rose-petal features, and he realized in that misty instant how alone she must often feel. What he knew of her story concerned loss, possibly even betrayal. She possessed a courage few could claim.

Gradually, she moved along the wall until her bonnet once again shielded her countenance from his view. He continued to watch, unable, unwilling, to cease.

As she made her way along the frieze, her slow, graceful rhythm and the inclusive hush of her supple body captured his awareness, focusing it, refining it until all else vanished into the glittering mist. In another land, in a different garb, she might have been a temple dancer, chosen and anointed, suffused with the sensual beauty of the unconfined female nature.

As if she had sensed his attention, she turned toward him. Her eyes met his, widening slightly.

"Mr. Tremayne," she said, her voice a bit breathless. She clasped her gloved hands in front of her, then shifted her weight.

As the heel of one half-boot caught the curve of a brazier leg, Isabel stumbled. Fox lunged to catch her, but he was too far. Her back hit the wall. Out went her feet. With a thump, she landed on her backside.

He closed the distance between them and went down on one knee beside her, grasping her shoulders in his hands. They seemed so fragile beneath his palms.

"Isabel, are you injured?"

Her lips twisted into a crooked smile, color high in her cheeks. "Only my dignity." She did not meet his gaze.

Fox stood and helped her to rise as if she were made of eggshell porcelain.

"I assure you, Mr. Tremayne—"

"Fox."

"Fox, I am not an invalid. Save for this painful bruise to my . . . pride, I am unharmed."

"I'm glad to hear it," he assured her. "Marble can be quite, uh . . . hard."

Jove, could he sound more idiotic?

Now she looked at him, her eyes twinkling. "I must agree with you, sir. I've put the matter to a test, and there can be no doubt. Marble *is* quite hard."

Feeling a little less foolish, he smiled.

Slowly, she smiled, too.

Fox watched as her full, mist-kissed lips curved. In that moment, as she smiled up at him, he found he could not live without tasting them.

He lowered his head, but paused a second. She made no move to withdraw.

He brushed his mouth softly over her slightly parted lips once—she trembled; twice—she steadied. Her lashes lowered. Fox settled his mouth over hers.

In this cold place, Isabel tasted of warmth, of sunlight, of life. Like a sweet, ripe wine, she heated his blood. Needing to feel her closer to him, he took her in his arms.

As he slipped the tip of his tongue along the satin inside of her lower lip, something darker, more innately sensual penetrated his flesh, reaching deep inside him. Like the glide of a searing feather, it smoldered in his brain, his spine, burning the hardened muscles of his belly, flaming in his loins.

Somehow her fingers had found their way into his hair, scorching his scalp. One hand clutched a lapel of his leather riding coat.

Fox pressed her to him, delving into her spicy mouth with his tongue. She hesitated, as if stunned. Then she met him with her own, more tentative, tongue. Soon, she grew as demanding as he.

In the recesses of his darkened brain, a faint cry of reason rang out. *I must stop this!*

This abrupt change of track befuddled his mind, confused his body, and generally went against every instinct he possessed. Only with determination did he succeed in lifting his head, in lifting his arms from around her, in taking a single step back.

The wealth of sable lashes ascended. Gray-green eyes stared up at him. "What—?"

As if she just realized what had happened, her stare turned to the hand that gripped his lapel. Then, with the slow reflexes of a sleepwalker, her fist released the wadded leather. Isabel regarded her open palm. Her fingers moved to her kiss-swollen lips. Lips Fox wanted to taste again.

He took another step back, trying to reduce the temptation to drag her back to him, to claim her delectable mouth. To claim much more than her mouth.

As he wondered what to say, his back lightly bumped against the solid statue of the goddess.

How did one apologize sufficiently for stealing kisses from an innocent, especially when one was not sorry?

His booted heel came down on an alabaster acanthus leaf trimming the bottom edge of the statue's base.

A more pressing problem was avoiding future theft of those sweet kisses. He might be a thief, but he did have standards.

The contradiction in that reasoning struck him at the moment a pronounced *click* echoed against the towering marble-faced walls.

Almost as one, he and Isabel turned to view the source of the sound.

FOURTEEN

Isabel's blood raced. Her heart felt as if it might soar right out of her body. She wanted the kiss to go on forever. Ever practical, she murmured distractedly, "What was that?"

Her lips felt tingly and swollen from Fox's kiss. From *their* kiss, Isabel corrected, since she had actively participated.

Fox glared at the source of the sound: the statue's base. "It sounded like a latch unfastening."

With a sigh, she glanced in that direction. What she saw surprised her.

"Look!" she exclaimed. "A hidden panel."

Fox muttered an oath.

Swiftly, she stepped to the stone base and prodded the marble panel open. "There's a tunnel!" She looked up at him. "I wonder where it leads."

"Probably an escape route. The builder of Willow Hall was a smuggler."

Isabel leaned into the ink-dark space. "How exciting! Let's see where it goes."

Fox placed his hands on her shoulders and eased her out and away from the tunnel. "I doubt that would be wise, Elf."

"Why?"

"Why?" he repeated. "Well . . . it has obviously been deserted for years."

"You weren't aware of this?"

"A complete surprise. Please come away from there, Isabel." He reached down and shut the panel. It clicked back into place. "Like as not it's filled with vermin, which would find it a snug place to make a lair."

"Lair?" Isabel's eyebrows rose as the image of a nasty, dark, smelly nest of indeterminate origin bloomed in her mind. Disgusted with her overactive imagination, she asked, "What sort of lair?"

"What sort of lair?"

She stared at him. "Have you been possessed by an echo?"

He gave her a look that she took to be a denial.

"What sort of lair?" she persisted. Absently, she put her fingers to her lips, which still throbbed with life.

His eyes followed her gloved hand. "Weasels," he croaked. "Polecats."

She knew weasels, when cornered, could be vicious.

"Beetles," he continued. "Possibly adders."

She made a face. "Sounds crowded."

"It will be dark and moist," he expounded, seeming to warm to his subject. "You know how slime and mold flourish in such places."

"Along with the beetles and polecats," she muttered.

"And the smell—"

"Please!" She swept her hand up in a halting gesture. "You've convinced me. No need to elaborate."

He gently clasped her arms to pull her from the entryway. "Exploring such a place would ruin your one decent gown."

"I possess *two* decent gowns, thank you." She eased back a step to counter the temptation to walk straight into his arms.

Fox released her with apparent reluctance. "You know," he told her in a low, intimate voice, "if you had that wardrobe I offered you, this would not be a problem."

"I certainly wouldn't wear one of those gowns out here,"

she said, hoping to avoid further discussion of the subject. "I would save them."

"For what?" he asked. "Your trousseau?" An edge in his voice sharpened that last word.

"No," she told him, "I would save it for London. I wouldn't want to embarrass Catherine by wearing my own two gowns."

He lifted an eyebrow. "But you wouldn't hesitate to embarrass me."

"I did not say that."

"You did not have to."

She turned and began to walk away. "I have no desire to embarrass anyone."

As they left the temple, he fell into step beside her, his hands clasped behind his back.

"Pride," he intoned. "It goeth before a fall, you know."

"So I've heard. And you are quite correct. I cannot afford to pay for an elegant new wardrobe, and I have enough pride not to go begging for one."

"I never heard you beg—"

"The wardrobe you initially suggested would have been far too lavish to be an appropriate gift from a gentleman bachelor. Even the one we settled on was too much." There, that ought to be the end to the subject.

"Ah."

She bridled at the tone of that single syllable. "I'm not," she informed him heatedly, "some . . . some *kept* woman, Mr. Tremayne—"

"Fox."

"Fox," she amended automatically. "And you are not my father—"

"Indeed not."

"—or brother—"

"Heaven forfend!"

"—or any other relation from whom I might respectably receive such largesse."

"Hm."

"Nor am I," she continued hotly, "a mannequin for you to dress at your whim."

"A mannequin? Elf, I would say you are much too ani-mated for that."

Isabel's foot came down on a lump of sod, and her ankle gave. Abruptly, she sat down on the brown, wet grass. An-noyed at her clumsiness, which seemed to manifest itself more than usual when Fox came around, Isabel vigorously adjusted her skirts. At a time when she wished to be, above all things, graceful, she had spent altogether too much time on her backside.

Ignoring the offer of his hand, she sprang lopsidedly to her feet. The miniature she wore flew up to smack the un-derside of her chin, then fell with a faint *thunk* against the base of her throat.

Frustrated, she closed her fingers around the ribbon, wanting more than ever to tear off the hideous picture and fling it away. Realizing how that might look, she reluctantly released the ribbon. When had the thing ceased to be a talis-man and begun to feel like an albatross?

"I do *so* appreciate your amusement, sir," she snapped.

"Amusement? I but mentioned my esteem."

"Oh, certainly." She made no effort to muzzle her sar-casm.

He stopped and put out a hand to halt her. His eyes met hers directly. "I would not find amusement at your expense, Isabel."

She found only still depths in his amber eyes. She wanted to believe. Oh, how much she wanted to believe him! Life's recent battering, however, made her shy away from belief.

Without comment, she set off again, in the direction of Willow Hall.

Again he stopped her with the touch of his hand on her arm. "You will accept a kiss from me, but not a gift of mere clothing?"

"There is nothing 'mere' about that wardrobe."

Why was he persisting in this discussion? The matter had already been settled at Madame Billaud's shop.

"You have not answered my question."

"That kiss did not *obligate*—" She stopped. That kiss had

expressed something deeper than even obligation. Deeper and more intimate.

A subtle shift came over his expression, making it unreadable. "I see. The kiss means less to you than a pair of shoes and a few yards of muslin."

"No!"

He tilted his head. "It means more to you?"

"The two cannot be compared," she told him, flustered. "One has nothing to do with the other."

"I believe many of the demimonde would disagree," he observed as he resumed walking.

She gathered her skirts and then limped after him at full speed. "Do you accuse me of something?"

"You have just said to me that a kiss means nothing to you." His gaze rested on the house ahead of them.

Isabel caught him up. "I said nothing of the sort."

Fox stopped. "Perhaps you will set me straight, then."

Choosing her words carefully, she frowned down at the now-grubby hem of her gown, swishing damply above the toes of her half-boots. "We have dissected the subject of the wardrobe to the point of tedium. But the kiss just . . . *is*. Must we analyze it?"

What had happened to mysteries of the universe? It was not *right* to tamper with one when it came along. The kiss she had shared with Fox had been breathtaking. She didn't want to spoil that experience. Not for anything. Besides, was that not supposed to be the test of a good kiss? The mysterious visceral reactions? The brush with heaven?

"I feel certain we should *not* analyze it," she stated firmly.

Fox stared at her a long minute. Then, without a word, he closed the distance between them.

"Precisely, Elf," Fox said softly as he lowered his lips to hers.

This kiss held the sweet, stirring magic of stardust. Isabel seemed to float, free of the earth, connected solely to Fox, to his beautiful, marvelous mouth, to the warmth of his breath on her cheek. It was all she wanted. All she needed.

He lifted his head. Taking in her dazed expression, he

smiled down at her. "Come," he murmured. "We should return to the house. I have no wish to injure your reputation."

"No," she mumbled, allowing herself to be guided by his
hand at the small of her back.

In even the plainest of gowns, Catherine and Isabel
would turn heads in London. Fox studied the collection of
finely stitched muslin, wool, and silk outfitting the long row
of dress forms arranged for show in Madame Billaud's
viewing room. In these gorgeous garments they might well
cause a riot among unwed men attempting to gain his aunt's
door first.

Perhaps it had been unrealistic of him to hope for a quiet
introduction to Society for Catherine. He hoped the notice
would not spoil what should be a time of triumph and pleasure for her, being, as she was, so painfully shy.

With a gimlet eye, he scrutinized the neckline of a dress
intended for Isabel.

"The bodice is not too low for Mademoiselle Smythe,"
Madame Billaud said, correctly interpreting his study. "I
'ave ensured that it is fashionable yet not immodest."

"By French standards, perhaps," Fox muttered.

Madame Billaud smiled. "It is true Frenchwomen are
more at ease with their bodies than the English *femmes,* but
I assure you, Monsieur Tremayne, this gown will be most elegant on her."

Fox's imagination furnished him with a vision of leering
lechers surrounding Isabel. Annoyed with himself, he gestured impatiently toward the long row of gowns, pelisses,
and spencers. "Please have them ready to be picked up at
three of the clock, Madame Billaud."

As he strode out of the mantua-maker's establishment, he
tried to turn his mind to his next appointment in Harwich,
but the visions of Isabel's bare throat and shoulders, alabaster against the black satin of her hair, undulated through
his head.

Feminine. Smooth.

And desecrated by that damnable miniature.

The thing was nothing less than ghastly. If Adkisson was

as lumpish as the artist had rendered him, Isabel's chances for handsome children were drastically reduced.

She had probably allowed herself to become affianced to Valfrid Adkisson out of sheer pity, and in return for this blessing of good fortune, the man had run off to make a fortune. Jove, that deserter didn't deserve Isabel's stout loyalty.

Hours later, Isabel watched with escalating dismay as Nottage built a tidy mountain of boxes on her bed. He made trip after trip to her chamber. He carted in diminutive green glove boxes; large, puce, rectangular boxes bearing Madame Billaud's distinctive tags; round, pink-and-white-striped, ribbon-trimmed hatboxes; shoe-sized, glossy blue boxes; and, it seemed, everything in between.

"These cannot *all* belong to me!" she insisted for what must have been at least the tenth time. "Most belong to Miss Tremayne, I am certain of it. *I* am expecting only a *few* things from Madame Billaud."

This time, Nottage didn't bother replying. Apparently he considered nine responses to her objection sufficient. She tried another tack.

"Please take these to Miss Tremayne's chamber *at once*." And when that failed to bring even a shadow of a response: "Why are you being so obstinate?"

Nottage placed what appeared to be the last box on the top of the rest, then turned to her. As ever, his black eye patch put her in mind of a pirate.

"Don't like upsettin' ye, Miss Isabel—"

She blinked. When had Nottage ever scrupled to be offensively blunt to her?

"—but the cap'n told me to put 'em in yer room. His exact orders." He pointedly eyed the dress she wore. Aware the garment was beginning to show its wear, Isabel felt her face go warm.

"There must be some mistake," she insisted heatedly. "He agreed—*he agreed*—to a small wardrobe."

"And did ye?"

"Did I what?"

"Order a wee wardrobe."

"Yes. Yes, I did."

Nottage waved a hand toward the hillock rising from her bed. "Well, then, I'm that certain it's there somewhere."

"Where *is* Mr. Tremayne?" she gritted through clenched teeth.

"Can't say. Moves about some, he does."

He left her glaring at the multitude of packages.

Despite her simmering indignation, curiosity drew her to the pastel pile of boxes. It had been so long . . .

She hesitated, then tugged at a tail of ribbon, untying the bow that secured the large box. With the tip of a treacherous finger, she prodded off the lid. For a long minute, she regarded the neatly arranged pink and silver tissue paper.

The elegant wrapping reminded Isabel of packages she and her mother had received from London before Papa had sailed to India. Before her mother had died of heartbreak. Before Rob had been flung into a Spanish prison.

Before they had been swindled.

She flipped aside a fold of the paper. Nestled in the box lay a gown of delicate white muslin. Twined along the edge of a short puffed sleeve and the neckline were embroidered silk leaves and vines of a rich moss-green—a hue that never failed to bring out the green in her eyes to best advantage.

Abruptly, she closed the box and stalked from her chamber.

Isabel passed briskly through the warren of corridors and rooms that comprised this floor until she reached the staircase. There she paused to take a deep breath. She patted her hair into place and rolled back her shoulders. Conscious of the placement of her feet on the treads, she managed to descend in a stately manner . . .

. . . into a corridor devoid of persons.

Fox Tremayne also displayed the discourtesy of being absent from both the library and drawing room. There was no sign of him in the dining room, the kitchens, the pantries, the stillroom, or on the front steps that led down to the water. In an ordinary country house, the master might be found in the stables, but Isabel knew Willow Hall's stable and carriage house stood in Felgate, and from Cook she had gathered the impression Tremayne remained on the island.

Frustrated, she cudgeled her mind to think of where next to look for him. "Coward," she muttered. If she hadn't known better, Isabel might have suspected him of hiding from her, but she could not, in truth, imagine him hiding from anyone, much less one relatively insignificant hireling.

Perhaps he had retired to his room. She knew the general location of the master's private chambers, but, of course, had never visited them. If this had been a normal household, she would have asked a servant to take a message to him. As usual in Willow Hall, there were none about and no efficient way to summon one.

Without thinking, she found she had entered the deserted hall outside the family's private rooms as if she had walked it countless times.

Isabel considered the closed doors around her for a long moment. Then, slowly, her slippers whispering against the India carpet, Isabel moved to the entry of what were clearly the master's quarters.

The consequences of a young, unmarried woman entering the personal chambers of an unrelated gentleman loomed in her mind. Since the night she had discovered Uncle Gilbert's villainy, she had lost nearly everything but her honor.

Honor, declared a small, indignant voice in her mind, *is precisely what you are here to* defend.

Well, not precisely, she reasoned, prodded by an irrepressible sense of honesty. Her honor had not actually been besmirched. More like threatened. Were it learned that Tremayne had purchased a lavish wardrobe for her, a female in his employ, someone would certainly leap to the conclusion that an impropriety between Tremayne and herself had occurred.

Society took pleasure in the fall of innocence. Once a good name had been stained by gossip, it never fully returned to its untarnished state.

Her fist hesitated, hovering inches from the paneled surface. She did not believe Tremayne had intended to do her reputation damage with his insistence on supplying her with a proper London wardrobe. Isabel sympathized with his desire to make all perfect for his sister, which would include the appearance of Catherine's companion.

She sighed. He must be confronted. Even the thought of someone speculating on what services she might have rendered the master of Willow Hall in payment made her stomach tighten.

Her fist plunged toward the door.

"Are you lost, Miss Smythe?" asked a voice from behind her.

With a gasp, she spun to face Croom, the peg-legged valet. Who other than Tremayne would engage a man with such a marked disfigurement as a valet? Valets were desired almost as much for their elegance of appearance as for their skills.

"Ah. Hello, Croom." Needlessly she smoothed the front of her gown. "I'm seeking Fo—Mr. Tremayne."

"Alas," Croom returned smoothly, "he is not in his chambers."

"Oh."

"May I bear him a message for you?" he offered, his expression bland.

"I would prefer you direct me to him, thank you. I desire to speak with Mr. Tremayne myself."

"This is not a good moment for that, I fear. Presently he confers with Messrs. Talloak and de Fortier."

From the casual attitude Isabel had observed between Tremayne and Croom, Isabel doubted "fear" entered into their relationship.

"Very well," she said. "I would appreciate your conveying to Mr. Tremayne my request for an interview."

Croom inclined is head fractionally. "Certainly. In the meantime, may I escort you to the east sitting room? There's now a nice fire on the hearth there, and I've taken the liberty of assembling your knitting items and ordering tea and cakes for you."

Isabel regarded the valet for a moment, long enough to

convey to him that she knew what he was doing. "Very thoughtful of you," she said dryly.

A corner of his mouth twitched, but he made no reply, merely stood aside so that she might pass.

For some reason she could not determine, Isabel did not worry he would spread it about that he had caught her at the master's bedchamber door. She did, however, feel certain Tremayne would be informed.

As she headed toward the east sitting room—the *only* sitting room in Willow Hall, to her knowledge, not abandoned to holland cloth and dust—Isabel reasoned this infelicitous incident might have worked out for the best. After all, she had not been compelled to enter Fox Tremayne's bedchamber, yet he would learn how strongly she objected to his largesse.

True to his word, when Croom opened the cream-colored, double-paneled door to the sitting room, a fire crackled on the grate, and a richly provisioned tea tray sat on a side table. Her knitting, which she had earlier left in the dining room, now lay on the striped sofa.

"Thank you, Croom," she said as she entered. "I'm sure I'll be quite comfortable here while I wait."

Croom's triangular face retained its neutral expression. "I shall inform the captain you are here, miss."

He left, closing the door quietly behind him.

Isabel eyed her knitting project: fine silk yarn taking shape as pantaloons in pale pink. Fortunately, unless she held them up, the shape was generally indistinguishable to others. When completed, they would warm her bottom and thighs under the light fabric of her skirts.

Isabel poured tea from the blue-and-white porcelain teapot, then lifted the cup to her lips. Bitter warmth spread over her tongue. She recognized excellent-quality tea when she tasted it. Through the pale curl of steam, her gaze returned to her knitting. Like the tea, the yarn was expensive. Unlike the tea, or even silk cloth, silk *yarn* was unlikely to be a popular item with either merchants or smugglers.

Yet when he had wanted it, Tremayne had seemed to

have at his fingertips an abundance of pale pink silk yarn. Fragrant tea. Obscure Swedish grammar books.

What else did he have at his fingertips?

Fox stood still and straight in the doorway to Isabel's bedchamber. His gaze moved over the neatly stacked packages on her tester bed. She had not opened so much as one of them. Not even one.

She preferred wearing her two mended, out-of-fashion gowns rather than accept these beautiful things from him. Isabel had objected so strongly, according to Croom, she had been ready to confront Fox in his private quarters.

He spun on his heel. Striding across this floor of the house, its silence disturbed only by the sound of his boot steps, he failed to notice the holland-covered furnishings and the cobwebs that swayed in the breeze of his passing. He took the stairs in short order, and stalked straight to the east sitting room. Setting his palm on the cold brass door handle, he entered.

Isabel sat knitting in a tall armchair arranged in front of a crackling fire. She made a pretty picture of domestic peace, and it tugged at a yearning deep within him. It seemed to him in that moment that a normal life might be within his reach after all. . . .

The glow of the flames kissed her fair skin with a blush of gold. As he watched, transfixed, she held her knitting to the light, examining it with an air of satisfaction.

Fox's eyes widened as he recognized the shape she held in her hands. "Just what are you making?" he demanded.

Isabel instantly dropped the silk garment into a shapeless mass in her lap.

"It is considered ill-mannered to sneak up on someone," she informed him curtly.

Swiftly, Fox came around the chair to confront her. He stabbed an index finger toward the pile of knitted pink. "Surely, neither you nor my sister intend to parade around in . . . in . . . *breeches*!"

"They're not breeches!"

"They are," he insisted hotly. "And being pink makes them no less so."

She shot to her feet. "These are *not breeches*. I believe I know the difference, sir. I have a brother," she added with lofty delicacy.

"I congratulate you, madam, but here, I *am* the brother!"

"How nice for you," she replied frostily. "Then you will be aware of a particular difference between what I am knitting and any breeches of yours."

Suddenly wary, Fox eyed the lump of silk knit. "Difference?"

She held up the garment for inspection and waited, a small, triumphant smile on her lips.

He had noticed only the outline of the article as she had held it to the light. Now he realized he might have been presumptive.

"Ah," he said, hoping it sounded as if he were fully aware of that particular difference.

She remained unmoved.

Fox rubbed the back of his neck. "I see a difference," he admitted.

Unlike his breeches, they possessed no fall.

"As I said," she reminded him, "these are not breeches."

"They are still indecent for a woman."

She rose to her feet. "I know it means nothing to your gender that females suffer from the cold in winter—"

"Untrue—"

"—but this item is meant to help prevent such suffering."

"I would not have you suffer, Isabel."

Standing there in the firelight, she looked like a raven-haired wood nymph. Her luminous beauty, her vitality, struck him with the power of a lightning bolt through the chest. He felt foolish, but more than that, he felt . . . curious. He wanted to know more about her. He wanted to know everything about her. And he wanted this moment with its hushed intimacy to last, spinning out into time until he had drunk his fill of it through every fiber of his being.

Her fairy eyes widened.

He cleared his throat. "Very well. They aren't breeches. What do you call them, then?"

And here they stood, discussing her intimate apparel.

Her cheeks appeared to pinken. "Why they are . . . they are, uh . . . warmers. Yes, warmers. They're not meant to be seen, you understand. Catherine and I will wear them beneath our gowns and will be less likely to take a chill and sicken."

Fox studied the *warmers*. He supposed females must feel the winter cold more sorely than men, insisting as they did upon wearing thin sarcenet or filmy cotton on even the coldest night. His gaze took in Isabel's violet wool dress.

Unexpectedly, the image of Isabel—tousled-haired, long-legged, and stunningly sensual, wearing nothing but pink silk warmers—blossomed vividly in his mind. Hot blood surged through his body with the pounding force of a tidal wave.

Casually, he moved to his left, placing himself squarely behind the high back of an armchair. "I'm certain you are right." His words came out low and husky.

High, rose-tipped breasts. Pink silk clinging to Isabel's long, gracefully curved thighs—

Fox's fingers curled into embroidered upholstery.

Isabel looked down at the toes of her slippers. Glossy black ringlets skimmed the pale shell of her ear. A ribbon around her throat bore that abominable miniature.

He drew a long breath through his nostrils. "You wished to speak with me."

She lifted her head. Her gray-green gaze turned up to him. "Yes. Thank you for attending me. I cannot accept your—your . . . largesse."

Within Fox, protective walls he had constructed over the past years slammed into place. He arched an eyebrow.

"'Tis generous of you," she continued. "I don't want you to think me unappreciative, but it wouldn't be—"

Why had he expected she might accept the wardrobe? The wardrobe he had left to the discernment of Madame Billaud, with a few stipulations. She had made it clear from the outset what she thought of him. To her, he was Traitor Tremayne.

"It wouldn't be what, Elf?" He had not meant for that note of challenge to rumble in his question.

"It would not be proper. We've had this discussion before. I thought you understood."

"I understand quite clearly."

"You understand, but you don't care. You insist on having your way." Slender black eyebrows drew slightly downward as she studied him. "Did you imagine," she said slowly, as if she were putting into words a thought only newly formed, "that because I agreed to take a position in your household, on an isolated estate, I might not be a . . . lady?"

"*My* household?"

She blushed.

"Did you then lower yourself to take employment with me, Miss Smythe?" He made the last word a hiss. By God, he was not the only liar in this room.

She gripped her hands in front of her. "Yes. No! That is to say, you do have a certain reputation. You must know you do. I—I cannot say it was one that put me at my ease."

He said nothing. Somehow, he had allowed her to flay his sensibilities, and his anger at himself, at her, simmered. He had no intention of making this easier.

"But then," she said, her voice and posture growing calmer, "you were kind to me."

Still he remained silent, but she seemed not to notice. Her gaze had turned inward, toward something only she saw now.

"I made a fool of myself, yet you were kind. I am certain you knew I needed work rather desperately—I saw the way you looked at my slippers. Even then they were looking the worse for wear. Yet you've never demeaned me, nor taken advantage of my situation. You offered fair wages for fair work." Her mouth moved in a slight, quick smile. "Catherine has become dear to me, and your aunt has been gracious. And now you press upon me clothes I would love to have."

Fox stared at his thumbnail.

"But I cannot accept them."

He knew she was correct. Had known from the beginning. Which only served to annoy him more.

"It wouldn't reflect well on either of us," she insisted.

"Therefore, the wardrobe will be a gift from my aunt. It is she, after all, who is sponsoring my sister's introduction into Society."

"But Madame Billaud and her seamstresses already know—"

"—that I have never before placed an order for a lady's clothing with them." He leaned his elbows on the back of the chair. "Madame Billaud will be informed that my aunt's London mantua-maker could not accommodate my aunt's entire order for Catherine's introduction into Society on my aunt's schedule, and with so much to tend to, Diana could not see to the matter herself. She was forced to entrust the important task to a paltry male."

Isabel appeared less doubtful.

"My aunt will support me in this claim, I assure you. She has every concern for the protection of your reputation." He shrugged one shoulder. "She would have insisted that you accompany them, instead of staying here, did Catherine's grandparents not have a dislike of strangers in their house."

"Oh."

"Which brings us to a subject I would like to discuss."

She resumed her seat with all the appearance of being attentive.

"Why did you tell me that your name was Smythe, when in fact, it is Millington?" he asked quietly, a contrast with the turmoil in his chest.

The embroidered pattern in the chair upholstery pressed roughly against the palms of his hands. On the hearth a flame crackled, piercing the dense silence like a shard of glass.

Isabel looked down at her hands, clenched in front of her. One thumb rubbed the knuckle of the other. Then she lifted her head, meeting his intent, waiting gaze.

Her words came out faint and hoarse. "I . . . I don't know what you mean."

Fox left the concealment of the armchair, walking over to the fireplace. He set his elbow on the mantel, and for a moment stared into the fire. "And I am the one people call liar."

Her hand went to the miniature. A slender thumb rubbed its porcelain surface. "I have not called you that."

Her gaze met his. She seemed to will him to see into her intention. Into her heart.

Fox waited. He caught himself holding his breath. In disgust, he drew a long breath. The sound reminded him of the night wind soughing through the sea of rushes that surrounded his island.

Her lashes lowered, she nodded. "I think perhaps that Traitor Tremayne is a bogeyman too terrible to have ever truly existed."

Traitor Tremayne. Fox had Kymton to thank for that shame. Once again, he wished fervently he had his hands around that noble swine's throat, pressing, squeezing, feeling the foul life seep away.

"Bogeymen do exist, Isabel."

She tilted her head slightly as she studied him. "I know." Oddly, she shivered slightly. "But I don't believe you are one of them."

The knot that lived in his gut loosened a little, and Fox felt distantly foolish for it.

"Tell me, Isabel Millington. Why have *you* lied?"

She swallowed. "I have not liked to keep it from you."

He waited for her to continue.

Thunderous pounding on the front door burst into the silence. Fox cast a glance at Isabel, who shook her head; she didn't know who beat on the door.

When the pounding did not abate, Fox stalked to the sitting room door, jerked it open, and stuck his head into the hall. No sound of hurrying footsteps met his ears. Nottage must still be laboring over the official-looking documents needed for the new operation. Croom would be deep in research, and Etienne would likely have talked Tsusga into learning how to use the printing press. The kitchen crew seldom ventured into the house past the butler's pantry.

Fox roughly excused himself to Isabel, telling her he would return.

He strode down the hall. On his way to the front door, he stopped at a closet to select a loaded pistol from behind a pile of linens. This he slid behind the epergne on the marquetry table in the entry hall, close to hand.

No new arrival was expected at Willow Hall.

He swung open the oaken door.

In front of him, standing in the candlelight pouring through the open doorway, a silver-haired bear of a man held a pistol to the head of Joe Brown. The boatman's small eyes had grown huge, but he seemed the calmer of the two.

"This is Willow Hall, *ja?*" the large stranger demanded. He stood but an inch or so shorter than Fox and outweighed him by at least sixteen stone.

Was that a Swedish, Danish, or Norwegian accent?

"It is," Fox replied politely. He knew through experience that it would take no less than a gun to Joe's head to induce the boatman to bring someone to this island without Fox's orders. "And you, sir, are . . . ?"

"Valfrid Adkisson."

FIFTEEN

Fox surveyed the older man's face in the flickering lamplight. "You look very unlike your miniature, sir."

Which, considering the walleyed weasel the artist had rendered, was no bad thing. But the subject of that damnable miniature was only two-and-twenty or so. The man with a gun to Joe's head was old enough to be Isabel's father. Had she ever *seen* her intended?

"You are Mr. Foxton Tremayne?" Adkisson asked politely, his pistol hand steady.

"I am." Fox hesitated to move for his own weapon with Adkisson's so close to Joe's temple. "How did you know?" he asked, stalling.

"She writes me you have few servants to run so large a house." His breath frosted the air. "And no one would mistake you for a servant."

Fox assumed by "she" Adkisson meant his betrothed. Apparently the letter Isabel had turned over to Tilly Lagden to post had reached him.

"Indeed." The word was crisp between Fox's teeth. He watched the pistol pointed at Joe's head. There were, in fact, no true servants, save some of Cook's young helpers. The fewer involved with what went on in Willow Hall the better.

Fox ignored the cold penetrating his wool coat and

breeches. "In what way may I be of service to you, Mr. Adkisson?"

Adkisson drew himself up. "I seek my niece, Isabel Millington."

Fox sucked in icy air. His niece? *His niece?*

From behind him a small voice said, "Hello, Uncle Valfrid."

The silver-haired man squinted into the shadows of the entrance hall. "Isabel? Isabel, is it you?"

She stepped forward, almost shyly, it seemed to Fox. Before he might stop her, she walked straight to Adkisson, who immediately embraced her with his one free arm, enfolding her into the breast of his greatcoat.

"Little Lamb, when last I saw you, you were a tiny babe in Annika's arms. In so few years you have grown into a beautiful woman!"

"Gilbert sent you a letter notifying you when Mama died. At least he said he did."

Emotion thickened his powerful baritone. "I was in Russia when my Annika died. I only returned to Göteborg two weeks ago. As soon as I received your letter, I came." He laid his bearded cheek on the crown of her head. "You are well? Herr Tremayne treats you well?"

Isabel smiled up at him. "Yes and yes. But what of Rob? What shall we do?"

"I have sent a courier to Robert's captors. He will soon be free."

She laughed, a thick, joyous sound. The wavering lamplight glinted on the tears brimming in her eyes. "Oh, thank you! Thank you, Uncle."

Adkisson chuckled as he gave her a little hug. "What else was I to do? He is my nephew! When he is released, he is to come to Felgate, where I have taken rooms at the Blue Dragon. Together, we will leave for Greenwood."

A gust of icy wind struck, and she shivered.

"Go inside," her uncle gently told her.

Jaw tight to prevent chattering teeth, Isabel complied, hugging herself, her wool gown little protection against the damp December cold.

Abruptly, Adkisson uncocked his pistol, lowering the muzzle to the ground. "I apologize for threatening you, sir," he said to Joe. "My only excuse for my behavior was my desperation to reach my niece." He took Joe's hand and laid a gold coin in its palm. Then he folded the surprised boatman's fingers closed. "I hope you will accept this as a token of my regret."

"Joe," Fox said, "go see Cook for a bite to eat in front of the kitchen fire. Mr. Adkisson, pray enter and warm yourself." He opened the door wider and stood back to allow passage.

At that moment Fox heard the sound of racing footsteps echoing through the halls, growing louder by the second. Croom, Nottage, Cook, Etienne, and Tsusga burst around the corner and charged down the corridor connected to the entry hall. Each bore a pistol. Three more men leapt out of a punt, which had just pulled into sight. They clattered up the wide staircase to the front door, muskets in their hands. They had come around from the back of the island, likely to surround the intruders.

"A bit late," Fox commented mildly to them all. "Perhaps we should work on security, hmm?"

Adkisson regarded the would-be rescuers with wide eyes. "What sort of place is this?" he asked. "Isabel, you are not a captive here?"

"No, Uncle Valfrid," she replied, darting a glance at Fox.

"I value my privacy," Fox said. He offered to take Adkisson's greatcoat and hat, which he handed to Nottage.

"Cook," he said to the burly, redheaded woman in a mobcap and apron, "I have told Joe you would find him something to eat and drink, and that he might warm himself by your kitchen fire. Would you also kindly have a tray for Mr. Adkisson sent to the east sitting room? Have your people set out something warm for our defenders to eat, please. Thank you, gentlemen," he said to the others, "I appreciate your coming to my rescue. I'll not keep you longer."

Etienne gave him a look of inquiry, and Fox knew his friend burned with curiosity. Tsusga's expression gave away nothing of what occupied his keen mind. With no further word, they left along with Cook and Joe and the three men who had arrived by water.

Fox retrieved his pistol and brought it with him into the east sitting room, where only a short while ago he had struggled to restrain himself from gathering Isabel in his arms to kiss her sweet mouth. Her sweet, lying mouth.

Now he faced Isabel and her uncle across the room.

"My intentions are peaceful," the older man said, lifting his open hands away from his sides. "I want only my niece."

"You will forgive me, sir, if I entertain doubts. You've come to my home with a weapon drawn."

"It was the only way anyone would bring me here. And even with my gun aimed at him, the boatman tried to mislead me. Only my sharp eyes and my familiarity with marshland foiled his plan. Your man remains loyal to you, Herr Tremayne."

"Joe is not my man."

"He considers himself so. And he was determined to wander about this marsh until I tired of the search. But I was as determined to save, er, find my niece."

Fox smiled coolly. "Ah. You bring up two points upon which I require clarification." He focused on Isabel, who gave him a look of apology. "From what is she to be saved, . . . and is it customary for uncles to wed their nieces in—what?— Denmark? Finland?"

The elder man stared at Fox in obvious astonishment. He was either an astute actor, or he truly did not know to what Fox referred.

"Uncles to wed their nieces—?" Adkisson sputtered. "I do not understand."

Isabel drew in a deep breath. "I lied," she blurted. The two words echoed faintly against the striped walls of the parlor. She looked at Fox, her dark eyes large in her pale face. "I did not like to."

"Then why did you?" he asked quietly.

She hesitated for a moment, then turned to her uncle. "I would like a minute to speak with Mr. Tremayne. He and his family have been kind to me. I . . . trust him."

*   *   *

They left Uncle Valfrid to the tray that had arrived as she and Fox had opened the door to step into the hall.

Fox led Isabel into the dining chamber, where he walked to one of the tall mullioned windows, his hands clasped behind him.

"Who sent you?" he asked without turning.

The question caught her before she could organize her scattered thoughts enough to begin her explanation. What it implied stung her.

"No one sent me."

"How did you find me?"

She shook her head. "I wasn't looking for you. You were a mistake."

He glanced over his shoulder at her. "How flattering," he said tonelessly.

Isabel moved to face him from across the width of the window where he stood. She would not have him believe she thought her time with him had been a error.

"No, not a mistake," she said, holding his gaze with all her might. "Luck, rather." She paused. "Destiny."

"Destiny," he echoed softly. "I would not wish my destiny on you, Elf."

As she surveyed his beautiful, bronze-fringed eyes, his marvelously sculpted lips, the small half-moon scar on his chin, Isabel managed a smile. "Foolish mortal. You have no choice in the matter. It is, after all, Destiny."

"You know me not, or you could not take the matter so lightly."

"I know you well enough to believe there must be an undisclosed truth in your past. I cannot believe you would have willingly done anything to cause the deaths of so many. Certainly not anything as dishonorable as disobeying an order."

His lids lowered, concealing his eyes from her. His square jaw tightened. "I did disobey an order."

"You are not guilty of losing the battle of Kurndatur, Fox."

"Pray, how have you come to this conclusion? Stop any

man on the street in London, or Leeds, or Bath, and you'll find you are in an exceedingly small minority."

"If you were responsible for the slaughter of more than a hundred of your own men, you would not now have the loyalty of Nottage and Croom."

"I pay them well."

"Were you guilty, I doubt any amount would prove sufficient inducement for those two."

"Some men can be bought." He looked out the window, into a dark distance invisible to Isabel or, she doubted, anyone other than Fox.

"Why are you determined to have me think the worst of you?"

Fox looked at her. "You were about to explain how you came here."

Into her confusion a ribbon of misery slowly unfurled. He held her confession of faith a matter of indifference. He remained untouched.

He reached out to softly trace the line of her jaw with his finger. As if catching himself in a criminal act, he dropped his hand. From the corner of her eye, Isabel saw his fingers curl into fist and press against his thigh.

Against all good sense, joy leapt within her. Fox was not indifferent to her! At the same time, a small voice lurking in the dark folds of her intellect predicted she would be better off to say nothing, do nothing that might open any gate between Fox and herself. Wiser to leave intact the rampart of distrust he had built around his heart. She had her own problems yet to settle.

Uncle Valfrid had begun the process to free Rob, which lifted an enormous weight of anxiety from Isabel, but they still had to find Mr. Syer and settle accounts with Gilbert.

"My name is Isabel Millington," she said abruptly.

"I have known that for some time."

"My parents are dead," she continued, intent on rolling out the truth, sick of the lies she had told. "My brother, Captain Robert Millington, is a prisoner of war being held for ransom by the Spanish." She hesitated, then plunged on. "I discovered that my father's brother, Gilbert, had been embezzling from Papa for years and successfully convincing everyone that my parents had spent every penny of Papa's inheritance. He refused to pay Rob's ransom, claiming lack of funds. After I found evidence that Gilbert had been stealing from us, I knew Rob would never be freed unless I could get the money Gilbert invested back from Mr. Syer. Mr. Syer," she added, "was the man who put together a couple of the investments into which Gilbert poured the embezzled money. I knew the chances of my recovering the stolen money were quite slim. So I contacted Uncle Valfrid, my mother's brother. He was my best hope of freeing Rob and possibly regaining at least a portion of my father's fortune. I knew I would never be allowed to contact my uncle—Valfrid, that is—as long as I remained in the same house with Uncle Gilbert."

"The evil uncle."

"Yes. The very evil uncle. So . . . I escaped."

"Is that how you came by those bruises? Your escape?"

"I incurred them before my escape."

Fox's jaw tightened.

"First I went to London," she said. "I intended to try to speak with Mr. Syer, but he was not at home to callers, and I couldn't tarry."

"Why?"

"I had little money. I knew no one in London with whom I might stay. And I was afraid Gilbert would find me."

Fox frowned. "If you had so little of the ready, how did you travel?"

"I walked. I rode farm wagons. For a short distance, I took a public coach."

"You *walked*? Rode farm wagons?" He began to massage the center of his forehead with his first two fingers.

"Yes. From my home, Greenwood, in Berkshire."

He closed his eyes and massaged more deeply. "Where did you sleep while you traveled?"

What did that matter now? "Under hedgerows, mostly. In barns, when I could. A couple of times at an inn," she answered patiently.

Isabel studied Fox's handsome features. If he could ever

open his well-guarded heart, he would father beautiful babies.

He groaned. "God, this tale grows better and better. Or worse and worse. A green girl sleeping by the road, hiding in barns, traveling with turnips and hens."

"Doves, actually."

He opened his eyes suddenly. "Have you any idea of the danger you courted, Isabel?"

"I *courted* nothing," she snapped. "Are you asking if I was afraid? Yes, I was afraid. But Rob once told me that courage is not being without fear. It is doing what you must despite your fear. What choice did I have?"

Fox sighed. "None that I can see."

"I perceive you do not suggest that I ought have reported my uncle's transgression to the authorities."

"No. I'm aware of how far that would take you."

"Directly back to my uncle."

"Precisely." His fingers restlessly returned to work on his forehead.

Tearing her gaze from the mesmerizing motion of his hand, Isabel attempted to continue. "My first priority was to reach Uncle Valfrid, who lives in Sweden, and whom I hadn't seen in years. I had no one else to turn to."

"Why did you not simply tell me that you needed help or wanted to contact your uncle Valfrid? Did you judge me a monster?"

"No. But I was a lone female, on the run from the temporary head of her family. Rob's life was at risk, perhaps even my own. I could not take the risk of telling you."

Fox walked over to the long mahogany table and appeared to consider one of the silver branched candlesticks with its lighted beeswax tapers. The aroma of the fricasseed rabbit and spiced stewed apples they had been served for supper lingered faintly, mingling with the honeyed fragrance of the burning candles.

When he finally spoke, his tone was collected, quiet. "I'm appalled at what you've endured." He turned his head to look at her. A smile hovered about the corners of his mouth, but never took possession. "And not a little impressed by your courage."

The unexpected compliment warmed her. "As I said, I saw no choice."

"So. Do you believe this elusive investment broker you tried to contact is in league with your uncle? The wicked one, that is."

"I don't know. But I do know the address of Mr. Syer. One way or another, I plan to find him."

By the time things had settled down at Willow Hall, the hour was late. Fox invited Adkisson to stay the night, and the older man consented.

When Adkisson discovered no proper chaperone for his niece, he made his opinion of Fox's neglect vividly clear. Fox explained the circumstances of Diana's and Catherine's absence, but that counted for nothing with the large, silver-haired, statesman-looking trader. Finally, Fox informed him that Isabel Smythe, who had been engaged as a companion and a language tutor, had represented herself as the daughter of a gentleman. She had comported herself as a gentlewoman and thus had she been treated.

At that point Isabel came forward to soothe her uncle, who was turning purple.

"He knows you're concerned for my reputation, Uncle, but what was he to do? Deny his grandmother what might be her dying wish?"

Adkisson opened his mouth.

"No, of course not," Isabel answered before he could speak. "Who, then, should be the defender of my reputation? Cook and her small flock of fledgling kitchen maids are the only other females on the island."

The scowl on Adkisson's brow remained.

"Uncle," she said softly. "I'm not a guest."

"Nor shall you be a hireling any longer," Adkisson announced. "Sir, I regret to inform you that my niece must end her employment with you." He added to Isabel, "I will leave instructions at the Blue Dragon for Robert to join us at the inn nearest Greenwood."

Faced with the prospect of Isabel hying off to Berkshire and out of his life, panic struck Fox.

"We had an agreement," he said. "One I fear only she can fulfill."

Adkisson looked disgruntled. "Eh?"

"I was to teach Catherine Swedish," Isabel explained.

"And," Fox quickly added, "be her companion during her stay in London."

Isabel looked stricken. "Oh, dear. Well, perhaps she'll be—"

"An agreement is an agreement," he announced loftily.

Adkisson sighed. "I must side with him on this, Lamb. If you have made an agreement with him, then you must keep your word."

Feeling triumphant, refusing to examine his feelings, Fox assumed a pious expression.

"I'm so glad you agree, Uncle Valfrid. I have grown fond of Catherine. While she's not as shy as she was, she is expecting me to accompany her to London, and I shouldn't wish to disappoint her. Lady Blencowe will have so much to do. What with the arrangements for the ball she will be giving and all the invitations to festivities given by others in Town, she might have little time to spend with Catherine."

"Who is this Lady Blencowe?"

"Catherine and Fox's beautiful aunt."

"Ah. Are you certain using Christian names is not improper?"

"Things are more informal on Frog Island," she informed him.

Both Fox and Adkisson chimed, "Frog Island?"

"This is Frog Island. At least, that is what I call it." Isabel's eyebrows drew down. "Uncle, are you certain you can manage without me when you and Rob haul Gilbert before the magistrate? You will have his letters and his journal as evidence, but—"

"When we make our move, we will receive justice. But for now, Isabel, I go with you to London."

Fox opened his mouth to object.

"An agreement is an agreement," Adkisson told him.

"But if you desire Isabel to keep her part of it, I go with her. I am, for now, the head of her family, and her protector."

Shortly after that conversation, Adkisson had been shown his chamber. It was one not far from Isabel's, on the same floor. It had been the most presentable room available on such short notice. Everyone in the kitchen, plus Nottage and Croom, had pitched in to clean it as well as possible. Then they had built a fire in the fireplace and made the bed with fresh linens and blankets while Fox, Isabel, and her uncle had carried on their discussion in the sitting room.

If Adkisson had thought the disuse of most of the rooms on that floor unusual, he had said nothing to Fox.

The next morning, Fox, Valfrid Adkisson, and Isabel took a boat to the Blue Dragon to retrieve Adkisson's possessions and leave word for Rob on where to find them in London.

As Fox poled the small punt through the cold, dark water, they slipped quietly through the mist. The only sounds were the muted splash of water made by the pole and the cries of marsh birds.

Fox brooded. What had happened to his relatively quiet life? Before Isabel had appeared at Mr. Syer's door, *he* had been in control of his private realm. Not everything always went as planned, but *he* made the decisions as to what actions must be taken to bring things back into line.

She had barged into his existence like a stone hurled into a still pond. No sooner had she passed the threshold of Willow Hall than she wormed her way into the affections of his sister, his aunt, and even, to Fox's astonishment, Nottage.

Everything she did caused tumult. Take, for example, the simple acceptance of a wardrobe. At first Fox had wanted her to have it so that she would not cause Catherine embarrassment, and to spare her own feelings whilst mingling with Society's razor-tongued wits and gossips. As time passed, however, he had found himself desiring to see her in beautiful gowns. He had even hoped to please her. Insanity! Look where it had gotten him. She had thrown it all in his face.

To what distant star had his sense fled when he had

kissed her in the Greek temple? Sense. Ha! It had completely deserted him. He had wanted badly to kiss her again.

He still did. A fact that had him gnashing his teeth. He was the prince of fools!

As if that were not enough, one of her uncles had embezzled her family's fortune and was now hunting her. Her other uncle—the *good* uncle—had appointed himself her duenna. Her brother, the soldier, would be joining Fox, his family, and Isabel with her odd chaperone, in London. All while Fox tried to conceal the existence of his less-than-legal business.

Worst of all, Fox had swindled the *evil* uncle out of Isabel's father's fortune.

It just keeps getting better and better, he thought darkly.

Finally, the inn loomed out of the mist before them. Fox brought the small craft to the quay and tied it off. Then he leapt out and assisted his two passengers to the plank walkway.

Valfrid went to pay his bill, to make arrangements with Mr. Densham to have his belongings transferred to Willow Hall, and to leave a message for Rob as to his whereabouts.

Isabel fretted over Rob traveling all the way to Felgate after arriving in England, then having to go on to London. He would be weary, possibly ill. Still, there was no way now to reliably contact him regarding the change in plans.

While she waited, Isabel looked for Fox, but he was nowhere to be found. In another time, she would have withdrawn to wait in a private dining room, but the few coins she possessed were too precious to be squandered on propriety. Besides, the common room was nearly empty at this hour, and she much preferred the openness of the beamed, cavernous chamber.

She seated herself at a table close to the fireplace, enjoying the heat from the flames after her trip through the frigid marsh.

"Well, and there you are!" exclaimed Mrs. Densham as she bustled out of the kitchen and around the tap, bearing a small tray with one cup and a steaming teapot. She stopped beside Isabel and off-loaded the teapot and cup onto the table. "I reckoned you would enjoy a nice cup of tea. Here, let me help you with your cloak. Men! Give them a task or two, and everything else goes right out o' their heads."

The cloak was draped over an empty chair.

"I'm pleased to see you again, Mrs. Densham. I hope all is well with you and your excellent family?"

Mrs. Densham plopped into the chair across the table from Isabel.

"Oh, la, child," she said, beaming, her cheeks pink. "We're to have a wedding in the family soon."

"How marvelous!"

"'Tis Martha. She'll be wedding the baker's middle boy."

"Please convey my felicitations to her. A wise girl, marrying the baker's son. She'll never be wanting for bread."

Mrs. Densham laughed delightedly. "Oh, and so I've told her! But he's a good boy, is Jack. He'll do right by her."

"His family is pleased, too, I should think." Isabel had never met them or their son. She was, however, acquainted with Martha, and believed that any man who took her to wife would be blessed. "Quite a coup for them, making an alliance with the most prosperous proprietors in Felgate."

"Good of you to say it, my dear. Do go ahead and drink your tea. Everyone is pleased all around."

"Think of it," Isabel said as she poured. "Martha a married woman. Are you going to have the nuptials announced in the gazette?"

"Gazette?"

"The Felgate newspaper. Will it not be a thrill to see the announcement there in print for everyone to see?"

Mrs. Densham chuckled. "Felgate has no newspaper."

Isabel stared at her.

"Oh, deary, we're much too small a village. What is there to print?"

"Elevating articles."

Mrs. Densham burst into laughter. "Elevating articles! We're not Colchester, you know, with so many people a body can barely draw a breath someone else hasn't already used."

"I suppose not," Isabel replied faintly.

"In Felgate, word of mouth gets around faster than any gazette could."

Mrs. Densham patted Isabel's hand, then rose to her feet. "I'll give Martha your felicitations."

She sailed back into the kitchen with her empty tray, chuckling. "A Felgate gazette. Ha!"

SIXTEEN

Alone in the common room, Isabel finished the tea without really tasting it. Her thoughts churned painfully.

Charade. Deception. It governed her relationship with Fox. She told him lies. He told her lies. Like two strangers in a courtly dance, they carefully executed each step and gesture; they wore formal smiles to conceal their thoughts and emotions. Every touch was prescribed, brief.

Except one. It had not been part of the dance. The instant connection had astonished her. Inexperienced in such things Isabel might be, but she had felt his surprise as clearly as she had felt her own.

Surprise and desire. Oh, such desire! An exaltation of taste and touch, a sweet, rushing chorus of inner flesh.

Threaded throughout that touch had been a hope of even greater, more enduring possibilities.

A touch. A kiss.

So much, yet not enough. Only in truth could that hope be realized.

Truth and then more kisses.

Isabel set the empty cup on the table. She rose slowly from her chair. Donning her mother's cloak, she drew the hood up over her bonnet. Then she went in search of Fox.

She found him sitting in the boat at the quay.

" 'Tis warmer inside," she told him.

"I'm quite comfortable, here, thank you," he said stiffly, not turning to look at her.

She studied the tall figure swathed in a multicaped box coat, boots, gloves, and broad-brimmed hat. "I suppose you are used to being out in the cold."

He cut her a sharp glance from beneath the brim of his hat. "What's that supposed to mean?"

"Well, you seem to prefer isolation."

"You know nothing about me," he said sharply.

"I know more than your average Englishman. Or woman."

"Which says you know little indeed."

Isabel shrugged her tight shoulders. "I comprehend there is more to you than you would have the world realize."

He turned his shuttered face to her. "You and your uncle should attend to your own problems. Meet your brother at the Blue Dragon, then go on to tackle your *evil* uncle at Greenwood. It would better for us all."

Her heart clenched.

"Have you told Uncle Valfrid so?" she asked, her voice husky.

"Not yet."

"Would it be better, Fox? Or simply easier?" She swallowed. "Easier than to deal in truths? You heard my truth last night. Would you send me away before I hear yours?"

Fox made no reply. He scowled out over the marsh.

"And the agreement of which you spoke last night?" she asked.

When she received no reply, she tried once more. "Was it solely for Catherine's sake?"

At Fox's continued silence, Isabel turned away. She climbed back up the concrete steps and took the footpath to the Blue Dragon.

Clinging to her pride for support, Isabel held herself upright and walked away as if her heart were not bleeding.

Inside the inn, she found her uncle ready to depart. Before she could reach his side, two of the Densham boys left through the back door, burdened with two trunks and a port-manteau.

"Where is Mr. Tremayne?" he asked.

"At the quay. It seems there is to be a change of plans, Uncle."

"*Ja?* How so?"

The smile she summoned felt wooden. "Mr. Tremayne believes it would be better for all if we kept with your original plan."

Valfrid lifted bushy silver eyebrows. "He does not desire you to fulfill your agreement?"

"He didn't say. But if you do not object, I would like to meet Catherine in London and stay with her for what remains of her introduction to Society."

"Certainly."

"Catherine is my friend. I wouldn't want to disappoint her."

He nodded. "Good, good. Such loyalty speaks well of you, Lamb. We will not disappoint your friend."

Valfrid looked more closely into Isabel's face. "You are pale. Are you certain you are not disturbed by this change of plans?"

"I'm quite all right, Uncle Valfrid."

Valfrid frowned. "This man, this Tremayne, he has not trifled with your affections, has he?"

Isabel slowly shook her head. "I'm just a bit tired. We were up late last evening."

"True. I will make new arrangements for rooms here. Then you can take a little sleep. While you do, I shall secure your belongings from Herr Tremayne's home."

The sound of footsteps on flags preceded the sight of Fox entering the common room.

"Your baggage has been stowed in the second punt, Mr. Adkisson, which will follow us. Are you and your niece ready to return to Willow Hall?" He did not look at Isabel.

"Did you not tell Isabel plans had changed?" Valfrid demanded.

"Perhaps I did not make myself clear."

Isabel regarded a point on the wall above his head. "You were clear enough."

"Then I must apologize. I fear sometimes I can be difficult to understand."

"Indeed, sir," she replied crisply. "A veritable mystery."

"Shall we return to Willow Hall?" he asked.

He turned his gaze toward Isabel. It seemed to her that his lion's eyes were asking something of her.

"Very well, Herr—no—*Mr.* Tremayne," Valfrid said. "Let us proceed."

As Isabel passed Fox on her way out the door, she said loftily, "In future, Mr. Tremayne—"

"Fox."

"—you really should labor to correct this problem of yours. A man who does not communicate is doomed to be forever misunderstood."

"Kymton is a growing problem," Fox said later that day behind the closed door of his office.

Also seated in comfortable chairs, Nottage, Tsusga, Croom, and Etienne sipped their choice of tea or claret.

Fox began to pace. As he did, it caught his attention that Nottage's ribs didn't seem to be paining him as much as they usually did during the winter.

"Has Cook fixed you up with some new concoction in your porridge?" he asked as he passed the older man. The concoctions almost always tasted foul and usually proved ineffective.

Nottage peered up at him, hesitating. Then he grinned and edged aside his waistcoat to reveal a glimpse of pink silk knit.

Fox blinked.

"Miss Isabel has a good heart, she does. 'Tweren't even polite to her," Nottage muttered, having the grace to look a little ashamed.

"She's known you long enough not to expect such extreme behavior, my friend."

Nottage glowered at Fox, who grinned.

"As I was saying," Fox continued, "Kymton is becoming

more of a problem. He has recently evicted several families to build his cannon manufactory. One of the Ladies is numbered amongst them. The manner in which the evictions were handled was brutal and not particularly legal."

"When has that ever stopped him?" Croom wanted to know. "The authorities aren't willing to touch him."

"Being a duke has its advantages," Tsusga said.

Etienne examined the ruby liquid in his glass. "They might be willing to enforce the law if—"

"Several of her possessions were burned," Fox went on, unwilling to discuss how one of the most corrupt dukes in Britain's history might be made to pay for his crimes. The subject was well-worn.

There was nothing Fox would like to see more. But he'd had firsthand experience in how the system worked. And when the dust had settled, he was being reviled by the public and avoided as taboo by those few who knew what had actually transpired—men who feared for their own careers and reputations. The duke manipulated the strings of his puppets in the government, persons one might naively assume to be equal in power to a duke.

Shadows, secrets, and sins were the Duke of Kymton's tools, and he wielded them with experience. To Fox's knowledge—which came through three years of silent, intense study—the nobleman's greatest weakness lay in his lust for the thrill that came with risk-taking. The most convenient way of satisfying that lust was gambling.

Fox continued. "The boy's arm was broken when he tried to stop Kymton's agent."

Etienne, Tsusga, Croom, and Nottage voiced their opinions of Kymton and his minions in tones and words that rumbled like the growl of an impatient tiger.

At one time or another, each of them had offered Fox his assistance in taking revenge on Kymton for what he had done in India. Fox had not taken them up on their offers, both for their sakes and for his. He had lost everything once.

"What of the Lady and her children now?" Croom asked.

"Settled in a cozy cottage nicer than the one she was forced from," said Etienne, who had made the arrangements.

"Regrettably, it is not close to her old home, but that is the way with long-lost cousins, is it not? The generous ones never seem to own empty cottages near one's old house and friends. These live far enough away not to attract notice."

Fox smiled. "Thank you, 'Tienne."

Etienne inclined his blond head.

"You've all met Mr. Adkisson," Fox said, "and by now you know he is not Isabel's intended."

"Aye," Nottage agreed. "But what's he for? Is it wise?"

"A man of all parts, is our Mr. Adkisson. He is a successful trader with business in Russia, the United States, Canada, the Baltic nations, and various other places around the globe."

"All the more reason to be cautious of him. If he is successful, he is probably intelligent," Tsusga pointed out.

"He may prove useful."

Fox knew there was no good reason to want Valfrid Adkisson here, and his own part in creating this situation rankled. Of course, Adkisson's presence kept Isabel at Willow Hall, too.

Fox rolled his head on his neck in an attempt to relieve some of the tightness in the muscles.

No good reason.

"How are your plans coming along for a new operation?" Croom asked.

They weren't. Fox was finding it difficult to focus on the construction of a new investment ruse. Try as he might to force his thoughts onto the correct path, he kept bumping into a wall. Usually so creative, he could not make his latest scheme come together as it should.

"I'm having a little trouble," he said, "but it will come to me."

The other men exchanged glances.

Fox noticed the looks. "What?" he snapped.

Etienne seemed to be silently elected spokesman. He cleared his throat.

"You have been greatly distracted of late. We have all noticed. Is it Kymton? We will help you rid the world of this vile creature. Concern over Mademoiselle Catherine's debut? You have but to speak the word, and we will effectively discourage any who would cause her an instant's discomfort."

Fox sensed that was not all. "Or?"

"Or is the source of your distraction the so beautiful Isabel Millington?"

Tension pinged down the muscles of Fox's neck and shoulders. "Isabel Millington?"

Again the other men glanced at each other.

"Ye seem taken with her," Nottage said bluntly.

Croom spoke up. "'Tis no secret that you've not enjoyed the company of a woman for three years now—"

Fox felt himself redden. "Jove! I didn't know anyone was keeping count!"

Even Croom's face pinkened. "We weren't really. But it was noticeable that there was nothing of which to keep count."

"It is not natural," Etienne declared.

Fox's eyes widened. "Are you saying you believe me to be *un*natural?"

Etienne's own eyes widened. "*Mais non!* Not in that way!"

"We've been waiting for you to find a woman and fall in love," Tsusga said calmly. "Three years ago you endured much. You were left bitter. Perhaps now you are healing."

"Aye!" Nottage agreed. "Tsusga has the right of it."

Fox rubbed the back of his neck. "There's nothing wrong with me."

"Or," Tsusga continued, "is it all only our imaginations?"

Fox dropped his hand. "Is what your imaginations?" he asked, narrow-eyed.

"Your attraction to Miss Millington."

"Whatever I feel for Miss Millington is not open to discussion."

"No one disputes your right to privacy, Fox," Tsusga said. "We want your happiness, but we also wish to remind you that any time a new member is admitted to the Assembly, there is risk to all of us."

"Do you think I don't know that?" Fox demanded.

"Better than any of us."

"We're here for any o' those other things 'Tienne mentioned, too," Nottage reminded him.

Fox sighed. "Yes. Thank you. I think."

Without another word, the others set down their drinks and filed from the office, quietly closing the door behind them.

For some time afterward, Fox sat at his desk in the quiet room. He recalled the first time he had seen Croom. The man had been as thin as a broomstick, with feverishly bright eyes and a grudge against the world. Nottage, who had served under Fox in India, had been found, unemployed, by Croom a year later and brought into the fold. A living-by-his-wits Etienne had followed, and then a quietly bitter, cynical Tsusga. Months after that, Fox had finally written his aunt Diana, who had promptly descended upon him with Catherine in tow. His lovely, shy little sister.

Admitting each of them had been a risk.

With Uncle Valfrid dozing in front of the sitting room fire and the men of Willow Hall conferring behind the closed doors of Fox's office, Isabel found herself with a rare moment of freedom. She postponed her visit to Oscar the duck and Lizzie Kesh and made for the stairs, up to the floor that housed her bedchamber.

First she stopped by her room to light her bedside candle. Then she carried the taper to the unused grand saloon. As she avoided tattered gray draperies of cobwebs hanging from the great chandeliers, her slippers whispered on the parquet floor.

In front of the column-flanked fireplace, she stopped. She looked around to ascertain she was alone. Then she set the candleholder on the mantel. Taking a deep breath, she carefully placed her splayed hand on the carved alabaster overmantel and pressed.

Nothing happened.

She moved her hand to a different place on the carved alabaster.

Nothing happened.

She slapped the overmantel.

Nothing happened.

Isabel stepped onto the hearth. Still nothing happened.

Determined, she began a methodical inspection. When she discovered no apparent mechanism, she began to press every alabaster blossom, leaf, vine, and acorn.

Midway across the overmantel, an acanthus leaf depressed with a faint *click*. The hearth, fireplace, and overmantel revolved, silently sweeping her out of the saloon and into a concealed chamber.

Clutching the carving on the overmantel, Isabel whirled to face the windowless room.

Gone was the printing press. The candle's flame revealed only bare stone walls. She peered into the gloom. Stone walls and a door.

Isabel carefully stepped down from the hearth and went to the closed door. She attempted to lift the latch on it, but the stout wood door would not budge.

To where had Fox moved the printing press? And, perhaps just as importantly, why had he moved it?

"I print things," he had said, when she accidentally discovered this hiding place.

He had also said, "I am working on the first newspaper for Felgate."

At the time she had thought it a kind, though doomed, undertaking.

Now she knew it was naught but a lie.

When Fox failed to find Isabel on the ground floor, he ascended the stairs. First he went to a window that looked out over the small park behind the house, in case she had gone for another walk. The view yielded no sign of her. He went to her chamber, but she wasn't there, either.

Room by room, he searched for her to no avail.

Finally he stepped into a bedchamber where a pastoral mural greeted him. He couldn't recall ever having entered this room. Elegantly attired shepherds and shepherdesses watched over a vast flock of sheep. But it was the sight of a solitary figure standing at the window that stole his attention.

If she had heard him enter, Isabel made no response.

He crossed the floor, passing holland-covered furniture, his boots thudding against the wood floor. He stopped behind her, well within touching range, but he quashed the urge to curl his palms over her shoulders and pull her back against him.

"What are you doing in this room?" he asked softly.

She continued to look out on dark water and brown reeds. "Thinking."

He started to ask her about what she had been thinking, but decided that might be dangerous ground after this morning.

"Oh," he said.

Now she turned from the window to face him. Her delectable lips wore a cynical smile that cut him like a knife.

"Do you want to know what I was thinking?" she asked.

"Uh—"

"I was thinking," she went on, ignoring his hesitation, "that I came to you and revealed the entire truth about me. I stripped my defenses bare before your eyes. And you have given me . . . nothing."

"You admitted the truth when it could no longer be hidden!"

"I could have given you more lies."

True.

"And I needn't have given you the whole truth of my situation," she said.

Also true.

He spread his arms in surrender—the surrender he had known he must face when he had walked out of his office to find Isabel.

"What do you want to know?"

Her gaze held his, fearful, hopeful, uncompromising. "The truth."

He nodded. "Then the truth you will have. But I doubt you'll like it."

Isabel looked around, then pulled the holland off a lyre-back chair facing toward Fox. Smoothing her skirts, she sat, clearly prepared for a long session.

He inhaled through his nose and huffed out the breath. "First of all, I am Mr. Syer."

SEVENTEEN

Isabel stiffened. "I thought I was to hear the truth."

"You are, Isabel. I'm Uriah Syer, man of business and broker for certain private investments."

When her expression warred between confusion and disbelief, he reeled off his Harley Street address.

"But that cannot be," she cried. "Mr. Syer is bent. He is *old*. With spectacles! You look nothing like him."

"And yet I am one and the same."

She shook her head. Dark curls trembled. "Why, Fox?"

He wasn't certain if she was asking why he disguised himself as Syer or why he had taken her family's fortune. Either answer was certain to bring him down in her estimation, but he had committed himself to the truth. Nothing less could provide them common ground. There they might discover trust. Or its impossibility. As with many things worth treasuring, it could be obtained only at terrifying risk.

"Perhaps it might make more sense if I started at the beginning," he said softly.

Dark eyes regarded him. "India?"

"Yes. India."

He sauntered to another chair and whipped off its covering. He set it down with its back facing Isabel. Then he straddled it.

"When first I was sent to India, I was posted in Calcutta. I was a young captain—"

"How young?"

"Two-and-twenty."

"Had you ever been away from home before?"

He shrugged. "Went to London on business once, with my father."

"I meant someplace a bit farther. Like Italy or France."

"A world tour, do you mean?" She nodded. "My heritage is ancient and proud, but it hasn't come with that kind of wealth in generations. We were sufficiently comfortable to purchase a commission in a respectable regiment for me and to endow Catherine with a nice dowry."

"So the innocent was sent abroad to India."

"Yes. And I found it all so exciting." He became more animated as he recalled the wonder. "India was a different world. Most of the Indians I met were hospitable and kind and willing to indulge my curiosity about their society and beliefs. When my superiors discovered that I had made friends amongst the local people, they cautioned me against it. Said it wasn't proper."

"Did you stop seeing your new friends?" Isabel asked.

"No, but I was quieter about it. That allowed my countrymen to turn a blind eye toward what they considered distasteful fraternization with natives."

Isabel remained silent, her dark eyes trained on him.

Fox ran the fingers of one hand over the smooth curve of the chair back, remembering. "One old gentleman even gave me the benefit of his wisdom in disguising myself and gaining information. His wife had died in childbirth, and he had never remarried. I think my interest in his former occupation pleased him. He had no sons to teach. He had been an agent, you see, and had learned to take on various identities."

"A spy, you mean."

"Very well, yes, a spy."

"Against his own people?"

"He didn't consider them his people. They occupied different towns, different territories far from his."

"So you met a spy who taught you how to be a spy."

Did he hear disapproval in her voice? Was he imagining something that wasn't there? "In so many words, yes. The disguises. The stealth. The use of certain weapons. Oh, all of it. It was a game for both of us. He was elderly and pleased to have someone to teach. I was young and eager to know everything. Neither of us ever expected me to *use* what he taught me. After all, I was a British officer."

Her fingers went to the place where the miniature used to sit at the base of her throat, and Fox felt himself bristle.

"Most of my time was spent amongst British soldiers," he said flatly. "And I was homesick sometimes."

"Well, of course you were," she said stoutly. "You missed your family."

He nodded, feeling a little confused. Maybe he should abandon any attempt to read her reaction. "Catherine was just a girl." He grinned. "She asked me to bring her back an elephant."

Isabel smiled. "That would explain all the elephant figurines."

"It was the best that I could do. Ship cargo officers disliked transporting the real thing." His grin faded. "And they were disinclined to accommodate me on my journey home."

"Calcutta was where you"—Isabel delicately cleared her throat—"met Miss Gilbard, was it not?"

"Ah, yes, the lovely Miss Gilbard," he replied. "I suppose all of Britain must know that."

She gave him a look of apology. "My brother was in London at the time you returned there. He wrote us."

Fox looked down at the wood his fingers stroked. "Then you probably know all that transpired upon my arrival in England."

"Some. I think even Rob was stunned by the cruelty you encountered. But he said only that you had been jilted, that all of London seemed intent on giving you the cut direct. And that the doors of the lending houses were closed to you."

Fox sat there woodenly as old humiliations were renewed in the presence of the woman who heated his blood and haunted his thoughts.

"Ariadne cried off in a letter that passed me by as I sailed from India. I called at her house still in ignorance, but the butler took great pleasure in informing me. I was turned away at the door."

Indignation transformed Isabel's elfin features. "Unforgivable!" She shot up out of her chair and began to pace. "Heartless jade! Such an *absence* of breeding." She whirled to face him. "You, my man, are fortunate to have escaped her net."

Her outrage on his behalf surprised Fox. He wanted to grab Isabel and kiss her.

"At the time, I felt somewhat less than fortunate," he said.

"The nerve of that female." She drew a long breath, then primly resumed her seat. "You were telling me about your stay in Calcutta."

"I was sent to an outpost in northern India, shortly after I reached the age of four-and-twenty. Sarojun, the local chief, who lived like a lord, maintained a friendly relationship with the British. Indeed, the governor-general believed so to the point of one day sending a major with little field experience to the post. Colonel Michael Montgomery remained senior in command, of course, but the new major took precedence over me."

"Did you have . . . field experience?"

"I did."

"Then why—?"

"Because he was Major Lord Everleigh, Marquess of Everleigh, sole heir of the Duke of Kymton."

"Kymton," she echoed, her brows drawn down. "I've heard that name before, though I cannot recall where."

"What does the name evoke in you?"

Isabel thought a moment. "An unpleasant reaction."

Fox's lips curved in a humorless smile. "Very apt."

"Everleigh . . . Everleigh," she muttered. "I've not heard the name."

"Perhaps it did not reach you in the country, but in Calcutta and, hence, London, he was said to be the hero of the battle of Kurndatur—the desired result of his father's machinations."

"So . . . he was not a hero?"

Slowly, Fox shook his head. "And perhaps he is naught but another victim of his father."

"I shouldn't think that would recommend him for command."

One corner of Fox's lips lifted. "In a perfect world, perhaps. But what the Duke of Kymton desires, the Duke of Kymton receives."

Isabel did not debate. Apparently, she was not so naive as to believe peers of the realm did not have special influence in the affairs of mere mortals.

"What happened?" she asked.

"Not long after Everleigh settled in, he was summoned to introduce himself to Sarojun—the chief—and his court. He dutifully complied. When he returned, he was full of praises for Sarojun and his courtiers."

"You did say the chief was friendly to the British," Isabel said.

"Up until then, they had never been quite that friendly. We put it down to one of those things. Sometimes persons simply find themselves compatible."

Her eyes intent upon him, she nodded.

Fox reached out to cradle her cheek with one hand.

She tensed.

He withdrew his hand.

Fox cast about his thoughts, trying to recall what he had been saying. "Sarojun requested Montgomery appoint Everleigh liaison to the court, a request Montgomery politely turned down. Colonel Montgomery had seen action in other parts of India, and he was a cautious man. I doubt he trusted Sarojun, but he couldn't find anything to justify that distrust, and so Montgomery was allowed to return to the palace periodically."

"Did no one accompany Major Lord Everleigh to the chief's court?"

"Yes, of course. It was unwise to travel alone with so

much rebel activity in the area. The British weren't universally admired, you see."

"So I've been told."

"Even I rode with Everleigh to the palace once. Each time he visited, he was separated from his escort, by various means, for approximately twenty minutes. Someone important in court would detach the escort by insisting on showing him the newest tiger or elephant, the most precious jewel in the chief's collection, or a glimpse of the treasure room. When questioned regarding the time he spent away from his escort, Everleigh said he was being shown the architectural wonders of the palace. Montgomery put a stop to the visits."

"I've seen drawings of Indian palaces," Isabel said. "Fabulous structures the size of towns, with fountains and gardens."

Fox snorted. "This one was a little more basic. It was built of brown stone blocks. Only the inside was painted. The courtiers lived in their own houses outside of the palace, inside the town walls. Only Sarojun, his family, his harem, his servants, and his elite corps of guards lived in the palace."

"Harem?"

"He had numerous wives and concubines. Until his daughters were married off, they remained with their mothers."

"Were they as beautiful as they are described in books?" Isabel asked. "Sloe-eyed, seductive, dripping with silks and jewels?"

Fox cocked an eyebrow. "What sort of books have you been reading?"

She pinkened. "The published journals of travelers."

"Well, I cannot speak for those published travelers, but *I* wouldn't know if those women were attractive or not. I never saw them. They stayed in the seclusion customary to harems."

"Good."

Ridiculous, but that one brisk word cheered him. "Well, I did see *one* of them," he admitted. "But it certainly wasn't intentional."

She made no reply, apparently waiting to hear him out.

"After Everleigh was forbidden to visit the palace," Fox continued, "things returned to normal at the post. One drill after another. Marching, marching, marching."

"You marched?"

"No, but my men did. Boredom was a problem. It led to intoxication and brawling. At times some of us would ride out to reconnoiter. There were dry plains and foothills combed with caves. The rebels seemed to know when best to strike at us, and they made use of the caves and ravines. If we hoped to catch them, we needed to learn the lay of the land, too.

"On one of those occasions, after we had bedded down for the night, I saw Everleigh slip from his tent and leave camp. He was good. Not even the sentry noticed."

Isabel leaned slightly forward in her chair. "Everleigh was a spy?"

Fox did not answer. In order for her to draw her own conclusions, she must hear the whole story. "I made use of some soot from the burned-down campfire, and then followed him. Among the rocks of the foothills, he rendezvoused with a woman."

Her eyes widened.

"I drew close enough to hear some of what they said. I heard endearments, and he called her Nishkala. I knew the chief had a favorite daughter named Nishkala."

Isabel drew a sharp breath. "Madness."

"I thought so, too. Dishonoring Sarojun's daughter was certain to lose us the goodwill of our only ally in the region."

"Not to mention Nishkala's when she realized nothing would come of her love affair," Isabel said dryly. "What did you do?"

"I returned to camp. The following morning I cornered Everleigh privately and confronted him with what I had seen. He vowed they loved each other. That she was paving the way for him to ask her father for her hand in marriage. I couldn't believe he thought Sarojun would ever consent. But

Everleigh was convinced that being the sole son of a promi-
nent British duke brought him eligibility."

"Did you report this to Colonel . . . ?"

"Montgomery," he supplied. "I had to. This business put
everyone on the post at risk."

"What did he say?"

"He was astonished. After all, who would suspect a
British officer could be so stupid? He summoned Everleigh,
who denied his assignation with Nishkala."

"Everleigh called you a *liar*?"

Fox's mouth hardened into a grim line. "Not in so many
words. But the end result was the same. He said I must have
had a dream. A *dream*!" He all but spat the word out. The
memory still rankled. "He implied I might have smoked
opium."

"Surely Colonel Montgomery did not believe anything so
outlandish."

"No. But his was not an enviable position. He ordered
Everleigh not to leave the post without his—Montgomery's—
express command. All anyone could do was hope that Sarojun did not learn of this affair, that it was an end to the
matter."

Isabel's gaze searched his face. "But it was not, was it?"

"No. That idiot Everleigh sneaked out of camp a few
more times. He must have bribed the sentries to look the
other way. At first, I took it upon myself to follow him."

"Did he meet with Nishkala again?"

"Yes. But I noticed something strange. Everleigh seemed
more emotionally involved with her than she was with him."

"How . . ." Isabel caught her bottom lip between her
teeth.

"How what?" he asked, his gaze occupied with the sight
of her lips, the glimpse of her white teeth.

"How could you tell she did not love him?"

"She said all the sweet words, but . . ." He shook his
head. "Something was missing."

Isabel seemed to study the clasped hands in her lap.
"Sweet words, like any others, can be hollow."

"Only if they're spoken that way," he said. "If they are uttered in truth, they can carry a glorious resonance."

"If you say so."

For a long moment, Fox found nothing that answered. A wistful tension filled the neglected room. Outside on the dark water, a marsh bird cried.

"How desperate to be loved Everleigh must have been," Isabel mused. "He remained blind to what even an eavesdropper could detect."

Fox stared down at the smooth wood of the chair back. How long had it taken him to recognize that very thing? To see through the titles and privilege to the sadness and want that haunted Everleigh? The pollution of Kymton's greed and arrogance had not spared his own son. Not that Fox had much pity for him.

"I stopped following Everleigh to his trysts, believing I had discovered nothing more than a bored princess with her lovesick British officer. If Montgomery would not put a stop to these meetings, I was wasting my time.

"Then Everleigh told Montgomery he had learned that the rebels planned to attack our next supply train as it neared Kurndatur. When Montgomery demanded to know where Everleigh had heard this, he was told only that it came from a reliable source."

"Nishkala."

"The bored princess. It was then that I reported all that I had heard. Montgomery sent scouts to the area where the rebels were purported to be gathering. They came back to confirm that Everleigh was correct. So we rode out, determined to protect our line of supplies and crush the rebels, hoping we could damage them sufficiently to put an end to them as a viable force in the region. My men and I were under Everleigh's command. His first real action."

Although she did not look at him, Fox sensed he had Isabel's full attention.

"Everleigh gave me the order to take my men amongst the rocks at the base of the foothills to await the right time to ambush the enemy. I tried to talk some sense into him, pointing out that we would be vulnerable to attack by anyone in the caves above, but he informed me that this time the rebels would not use the foothills for cover. Even the scouts had reported no sighting of enemy there. Everleigh's source had confided that this was to be a surprise move on the rebels' part.

"Nishkala lied," Fox said tonelessly. "She lied at her father's command. Not only did an enemy force come from the direction she had said they would, they were crawling all over the foothills. The chief's own army joined them, giving them an advantage in numbers over us."

"Sarojun had turned coat," Isabel said.

"Too late, we discovered he hated the British. He had always sympathized with the rebels. He simply didn't support them publicly until they had a chance to wipe us out, effectively returning control of the region to him."

"And Nishkala?"

"A strong rebel sympathizer. She did not regret her part in the massacre," Fox continued. "Rebels did use the caves above us. Many of my men were slaughtered, as I had feared. The attack was progressing just as Sarojun had planned. Nishkala's betrayal paralyzed Everleigh. He couldn't believe she had lied to him. He refused to give the order that would let us retreat from our position and then outflank the enemy on the other side of the supply train to help our men there. Finally, I gave the order to move, though by then there had been over a hundred casualties. I led the men, despite Everleigh screaming at us to maintain our positions.

"In the end, we drove off the rebels and then managed to get what was left of the supply wagons to the post. But we knew it was only a matter of time before we were attacked. The rebels' only hope was to finish the job they had begun before reinforcements could reach us. Now that Sarojun had shown his true colors, he had no choice but to try to exterminate us."

Restless, Fox rose from his chair and began to wander around the chamber. "That worry proved less trouble than we feared. Sarojun had been killed by his cousin, who refused to send the remnants of the imperial—though small—

army against us. We had managed to inflict damage on the rebels, who, without the aid of the new chief, hadn't a prayer of defeating us. They crawled off to lick their wounds."

He twitched aside the covering over what turned out to be an ornately carved mirror. He jerked the holland back into place. The last thing he wanted to see was his own image.

"You saved lives," Isabel said. "By disobeying Everleigh's orders, you saved lives and aided in turning the tide of the battle."

"I saved lives," he agreed softly. "But I disregarded an order."

"What . . . what occurred next?"

A muscle jumped in Fox's jaw. "Everleigh was promptly summoned to Calcutta. The real story was quashed and a new one put about. The official line was that my disobeying Everleigh's order was responsible for the high death toll, that I had turned coward. Montgomery tried to intercede for me. That was cut short by something he received from Calcutta."

"What was it?"

Fox flipped aside a dusty cloth to reveal the carved mahogany leg of a writing table. At its bottom, a lion's claw grasped a small Earth. "A letter. Probably from the Duke of Kymton's agent. I've often wondered what it said. Since Montgomery is an honorable man, it most likely spelled out the futility of any attempt to continue as my champion. Perhaps it included a threat aimed to one of his family. Based on what I now know of Kymton, that seems likely. He would have made good on any threat, too."

Isabel's face grew paler. "Despicable."

"I was given a quick court-martial and drummed out of my regiment. Out of the Royal Army. I came home." He shrugged. "The rest you know."

"Oh, Fox," she murmured, her eyes large and liquid.

He steeled himself. "The rest you know, that is, up to a point."

Absently, she slipped off the holland cloth covering a black lacquered cabinet sitting on a stand. "Kymton should be stopped."

"I agree."

She ran her fingertips over an ornate brass hinge. "Have you tried?"

"No."

Isabel cocked her head. "I should think you would want to."

"I do. I imagine there are many who would like to."

"Then why do you do nothing?"

"Because I'm not a fool."

"You sound so cool, so controlled."

He lifted more of the cloth to reveal a silver inkwell black with tarnish. "I've had three years to learn that control, Isabel."

She traced a circle around the engraved brass lock, never touching the red-tasseled brass key that stood in it. Fox watched, unable to take his eyes from the slim, fair fingers.

"Is it true you lost your ancestral home?" she asked.

This was becoming more difficult than he had anticipated. "Tregarn. Yes, I lost it." Too often he had imagined what his father's reaction to that loss would have been.

"The portraits in the gallery are from Tregarn."

"There was a great deal of debt attached to Tregarn when I arrived home. No one would lend me money." More remembered humiliation.

"Did you . . . did you take up . . . smuggling?"

Fox's eyebrows lifted in surprise. "Smuggling?"

Isabel's face went pink. "I just assumed. . . . That is to say, you live out here, by a waterway, close to a river and the sea. This island *was* built by a smuggler."

A wry smile tugged at one corner of his mouth. "Yes, but some time ago. I have not followed in his footsteps. Not exactly."

EIGHTEEN

"What do you mean by 'not exactly'?" Isabel asked.

"Well—"

"And another question comes to mind, one I've been meaning to ask. When you said you had known my real name for some time—how long? And how did you learn it?"

Fox's statement had surprised her at the time, but the excitement of Uncle Valfrid's arrival and her desire to sweep away the burden of lies had distracted her.

He leaned a shoulder against the wall, arms folded across his chest. "You do not seem surprised to learn what happened in India."

"I told you I had faith in you."

"Yes. Yes, you did," he said, his eyes concealed by thick, burnished lashes.

"Did you not believe me?"

Had he been wounded so many times he refused to accept that someone who had not known him before that fateful incident in India might believe in him? In his essential kindness and courage?

Isabel considered that tall, self-contained figure standing halfway across the room. They had come a long way from their initial meeting at the Blue Dragon. Was she willing to walk away, to leave with her uncle and brother without a backward glance? Or did she want more from Foxton Tremayne?

She took a breath and took a chance. "When I confessed my faith, and you made no reply, . . . I thought you found it a matter of indifference."

He did not respond immediately, and her heart sank.

"No," he said in a voice so low she could scarcely hear it. "I was afraid to believe. And . . . there is much you don't yet know about me."

Isabel wanted to hold him, to be held by him, but she knew the time for that had not arrived. Instead, she sought to drink him in with her eyes. What could he possibly say that would offend her? "Tell me."

"When I could not earn my bread through honorable methods, I became a thief."

She blinked. "You stole?"

"I steal."

"Then you are a smuggler?"

"No."

"You . . . break into people's houses?"

"No. What I do is somewhat more complicated than that. I take from the greedy and corrupt. The money is spread amongst many who have suffered at the hands of such persons, myself included."

"Like Robin Hood?"

"The comparison has been made, but I believe it too simplistic. And too noble."

"Too noble? Why? Is there an element of revenge involved?"

His lips curled into a cynical smile. "Clever girl. Yes. There is an element of revenge."

"Does it give you satisfaction, taking from the corrupt?"

She had expected a prompt reply, but he paused, as if giving her question some thought.

"Yes," he said at last, "but not as much as it used to."

"Have you robbed the Duke of Kymton?"

Isabel sensed a tightening in him, a drawing inward. "No."

Did he not lust for revenge against Kymton? *She* would. She believed Fox did, too.

He was intelligent. Isabel believed he could outwit Kymton if he chose.

"I could never rob Kymton of enough," Fox continued. "I couldn't take his reputation, his honor, and his family home. Not even enough of his money to wound him."

"Have you wounded his son, then?"

He shook his head. "I think sometimes his son is wounded enough. Everleigh resigned his commission shortly after I left India. I've encountered him a few times over the years, though most of those times he would not have recognized me. The fellow even tried to apologize once, but he couldn't contrive it without implicating his father, so the attempt ended with a pathetic pleading look on his face and his retreat. He is approximately my age, but he looks a score of years older."

"Perhaps guilt does that."

"Perhaps. I doubt the duke has lost a minute's sleep over what he did to me. I am but one of many over whom he has marched."

"And will continue to march until someone stops him."

A bitter note rang in Fox's bark of laughter. "That someone will not be me, Elf."

What was bitterness if not anger? she thought. An anger that hurt Fox far more than it hurt the duke.

"Isabel? Are you listening?"

Reminded, she asked, "How did you know my name?"

Fox gave her a blank look. "You told me."

"No. You told me that you had known my real name for some time."

He looked up at the plastered ceiling. "This is where the story becomes somewhat ticklish."

Made restive by his reluctance, Isabel left the cabinet to pace. What could be worse than learning he was a thief? Even a *good* thief. "I am all attention."

Without taking his gaze from the ceiling, he inhaled abruptly and exhaled with equal sharpness. "I had you investigated."

She halted abruptly and discovered she again stood in front of the black lacquered cabinet. "I am certain I mis-heard, Fox. I thought you said you had me investigated."

"You did not mishear," he answered heavily.

Isabel scowled. "Investigated. I cannot say I appreciate being treated like the worst of criminals," she informed him. "*Spied* upon. I have had faith in *you,* but clearly it is not re-ciprocated. Indeed, sir, I am mortified!"

He dropped his arms and pushed away from the wall to start toward her. Instantly, she thrust out her arm, palm flat in a warding-off gesture.

"It was the handkerchief, was it not?" she demanded. "My initial on the handkerchief I loaned Catherine. Dear God. Does Catherine know I have been investigated?"

He opened his mouth.

Before he could speak, she asked, "Had you so little trust in me that you could not believe there might be an innocent explanation for that *M*?"

"Is there?"

"That is beside the point!"

"I am Mr. Syer," he said simply.

Now that knowledge pressed on her with the weight of an anvil. "And you robbed Gilbert."

He hesitated, then nodded.

"Well, you were right," she said numbly. "He is corrupt. But the fortune you stole from him he had embezzled from my family."

That embezzlement had set off a chain of events that had taken everything from her.

Fox took three steps toward her, but the look she cast his way stopped him in his tracks. "I did not know that," he vowed. "He was brought to me by a crony of his, a bribe-taking magistrate."

"Probably the same one who would have sent me back to Gilbert if I had gone to the authorities when I had uncovered my uncle's odious deed," she said dully.

"They thought they would get rich. The avaricious al-ways do. But the investments do not work that way. The marks—my targets—make a small profit, just enough to keep them from becoming awkward for me. The bulk of the money is distributed—"

"To the poor, I know." She lifted her eyes to him. "I am now one of them."

"No!"

"Look more closely at your 'marks' next time, Fox. You will probably find the money you take from them in revenge was pilfered from someone who does not deserve your anger."

With as much dignity as she could muster when she felt as if a sword had pierced her heart, Isabel turned from Fox and walked from the chamber.

Oscar the duck nibbled greedily at the bread crumbs in Lizzie Kesh's outstretched hands. The little girl giggled.

It had been two days since Fox had confided in Isabel. Anger and sympathy churned inside her. The love she felt for him only muddled what she had learned. Unable to look at him without choking on welling tears and indignation, Isabel had done her best to avoid him.

She had managed only to a point. While she might not encounter him in person, he filled her thoughts and stirred a sorrowful tumult within her breast.

When Isabel had confronted Catherine with what she knew, the young woman had burst into tears. She had hated keeping secrets from Isabel. She had never expected to become dear friends with her. She had only wanted to be more included in her brother's life. And there was not now, nor had there ever been, an "intended" who might whisk Catherine to Sweden.

Catherine's tears had drawn Isabel's own. In the end, the two had held hands as they wept, apologizing and forgiving.

"Your apron string is trailing in the mud," Isabel now told the squatting child.

"Maybe Oscar will think it a worm," Lizzie suggested optimistically.

Isabel smiled at the small scullery maid. "Do you believe that?"

Lizzie sighed. "No. It would be a dead worm, and Oscar won't eat them."

Having finished Lizzie's offering, the duck waddled over to guzzle crumbs from Isabel's hands.

"Our Oscar is too discriminating for that," Isabel said.

Drying her hands on a cloth, Mabel Cook walked out the kitchen's back door to join them.

It had come as a surprise to Isabel to learn that when Catherine or Fox or Nottage or Lady Blencowe referred to "Cook," they weren't merely substituting the robust woman's title for her name, as happened in so many houses of the privileged. In this case, her name was really Cook.

Mrs. Cook glanced fondly at her niece. "We thank you again for that lovely cap, Miss Smy—Millington. It fits right nice under her mobcap, like, and keeps her little ears warm. Don't it, Lizzie?"

Lizzie's grubby face lit. "Oh, yes, Miss Millington. My new cap keeps me *very* warm. 'Cause it's *pink.*"

"Pink *silk,* my girl," Cook told her niece. "Very fine indeed. It's not every tyke as has a silk cap knitted by a lady."

With one small index finger, Lizzie touched the hat Isabel had given her, its pink edge the only thing showing under the more voluminous mobcap.

Cook swooped down on the child, only to carefully catch hold of the finger and give it an affectionate squeeze. "Do not be handling your present in such a state, sweeting. You'll get it dirty. Go on back to your work, now, else your cousins will start complaining that you're not doing your share."

Lizzie made a face, indicating her feelings about her cousins' complaints, but obediently skipped back to the kitchen.

Isabel stood, brushing at her skirts. "How many cousins does she have working in the kitchen, Mrs. Cook?" All of them were years older than Lizzie.

"Four."

"Are they all your nieces and nephews?"

Mrs. Cook withdrew a fistful of crumbs from a cloth sack and handed it to Isabel.

"Yes," she replied. "My own children are grown and

gone. Ambitious they were. Moved to the colonies in America. These belonged to my sisters, both taken two years ago when the Cough came to their village."

"Good heavens. *Five* children. I am all admiration, Mrs. Cook. Not many women would have taken them in."

Not many *could* have taken in what amounted to a whole other family. So many mouths to feed . . .

Isabel smiled. "You are an exceptional person, Mrs. Cook. A kind and caring soul."

Mrs. Cook's ruddy face turned even pinker. "Oh, go on with you. It's the cap'n as makes it possible. Provides us all room and board, he does. Pays me a right good wage. Even pays the little ones wages, which I set aside for 'em, for when they get older."

Oscar nibbled at Isabel's hem. Absently, she tossed him some crumbs. "It seems Mr. Tremayne has many facets to his character. Why do so many address him 'Captain'?"

He had been stripped of that honor. Surely it must serve as a painful reminder every time he was called by his former rank.

"We do it out of respect for him," Mrs. Cook said firmly. "He was robbed of his position."

Isabel nodded. Instead of a painful reminder, it was meant as a vote of confidence, a show of support.

"Did you know him before he was . . . robbed?"

"My man did. Jim lost a hand at Kurndatur. Didn't stop the cap'n from finding a place for him, though, when Jim come to him. An upright man is our cap'n."

"Hmph."

Mrs. Cook chuckled. "Heavens, if you two aren't peas of a pod. Both of you can see what's good for everyone but yourselves."

"I am Miss Tremayne's Swedish teacher, not a pod-sharing pea."

"All I'm saying is that a body would have to be blind not to notice the way the two of you look at each other."

Isabel stared at Mrs. Cook, embarrassed.

"We're all glad to see it. That's all I'll say on the matter."

It seemed to Isabel that Mrs. Cook had said more than

enough. It would be difficult to face anyone in Willow Hall without wondering if they, too, had observed the potent attraction between Fox and herself.

"Ephraim showed me what you did for him, Miss Millington. Very kind of you."

"Ephraim?"

"Mr. Nottage."

"Oh. Well. The cold hurts his ribs."

"It does. It does, indeed. They were broken in his younger days." Mrs. Cook negligently waved a hand. "In one battle or another. Age, you know. It pains us all, and it's worse in the winter. Take my right elbow, for instance. Beating all those cake batters and lifting all those hams 'n such."

Isabel dutifully regarded the elbow joint revealed to her.

"You've been making tonics for him, have you not?" she asked.

Mrs. Cook gave her a sidelong glance. "I have."

"Just hearsay."

The older woman thought a minute, then said, "My Jim has been gone above a year now, and I have a soft spot for Ephraim. I don't deny it. He may be gruff, but at heart he's a good man."

A tall shadow fell across Oscar's duck palace.

"Oh, mercy me," Mrs. Cook exclaimed, thrusting the bag of crumbs into Isabel's hands. "Look how time does fly! Back to my kitchen for me, my dear."

She hurried back into the house, shutting the door with a loud thump.

"I've been looking for you, Isabel," Fox said quietly.

The late afternoon sun stood at his back, touching his hair and eyelashes with fiery shots of copper, sienna, and gold.

Isabel's heart beat faster. She wished she were better at resisting the effect he had on her. "Good day to you, Mr. Syer."

"I will make good the money Gilbert invested with me."

"Crime certainly pays well, does it not? My uncle invested a fortune with you."

She could not read what was going on behind that shuttered face. How she wanted to reach out her fingers to touch those high, slanting cheekbones, that sensual mouth. Isabel kept her fingers tightly clutched around the bag.

He stayed out of range of her touch. "I have said it will be done."

"According to my lying, cheating uncle, his money with you will be tied up for some time to come."

"According to his lying, cheating investment broker, the money will become available to you quite soon."

His ruthless appraisal of his part in her family's misfortune slashed at Isabel.

"Don't," she said, her throat clogged with unhappiness.

God help her, she loved this man.

"Don't what?" he asked harshly.

She frowned down at the crumbs in the sack. "Do not speak of yourself in such a way."

"Why? It's true. I make my living lying and cheating. And now it's come home to me."

Isabel lifted her face. A tear trembled on her lower lashes. It broke away to roll down her cheek. "It hurts me when you are cruel to yourself, Fox."

With swift strides, he closed the distance between them, taking her into his arms, crushing her close.

She clung to him.

"You do good things, too," she declared into his shoulder. "So many good things. And *you've* been robbed."

"And I had you put off the coach to Harwich and directed to Felgate."

His announcement left her speechless. She felt him tense. Finally, she found her voice. "You *what*?"

He cleared his voice. "I had you put off—"

"I heard you!"

She struck him an ineffectual blow on the back.

"Wretched man! Why would you do such a thing? I was trying to reach my uncle in Sweden."

"You had come to my house on Harley Street seeking Mr. Syer. Your speech gave you away as a well-bred woman, and you issued a calling card, yet you had dirt on your face and scuffed half-boots. You wore an expensive cloak, but you were on foot, carrying a portmanteau you had hidden in the bushes. In my profession, one must be very, very cautious."

With the same loose fist, she hit him again, this time with even less force.

"Your uncle Valfrid wasn't in Sweden," he pointed out. "He was in Russia—"

"On his way home from Russia," she insisted.

"On his way home from Russia. What if you had succeeded in reaching Göteborg? You would have been alone and penniless in a foreign land."

She sniffled. "Are you suggesting that you saved me?"

He tucked her head beneath his chin. "Yes, indeed," he murmured. "Saved you from discouragement. Perhaps even saved you from a Fate Worse Than Death."

"Dear me. I had not considered."

"Of course you hadn't," he sympathized. "You had learned your uncle was a villain. Your brother was held captive by the enemy. Your only thought was to reach someone who might be trusted to help."

"So true."

"Alas, you didn't know that you had already reached such a person."

She tried to lift her head to give him a gimlet eye, but he adjusted his embrace to prevent her. He stroked her back.

"Uh-huh." She imbued the two syllables with skepticism.

"You did say I was kind," he reminded her.

"That was before I knew you had put me off the coach. That was also before I remembered I was forced to hike two miles in my best gown, carting a portmanteau."

"You had already hiked a great many more than two miles with that portmanteau. And your best gown has been replaced with several new ones."

"It seems you have an answer for everything."

He nuzzled her ear. "I've given the whole matter a great deal of thought."

Her heart quickened its beat. "Have you?"

"Mm-hmm." He kissed the rim of her ear.

Isabel closed her eyes, thrilling to the touch of his lips. "And . . . at what . . . conclusions . . . have you arrived?"

He kissed her temple. "That a wise man should never let go of a woman who feeds his duck."

At that moment, the outside kitchen door banged open. Mrs. Cook tactfully called out from within the kitchen, "Cap'n, your sister and aunt have arrived home."

With a deep sigh, Fox stepped back from Isabel, but slipped his hand to the small of her back, as if refusing to relinquish touch.

"Thank you, Cook," he called back.

Reluctantly, they returned to the house. Inside they discovered trunks and hatboxes being carried in from several punts lined up at the bottom of the front outside steps.

"I am *so* glad to be back, Fox!" Catherine exclaimed, throwing her arms around her brother's neck, one hand encased in a large swansdown muff.

Fox laughed, pleased with his sister's show of affection. She had not done such a thing since he had left for India.

"So I would imagine," he teased. "What torment to be doted upon day after day!"

Catherine stood back in the embrace to give her brother an admonishing look. "You know very well it was not like that. Well, not quite."

He gave her hand a small squeeze. "I know. You are a good granddaughter to humor an old woman's fancies."

Diana kissed Fox on the cheek as she swept by him on the way to warm herself by the sitting room fire. She, too, wore a muff, though hers was sable.

"You were much missed, Fox," she announced. "Having the full attention of both my mother and father is a daunting experience. Is it not Catherine?"

Catherine pecked Fox on the other cheek, then turned to Isabel to give her an affectionate hug and kiss. Then she hurried to the fire.

"One has only so much to tell," Catherine said. "I drew out what I did have and played it up as much as possible, but being the object of their focus makes me feel as if I should be spitting out diamonds and pearls instead of words."

"Indeed, Little Sister, they probably believed your words to be diamonds and pearls."

Catherine made a face. "Doubtful. I fear I am destined to remain an innocent—or a dolt—in their eyes forever. Nothing will do but that I heed their continual servings of wisdom. Even Aunt Diana could not please Grandmama. Nor Grandpapa, either."

"Did they at least admire your new gowns?" Isabel asked.

"Oh, yes. Even though Aunt Diana had not seen fit to use Grandmama's mantua-maker"—she rolled her eyes, and Diana laughed—"they were still 'rather pretty.'"

"Perhaps my taste is not so exquisite as your grandmother's," Isabel said, "but I find your gowns exceptionally beautiful."

"Oh, they are," Diana agreed. "Mother comes from another age."

Isabel excused herself to find her uncle.

After she had gone, Fox explained to Catherine and Diana everything that had occurred in their absence, and how it had come about.

"And Isabel was so concerned for you, Catherine," he said, "that despite all their own troubles, she persuaded her uncle to allow her to stay with you through your time in London."

Before anything else could be said, there was a tap at the door.

"Come," Fox called.

Isabel entered, followed by her uncle. When the introductions were performed, Adkisson would have done any courtier proud, so gracefully did he bend over the hands of Catherine and Diana, so elegantly did he turn a compliment. But then, as he had told Fox, his business had taken him to the royal courts of various lands.

Fox noticed a subtle difference in his aunt. She didn't hold herself any differently that he could see. Her expression indicated no more than pleasant interest. Yet, upon being introduced to Adkisson, she, well, *radiated*. He sensed an intensity, an alert interest that he had not noticed before.

He turned his gaze to Isabel. She, too, radiated, though he perceived a difference. Was this some female thing he had not noticed before? It had been so long since he had cared.

Under his study, Isabel's cheeks pinkened. The long, thick lashes lifted, and she looked up at him.

Fox felt as if an arrow sped with her gaze, an arrow dipped in some mystical, intoxicating elixir. It pierced him to the heart.

He grinned.

She smiled at him, and his grin broadened.

Catherine moved across the room to join them.

"Isabel," she said. "Isabel, are you well? Did you hear me?"

She turned to Fox, ready to say something. Abruptly her eyes widened. "Oh."

Catherine looked from Fox back to Isabel, and then a knowing smirk slowly spread across her face.

The remaining shred of Fox's dignity shouted, *Snap out of it, man!*

Reluctantly, he turned his attention to his sister. "Did you have something you wished to ask?" He gave her his fiercest scowl.

She giggled. "No," she replied in a low voice. "I was wishful of speaking with Isabel, but I will wait until you two have finished staring into each other's eyes. Isabel, I'll be in my chamber with, I hope, a tray of something warm."

With an easy grace, she assured Adkisson it had been a pleasure to make his acquaintance, then took her leave of the room.

Fox watched her go. What had become of that timid mouse of a girl who, only a mere month ago, had moved about Willow Hall like a shadow?

Hearing a deep, masculine chuckle, Fox looked across the room. Near the fire, Adkisson and Diana appeared engaged in an amusing conversation.

Isabel, her cheeks pink, placed her hand upon his arm to draw his attention. "I do not wish to interrupt my uncle and Lady Blencowe. I go to see what Catherine desires."

He lifted her hand to his lips, pressed them to its back. "I've no doubt she'll quiz us both."

"No doubt at all."

He smiled. "Be strong."

She gave him a snappy salute, then departed.

"So, it is settled," Diana said, lifting her voice to be heard throughout the room. She turned to discover Catherine and Isabel gone. "Where did they go?"

"To Catherine's room," said Fox. "What is settled?"

"We will leave for London directly after the New Year," Diana announced.

NINETEEN

Christmas brought a feast prepared by Mrs. Cook and her helpers. A roast goose, cooked to perfection, vied with the plum pudding for the title of crowning glory. Lizzie assured Oscar he was safe and loved, and that the goose with the crisp, golden skin was no relation to him.

Simple gifts were exchanged: pretty boxes and bags of confections, fine handkerchiefs, knitted elbow-warmers, and nightcaps. After dinner they gathered in the saloon and sang to the music that Catherine and Isabel played on the pianoforte. Everyone went to bed filled with good food and convivial spirits.

As planned, Catherine, Lady Blencowe, Valfrid, and Isabel departed for London directly after the dawn of the New Year, at the head of a cavalcade of carriages filled with trunks, bandboxes, and portmanteaus.

Lady Blencowe's London house might not be as vast as that of the Prince Regent or his wealthier associates, but its Mayfair address made it desirable even before one glimpsed the elegant Palladian building designed by the Adams brothers, with its graceful horseshoe staircases leading to the front door, the orderly pedimented windows, and the marble Corinthian columns flanking the front door.

On the night of the ball introducing Catherine to Society,

the front of the mansion was aglow with lanterns and torches. Uniformed footmen helped guests hasten out of the cold London night into the warmth of the baroness's abode.

Not a little of that warmth was generated by the number of guests. It seemed an invitation issued by La Baroness was not to be declined. And, of course, in gray and snowy January, when those involved in Parliament and other government posts traipsed into Town from their country estates, even a ball honoring an outcast's sister offered diversion. Isabel could see the fine hand of Lady Blencowe behind the timing of this affair.

Having completed the formalities of the receiving line, Isabel now stood beside Catherine, not far from a table bearing etched-glass bowls of milk punch, tea punch, and ratafia, and fragile goblets of negus. Catherine held a dainty cup of tea punch in one gloved hand, though she had been given no opportunity to taste it.

Isabel languidly applied her lacy fan, enjoying the cool puffs of air as she watched her friend. Catherine glowed with demure excitement as one well-dressed young man after another presented himself to request the honor to stand up with her when the dancing began after dinner. Most of them then stayed to vie for her charming smile.

Isabel found herself looking around for Fox. Had he decided to stay away? It would be like him to make such a sacrifice if it might help ensure a perfect evening for Catherine. He wanted for his sister all the happiness the world could offer.

"Don't worry," Catherine whispered in her ear. "He'll come. Fox always keeps his promises."

"I wasn't aware I'd been so obvious."

"Oh, you haven't been. Not at all," Catherine assured her. "It is only that I've been looking, too."

"So he promised you he would attend tonight?"

What courage that took. A different kind of sacrifice.

Catherine smiled impishly. "I became a horrid nag until he agreed. But my introduction ball could not be complete without my brother." She dropped her gaze to the mother-of-pearl and lace fan she held in her gloved fingers, as if suddenly assailed by a depressing thought. Then she brightened. "Fox will find a way."

Isabel lightly squeezed her friend's wrist. "Of that I have no doubt." Just how Fox would fulfill his promise without destroying his sister's important evening remained a mystery. "Your brother is most devoted to you."

Catherine's smile softened. "He is, isn't he?"

"Have you ever doubted it?"

To Isabel's surprise, Catherine nodded slightly. "Yes. Years ago. After my father died, and Fox did not come home. I was a child then and had no idea of how far it was between England and India, or what Fox was enduring. So selfish . . ."

"So *young*," Isabel corrected gently. "How could you know what was going on in India?"

Catherine searched Isabel's face. "Do you believe Fox was responsible for all those deaths? That he buckled in the heat of battle?"

Never before had this subject been brought so clearly out in the open between them. Almost as if by unspoken agreement they had skirted it. Now, on this night of her entering the adult world, Catherine wanted to know where Isabel stood on this important subject. And she deserved an honest answer.

"No, I do not," she said simply. Her emotions regarding Fox felt far from simple.

Before she could murmur another word, a fresh-faced young man in a scarlet waistcoat arrived from the refreshment table with cups of milk punch for Catherine and Isabel, only to notice they already held cups full of beverage.

The subject of Fox refused to release its hold on Isabel's thoughts. She permitted Catherine to carry the conversation with the growing cluster of men and young women.

The Duke of Kymton and his reckless son had stripped Fox of his career, of his social consequence, of his hope. Yet *they* probably did not hesitate to show their faces in public, Isabel thought resentfully.

"Pardon me, madam," a masculine voice said behind her. "You seem to have been separated from your companion."

Shaken from her reverie, Isabel saw that she had been displaced to the edge of the chattering group surrounding Catherine.

Catherine appeared immersed in merry conversation with young men and women her own age, and Isabel didn't have the heart to interrupt. For too long the girl had been deprived of such companionship.

"Thank you, sir, but Miss Tremayne is an intelligent and trustworthy young lady," Isabel said as she turned to face her informant.

He was tall, approximately six feet three inches in height, and broad at the shoulder. His cropped mouse-blond hair was thick and curly, with pronounced side whiskers. Below darker mouse-blond eyebrows he wore spectacles.

"I am pleased to hear it," he replied. "So you are not, in fact, her chaperone?"

Something about the fellow's voice caused Isabel to cast another glance at him. How could she find anything familiar about someone whom she had never seen before? Had he come through the receiving line, Isabel felt certain she should have remembered him.

"I'm her friend and her companion, sir. I am also her chaperone," she informed him.

"Indeed?"

Isabel turned a fond smile on Catherine as the latter giggled with two other girls. "Yes."

"You look scarcely old enough to be Miss Tremayne's chaperone, if you will not mind me saying so. You cannot yourself have been long out of the schoolroom."

Was the fellow flirting or criticizing?

Well, it didn't matter. They had not been introduced, and she had no intention of allowing him any closer to Catherine. With a jerk of her wrist, she snapped her fan shut. Any nincompoop could spot her as the companion, hence less financially, and perhaps even less socially, desirable than Catherine. Or at least they would have been able to if Fox had not insisted upon Isabel having such a lovely wardrobe.

"I'm sorry, sir," she said coolly. "We have not been properly introduced. I must consider Miss Tremayne."

He inclined his head. "Very right of you."

Did she detect suppressed laughter in those eyes behind the spectacles? Before she could study his expression, he withdrew into the crush of guests.

As Isabel made her way to stand again beside Catherine, something about that man continued to niggle at her. What was it that made her feel they had met before tonight? His erect carriage? His husky voice? The firm angle of his jaw? His perfectly sculpted lips?

Merciful heavens, she was looking at a stranger's mouth!

Isabel rolled her eyes in disgust at herself. She would think no more of the stranger with mouse-blond hair.

She surveyed faces in the sweltering crush around her. Gilbert's name had not appeared on the guest list, but that had not surprised Isabel. She could not imagine that his connections extended to such exalted circles as Lady Blencowe inhabited. Still, it was not uncommon for uninvited guests to intrude on fetes such as these. What if she was seen by someone who knew Gilbert was searching for her? Her uncle was capable of inventing any manner of lie to explain her escape and the need to retrieve her. Would Uncle Valfrid prevent it? Isabel wanted to trust him, but she did not know him well. Had he even sent the gold to free Robert?

"Ah, there you are," a male voice said from beside her.

It was The Stranger. A warm tingle traveled up her exposed nape.

He gestured to a slender man who accompanied him. "You were introduced to Sir Mumfry Davidson in the reception line, were you not?" Mr. Mouse-Blond Curls with the perfect mouth inquired.

She did remember meeting Sir Mumfry Davidson in the reception line. "I was."

"Mums," the persistent stranger said to Sir Mumfry, "will you please introduce me to Miss Millington? I've heard her name, and I've admired her from afar, but she will not speak to me because we've not been introduced."

"Quite proper, quite proper," the slim gentleman said. "This is what comes of skipping past the reception line,

Fullarde." His freckled face split in a grin. "Never thought you had it in you! Always one to follow rules."

He introduced Simon Fullarde to both Catherine and Isabel. "The man seldom comes to London," he declared, "and I don't remember the last time I met him at a party."

"We're delighted you decided to accept my aunt's invitation," Catherine said.

"So kind of her to think of me," Mr. Fullarde replied.

From behind the slow motion of her fan, Isabel once again found herself scrutinizing Mr. Fullarde. Were it not for all the hair—the abundant curls, the side whiskers, the thick eyebrows—he might be a strikingly handsome fellow, but it was hard to tell with so much covered. His slightly tinted spectacles obscured his eyes sufficiently to make it impossible to tell anything about them.

How could he remind her of Fox? The mouth, of course. And the height. And that narrow-hipped build. But Fox's voice was a clear, mellifluous baritone, while Mr. Fullarde's was husky. Perhaps he was a distant relative of the Tremaynes.

"I hope you will pardon my curiosity, Mr. Fullarde," she said, "but are you related to the Tremaynes?"

"Yes," Catherine chirped promptly. "Mr. Fullarde is a distant relation."

"Why, Fullarde, this comes as news. You've never said," Sir Mumfry declared with a sharp glint in his eye.

Mr. Fullarde smiled smoothly. "The connection is, as Miss Tremayne has stated, distant."

"One of Lady Blencowe's cousins married one of his cousins ages ago," Catherine said.

Sir Mumfry nodded. "Up for a hand or two of whist after dinner, old man?" he asked Mr. Fullarde, who declined.

Sir Mumfry excused himself to go find others interested in playing whist. When he was gone, Mr. Fullarde turned to Isabel.

"Your question puzzles me, Miss Smythe. Why did you ask?"

Isabel cocked her head as she regarded him. "You remind me of someone. A Tremayne."

"Ah. Might I inquire this person's name?"

"Foxton Tremayne," she said, feeling a spark of defiance at the awareness that most persons would not appreciate such a comparison.

At the softly spoken name, conversation buzzing around the trio died away. There was a sense of men and women leaning closer, listening intently for any crumb regarding the infamous outcast.

"Never met the fellow," Simon Fullarde said crisply.

"This is only the second time I've seen Mr. Fullarde," Catherine said in a rush.

What was wrong with the girl? Since Mr. Fullarde had arrived, she had become oddly gushy and breathless.

Catherine added, "That was when Fox was . . . away."

"We met in Bath. I remember the occasion well, Miss Tremayne," Fullarde said gallantly. "You were as pretty as a flower."

The buzz of conversations around them resumed.

Isabel fingered her fan, sliding her forefinger up and down the delicate, enameled pear-wood stick. Was Catherine taken with her distant cousin?

As she watched, Catherine lifted her face to smile up at Mr. Fullarde. It set an alarm ringing in Isabel, for the smile was nothing short of adoring.

Isabel stepped closer to Catherine. She gave her a surreptitious nudge with one gloved elbow.

Catherine blinked. "Oh!" she murmured, as if realizing what she had been doing.

"There will be dancing after dinner," Mr. Fullarde said. "May I reserve a dance with each of you ladies?" His gaze moved between Catherine and Isabel.

Once again, an image of Fox flashed through Isabel's mind.

"Certainly, Simon," Catherine replied, recalling Isabel from her odd thoughts.

Simon! A bit intimate. Then, he *was* Catherine's cousin. Still, they had initially appeared not to be well acquainted. Isabel's fretting over whether or not Mr. Fullarde might take ideas into his head because of Catherine's more casual form of address screeched to an abrupt halt as his request registered.

Disapproval burst into panic. "Dance?" she uttered stupidly.

Despite all those hours of dance lessons, and all her determined practice, what Isabel recalled was the awkwardness, the nervousness, the embarrassment. She thought of the times she had tripped on her hem, and worse, that hillock of mugs she had sent tumbling in the alewife's kitchen, and knew she still possessed the grace of an inebriated ox.

Making a fool of herself at a small local assembly or a party at Greenwood had been mortifying enough. The thought of committing such an atrocity here, within view of tenderhearted Catherine, Lady Blencowe, Uncle Valfrid, Mr. Fullarde, and half of London strangled the breath in her throat. The temperature in the room seemed to soar.

"Dance," Mr. Fullarde repeated. That perfect, somehow familiar mouth tilted up at the corners. "Will you dance with me after dinner?"

"Oh—I—" *No!*

At that moment, dinner was announced. Like a tide pulled by the moon, the crowd ebbed toward the dining room.

His eyes crinkled at the corners. "I'll take that as a 'yes.' Ladies, please allow me to escort you to dinner."

Fretting silently, Isabel allowed herself to be guided into the vast dining room, where several long tables had been draped in damask and set with china, silver, and German glass. When everyone had been seated, liveried footmen moved swiftly about the elegant hall, ladling, forking, and refilling.

Isabel had been seated between a bewigged elderly gentleman and a well-dressed young woman of about eighteen or nineteen years. The gentleman turned out to be hard of hearing, but good-natured. For the most part, the woman on the other side of him commanded his attention. The miss on the other side of Isabel had seen Mr. Fullarde and wanted to know more about him.

"He is quite handsome, don't you think?" she asked Isabel. "Even with those spectacles."

"He is attractive, yes." Privately, Isabel believed he could not compare to Fox. Though he did have a very fine mouth. Like Fox.

"Do you know where he's from?"

"No."

"Well, who are his people? Did he say?"

"No."

"He seems acquainted with Miss Tremayne."

"They are distant cousins."

Isabel scarcely tasted the food on her plate or the wine in her glass. All she could think of was the dancing and the humiliation yet to come.

Her gaze traveled down the table to where Catherine sat. Catherine was smiling at someone midway down the table from her. Following the direction of that smile, Isabel arrived at Mr. Fullarde, who gave his pretty cousin a nod—and a wink!

Isabel's fingers tightened on her fork. The cheek of the man! A wink indeed! And there was Catherine, smiling on Mr. Fullarde as if he had granted her fondest wish. Isabel glanced over at the baroness, who appeared to be unaware of what was going on between her niece and Simon Fullarde.

Uncertain if the situation was acceptable to Catherine's aunt or if it was being left to her to resolve, Isabel finally felt too nettled to pretend to eat. The matter must be settled now.

Excusing herself to her dinner companions, she tossed her serviette onto the seat of her chair and swept down the aisle between the long tables, dodging liveried and bewigged footmen bearing tureens, heaping platters, and bottles of wine. When she arrived at Mr. Fullarde's shoulder, he stared up at her, clearly surprised.

"A word, please, Mr. Fullarde," she said severely.

"Miss Millington! A pleasant surprise." He grinned, and her silly heart flipped.

Nonplussed, Isabel failed to answer his welcome with one of her own. Instead, she fixed him with a stern eye. "Mr.

Fullarde, you may not mind making a cake of yourself, but please do not involve Miss Tremayne in the process."

The grin fled his face. From beneath thick lashes, he checked to see if her statement had been overheard. Apparently, it had not. "A cake?"

"I've seen you winking and smiling at her. It must stop immediately." Isabel's ire over the matter skirted a little too closely to jealousy for her comfort. She wasn't jealous, of course. The mere thought was ridiculous. She scarcely knew the man.

Swiftly, he rose to his feet, towering over her. "This development is news to me," he informed her in a low voice. "We should discuss this in private."

The last thing Isabel wanted to do was anything private with Mr. Fullarde.

"That won't be necessary, sir," she informed him brusquely. "I trust you will allow your conscience to be your guide." Not that her trust would extend very far.

Taking a gentle, yet firm, grip on her elbow, he steered Isabel toward the door. "No, I believe we should discuss this."

"Really, Mr. Fullarde!" she objected in a low, indignant voice as they passed from the dining chamber into a stately corridor. "This is not necessary at all if you will behave as a gentleman toward Miss Tremayne."

He opened the door to a small sitting room, steered her inside, then closed the door behind them.

Outraged, Isabel jerked her arm from his grasp and whirled to confront him. "This is *most* inappropriate. Open that door at once!"

"Not until we've settled this," he told her mildly.

"There is nothing to settle. You've cozened Miss Tremayne into smiling like a mooncalf. She is a good girl, sir," Isabel declared. "Treat her accordingly. I'll not allow you to start people's tongues wagging. The poor darling doesn't need trouble from you. She does not deserve it!"

As her impassioned statement faded away, the only sounds in the room were the faint clatter of cutlery against dishes and the riverlike murmur of voices from down the hall. As Isabel and Mr. Fullarde stood facing each other, even those noises faded out of awareness.

"I know better than anyone she does not deserve it," he said, his baritone no longer husky, but flowing like golden magma.

Isabel stared at Simon Fullarde. Without a second thought, she went to him. When she reached up to lift away his spectacles, he made no move to stop her.

Amber eyes regarded her. They appeared a bit more brown than usual, but perhaps that came from his lashes having been darkened. For whatever reason, they remained heart-stoppingly familiar.

"Fox." Catherine had been right. He did always keep his promises.

"I told Catherine I would come. If it is within my power, I will never disappoint her."

"But at such a risk. To both of you!"

One corner of his mouth lifted in a faint, sad smile. "We know the risks."

Isabel knew she would want Rob present were she in Catherine's place. And she believed that like Fox, Rob would not have disappointed her. She could think about such things now that she hoped he was on his way from Spain.

"It seems as if you live your life in the shadows," she said.

Fox softly traced her jaw with the side of an index finger. "I might keep somewhat to the shadows, but life goes on. For the most part, my family and I are left to ourselves."

"It is not right. It is not *fair*."

"I fear those who depend upon Fate to be fair are doomed to disappointment. When is the last time you trusted Fate's mercy?"

Although it seemed like a lifetime ago, it had been less than a year since her family had fallen into genteel poverty, and little more than a month since she had discovered Gilbert's betrayal. In that time, she had undertaken actions of which she would never have dreamt when all had been right with the world. She had not trusted her future or the future of her brother to Fate, but in the end, Fate had not been entirely harsh.

"For my part," she murmured, bathing in his golden gaze, "I will not claim Fate has been merciless."

He moved closer. "A mistake, perhaps?"

"No, not a mistake. Destiny."

As carefully as if he were approaching a wild doe, Fox cupped her face in his hands. He kissed her.

Isabel's world telescoped into the warm caress of his lips across hers, the heat of his palms on her cheeks. Her eyes fluttered closed.

As Fox deepened the kiss, her blood seemed to fuse into spiced wine, and she twined her arms about his neck. Under the urging of his tongue, her lips parted.

His hands moved to her bare nape and then to her shoulders. They roamed her back.

She pressed closer as his tongue stroked hers. Her breasts tingled. In that harbor between her thighs, heat pulsed.

Against her hip she felt hard evidence of Fox's desire.

A knock sounded on the sitting room door.

As if interrupted from a deep dream, Isabel blinked. Her body moaned with disappointment.

"Out with you," Uncle Valfrid ordered through the barrier in a low bass. "I'll not have you sullying my niece's reputation."

Fox sighed softly and lowered his forehead to hers. "Your uncle is vigilant."

"So it would seem," she muttered.

"Besides," Valfrid informed them in a less formidable tone, "the musicians are tuning up. It is time to dance."

"Coming," Fox called. Then, without taking his gaze from her, he said to Isabel, "You gave me no answer before. Tell me now that you'll dance with me."

"You should dance with Catherine," she evaded.

"I shall. But I also want a dance with you."

A vision of her sprawled on the dance floor, and Fox's stunned expression, blossomed in her mind with fine, agonizing detail. Isabel swallowed dryly.

Mouse-blond eyebrows arched upward. "Have you already promised all your dances?"

"No," she croaked.

He paused as he replaced his spectacles. "Are you trying to tell me that you don't wish to dance with me?"

"Of course not."

"Then . . . ?"

Isabel wanted to dance with him, she truly did. What sensible woman would not? Dancing with him could almost certainly guarantee a tantalizing flash of mirth in those tawny eyes, or contagious laughter simmering behind an innocent curve of sculpted lips. The warm touch of his hand on hers.

"I will dance with you, Fox."

The door to the sitting room flew open, and they were confronted with a glowering Uncle Valfrid.

"I was just securing the promise of a dance," Fox told him.

Without a word, Uncle Valfrid stood aside, indicating that Fox and Isabel should exit the chamber before him.

The ballroom was an elegant hall of generous dimensions. Pink silk covered the walls, and three lead-glass chandeliers hung from a ceiling painted with frolicking classical gods and goddesses. Light from the myriad tapers in the chandeliers combined with that provided by candles in wall sconces and the silver branched candlesticks on draped refreshment tables. Their capering flames reflected in tall pier mirrors that punctuated the length of the walls, accompanied by palms in Oriental urns and benches upholstered in ivory damask. As the hall filled with the murmurous flood of guests, wineglasses, crystal beads on gowns, and jewels of every kind sparkled.

The three located Catherine and Lady Blencowe, who were surrounded by admirers seeking their pledges for the evening's dances.

Fox stepped forward to claim his sister's hand and was met with protests from would-be beaux. He smiled good-naturedly, then ignored them.

"Cousin," he said to Catherine, "you did promise me this first dance long ago."

Catherine twinkled up at her brother. "Indeed, sir, I remember the moment well. I clutched a toy elephant in one hand and my nurse's skirt in the other."

A chuckle arose from Catherine's admirers and the ladies in the group. They parted to clear the way when Fox led his sister onto the dance floor. The musicians struck up a lively country dance. Nothing that might cast a shadow onto Catherine's reputation could be permitted here this evening. That included the controversial new Continental dance. Tonight in Lady Blencowe's exquisite house, there would be no waltz.

Valfrid bowed over Lady Blencowe's hand, beating out several other well-dressed men. Isabel thought he looked quite handsome for an elderly gentleman of two-and-fifty. His thick silver hair and stylish cheek whiskers showed his blue eyes to best effect. His midnight-blue coat set off his pristine neck linen, white silk damask waistcoat, and dark gray breeches.

Lady Blencowe smiled her acceptance, then placed her gloved hand lightly upon his arm. With an answering smile that Isabel thought must have charmed all the ladies in Moscow, Valfrid led the baroness to join the other dancers.

Isabel gently excused herself from the gentlemen who asked her to partner with them on the dance floor, claiming the closeness of the room had made her quite dizzy.

She slipped up the gracious staircase. In the deserted, dimly lighted gallery on the floor above, she stood at the railing, where she watched Fox and Catherine, Lady Blencowe and Uncle Valfrid, along with the other dancers twirl and merrily promenade over the polished parquet floor.

Isabel knew the steps to this dance and probably to most of the others that would be performed this evening. As a schoolroom miss she had practiced them often enough, though there had been no pleasure in the drill. She had fretted over the all-too-excellent chance that she would stumble or bungle a step, distracted by her enjoyment of the accom-

panying music. Experience had taught her that music and
movement did not promise a happy combination for her.

Up here, she relaxed. Lady Blencowe had engaged musicians of skill, and within minutes of resting her elbows on
the balustrade's top rail, Isabel found herself tapping one
slippered foot in time to the lively melody. Below, the glittering crowd had gathered around the polished dance floor
to watch the row of men and the row of women bow and
meet, only to part again. But the hum of a multitude of conversations and the clink of wine and punch glasses indicated
the country dance under way did not possess the undivided
attention of all.

It did hold Isabel's attention. From the shadowed gallery,
she watched her uncle and friends enjoying themselves. But
mostly she watched Fox. He was taller than the other men
on the dance floor. His impeccably tailored clothing revealed his broad shoulders, flat abdomen, narrow hips, and
long, muscular legs. He moved with an athletic grace. She
could not see his expression from this distance, but she did
notice the heads of several females of all ages had turned in
his direction. A mouse-blond wig, false eyebrows, and tinted
wire-rim spectacles could not conceal his masculine magnetism.

As the dance came to an end, the women curtsied and the
men bowed to their partners and to one another. Before
Catherine could even quit the floor, she had been claimed as
a partner for the next dance. It seemed to Isabel that Uncle
Valfrid relinquished Lady Blencowe with reluctance.

With both Catherine and Lady Blencowe involved in another dance, Isabel could stay in the peaceful gallery a little
longer. She surveyed the crowd, looking for one man in particular. When she spied him, his back was toward her.

As she focused on Fox, he went still. Then he turned
around. He looked up.

TWENTY

At this distance, she could not make out Fox's expression. He abruptly turned and then headed toward the towering paneled door. When Isabel heard footsteps coming up the curved sweep of stairs, she knew to whom they belonged.

She backed away from the balustrade, out of view of those down in the ballroom. Then she marched toward the stairs, ready to return to the gathering. It would never do to be alone up here with Fox. Up here where shadows and an air of intimacy seemed to close around one like cotton wool. Here, where she would feel the full potency of his magnetism. Isabel had little faith in her powers of resistance when it came to this man.

Fox smiled and spread wide his arms, effectively blocking her from scuttling by him in unvarnished retreat.

"I'm flattered, Elf," he told her, laughter lurking in his voice. "Every man dreams of a beautiful woman rushing to greet him."

Isabel backed up one step, two steps, then caught herself. She lifted her chin, but flipped open her fan and fluttered it nervously.

"I was just leaving," she announced.

He approached her with a soft, slow tread, as if she were

a wild creature, ready for flight. "What? So soon? But I've only just arrived."

"I must resume my duty to your sister."

"My sister is dancing now. As is Diana. It is my aunt I should worry about. This is the second time she has stood up with your uncle. Catherine's reputation is quite safe for the moment."

"Very well, *my* reputation is in danger."

Mouse-blond eyebrows lifted in mock astonishment, but his advance did not falter. "Not from *me,* Miss Millington, surely?"

"From you precisely, Mr., er, Fullarde."

"You wound me, lady."

She retreated another few steps and bumped into a pedestal. The statue of a lyre player teetered dangerously. Fox reached around her to steady it.

"'Tis not my desire to injure your feelings," she told him. "You know I would never willingly hurt you."

"Heartless jade," he murmured in a low, melting voice.

Isabel felt some of her resistance seep away. "Fox, you do know I would never willingly cause you pain, do you not?" she asked earnestly.

Gently, he cupped her bent elbows in the gloved palms of his hands. "So you say," he said as he lowered his face close to hers.

She allowed him to coax her closer to his body, unable to resist her desire to be near him. Very near him. His warm hands slid up the backs of her arms to rest on her shoulders.

Her fan dropped from her gloved fingers.

"Have you come here to hide from me?" he murmured, his gaze caressing her face, to settle on her parted lips.

"Of course not." Her voice caught in an unconvincing squeak. "I wanted a moment of peace away from the crush is all."

"Then you were not trying to dodge our dance?"

"That . . . that would be . . . cheating."

His long, blunt-tipped fingers splayed against her muslin-clad back, softly flexing, setting off tiny ripples of sensation in her skin.

"Yes," he whispered. "It would."

She wanted him to kiss her. She longed for another kiss like the one they had shared in the misty temple on Frog Island. Or the sitting room downstairs. She only hoped he could not guess her thoughts, because then he might actually give her that kiss she wanted. *Needed.* So very badly. Now.

His breath stroked the crown of her head.

Isabel tried to convince herself this was neither the time nor place for kisses, yet she found herself lifting her face to his. Even as she made that small, subtle movement, a small, insistent voice within her reminded Isabel that her reputation was not the only one at risk. Indeed, *she* might be granted more leeway.

"Catherine," she croaked.

Fox closed his eyes. He drew in a long breath and released it slowly. Then, with obvious reluctance, he released Isabel. He opened his eyes and stepped back. "Catherine has a good friend in you."

Isabel nodded dumbly.

He retrieved her fan from the carpet, and slipped its silk carrying loop over her wrist. Then he took her fingertips and placed them on the back of his gloved hand. "Come. If you do not wish to dance tonight, I'll not press the issue. But you owe me a dance. Soon."

Saved from disgracing herself, relief flooded Isabel. She smiled.

By mutual agreement, she returned to the ballroom, while Fox went to the saloon where guests played cards.

Isabel threaded her way through the crowd until she located Uncle Valfrid, who was engaged in conversation with Lady Blencowe. Out on the dance floor, Catherine curtsied to a new partner.

"Why are you not dancing, my dear?" Lady Blencowe asked. "You are certainly not at a loss for partners." She eyed the men making their way toward them.

"I prefer to watch," Isabel said.

Lady Blencowe cast her an unfathomable look. "Indeed."

"Perhaps she is shy of these strangers," Valfrid said. "Will you dance with me, Niece?"

Isabel felt hunted. It appeared that she would dance, one way or the other this evening. There came a point when refusing again became just plain ill-mannered, and she guessed that point had arrived.

A liveried footman appeared to murmur a message to his mistress. Lady Blencowe replied. Then she turned to place a hand on Valfrid's coat sleeve. He leaned closer and listened to her low voice. He nodded.

Lady Blencowe caught Isabel's eye.

"Isabel, dear, please go with Meachum," she said, gesturing toward the footman.

Isabel hesitated, sensing there was something more going on.

"Run along, Niece," her uncle said with a smile.

Clearly no one was going to tell her why she was being directed to follow Meachum. She trailed behind the footman, heading once again toward the main entrance into the ballroom.

The footman led Isabel to the sitting room where Fox had kissed her. Meachum opened its door.

Still puzzled, Isabel walked inside. The door closed silently behind her.

A tall, dark-haired man stood in front of the fire, his back to the room as he gazed down into the crackling flames in the fireplace.

He wore a blue dolman and, over one shoulder, a fur-edged greatcoat of matching blue. Around his spare middle a red barreled sash topped white breeches and polished black boots. Under one arm, he carried a fur busby. A detested fur busby.

Recognition leapt through Isabel's heart.

"Rob?" His name was little more than a jolt of breath.

The man turned.

"Oh!" she sobbed. She threw herself into his arms and clung to him.

He hugged her tightly to him. Her cheek rasped against the white braid and the wool of his uniform. He laid his cheek against the crown of her head.

"God, Bel, I feared I'd seen the last of you," he said raggedly.

The grinding anxiety and cold fear that had gnawed at her these past two months eased. Into the raw void left behind bubbled a tight giddiness. Tears coursed from her clenched eyes. "You're safe."

"Thanks to you."

She looked up at him. "I was so afraid. . . ."

"You? Afraid?" He wiped her tears with his thumb. "I think not. My little sister has grown up into a beautiful, incredibly brave woman. You saved me, Bel."

"Uncle Valfrid—"

"—would not have known anything about me if *you* hadn't gotten word to him. He said as much himself in the letter to me that he sent with the ransom gold."

"He came to our aid when we needed him."

"Of a certainty. I'll not discount his part in gaining my release. Considering that he doesn't truly know us, he's been generous indeed."

"He's a good man, Rob. I think he regrets not having kept in touch with Mama and with us. He travels so much, to distant places, but he does go home to Sweden. But we can share in the fault. We should have corresponded."

Isabel studied her brother more closely now. "You are but skin and bones, Rob. Those filthy Spanish!"

"I'm alive, and I'm home in England." He gave her a lopsided grin. "Your prayers have been answered."

"Yes," she agreed wholeheartedly, "they have."

"In his letter, Uncle Valfrid repeated to me what you had told him happened after Father died. About Mother . . . pining away. And what you discovered about our dear uncle Gilbert. How you were forced to flee your own home. Dear Lord. Female, alone, and impoverished!" His lips thinned into a hard line. "I'll get him, Bel. Never you worry. I'll get the swine."

She curled her fingers over the tops of his shoulders and lightly shook him. His uniform fit him so loosely now.

He winced.

Horrified, she unbuttoned his collar, impatiently brushing

away his hands when he would stop her. She glimpsed the white cotton gauze of a wound dressing before he gathered her fingers firmly in one hand and rearranged his clothing with the other.

"You're hurt!" she accused. "Why did you say nothing? What happened?"

"I caught a bayonet in my shoulder while trying to escape this last time. It's healing, Bel, and I feel a clumsy fool, so do not make a fuss."

"Have you a salve to apply?"

He nodded.

"I would like to see it, please. You know what quacks so many of these doctors can be."

"Later."

"When was the last time your dressing was changed?"

"On the ship, as it set anchor. I just arrived in London. Bel, stop hammering at me."

"Oh," she said in a small voice.

Immediately, he was contrite. "I am sorry. It is just, well, I've been half-crazy since I received Uncle Valfrid's letter. My little sister running about England on her own. Only the fact that I had the opportunity to speak with some of the men who fought at Kurndatur kept me from going crazy with worry. I feared you had taken employment with one of the worst scoundrels in Britain's military history, but they gave me the true story."

Relief flooded Isabel. "Then you know it was the Marquess of Everleigh who was actually responsible? That his father covered it up by blaming Fox?"

"Fox?"

"I love him, Rob."

Rob sighed. "He is not a marriage catch, Bel."

Isabel made no reply.

He sighed again. "I recognize that look."

At that instant the sitting room door opened, and in strode Valfrid with Lady Blencowe.

Isabel wasn't yet ready to share Rob. There was so much to tell him, so much to hear! Instead, she settled for making introductions.

"I asked that you be escorted to a private room, Captain Millington," Lady Blencowe said, "because I believed you would not wish to make your return known until you have decided how to approach the situation with your father's brother."

Rob's expression hardened at the mention of Gilbert. "Very wise of you, Lady Blencowe. Thank you."

Isabel again noticed her brother's haggard aspect. She sent Lady Blencowe an anxious glance. The older woman acknowledged it with an almost imperceptible nod.

"I expect you might welcome a hot bath, a meal, and a soft bed, Captain Millington, after your long travails?" she queried gently.

A weary smile curved Rob's wide mouth. "With cries of gladness, ma'am."

Lady Blencowe and Valfrid chuckled.

"I shall see you in the morn," Lady Blencowe said. "Meanwhile, I'll arrange for the amenities if Isabel will be so good as to show you to the green guest chamber." At Isabel's agreement, she bade Rob sleep well, then left.

Rob turned to his uncle. "It is good to see you, Uncle Valfrid." He offered his hand. "I owe you more than I can ever repay. But I will try, sir. I will most certainly try."

Valfrid seized his nephew's hand and pulled him into an ursine hug. It was clear from what branch of the family Rob took his height. After less than a second's hesitation, Rob hugged him back with every bit as much emotion.

"You owe me nothing," Valfrid avowed in a rough voice. "You are my nephew. You and Isabel are my family. You are all I have left of Annika." The older man's eyes shut tightly for a moment. They were suspiciously moist when he abruptly opened them. Valfrid released Rob, still holding the younger man at arm's length, as if he could not bring himself to fully relinquish his only sibling's child, so nearly lost forever. "We will talk more later, eh? Now is the time for you to rest, to heal. When you are ready, we will settle with Gilbert Millington."

Rob nodded.

After another swift, fierce embrace, Valfrid released Rob, placed a kiss on Isabel's forehead, then departed.

Isabel led the way to the green guest chamber, bypassing the public areas of Blencowe House. Rob, tired as he was, seemed to take in everything, which inspired her also to notice the rich furnishings, the liveried servants, the distant melody of a country dance played on pianoforte, violins, and flutes.

"Grand, is it not?" asked Isabel with the shadow of a smile.

"Quite."

He had not seen Greenwood since it had been stripped of most of its manifold luxuries. During the cold journey from Spain, had Rob yearned for home? Isabel slipped her arm through his.

The green guest room had earned its name by the simple fact that its walls were covered in silk of a soft green hue. The upholstered satinwood side chairs and the bench at the foot of the canopied bed, as well as the draperies on the bed itself and the tall windows, were done with a heavier weight of silk in a deeper shade of green. A shaving stand complete with looking glass, porcelain ewer, and basin had been placed in one corner of the commodious space, where the natural light from the windows could be of benefit during the day. In front of the red-porphyry fireplace, where a cheerful fire burned, stood a partially filled bathtub. Beside it, a stool bore a pile of folded linen towels, topped with a cake of fine-milled soap.

"Your needs have been anticipated, Rob," Isabel said.

Even as she spoke, a footman appeared in the doorway burdened with a copper of hot water. At Isabel's nod, the man emptied the steaming contents of his copper into the tub, then left.

There were so many things she wanted to tell him, to ask him, but he looked pale and exhausted. Fortunately, he didn't look feverish. She laid her palm on his cheek. He didn't feel feverish, either. She decided that she had waited this long to be reunited with Rob, she could wait a few more days while he rested and ate his fill.

"You've been my champion," he said with a weary smile. "Are you now to be my nurse as well?"

"If I decide you need one," she replied.

Fretting over her brother's gaunt condition, Isabel went directly to the marquetry table to lift the cover off a tray. She revealed a bowl of fragrant soup, bread and butter, and slices of roasted chicken.

Under her urging, he sat down at the table. "Will you join me, Bel?"

"I've already dined, but I will bear you company as you sup." She sat in the chair across the table from him.

As if by mutual consent, they talked of trivial things as Rob slowly consumed the food on his tray. Isabel did her best to make him laugh and even succeeded two or three times. Throughout the meal, servants continued to fill the tub with hot water.

When Rob had finished the last crumb on his plate, Isabel came around the table to wish him a good night.

"I will leave you in peace now," she said, placing a kiss on his cheek. "Everything is better now that you are returned, Rob. Soon everything will be put to rights."

"We'll talk more tomorrow." Rob hugged her. "My brave little sister."

As she left his chamber, her heart felt lighter than it had in many a month.

First Isabel walked through the rooms designated for card games, but she found no sign of Fox. Returning to the ballroom, she found him waiting for Catherine, who was being escorted off the dance floor by her attractive partner.

"Rob is here," she told him. She could scarcely contain herself. "He is finally *here*!"

Before he could respond, Catherine swept up to them, breathless and merry.

"Isabel, you haven't danced once," she pointed out. "Do you not find the ball marvelous?"

"Very marvelous—"

"Then you must *dance*," Catherine exclaimed in a low voice matching Isabel's, her face alive with delight.

"My brother is here," Isabel blurted.

Catherine's eyes widened. "You've seen him?"

"I have. He looks dreadfully ill-used, but at last he is safe on English soil. We do not want this known, though, so say nothing. Gilbert must not learn Rob is home, or we will lose the element of surprise."

"My lips are sealed. How relieved you must feel!"

Isabel felt the tears she had managed to hold at bay threaten. "So relieved I believe my knees have turned to jelly."

She felt Fox's hand give her elbow a small, concealed squeeze.

Catherine clasped Isabel's hand. "You've been wondrously brave, Isabel. I much doubt *I* could have been so brave were Fox captured by the Spanish or—or . . . anyone else."

"Miss Tremayne," a smooth, unfamiliar voice behind them said, "I take it congratulations are in order."

Fox's gloved hand withdrew from Isabel's arm.

Catherine and Isabel turned as one to discover a short, slender man of approximately sixty years. His sparse blond hair was pomaded and styled à la Titus with side whiskers. A superbly tailored coat of claret superfine topped a white-on-white patterned waistcoat, a ruffled cambric shirt, and buff pantaloons. A touch of Venetian lace made an appearance at wrist and throat.

Isabel searched her memory for his face in the receiving line, but came up with a blank.

"I fear you have the advantage, sir," Catherine told him. Clearly she did not recall meeting him, either.

He performed a slight, graceful bow. With the motion, his stickpin caught the light. Isabel had never seen its like before. Nestled upon the impeccable knot of his cravat gleamed a jewel more subtle than any of the diamonds, emeralds, or sapphires worn by the baroness's guests this evening, and far more costly: a black pearl.

"I am come late to your little entertainment," he said.

Lady Blencowe arrived, her lovely face as set and as impassive as a marble statue's. "Lord Kymton," she murmured, her words civil, but lacking her ususal warmth.

Isabel felt Catherine stiffen beside her.

So, this was the powerful Hugo Foss, Duke of Kymton. Before her conversation with Fox, the peer had been only a title and a name to Isabel, though one associated with dark rumor. Now she knew not all of it was rumor.

From behind the leisurely movement of her fan, she studied him as one studied a venomous snake: with caution.

"Lady Blencowe." Kymton's full lips almost curved into a smile. "My invitation seems to have gone astray."

Was that the suggestion of a hiss Isabel heard?

"I did not presume to believe you would interest yourself in my humble gathering," Lady Blencowe replied coolly.

"Perhaps not usually, but in this dull time of year one suffers a pall of boredom. Any diversion finds welcome."

"Why, thank you, Your Grace."

No one with an ounce of perception could miss Lady Blencowe's displeasure. It appeared to amuse the duke.

Kymton chuckled. "You know very well your reputation for stimulating diversions, Lady Blencowe. No person of discernment would miss one of your salons. Even your musicales are much talked of for days afterward, and I do so abhor musicales."

"You flatter me," Diana said, not appearing the least bit flattered.

"Will you introduce me to these charming ladies?" It was not a request.

Diana regarded him steadily for a moment. Tension strummed the air. From those around them, Isabel heard a nervous cough, the shuffling of feet.

Briskly, Diana performed the introductions.

The Duke of Kymton deigned to bow. Isabel and Catherine gave him the acceptable abbreviated curtsy.

"Lovely," he murmured absently, scrutinizing them one at a time through a beribboned quizzing glass. Finally he concentrated his ice-blue gaze on Catherine. "So. This is the sister of the infamous Traitor Tremayne."

Isabel—and several other guests—gasped at the man's audacity. Tension radiated off Fox, sending a prickle along her skin.

"Perhaps, sir," Lady Blencowe told Kymton icily, "you would prefer to play cards rather than slash a young woman's sensibilities."

He glanced up at her. "No." His voice was pitched so that only those closest to him might hear. Then his lips curved upward, parting to reveal a missing canine. "You see, I am conducting an experiment."

Lady Blencowe did not oblige him by inquiring about his undertaking, and he looked faintly annoyed.

"Are you not curious as to the nature of my little project?" he finally asked.

"I cannot think I will approve."

"No, perhaps not," he agreed. "I intend to see how many generations can be made to suffer for one man's mistake."

The musicians struck up the jaunty melody of a country dance.

Lady Blencowe seemed not to hear. "Who, may I ask, has made the mistake?"

"Why, your nephew, of course."

The bow of Lady Blencowe's mouth tightened. "Lord Kymton, we both know he made no mistake."

"Oh, but he did."

Catherine casually took a step closer to Isabel, so that both of them stood between Fox and Kymton.

Lady Blencowe appeared as composed as the duke. "I cannot imagine what that might be."

Kymton examined the lace at one wrist. "He aspired to foolishly high moral standards, and, somehow, he infected my son with his beliefs." A throbbing vein in his forehead belayed his casual tone. "The infection has turned my son from me. This I cannot, will not, forgive." He shrugged. "Since I cannot find Tremayne himself, I am left with no choice but to vent my displeasure on his sister and, eventually, her husband and children."

Isabel stared at him. How could this one, rather ordinary-looking man possess such monstrous evil?

"Thoughtless of my nephew, to be a moral and courageous officer." Lady Blencowe's fan moved with warning briskness.

Kymton's eyes narrowed. "He caused me more trouble than I expected. And that colonel of his. Monmercy or some such name. He wrote letters, sent messengers to the governor. A veritable champion for the ill-accused." He smiled. "His career went the way of your nephew's. Last I heard, he was working off his passage to Georgia as a common sailor." His smile slithered into a grin. "How the mighty fall."

Lady Blencowe made no reply.

"Where has Tremayne taken himself? I've heard nothing of him since he became bankrupt."

"He has gone where you cannot reach him."

Kymton mimicked a look of surprise. "Indeed? He is dead, then?"

"No."

"Ah, America then." He shrugged. "No matter." He inclined his head toward her. "Your servant, madam."

He turned toward the saloon where guests played cards.

Isabel heard gusty exhalations and realized she had been holding her breath. She glanced quickly up at Fox. His disguised features revealed nothing of what must be churning in his mind, but a muscle jumped in his jaw.

Before the duke could move away from them, a woman's indignant exclamation and an earnest, if slurred, "Sorry!" heralded the appearance of a tall, expensively attired man.

Isabel guessed him to be in his thirties. Mussed blond hair and disheveled cravat and collar points framed a face that bore a striking resemblance to Kymton's.

"You couldn't leave them alone, could you?" he demanded of the duke. "By God, I didn't believe it when Byrd told me you were coming here!"

"Lower your voice," Kymton ordered.

Guests in the immediate area again fell silent. They turned toward the two men.

The younger, inebriated fellow took a step forward, towering over the duke, his hands bunched into fists at his side. "Damn your eyes!"

"Lady Blencowe's gathering offered a diversion tonight," Kymton said casually. He withdrew a snuffbox from his coat pocket. "You know how dull Town is this time of year. Oh. I *am* sorry. I forget you cannot be bothered to stay out of the brandy decanter long enough to interest yourself in the workings of your country's government."

Now the only sounds in the vast chamber were a few voices on the far side, near the dance floor and the music.

"Unlike you," the other sneered, "I haven't desired to learn every minister's, admiral's, and general's dirty secrets."

A dangerous light glittered in the duke's pale blue eyes. "Silence," he hissed.

The younger man locked gazes with Kymton for a long moment. Then his face spasmed in self-fury. He whirled and fled, sending stately company scrambling from his path. The door out of the ballroom thundered shut.

Abruptly, everyone found something other than the duke at which to look. Conversations did not fully resume until Kymton departed the ballroom.

Lady Blencowe betrayed nothing of her true reaction to the startling scene that had just played out before them. "I really must start posting a few large footmen outside the front door when I entertain," she muttered.

Valfrid made his way to them from the dance floor. "What did I miss?" he asked. "I heard angry voices."

The baroness closed her fan. "You just missed a confrontation between the Duke of Kymton and his son and heir, the Marquess of Everleigh."

Catherine's eyes met Isabel's. Everleigh.

Neither spoke, surrounded as they were by persons only too eager to hear what they might say regarding that which had transpired. The confrontation between the duke and his son that had played out in Lady Blencowe's elegant ballroom on the night of her niece's introduction to Society would be savored over tables and tea trays around London for no less than a sennight.

And by tomorrow morning, everyone in Town would know that Miss Catherine Tremayne was not only the sister of the notorious former captain, but the particular target of a powerful man's displeasure.

The Duke of Kymton had begun his experiment.

TWENTY-ONE

Isabel followed Fox from the ballroom, slipping out of the closing doors behind him.

She motioned to the servant for her pelisse as soon as Fox had been given his greatcoat and left to await his carriage. In the shadows outside, she shivered until his equipage was brought around, and he stepped into it. Then she darted from her concealment, following on his heels.

She entered the carriage behind Fox. The footman closed the door behind her without a word, then took his place on the back of the carriage.

Fox sat back against the squabs in lethal silence. The vehicle jolted into motion, rattling over the stone pavement.

"May I inquire what you are doing here?" he finally asked.

"I thought to speak with you."

"Then speak. Have your say so that I can take you back to Blencowe House. Catherine will need you now more than ever."

"She needs you also." Isabel shivered.

With a sigh of resignation, Fox drew one of the lap rugs around her, tucking the rug up around her shoulders.

"Why are you not wearing your warmers?" he grumbled.

"I am."

His hands stilled. He eased back into the squabs.

Isabel noticed his withdrawal. "What is wrong in my wearing warmers?"

"Nothing wrong in wearing them," he said, adjusting his coat. "However, *thinking* about your warmers, about how you look in them, what they . . . cover, is."

"Oh."

The single breathless word was all she could manage. The thought of Fox thinking about her wearing her warmers . . . the pale, shimmering, pink silk sliding against the bare flesh of her hips . . . her thighs . . . her buttocks. The secret place that grew warm when he kissed her, when he held her . . .

"Oh," she croaked.

A streetlamp cast a quick caress of light across Fox's lower face. Those lips, those perfectly sculpted, masculine lips burst into her view, then vanished into the dark that wrapped around Isabel and Fox like black satin.

"Why did you come here, Isabel?" His rich baritone lapped at her from across the darkness.

"After the duke made known his experiment . . . I thought you might need someone now."

"Might need someone for what purpose?" His tone was as hard as a diamond.

As he had stood behind her in the ballroom, she had sensed the tension radiating from him. She felt it still, that barely leashed fury.

She had not thought when she followed him from the ballroom. She had simply acted on instinct. He needed her; Isabel knew he did. She felt it in her gut. She felt it her heart. But in the presence of this remote Fox, uncertainty assailed her.

"I ask you again, Miss Millington: For what purpose might I need someone now?"

"To—to bear you company?"

"I need no company."

"Yes, you do," she insisted. "Lord Kymton has done you damage. You have done nothing to restrain his abuse of power, and now he proposes to bring trouble to Catherine."

"I'll tell you what I do *not* need now, and that is a sharp-tongued female who knows nothing of the full extent of that monster's power."

"Sharp-tongued I may be, Fox," she admitted—at least for now. "I own I do not know precisely how powerful the duke is, but I know that you are an intelligent, resourceful, strong-willed man with a strong sense of right and wrong. A man with some useful skills. What you need is—"

She heard a rustle of movement, caught the scent of sandalwood. Fox sat close beside her, placing one arm across the cushions, brushing her shoulders.

"What I need *now,*" he said in a low, rumbling purr that stirred the tendrils of hair at her temple, "is a sympathetic woman."

His enveloping presence turned her breathless and edgy. She strove to discern his features, but his face remained indistinguishable. In the darkness, there remained only smell, sound, and touch.

"I am not . . . unsympathetic," she replied.

"Ah, but that is not at all the same. Here. Let me show you."

He leaned his body closer. Butterflies scrambled to flight in her belly.

His lips grazed the edge of her ear with the impact of a sigh. Isabel struggled to keep from melting.

"Is a sympathetic woman expected to accept this . . . ear thing? Or is she required to . . . to perform it?" she asked, her voice acquiring a squeak near the end.

"Both. But there is more."

"More?" she echoed faintly.

She felt the kid leather of one gloved fingertip on her chin. He turned her face toward him.

With uncanny accuracy, he set his lips over hers.

Hunger drove his kiss. Hunger and rage.

Isabel flattened her palms against his shoulders. His embrace tightened.

She shoved at him. He pressed his lips more firmly against hers, his breathing labored. Hard evidence of his arousal pressed against her thigh.

"No," she mumbled into his mouth. "Let me go."

There was something other than desire for her in his rough actions. She did not intend that their passion and his anger should become tangled.

She turned her head from his. He caught her jaw in a firm grasp and turned her face back to his.

"Release—!"

His mouth cut off her demand.

She bit him.

He jerked away, cursing.

She sprang to the other side of the compartment, where she fumbled to gain her bearings. Then she pressed against the farthest wall, her chest heaving.

"Bloody hell," he exclaimed. "I believe I'm bleeding!"

"Good," she snapped.

"Good?"

"I'll not be manhandled just because you are in a temper."

"Oh! So you would not mind my so-called manhandling if I were not in a temper?"

"There was nothing 'so-called' about it. And I told you to release me. You ignored me!"

Furious, she groped her way to where he still sat, hauled back her arm, and then slapped him for all her worth. Her open palm connected with his cheek and jaw.

He received her blow with a grunt.

She scuttled back to the far side of the other seat to nurse her smarting hand.

"Damn, woman, could you not have pulled your punch?" he complained.

"Be glad I did not kick you as well," she told him, her voice shriller than she had intended.

"Cap'n? Cap'n Tremayne?" the coachman called. "Is all well wi' ye?"

Fox did not immediately reply. "Is all well with us now?" he inquired politely of Isabel.

"It is *not*," she informed him primly, relaxing enough to sit. She hesitated.

"But that is not your driver's worry."

"Cap'n?" came the coachman's voice.

"All is well, Ben."

"Aye, sir."

Isabel and Fox rode in silence for several minutes.

"Isabel—" he began.

"I will not be your whipping boy!"

"You are entirely correct. I apologize for my brutish behavior." There was a humble note in his voice Isabel had never before heard.

"I should hope so." She tugged her skewed pelisse and gown back into place. She hoped.

"Well, I do," he said.

Isabel nodded, then realized he could not see her in the dark.

"The next man who grabs me," she said clearly, "receives something heavy over the head."

"Who else has grabbed you?" he growled.

"Gilbert."

He muttered an oath.

"I was distressed for you, Fox. *That* is why I intercepted you. With England so involved with stopping Napoleon, it is missing a malignancy breeding in its own bosom." She moved to the edge of her seat. When Fox did not reply, she continued. "You have the skills and resources to prevent Kymton from hurting Catherine. You've been perfecting them for the last three years with lesser villains like my uncle."

"Or I could take Catherine with me to live in the United States of America."

Isabel stared into the dark. "You would run? You might be the only one capable of stopping Lord Kymton, and you would run away?"

No reply issued from the other side of the passenger compartment.

His lengthening silence seemed to refute her disbelief.

No, she thought. *This man is no coward.*

"I am not a coward," he said, as if he had read her thoughts. "But neither am I a fool. Isabel, I've had a taste of what Kymton can do. One day I was the son of a respectable, landed family with a good military career. The next day I was spat upon in the street, dishonored and penniless. The only friends who did not slam their doors in my face were those who had known me in India. A rare few who knew me before even that: Etienne and Tsusga. Most did not want to risk association with me."

Isabel plucked up the lap blanket that had fallen on the floor. She wrapped herself in it, suddenly more chilled than ever.

"Time has stopped for you, Fox," she said, misery pressing against her heart. "You dwell in the past."

"Do not say that."

Raw with grief for the man she had come to love, Isabel forged on. "Oh, Fox, you have surrounded yourself with it. The people with whom you associate. The widows and children you support—yes, I know about them. Nottage told me. 'Tis a noble thing, but they, too—or rather their husbands—are associated with a time before your misfortune. You live in an old house in the most isolated place I have seen. Have you been seeking to escape the notice of the authorities, the Duke of Kymton . . . or the present?"

"Damn you, this is all rubbish. I live in Willow Hall because—I don't have to explain my decisions to you. Why are you even here? Do you not have an evil uncle to prosecute?"

"Yes, one you tricked. Gilbert is no fool, yet you tricked him, Fox."

"And robbed you and your brother in the process! Oh, but I make an excellent god of retribution, do I not? Sorry, my dear, but that dog will not hunt."

"Kymton took you unawares. You were an innocent in the ways of such a creature, but now you are stronger and wiser. You've honed the skills your Indian friend taught you. You have people who will stand by you."

A bitter bark of laughter burst from the dark. "Someone stood by me three years ago, and look where he is now. Swabbing the decks of a ship for the price of passage."

"You also have someone who . . . cares for you," she said hoarsely.

"I thought I had someone who cared for me then, too."

Isabel felt as if she had been slapped. "Did you . . . did you love her?"

Outside, the clatter of hooves against paving stones echoed in the snow-laden street.

"At the time, I thought I did."

She waited for him to offer something more. Something more relevant to the past several weeks. Her hands crushed fistfuls of blanket as Isabel struggled to breathe silently.

But Fox offered no further word.

Finally she spoke. Each word felt as if it weighed a ton upon numb lips.

"Please return me to the ball."

After returning to his quarters from Catherine's ball, Fox sat at the dressing table occupied by an organized array of covered jars, pots, and small boxes. He glared into the look-ing glass without really seeing the face of Simon Fullarde minus his spectacles and with a swath of different skin tone striped across his forehead. A blotch of Simon's slightly dif-ferent color resided on the cloth forgotten in Fox's hand.

Bastard!

His fists sat on the edge of the table. It took no small re-straint to keep from driving them into the silvered glass in a fit of rage.

That puffed-up, skulking, *evil* bastard.

He meant to ruin Catherine. Lovely, intelligent, sweet-natured Catherine, who had never hurt so much as a fly.

Catherine had already been made to pay once for the ac-cident of Fox's being in the same company as Everleigh.

Catherine, I am sorry.

She had lived like an outcast, away from the company of her peers, but at least she had remained safe. Now that Kym-ton had decided to conduct his hellish experiment, Fox could not be certain that even isolation on Frog Island would protect his sister.

Catherine had not been the only one made to pay. Colonel Montgomery had not come of a wealthy family. His career had been all that he had.

Isabel had been right. Tsusga, 'Tienne, Croom, and Nottage had been right. And, of course, Diana. His wise aunt was a good judge of people.

Only Isabel, however, had left him feeling so raw. She made it sound as if he were neglecting his patriotic duty by refusing to try to bring Kymton down. Indeed, to hear her tell it, Fox Tremayne was the only man in the kingdom who *could* bring Kymton down. Ha! Besides, what did he owe this country that had turned its back on him? If he took Catherine to North Carolina, that would be the end to the matter. He could make a new start, and Catherine would be safe.

Trapped in time. She had told Fox that he was trapped in the past. That rankled. He was simply being cautious, that was all. If those he had chosen to trust happened to be persons he had known before Kurndatur, it was nothing more than coincidence. After all, he had not known *her* before the battle. . . .

He sat in front of the mirror for a long time, thinking.

The following morning, several guests, who had traveled to Blencowe House from their estates outside London to attend the ball, joined Lady Blencowe, Catherine, Valfrid, and Isabel to break their fast.

Isabel had already gone to see Rob. To her relief, his color had improved, and he appeared less haggard. His uniform fit too loosely, but, as Lady Blencowe had told her, time and good food would remedy the matter. That and the tailor Valfrid had summoned, making his selection from a list provided by Lady Blencowe.

Isabel could not help but notice how often her uncle and Lady Blencowe sought each other's opinions, and how content they were with the responses they received. In truth, Isabel believed they made an attractive couple.

As she watched them together, the wound of Fox's refusal pained her afresh. Oh, she understood his reasons for deciding to emigrate to the former colonies rather than undertake the perilous office of avenging angel. Kymton must possess some interesting enemies in America if, as he had admitted the previous night, he could not touch Fox there.

Isabel sighed. More lay at stake in the matter than a young woman's social success. The Duke of Kymton possessed no ethics—a distinct disadvantage in an adversary. Doubtless, with his resources, he would uncover Fox's investment schemes, which would open Fox and his partners in fraud to severe consequences.

Such as the noose.

Perhaps she expected too much. He had, after all, endured so much injustice.

Yet, Fox, with his lion's heart, his intelligence, and his innate nobility, had not only captured the admiration of those who actually knew him, but he also anonymously supported other victims of Lord Everleigh's misplaced faith. In addition, he had managed to extract a handsome living from the fleecing of villains. Of course, the lucre he accrued might, in fact, have ultimately come from nefarious acts perpetrated on the innocent. Her family had been just such innocents.

Isabel had given the matter much thought in the sleepless nights since Fox had revealed the truth to her. She had been forced to come face-to-face with realities she had managed to avoid until now. The realization of just how sheltered most of her life had been came as an unpleasant awakening, one she would have fervently wished to avoid.

If only she had never stepped into the Blue Dragon's private dining room in her wrinkled blue gown, queasy with anxiety.

If only Fox had not been so kind. So beautiful, so clever, so caring.

A hiccup of laughter caught in her throat. If only she had not seen that *silly* duck waddling lovingly after him.

If only she had not lost her heart to him.

In the soul-shriving solitude of night, Isabel had come face-to-face with the fact that she and her family had been victims long before Gilbert had chosen to invest with Mr. Syer.

Isabel picked at a spicy, wedge-shaped roll on her plate, finding little appetite for it or the kippered herrings, which seemed to stare at her with their tiny black eyes.

To her mind, no one was better equipped than Fox to

bring Kymton low enough to make it impossible for the duke to inflict further damage on his fellow man. Which included Catherine.

She swallowed against the thickness of tears, willing the moisture to dry before mortifying her by dropping down her cheeks.

He planned to run away.

Liveried footmen entered the room with the morning's newly arrived correspondence. Silver salvers piled with notes and invitations were presented to Lady Blencowe and her guests.

The tray delivered to Catherine, who ought to have been the toast of London and in demand by hostesses, bore only two envelopes.

Isabel squelched the urge to reach out to her friend, who stared at the nearly empty salver. Catherine swallowed. Then she accepted the envelopes with quiet dignity, thanking the footman, who looked as if he were torn between weeping for her and charging out to extract revenge. To his credit, he nodded, then turned to stalk out of the dining parlor.

On a quiet sigh, Isabel told herself the time would come for comforting after Lady Blencowe's other guests had taken their leave. Judging by the rate at which many excused themselves from the table, that would not be long.

In the meantime, it seemed as if Isabel would not be left to push her food around her plate, for Valfrid leaned toward her and informed her in a low voice that Rob expected them in his chamber.

At Uncle Valfrid's knock, Rob bade them enter. They found him dressed in his uniform—the only suit of clothes he yet owned—and seated at a small table beside the cheery fire, drinking coffee. He rose as they entered.

"Let me say again, Rob, you appear better rested than you did last night," she told him.

"It was the shock of lying down in a real bed. It stunned me to sleep."

Isabel hugged Rob. "I am so relieved you are home, safe and sound."

Rob chuckled as he hugged her back. "As am I."

"I will be leaving with you and Uncle Valfrid," she announced, the weight in her heart growing heavier still. "This morning, before we broke our fast, Lady Blencowe and Catherine told me of their decision to return to Willow Hall before Kymton has the chance to do more harm to Catherine. As I was at Greenwood when Gilbert committed his crimes, perhaps I can be of some help to you."

Rob brightened. "Bel, that's splendid!"

"And now we must decide how to retrieve your inheritance," Valfrid said to them both as he drew out a chair for Isabel.

An hour later, the three left Rob's chamber. After much discussion, it had been decided that approaching the justice of the peace who held Greenwood in his jurisdiction might be a mistake. Since taking up residence in the mansion, Gilbert had not lost any opportunity to ingratiate himself with the man. Instead, they would retain a London lawyer to advise them. Doubtless Lady Blencowe's steward could give them the name of the finest lawyer in Town. They would call on the fellow on their way out of London.

The following morning, they found Lady Blencowe and Catherine in the south saloon, a lofty, graciously appointed room. On a green-and-gold-striped upholstered sofa with a delicate gilded frame, the baroness and her niece sat together murmuring to each other. Today, Catherine had received no invitations.

Neither Valfrid, Rob, nor Isabel inquired where all the guests had gone. Rob went to Lady Blencowe, whom he had met the evening before, and bowed.

"Lady Blencowe, your generous hospitality has afforded me the first good night's rest I've had since my capture. My deepest thanks."

"We are all happy you are returned to England, Captain Millington," she replied with a smile. "I am sorry you are leaving us. You are all welcome to accompany us to Willow Hall."

"You are generous."

Lady Blencowe stroked her niece's arm in a comforting

gesture. "We have grown attached to Isabel and Valfrid, and we would enjoy the opportunity to further our acquaintance with you."

Rob bowed over Catherine's hand. "By all rights, you should be the toast of London, Miss Tremayne."

Isabel's heart went out to Catherine as the young woman smiled bravely up at Rob. "You are too kind, sir." She reached out to Isabel, who took her hand in her own. "You are fortunate in your sister, Captain Millington, and I am fortunate in my dearest friend. Were I a writer, I would pen a novel of her intrepid exploits." Her smile widened. "I am certain it would sell well." The smile wavered. "I shall miss her."

"And I, you, Catherine," Isabel said thickly.

She gave Catherine's hand a little squeeze, struggling to ignore the emotion that knotted in her throat. The inhabitants of Willow Hall had grown dear to her. Catherine had become the sister Isabel had always wanted.

And where was Fox now? Did he even know that she would leave London this day? She swallowed hard against her tears.

"What do you propose to do?" Rob asked Catherine.

Lady Blencowe spoke for her. "We have an option or two to consider. But for the moment, I believe we need some cheering music. Let us send you on your way in better spirits."

She rose from her place on the couch and beckoned her niece to rise as well. "Play for us, Catherine. Some new sheets of music arrived two days ago, and I am longing to hear them played on the pianoforte." The baroness took Rob's elbow and guided him and Catherine to the elegant pianoforte. From the bench, she removed several music sheets and thrust them into Rob's hands. "Will you turn the pages for Catherine, Captain Millington?"

"It will be my pleasure," Rob replied gallantly. He took his place, standing beside Catherine.

As Catherine's slender fingers moved upon the keyboard, a cheerful, three-quarters-time melody filled the saloon. It could not have been more alien to their mood, which was,

Isabel thought as she noticed Catherine's glistening eyes, probably wise.

Valfrid asked Lady Blencowe to dance. The two of them presented a handsome sight as they bowed and twirled, Isabel decided. She watched them with a smile fixed upon her face, surrendering to the numbness she had fought since her parting with Fox night before last.

The next tune was a waltz, and it was decided that Valfrid and Lady Blencowe would dance it before taking over at the pianoforte so that Rob and Catherine might have a dance or two.

As the music and dancing lifted moods, Isabel slipped unnoticed from the saloon. She made her way down the hall, remembering how Fox had wanted to dance with her, and how her fear of making a cake of herself had kept her from accepting.

She ought not to accuse him of cowardice when it ruled her own life in so many ways.

A hand shot out and grasped her arm, drawing her into a room lined with packed bookshelves and furnished with leather-upholstered wingback armchairs. Thin January sunlight crept through partially pulled draperies, illuminating the chamber with a shadowed half-light.

It might have been midnight-dark, and she would have recognized that masculine scent, that sweet caress of breath against her skin.

Fox leaned against the closed door as he held her in his arms.

Through the walls, and through the saloon's open door, the music swirled its way into the library.

Her ear laid against his chest, Isabel found the only music that interested her was that of Fox's rapidly beating heart.

He lowered his head to kiss the top of hers. "Dance with me."

"No," she replied automatically. These might be her last minutes with him. She refused to mar them with her lack of grace.

He pressed her nearer. "Dance with me, Isabel," he whispered close to her ear, sending a shiver of delight through her.

She found herself nodding as her gaze moved over every dark-obscured detail of his beloved face.

In an instant, he swept her into a waltz. Surely he should not hold her so close, she thought distantly as she was seized by a heady euphoria.

It did not matter, she realized. She did not care what might be proper. Not with Fox. Never again with Fox. For they had only this moment left together.

Isabel loved him with all her heart. She did not expect to ever again love a man as she did Fox. But he had made his decision, and she had made hers. He would go to America to escape the destructive poison spewed by that deadly spider, Kymton. She would stay to fight alongside her brother to regain their inheritance. Or what might be left of it.

She inhaled deeply, wanting to impregnate her every sense with the essence of Fox Tremayne. O glorious male! Honorable, brave, beautiful man.

Here in this shadowed room lined with rows of books, she held him in her arms. For now, he was hers.

To her amazement, her feet moved in perfect time with his, following their direction. She smiled up at him as she swayed, feeling, for the first time in her life, like a swan gliding over glassy water.

He smiled down at her, looking as entranced as she felt.

His heel bumped against a chair leg, jostling them both. He apologized as they moved back into the dance.

"You dance well," he said. "Why did you refuse me?"

"I dance well with *you*. Usually I am not so . . ."

"Comfortable?" he supplied. "Confident?"

He collided with the corner of a library table. "I *am* sorry. Normally I'm a bit more—"

"Graceful?" she supplied.

He trod upon the hem of her gown and bit back an oath. "Coordinated, I was going to say. I know not what has gotten into me."

"Think nothing of it," she told him easily as her slippered

feet glided over the polished wood floor. "Happens to the best of us."

He muttered a response, then spun her into a wide arc, circling, circling, until she began to grow a bit dizzy.

"Enough," she laughed. "Enough."

He slowly came to a stop in the middle of the chamber. "No," he rumbled softly, lowering his face to hers.

Fox brushed her parted lips with his. "Never enough, Isabel. I will never have enough of you."

His kiss gave her more pleasure than the most exquisite confection she had ever tasted, than the most stirring horse ride of her life, thrilling her at the same time it sent whorls of heat curling through her body. "Mmm."

His lips now moved more slowly, his tongue delving, stroking, driving the kiss deeper and deeper. So deep her breasts ached for more. A pulse took life between her thighs.

His skin warmed under her touch. Her breathing matched his, filling her ears along with the quickened beat of her heart.

"Isabel," he whispered, dropping kisses on her forehead, on her cheeks. "Dear God, I love you."

His ardent words sent her heart soaring.

"Oh, Fox. I have loved you since . . ."

He paused amid his kisses. "Since when?"

She smiled. "Since I saw you with Oscar."

"You love me for my *duck*?"

She chuckled and dropped a tongue-teasing kiss on his throat, above his cravat. "No, my silly man. I love you for many reasons, but the devotion Oscar shows for you, your act of kindness in saving him . . . what woman could resist?"

He moaned softly as her lips caressed his warm throat. "I can think of a few."

"Fools," she muttered.

Fox splayed his hand across the small of her back. "Lucky for you, eh?"

She nipped his flesh, careful not to inflict real pain, and he laughed.

With one hand, he loosened his cravat, then tossed it aside. "I love you, Isabel." He pressed his lips to the curve between her shoulder and neck. "I love you." His mouth moved to the base of her throat. "I love you."

Isabel tilted back her head, her fingers in Fox's hair, adrift in a turbulent convergence of happiness and desire.

Lips and tongue and teeth lowered to the cleft between her breasts. She drew a shuddering breath.

"Marry me, Isabel," he urged. "Marry me."

Isabel found it impossible to focus with his fingers brushing her nipple, found she didn't want to focus, didn't want to think beyond his touch and his proposal.

"Yes," she whispered. "Yes!"

They would be together always.

Then he wrapped her in his arms and wielded his mouth and hands and body with lightning skill. She yielded to the tidal rush of passion, to the explosions of sensation that eclipsed all time and reason.

When at last they lay panting and disheveled on the library table, Isabel snuggled deeper in Fox's arms.

"You will love North Carolina, Elf," he murmured. "We'll build a handsome house from which we can watch sunsets and our children playing in the gardens."

Minutes later, his breathing assumed the regular pattern of sleep.

Gently, Isabel eased from his embrace. For a long time, she gazed upon his slumbering figure. She drank in the beloved details of his face: the lock of golden brown hair over his forehead; the curve of thick, bronze-colored eyelashes against his cheek; the shape of his sweet, sweet mouth.

He had not changed his mind after all. Fox would take Catherine to safety in America, where Kymton would not follow.

Isabel rejoiced for Catherine, relieved that her friend would escape the duke's malice.

But Isabel grieved for Fox . . . and for herself.

Until he could face down the betrayal and horror of what had happened in India, it would continue to haunt him, casting a shadow over every decision he made.

Fox loved her, of that Isabel had no doubt. But how long

before the simmering rage over the betrayal and treachery he had suffered, in India and then in England, showed itself in North Carolina? Would Fox withdraw, building that wall around his heart again? What if Kymton found a way to reach Fox in his new home?

Nothing had been resolved, and it seemed to Isabel that once Fox was in America nothing ever would be.

As she quietly closed the library door behind her, her fingers trembled on the brass knob.

She would miss him every day for the rest of her life.

TWENTY-TWO

It was an early-March night with a new moon, heavy with stygian gloom. Mist swirled about them like starving wraiths. With a solicitous Tsusga at his elbow, Fox, in his guise as Uriah Syer, hobbled toward the offices of Leopold Ames, Esquire, the only visible evidence of a building being the feeble flame of a lamp. It was here that the investors whom Fox had gathered with exquisite care—and not a little pleasure—were to have their final secret meeting. Gilbert Millington was one investor. The other was the Duke of Kymton.

Gilbert Millington had been easily enticed to invest again with Mr. Syer, particularly after Isabel and her brother had failed in their suit to charge their uncle with embezzlement. Clearly, Greenwood was Rob's, but it was a mansion stripped of most of its furnishings, and an estate barren of funds to make necessary repairs and improvements.

Gilbert, like Kymton, had not been made to pay for his crimes, and, consequently, was free to continue committing them.

Tempting the Duke of Kymton had required somewhat more finesse, but the excitement of defying upstanding morality and the lure of rich returns to replenish his diminished private coffers had done their work.

The rest of the group, using various disguises, were, of course, members of the Assembly. In all, the exclusive gathering numbered seven, counting Tsusga, Fox, and Reginald Padbury, a member of the Assembly who had been a lieutenant under Fox in India. Reggie was the son of a gentleman driven into bankruptcy through the devices of a corrupt banker and his conspirator, a lawyer. His father had taken his own life over the humiliation. After that, Reggie had made a point of learning the lawful practices of both professions. Now he often played the part of a lawyer or a banker—most convincingly—during operations. Leopold Ames was but one of his personae.

Nearly two months ago, the night of Catherine's ball, Fox had begun to envision an operation that would topple the Duke of Kymton. That man had threatened Catherine, had even threatened the children she might eventually bear.

Europe and most of the rest of the world had grown accustomed to arrogance and corruption, and thus tolerated them. Kymton operated successfully out of many countries. There was only one place where Fox's sister might be relatively safe from Kymton's reach: the United State of America, particularly the state of North Carolina, where Kymton's arrogance and dirty dealing had angered too many who had come to power. They had not forgotten their old enemy.

Tonight was part of Operation Plum Pit, the proposal for which had received astonishing enthusiasm from the Assembly. Fox wished Isabel were here beside him tonight. She had been right about his desire, his need to extract justice from Kymton. And maybe she had also been right when she had told him that he might be the best man for the job of bringing about that justice.

But she had left him. She had agreed to be his wife and then walked away. It had taken time for Fox to admit it, but perhaps Isabel had done the wisest thing. That morning, that night, that sennight, he had not been certain of anything. Even now he had his moments of doubt.

When his head and his heart had cleared enough for him to see sense, he had realized that this might be his only chance to broadside Kymton. Political events might never again present such an opportunity. And while Catherine might be safe in North Carolina now, there was no guarantee the situation would continue. Then there was the matter of Fox's other relations and friends, who could not or would not emigrate to America. Deprived of his two prime targets, would he go after them?

The fog muffled the shriek of the wrought-iron gate as Tsusga swung it aside. They proceeded up the brick walkway to the front door.

After Tsusga rapped out the agreed-upon code-knock, the door opened to them. There stood Reggie, attired in the dark broadcloth and wool of a respectable country lawyer, complete with a plain, white neck cloth and gray bagwig.

"Ah, good evening, Mr. Syer, Mr. Lonepine. Everyone is here."

"Excellent, excellent," Fox said in his rusty voice. "Thank you, Mr. Ames," he added as Reggie helped him out of his box coat and then hung it on one of the pegs by the door, along with the other, more elegant, cloaks and coats.

Fox and Tsusga followed Reggie down a hall to a commodious chamber featuring a long mahogany table and a sideboard decked with full decanters and glasses that sparkled in the candlelight. Around the table sat three men and one woman. Two of them were members of the Assembly disguised as investors of means.

"Mrs. Blue," Fox said with a creaky bow to the sole woman, whose flawless skin, quality gown, and perfectly matched pearls marked her as a lady.

Everyone in the room accepted that Mrs. Blue was an assumed name. In addition, the two genuine investors had been carefully led to believe that she was a member of the Scottish nobility.

"You're in fine looks this evening, ma'am," Mr. Syer added.

She gave him a regal nod. "Verra kind of ye, to be sure."

"Allow me to introduce to you," Fox continued to the entire group, "Mr. Charles Lonepine of the Concha Clan of the Cherokee. He has been good enough to accompany the lumber all the way from our former colony. Mr. Lonepine represents his people in our enterprise. As I told you at an earlier meeting, I have worked with him several times before, always to our mutual benefit."

Fox suspected that only the duke's love of risk had brought him to these clandestine meetings instead of his agent. It was what Fox had counted on.

Kymton raked his gaze up and down Tsusga, who regarded the duke with a bland expression.

"A savage in a suit of clothes," Kymton drawled.

Suppressing his temper, Fox shook his silver-haired head. "Mr. Lonepine has been educated in France, and he is as well-read as you or I. His people own thousands of acres of prime timber."

Lord Kymton shrugged. "Savage or sophisticate, what matters the man, I suppose, when the goods are delivered." Lord Kymton smiled. "You will forgive me," he said to Tsusga. It was not a request.

Tsusga inclined his head, his expression unreadable.

Formal introductions were made, although in reality everyone but the duke and Millington already knew Tsusga.

"What cruel irony," Millington murmured, almost as if to himself. "India killed my brother, who made me rich, and now an Indian will be instrumental in making me richer."

Fox regarded Millington from under silver-gray eyebrows adhered over his own, making his brow feel tight. "Irony, Mr. Millington? Mr. Lonepine is not from India."

"Er, of course not."

Fox hobbled to the sideboard, where he poured himself a small glass of Madeira. "With the money you make from this investment, Mr. Millington, you can set yourself up in an estate in the New World *and* in India."

Millington picked up his near-empty glass and tossed back the remainder of his brandy.

"India," Kymton spat, as if the word were poisoned. "England should drain it of every ounce of gold and silver, every gem and bolt of silk."

Fox raised a stiff eyebrow. "I was under the impression that was precisely what England was doing, sir."

"Not quickly enough to suit me," Kymton muttered.

Fox announced to the room at large, "Let us begin this meeting."

"Aye, the sooner we be quit of here, the less chance of discovery," said "Mr. Charnley" with a heavy northern accent.

"Hear, hear," Mrs. Blue agreed.

"Mr. Eddison" poured himself a glass of port and took his seat at the table with the rest of them. "I've naught done anything like this before. The risk makes me uneasy."

Millington nodded.

"Are you implying the rest of us have done this sort of thing before?" Kymton demanded.

Mr. Eddison blinked. "No, of course not. I was just saying—"

"I believe we know you meant no such thing," Fox soothed. "We are all unsettled. The vast fortune to be made brings us here, nothing else. Once our . . . transaction . . . is accomplished, we'll all go our separate ways, to spend—or save—our new wealth."

Millington smirked. "Always the consummate investment broker, eh, Syer?"

Fox merely smiled. Operation Plum Pit would bring the end of Uriah Syer.

"I have seen enough financial opportunities to know a rich one with relatively little risk of failure," he said.

"The pivotal word bein' 'relatively,'" Mrs. Blue said. "Gentlemen, we've established the fact that we are all somewhat nervous. Treason has serious consequences. Now, if we might get on with the real business at hand. . . . ?"

Fox inclined his head toward the lady. "Thank you, Mrs. Blue. As we previously discussed, the French know they have no hope of winning a sea war with the British without new ships. 'Tis my personal opinion that they stand no chance of winning such a war with Great Britain no matter how many ships they have, but they most assuredly stand none without *more* ships. Building new ships requires timber and a great deal of it. The French are desperate for high-quality lumber—desperate enough to pay well, very well."

He turned toward Tsusga. "Mr. Lonepine's people own thousands of acres of forest. Prime timber. They desire to convert some of their bountiful resource into gold. Mr. Lonepine has persuaded them to sell to *us* at a most reasonable price." He smiled. "Of course, our price to the French will be somewhat less reasonable."

"Yes, yes, we are already acquainted with the facts, Syer. Get on with it."

"So when do the Froggies pay up?" Mrs. Blue asked.

"I have met with the necessary French director. They have sought timber from other sources, of course, but their choices are extremely limited. As I said, gentlemen, Mrs. Blue, they are desperate, and becoming more so with every battle British ships win. In short, there will be payment upon delivery, and we can deliver now."

This caused a congenial murmur around the table.

So Mr. Syer gave them the new figures he had prepared. With *this* financial arrangement, he did not hand each investor the usual impressive, ribbon-tied portfolio containing, in lavish script, every aspect of the investment. Well, *almost* every aspect.

Tonight was different. Tonight he read aloud the faux facts and figures. Each investor must make his own notes according to need. The fewer bits of evidence outside Fox's control the better. This venture involved the risk of a traitor's death.

In the shadowed chamber, pens scratching against stationery sounded preternaturally loud. From behind his clear-glass spectacles, Fox watched as Millington and Kymton scribbled. They gripped the quills more and more tightly. Their eyes grew brighter, slightly narrowed as the figures Fox gave them grew increasingly splendid. Almost imperceptibly, their breathing hastened.

Fox had presided over too many investor meetings not to recognize the signs. He knew what the two men were feeling: elation over anticipated wealth. Greed. And tonight there might also be a fear-based thrill of excitement that would not have attended meetings involved with previous Assembly undertakings.

Outside, an owl hooted.

Neither Isabel's uncle nor Kymton appeared to notice. It revealed the measure of the two men's commitment . . . or avarice. Either motive worked to the advantage of Operation Plum Pit.

Over the past three years, owls had unsettled more than one of Fox's wealthy targets, who had believed them, as did many, harbingers of ill fortune. Fox harbored an affection for the nocturnal hunters; they disposed of rats.

Regretfully, Operation Plum Pit could not provide such a final end to the powerful Kymton. Millington might eventually swing, but the nobility of Kymton's title and the long reach of his influence made unrealistic any hope for his execution as a traitor. Both men, however, would be the engines behind their own financial and social ruin.

Since the law had seen fit to dismiss, allegedly for lack of evidence, Robert Millington's case against Gilbert, at least he and Isabel could take what little comfort there was to be found in knowing Gilbert would not enjoy his ill-gotten gains, nor would he be likely to swindle anyone else.

If everything went as planned.

In order not to jinx the operation, Fox refused to allow himself the pleasure of anticipating that ruin.

Soon enough, a king's man would be led to the supply of lumber, just in time to stop its receipt by the French republicans. Notes taken by Kymton himself and genuine witnesses, who had believed they had been doing business with Hugo Foss, would find their way to the correct authorities. And Hugo Foss, as almost every Englishman knew, was the birth name of the present Duke of Kymton.

For now, Fox must continue to concentrate on each chessboard move of the plan.

And later tonight, as he did every night, he would pour himself a large glass of brandy and let loose to haunt him the memories of Isabel.

"Bel! Bel! Where *are* you?"

At the sound of her brother's excited voice, Isabel wiped at her wet eyes with the backs of her gloved hands, then hurried from the garden. She stuck her head in the open top half of the kitchen back door.

"Rob, what is it?" she called.

"There you are!" Clad in work clothes, his shirtsleeves rolled up on his forearms, he rushed into the kitchen, waving a letter. When he saw her, his brows drew together. "Ah, Bel. You've been crying again."

She sniffled. "No, I haven't."

His expression softened. "You've smeared your tears with garden soil."

"Oh." She brushed at her cheeks with her fingers.

Rob opened the door for her to step into the kitchen. "Why do you not simply go to him?"

She shook her head. They had been over this subject countless times. Fox had made his decision not to free himself from the demons of his past, and Isabel was stuck with her decision, though she had doubted it so many times since she had left Fox in the library at Blencowe House. How he must loathe her now. . . .

With a grunt of disgust, Rob thrust the letter at her.

Quickly she removed her begrimed gloves to toss them outside on a chair by the door. Then she accepted the epistle. It had been franked, which told her it came from Lady Blencowe. The baroness always took the trouble to have her correspondence to Isabel and Rob franked, which saved them the cost of postage and was wholeheartedly appreciated.

"Kymton has been found guilty of treason!" he exploded before she could read the news herself.

She stared at him.

"Truly, Bel!" he insisted. He snatched the letter from her fingers to scan it. "Ah! She says right here—"

"He did it," Isabel said in a stunned voice.

"Eh? Yes, of course he did it. And now he will pay for his crime."

Isabel struggled to collect her wits. "Not Kymton. *Fox. He* did it. He worked his magic to draw Kymton's fangs."

"Magic? Drawing fangs? What—?"

"You know Fox was successful at initiating—and pulling off—several confidence games—"

"Yes, yes. He told me the morning we left Blencowe House. And Lady Blencowe, Miss Tremayne, oh, and *you* told me. But it was to be a secret, of course."

Isabel scowled. "You were my brother, and Fox was moving to the United States, where he no longer planned to conduct, er, investments." She snatched at the letter.

Rob lifted it out of her reach, ignoring her swipes at it.

"So you believe," he said consideringly, "that Tremayne exposed the duke's treason? Which was, by the by, selling timber to the French to enlarge their navy." He shook his head in disbelief. "A peer of the realm. Who would have thought?"

"Anyone with the misfortune of ever having known him."

"Hmm. True. I never met the man—never wanted to—but word gets about. He's a bad egg."

Isabel gave up trying to wrest the letter from her brother. "Did she say anything about . . . about . . ."

Even now, three months after she had left Fox asleep on the library table, she found it difficult to mention his name without her throat tightening.

"Tremayne?" Rob asked gently. "No. But wait! Here she mentions our dear uncle Gilbert."

Isabel stared unseeing at the ceiling, blinking rapidly. "Oh? Has he, perchance, stepped in front of a speeding carriage or other good news?"

"He, also, has been found guilty of treason."

For a moment, Isabel stood silent.

"Do you believe this might be another feat of Tremayne's magic?" Rob finally inquired.

"Do you not believe it possible?"

"Oh, indeed I do. Any man capable of seizing and holding my little sister's heart must be a trickster of great power."

She walked into his comforting embrace. "Oh, Rob." She sniffled. "I miss him."

"I know, Bel."

"I love him, you know."

"I know, Bel."

She thought a minute. "I've got to find him, Rob. *Now*."

Rob sighed. "I know, Bel. I have suspected all along that it was just a matter of time; only I always thought he would come looking for you."

"Including Gilbert in his operation was a signal," she said, slowly brightening. "It was a signal to me."

Rob gave her the letter. "And what was tricking Kymton into betraying his true nature to regent and country?"

She smiled, and for the first time in months, it felt . . . genuine. "Oh, that was not a signal to me. That was a signal to himself. A sign. A declaration."

"I own I do not understand."

She went on tiptoe to plant a kiss on his forehead. "I do. He still loves me after all. And the past—oh, never mind! I must pack."

"We've got the coins Uncle Valfrid gave us before he returned to Göteborg. And most of what Fox reimbursed us."

"I'll take no more than I need," she promised. She hastened from the kitchen, but before she did more than pass through the door, going toward her room, she heard Rob call her again.

She stopped. "Yes?"

"You know war is coming to the United States."

Because of Fox's interest in that country, she had kept abreast of its events. Its ships fell prey to pirates and the navies of other nations around the world.

"I know."

She only hoped Fox had not left England yet. Not without her.

London was closest to Greenwood, so it was to Blencowe House that Isabel first went. The angels were smiling on her, because she would have missed Lady Blencowe had she arrived two hours later. The furniture was draped with holland cloth, and carriages were being loaded with her trunks. Even though the Season had begun, Lady Blencowe intended to take up residence in Riverside, her primary estate.

Despite the commotion wrought by the move, she ordered tea to be served. It arrived in a matter of minutes.

When the butler had withdrawn, closing the pocket doors behind him, Lady Blencowe spoke as she poured.

"You know, of course, that the Duke of Kymton and your aunt and uncle have fled the country. I expected it of Kymton, who has resources, but how your relations contrived to escape, I know not."

Isabel considered this revelation as she sipped her tea, enjoying the sweet warmth on her tongue, in her throat.

"Like you, I am not surprised to find the duke has gone into self-exile rather than face the gruesome death of a traitor. As to my uncle, all I can say is that he is clever. And I'm rather glad to hear that he will not die, dislike him as I do. I doubt he will live well, which also pleases me. Alas, the duke undoubtedly will manage to dwell in style. A creature such as he would have been stashing money outside Great Britain for years."

Lady Blencowe nodded. "But he would have been forced to leave behind the greater portion of his fortune, gleaned from blackmail and bribery. The Crown has frozen his assets. What they can lay hands on, he will lose. And who will now trust such a traitor?"

"And his son?"

"Well, of course he will inherit nothing from his father. No title, none of the duke's property, entailed though most of it probably is. His maternal grandmama has, however, endowed him with a vast fortune, greater than anything he would ever have received from his gambling papa."

Isabel smiled. "How fitting that the duke has been judged a traitor."

Lady Blencowe's eyes laughed over the rim of her cup.

"But you have not come to chat about Kymton, surely," the baroness said as she set her cup and saucer on the tea tray in front of them.

"I have come to discover where I can find Fox."

"Ah."

"Since I've seen no sign of Catherine, I judge she is with him?"

"She would consider nothing else. You have left her with a taste for adventure."

Nothing was said for a few drawn-out minutes.

"Has he sailed for North Carolina?" Isabel finally said.

Lady Blencowe smiled. "Not yet."

"Please tell me where I can find him, Lady Blencowe."

"You may call me Diana. May I address you by your Christian name?"

"Certainly," Isabel replied, struggling to suppress her impatience.

Diana seemed to consider something for a moment. Then she asked, "Do you love him, Isabel?"

"With all my heart," Isabel replied without hesitation. "Now I must find him and tell him so."

"Then, my dear, you are likely to discover him at the Dolphin Inn in Portsmouth. He and Catherine are awaiting the ship that will take them to a fresh start in the New World. But you must hurry."

Isabel set down her cup. "Thank you, Diana. I will take my leave now."

"You might not make it in time if you take public transport. If you can tolerate the wind in your face, I'll have a groom take you to Portsmouth in my phaeton."

"Thank you!"

Diana smiled. "Oh, my dear"—she kissed Isabel's cheek—"thank *you*."

Clearly Diana had impressed upon Tomkins, the groom, a need for haste, because never had Isabel been transported with such a concentration for maintaining speed. Tomkins kept the horses to a goodly clip, changing them at every posting inn. At each stop, Isabel had just enough time to wash her face, attend to nature's call, and to procure them meals, to be consumed as they traveled.

Despite their swift pace, Isabel fretted. What if Fox's ship arrived before she did? The coins in her purse would not provide the sum required for passage to North Carolina.

Finally, finally, they entered Portsmouth. Dusk tinted buildings and streets with its golden brush. Shops were closed for the night. Traffic had dwindled to a few carts and an occasional carriage.

Isabel's impatience raged as they stopped to ask the way to the Dolphin Inn. By the time they had followed the directions given, it was well past dark, and she thought her head would pop off. To Tomkins' distress, she leapt down from the phaeton and ran inside as soon as he pulled into the inn's courtyard.

Fortunately, this inn possessed a front desk, complete with a large logbook of its guests. Unfortunately, no one stood behind the desk.

Feverishly, Isabel thumbed through the pages of the ledger until she found the most recent entries. Running her gloved finger down the lines of signatures, she located Fox's. He had used his real name.

The tension in her wound tighter.

He registered at the Dolphin. Please, please, *Lord, let him still be here!*

Where was the innkeeper?

From the corner of her eye, she caught sight of a tiny bell. Attached was an even tinier sign: RING FOR SERVICE.

Snatching up the bell, Isabel rang it. She continued to ring the bell, unceasing. As she did, she caught a glimpse of herself in a framed mirror on a wall. Two gray-green eyes glared out of a mask of road dirt.

"Yes, yes, yes!" grumbled a thin, aproned man, hurrying in from the common room. "I hear!" He recoiled at the sight of her.

Undeterred, she told him, "You have one Foxton Tremayne here."

"Madam, it is not our policy to give out information about our guests," he informed her haughtily.

"It was not a question," she replied coldly. "He registered here. I must speak with him. Now."

Tomkins arrived. He looked from the fellow behind the desk to Isabel.

Apron Man glanced at the logbook and then inquired indignantly, "Did you look in our guest ledger? That is not done, madam, *not done*. Really!"

Desperate to find Fox, aware of every second that passed, Isabel lunged across the desk to grab the man's shirt in her grimy fists. She jerked him closer. His rosy nose trembled at the end of her brown one.

"Hear me well," she growled. "I—must—speak—to—Foxton—Tremayne. *Now*."

"Why did you not say so?" the fellow said in a small voice.

Tomkins closed in on the man. "Do as the lady says."

"Of course, of course."

Isabel released the fistfuls of shirt, shocked at her own behavior, but too anxious to cease.

"If I am not looking at Mr. Tremayne in ten minutes, I will go from door to door in this inn and rouse all of your guests until I find him myself."

The prospect of a woman disguised as a dirt-creature knocking on each guest chamber door, demanding word with Mr. Tremayne, seemed to be the final straw. He scuttled away, it was to be hoped, in search of Fox.

Aware of Tomkins' steady gaze, Isabel shifted from one foot to the other.

"The man tried my patience," she said.

Tomkins maintained a bland expression on his own dust-covered face. "A fact miss made quite clear to him."

When Apron Man did not return in a few minutes, Isabel straightened her bonnet, rolled back her shoulders, then went in search of the guest quarters. Tomkins marched right behind her.

She climbed the narrow stairs that led from the common room to the floor above. There, in the wavering light of three wall lamps, she surveyed a hall lined with doors.

Isabel decided to visit the last door in the hall first, thereby keeping open the line of retreat down the stairs, in case she needed to leave quickly.

She paused in front of the door, breathing deeply. Then she knocked.

And knocked again. No one answered.

Before she could move to the next chamber, the first door was snatched open.

There stood Fox.

He stared at Isabel. "Elf?"

Suddenly feeling shy and all too aware of her appearance, she nodded. She looked over her shoulder at Tomkins. "Please go to the common room and order dinner and refreshment for yourself. I will see you shortly."

After he had left, Fox motioned her into the chamber and closed the door behind her. His window was open to the spring night air. The faint, salty smell of the sea wafted in.

"What are you doing here?" he asked quietly.

"You asked me to marry you."

Fox scowled. "You left."

"I've returned. Is the . . . is the offer still good?"

He looked down at her upturned face, his gaze seeming to take in every feature, his scowl fading. "Do you want it to be?"

"Yes," she breathed. "Oh, yes."

He took her shoulders in his hands. "Why did you leave, Isabel?"

"You had not made the decision to confront your past."

"And now that I have . . . confronted my past, as you put it?"

She smiled up at him. "Now you have a greater chance at finally being content, perhaps even happy."

His palms moved up and down her back. "I require but one more thing to guarantee my happiness."

"Tell me."

"You. As my wife."

She kissed him, leaving a smudge on his chin. "I hoped you would say that."

EPILOGUE

North Carolina, 1813

Spring touched the dogwood blossoms with a delicate blush. From her bower of climbing roses covered with fragrant pink blooms, Isabel knit and regarded her garden with satisfaction. It glowed with color.

Knitting was about the only work Fox would allow her, now that she had become large with their first child.

Catherine would come to childbed at about the same time as Isabel. Isabel smiled. Her friend must have become pregnant on her wedding night or very shortly after, she thought, to be so far along. But that came as no surprise. She was passionate about her handsome, strapping husband, David Napier, who owned the estate bordering that of Fox and Isabel.

He had come courting shortly after he had laid eyes on Catherine at a neighbor's dinner party. That had been before work had concluded on the large house, which now stood across the garden from Isabel. A handsome, columned structure, it was Fox's pride. He had designed it.

Unlike the old Willow Hall, every room here at the new Willow Hall was used.

Fox strode down the brick path that wandered through

the draping willow trees, Oscar waddling happily at his heels.

"News," Fox called as he waved two letters. With the war on, mail from England arrived irregularly.

When he entered the bower, he bent to give Isabel a long, tender kiss. Oscar nibbled at the hem of her gown.

"We received word from Aunt Diana," Fox finally said, "and George Foss." All George's father's titles and dignities had been stripped away.

"Did Diana's letter come from Sweden or from England this time?" Isabel asked.

"England. It seems my aunt has prevailed upon your uncle to move the seat of his trading empire to London."

"They both like London."

"That they do," he agreed. "I suspected things might fall that way when they wed last year."

"Besides the move, of what does she write?"

"Your brother. When last she and Valfrid visited him, it seems they discovered Rob's partiality to a local lady. Frannie Twickham, the eldest daughter of the late Earl of Merlawe."

"I know her! We grew up together. Attractive, excellent manners, a delightful sense of humor. Oh, I hope it takes! I wonder if I should send him felicitations."

"I would wait to hear the announcement from him first."

She sighed. "Yes, I suppose."

"What troubles you, Elf?"

"'Tis only that I desire Rob to be as happy as I am."

"He will be, love, he will be. My guess is he has been waiting until Greenwood finally showed a profit. Now that it has, he is free to consider taking a bride."

She nodded. "That makes sense."

"The letter from Foss says he and his mother are keeping up the good work started by the Assembly—"

"By *you*."

"Not entirely. He says—again—how much satisfaction they take in it. You do know that Foss's mother's parents were hiding money for her, don't you? So Kymton couldn't squander it. Foss and his mother see their new work as a way of trying to make up for the damage the duke did. I've received a detailed report from them on everything. And Etienne is keeping an eye on things. Foss says they greatly rely upon him."

Isabel plucked at the baby shoe. "I hope they pay him well."

"They do."

"Do you think he will ever wed?"

Fox shrugged a shoulder. "Who can say? *I* was not thinking of marriage when I first met you."

She nuzzled his neck.

He put his arm around her. "Come. Cook has made lemonade and apple cakes to celebrate Nottage's birthday."

Isabel smiled as he helped her rise to her feet. "There is one union that is a pleasure to consider."

Fox grinned. "Nottage and Mrs. Cook."

"Mrs. Nottage, now."

"Who would have thought a curmudgeon like Nottage would find a mate?"

"Oh, he is an old softy when one comes to know him."

Fox laughed. "Sometimes."

He swept her up in his arms, and she reveled in his obvious joy, in the lush beauty of their new place in the world. A place of honor.

A place of love.

All your favorite romance writers are
coming together.

SIGNET ECLIPSE